FOREIGN AFFAIRS

Blazing attraction...

Sizzling seduction...

The world's most eligible men!

Dreaming of a foreign affair? Then, look no further! We've brought together the best and sexiest men the world has to offer, the most exciting, exotic locations and the most powerful, passionate stories.

This month, in *Outback Husbands*, we bring back two best-selling novels by Margaret Way and Marion Lennox in which rugged Australian men prove themselves perfect marriage material. And from now on, every month in **Foreign Affairs** you can be swept away to a new location – and indulge in a little passion in the sun!

And there's temptation in paradise next month in
PACIFIC PASSIONS
by Anne Mather & Robyn Donald
Don't miss it!

MARGARET WAY

Margaret Way takes great pleasure in her work and works hard at her pleasure. She enjoys tearing off to the beach with her family on weekends, loves haunting galleries and auctions and is completely given over to French champagne "for every possible joyous occasion." She was born and educated in the river city of Brisbane, Australia, and now lives within sight and sound of beautiful Moreton Bay.

Look out for Margaret Way's next book *Strategy for Marriage* in July 2002 in Tender Romance ™!

MARION LENNOX

Marion Lennox is a country girl, born on a south-east Australian dairy farm. She moved on – mostly because the cows just weren't interested in her stories! Married to a 'very special doctor', Marion writes for Medical Romance™ and Tender Romance™ (she used a different name for each category for a while – so if you are looking for her older books search for author Trisha David as well!)

In her non-writing life Marion cares for kids, cats, dogs, chooks and goldfish. She travels, she fights her rampant garden (she's losing) and her house dust (she's lost). After an early bout with breast cancer she's also reprioritised her life, figured what's important and discovered the joys of deep baths, romance and chocolate. Preferably all at the same time!

Look out for *Adopted: Twins!* by Marion Lennox on sale in January 2002 in Tender Romance™ and *The Doctors' Baby* in Medical Romance™ in May 2002!

outback husbands

MARGARET WAY & MARION LENNOX

THE FIERY HEART OF AUSTRALIA

MILLS & BOON®

*All the characters in this book have no existence outside the imagination
of the author, and have no relation whatsoever to anyone bearing the
same name or names. They are not even distantly inspired by any
individual known or unknown to the author, and all the incidents are
pure invention.*

Harlequin Mills & Boon Limited,
Eton House, 18-24 Paradise Road, Richmond, Surrey, TW9 1SR

Outback Husbands © Harlequin Enterprises II B.V., 2002

Her Outback Man and *Bush Doctor's Bride*
were first published in Great Britain by
Harlequin Mills & Boon Limited in separate single volumes.

Her Outback Man © Margaret Way Pty., Ltd. 1998
Bush Doctor's Bride © Marion Lennox 1996

ISBN 0 263 83183 3

126-0102

Printed and bound in Spain
by Litografia Rosés S.A., Barcelona

outback husbands

HER OUTBACK MAN

MARGARET WAY

CHAPTER ONE

VAST as the homestead was, everywhere Dana looked there were people; in the drawing room, the library, Logan's study, the entrance hall of grand dimensions, even the broad verandas that surrounded the marvellous old homestead on three sides were crowded with mourners. There must have been four hundred at least. They had been arriving since early morning in their private planes and their charter planes set down like a flock of birds on the station's runway, or in the small army of vehicles that had made the long hot trek overland; all of them come to pay their last respects to James Tyler Dangerfield, second son of this powerful and influential landed family, dead at twenty-eight, killed in a car crash after a wild all-night party. Not many people would know that. Logan, as always, had taken charge very swiftly, gathering them all in, issuing a brief statement to the press, making all the arrangements while the entire Dangerfield clan, pastoralists, judges, scientists and politicians, one a Government minister, closed ranks behind him.

Logan was the cattle baron. As direct descendant of the Dangerfield founding father in colonial Australia, he was head of one of the country's richest families and Chairman of the Dangerfield pastoral empire and a network of corporations since the death of his late father, Sir Matthew Dangerfield some two years earlier. Jimmy had been the playboy, the second son, forever doomed to walk in Logan's tall shadow. Logan was the *real* Dangerfield, Jimmy had often said, never quite able to conceal his envy and a kind of half-bitter, half-wry re-

5

sentiment at his being second best. Jimmy, with his easy, happy-go-lucky charm, spoiled by the family fortune. Logan was the chip off the old block. The son with unlimited skills and matchless energies. Sir Matthew had worshipped Logan, Jimmy had told her, and Dana had seen that with her own eyes. It had always been perfectly obvious Jimmy could never hope to measure up to his big brother.

Stepbrother.

Logan's mother, Elizabeth Logan Dangerfield, had died giving him birth, something that would not have happened had she elected to have her firstborn in hospital instead of on historic Mara Station to please her husband. Matthew Dangerfield had married Jimmy and Sandra's mother, Ainslie, a few years later, a marriage as nearly a business merger as the first one had been an ecstatic romance. Both Jimmy and Sandra favoured their mother's side of the family, with their golden-brown colouring. Logan was all dark, dangerous Dangerfield, which was to say, unfairly endowed with all of Nature's attributes.

Her expression bleak, Dana turned away from the elegant white wrought-iron balcony to look over to where Logan stood, perhaps on this awful day a little stiffly, his head characteristically thrown up but in perfect control of his emotions as was expected of the head of the family.

Logan, strikingly handsome in his formal dark clothes relieved only by the immaculate white of his shirt, thick blue-black hair, a piercing regard, not that "piercing" fully described the beauty of his sapphire eyes, at six-three, towering over the people around him, a lean and splendid physique. One might have thought it unnecessary to endow him with other qualities, but he had a razor-sharp intelligence he never bothered to conceal and a natural air of command; a capacity for leadership he hadn't developed but had been born with. If there were scores of people who adored Logan Dangerfield, scores more *women,* Dana wasn't one of them. She and Logan looked on one another with a mixture of feelings. Liking wasn't one of them. In the six years since she had first met him they had maintained an uneasy and often electric truce.

The thing was, she would never have moved into his rarified world if it weren't for Melinda. Melinda was her cousin, orphaned child of her mother's sister. Melinda's parents had been killed in a train accident when Melinda was eight and Dana six, and Dana's mother had insisted Melinda come to them. Pretty as a picture, blond-haired and blue-eyed, strangely no one else in the family had wanted her, so Melinda arrived. More than a cousin, a sister, settling into the house as softly and quietly as a little cat. Dana knew better than anyone all about Melinda.

When they were at University, Melinda, two years ahead of eighteen-year-old Dana, had met the Golden Boy, Jimmy Dangerfield, a playboy even then. Jimmy was studying for a degree in Commerce, though he cared little for study. Jimmy was a "dabbler" with no interest in getting on with his work yet he had a perfectly good brain. Something he apparently liked to keep to himself. But Jimmy always had all the money he needed. He got to all the parties and he always had the pretty girls. Jimmy thought being serious about anything was dull and boring. When it was all said and done, all he wanted out of life was fun.

He hadn't really wanted Melinda, though his roving eye had singled out her soft, seemingly vulnerable prettiness. He had taken her out for a time without the slightest awareness of what Melinda was really like. Melinda had an overriding ambition in life. To find *security.* No doubt a consequence of her early traumas. Not

the security that mattered, but *money* above all else.
Golden Boy Dangerfield was the beginning and end of
her search. Known for his love of freedom, Melinda had
set Jimmy a trap. She deliberately got herself pregnant,
feeling no guilt when Jimmy was forced into a marriage
he didn't want, though to his everlasting credit he rec-
ognised his responsibilities to Melinda and his coming
child. This child was a Dangerfield. He would never
have been forgiven had he turned his back on her.
Melinda was pretty, intelligent, and from a respectable
background. Jimmy had believed she loved him passionately. It wasn't long into the marriage before Jimmy
found out she didn't.

Melinda.

At this moment she was lying supposedly sedated in
one of the upstairs bedrooms, unable to attend the service, which had been held in the old two-storeyed stone
chapel some distance from the homestead, or see her
young husband laid to rest on Eagle's Ridge, the family
plot surrounded by a six-foot-high wrought-iron fence
with ornate double gates. Melinda wasn't prostrate from
grief. Dana knew that for a fact. Melinda needed to hide
away from all the condemnatory eyes. Dana, who had
had a lifetime of fronting for Melinda, was acutely aware
of all the subterranean surges and the long speculative
glances levelled at her. Everyone knew who she was just
as they knew "Tyler's" marriage had not been a happy
one. Inevitable some would say when it had started out
so badly.

Dana couldn't bear to look back on those days. The
image of Melinda, her face paper-white, blue eyes blazing, smiling at her in a sort of conspiratorial triumph.

"He doesn't really want to but I pulled it off, didn't
I? He's going to marry me. I'll be a Dangerfield. I'll be
rich and important. Mara is *famous.*"

Dana then as now felt a sick dismay but she had little

room in her heart for condemnation. Melinda's dream
had turned to ashes. Jimmy had been laid to rest. Life
might have been very different for both of them had
Melinda been more a woman of heart and mind. Going
over to visit them mostly for Alice's, her beloved little
goddaughter's sake had been like going onto a battle
ground. Jimmy had not finished his degree any more
than Melinda had. After an initial period of trying,
Jimmy had quickly settled back into having a good time
while Melinda, to everyone's horror, turned into a shrew,
complaining bitterly to anyone who would listen, having
Alice had caused her to miss out on her youth. Small
wonder Alice growing up in such a household was as
troubled a child as she could be. Dana was her refuge
and they both knew it. Dana could never abandon Alice.
Especially *now*.

What to do with the pain? Dana thought. What to do
with the pain?

She knew Logan blamed her for lots of things, but he
had only said it once. The night of the wedding. The
first time she had ever laid eyes on John Logan
Dangerfield.

CHAPTER TWO

THIS wedding was different. He had known instinctively something was wrong when Tyler came home crowing with delight he had fallen love and wanted to get married immediately.

"She's my blond enchantress," he told them, shocking Ainslie, who had different plans for her son. "I've never met anyone like her. So cool and clever."

It didn't fit the description of the young woman who later flew in to meet them with her coy almost cloying prettiness and shy downcast eyes. The disturbing beauty and the cool intelligence belonged to her cousin. He could never understand how Tyler had looked beyond Dana until it all became clear. But on that day Tyler had his eyes firmly set on Melinda, his young wife, soon to be the mother of his child. Logan had managed to get that out of his beleaguered brother almost at once, backing Tyler's wish to have a quiet wedding on the station attended by family and a few close friends; something that upset Melinda terribly. She had wanted a big wedding with all the trimmings, but the family took no notice of that. It was, after all, a marriage that had been manipulated from the start. But in all fairness, though bitterly disappointed, Ainslie had arranged a wedding pageant and they all did their level best; about fifty in all, to make it a festive occasion. The bride wore virginal white, a soft flowing dress cut to skim the waistline, her pale face hidden by her veil; the cousin wore the same sort of fabric, silk chiffon, he later learned, but in a frosted gold, the bodice leaving her shoulders bare, the long skirt billowing from a small cinched waist. Like the bride, she carried an exquisite bouquet of roses from Mara's home gardens combining all the creams and yellows and golds...

He had been caught up on one of the outstations all morning. The manager there had been foolish enough to try to make a bit extra for himself periodically selling off a few head of prime cattle, so he had to attend to that, a rough confrontation out in the bush, flying back into Mara just over an hour before the ceremony in the family chapel was due to begin. He had never felt less like attending a wedding in his life, knowing Ty, for all his efforts to put on a good face, wasn't happy and he himself was deeply uncomfortable with the idea the bride wasn't just a kitten-faced innocent caught up in an all too common situation but a first-rate opportunist. The cousin she had lived with from childhood was probably the same. He had left before the cousin's flight was due in. She had paid for her ticket to the domestic terminal herself. Something that had surprised him. Melinda had taken to being "looked after" like a duck to water.

Feeling strung out and dishevelled, he had entered the house at the precise moment a young woman in a beautiful strapless gown set her foot on the first landing of the central staircase. She was young, very young, perhaps eighteen or nineteen, but her expression as she looked down at him was one of dignity and maturity.

Tyler's *enchantress,* he thought in one revelatory second, while something hot and hostile flared behind his rib cage.

"You must be Logan," she said sweetly, an answering heat in her flush. "I'd heard you'd been called out."

Her voice, too, was alluring and he gave himself a moment to level out. "To one of our outstations, as it happens." He didn't smile, the formality of his tone in sharp contrast to her natural warmth. "And you must be

Dana?'' Stupid. Of course she was Dana. The cousin.
Yet he couldn't quite believe it. She was blond, like
Melinda, but an ash-blond, very nearly platinum, her
long, thick, straight hair caught back from her face with
a sparkling diadem and allowed to fall down her back.
But where one might have expected Melinda's white
skin and blue eyes, this girl's skin gleamed ivory, her
eyes set in a slight upward slant like the wings of her
eyebrows, velvet brown. It was a stunning combination.

What was even more stunning was the fact he was
staring, but her physical beauty seized his imagination.
Woman magic. A quality that could bring great joy or
havoc or both in equal measure.

She hesitated, perhaps baffled and a little alarmed at
his attitude, while sunlight from the high arched case-
ments lent a startling radiance to her hair and her gown.
He almost felt like calling out, ''Come down, I won't
bite you,'' when she suddenly descended the stairs in
cool challenge, holding up the folds of her skirt with one
hand, the other outstretched towards him.

''How do you do, Logan,'' she said with the utmost
composure. ''I'm so pleased to meet you at last. Jimmy
speaks of you all the time.''

Jimmy. Who was *Jimmy?* To the family, he was Tyler.
He knew from the glitter in her velvet eyes she was
suddenly angry, as hostile in her fashion as he was. Even
the brief contact of hands sent out warning signals as if
to say we may never be open about it but we will never
be friends.

Friends with this young woman? One might as well
be friends with some creature who wrought spells. The
danger was plain. He felt a powerful urge to question
her, to try to get to the bottom of what had happened to
his brother, only it was all too late.

''Please *don't,*'' she said, surprising him, her upturned
face betraying a certain anguish. *Guilt?*

"I'm sorry. I don't follow," he lied, every nerve jangling.

"I think you do." She took a little breath. "We both want Jimmy to be happy."

His voice when it came was so sharp it was like he had splinters in his throat. "You speak of *Tyler* as though you know him very, very well."

Something flickered in her eyes and she flushed as if knowing he had insulted her. "Jimmy is my friend." Still she remained controlled. "I have a warm feeling towards him as befitting someone who is to marry my cousin. I don't want to see him hurt. Melinda, either."

That touched a raw spot. "Are you suggesting *I* do?"

She half turned away from him so he could see her delicate winging shoulder-blades above the low back of her gown. For a moment disconcerted and thoroughly on edge, he felt a strange piercing tenderness for her youth, her beauty, and the fact he had offended her.

"I can look behind your words," she said. "I can see into your eyes. You're upset about the whole situation. Your family, too."

"Well you would know better than anybody how it all came about." He answered too harshly but he was unable to prevent himself.

Her eyes went very dark. "*I* had little part to play in it."

"Well you know," he retorted crisply. "You fit the role of enchantress."

She managed to appear genuinely bewildered. "Why ever are you saying *that?*"

"When Tyler came home he told us he'd fallen hopelessly in love with a *blond enchantress.*"

Her delicate brows rose. "Melinda *is* very pretty."

"So she is, in a conventional way," he replied bluntly. "You on the other hand have a quite different look."

Her expression gained a dismayed intensity. "You surely can't think Jimmy and I shared a romance?"

"I'm sure you dazzled him." He smiled at her, looking very dangerous and powerful, but that simply didn't occur to him.

She appeared, for her part, appalled. Perhaps she was. At being found out. "We simply didn't move in the same circles. I barely knew Jimmy until Melinda started going out with him."

"This isn't actually how she tells it." He didn't quite know *how* Melinda was telling it, but she had certainly thrown out lots of veiled hints.

One of the girl's hands fluttered to her breast. She looked for a moment enormously vulnerable. "I can't imagine what Melinda said, but I assure you you've misinterpreted it. This is ridiculous."

"Yes it is." His tone was laced with irony. "Especially as my brother is to marry your cousin in—" he lifted an arm and glanced at his watch "—under an hour. What I really have to do is shower and change. We can talk again."

The chapel was luminous with white flowers, roses, lilies, carnations, stephanotis, great clouds of baby's breath literally transforming it into a fairyland. The bride and her attendant looked as lovely as anyone could wish, the reception in the homestead's ballroom was sumptuous, but hectic circles of colour burned on the bridegroom's cheeks and Logan had to tell him very quietly he was drinking too much.

"Nerves, J.L.! It's not every day a man finds himself married."

Ainslie and Sandra quietly cried into lace-edged handkerchiefs. On the air was a kind of sulphur, like after a thunderstorm. The happy couple, Melinda *did* appear radiant, were to leave on the first leg of their honeymoon journey that would take them to Europe, only at the very last minute Tyler pulled their bridesmaid to him and kissed her full on the lips with a kind of mad jubilation. Something that made Dame Eleanor Dangerfield turn to Logan with consternation on her imperious old face. The girl, Dana the cousin, had made a singularly good impression on her, but what in the world was *that* all about?

Logan faced Dana with it hours later when the household had finally settled. He caught her hand, risking those warning tingles, drawing her into his study and shutting the door. "I have to be gone fairly early in the morning, Dana, so I'll say my goodbyes now. Your charter flight has been arranged for 1:00 p.m. I've taken the liberty of securing you your on-going ticket. You'll find it waiting for you at the terminal."

"I didn't want you to do that," she protested, as much on edge as he was.

"Nevertheless I have. My pleasure. Everything went off very well."

"It was a beautiful ceremony and the reception was superb. I must tell you Melinda and I are very appreciative of everything you've done. She was too emotional to begin to tell you."

"Perhaps she was marvelling at that kiss Tyler gave you just as they were leaving?" he said in a tone, half silk, half steel.

Colour stained her cheeks. "Tyler scarcely knew what he was doing."

"My God, the rest of us did." Now came the hard irony.

"Please, Logan, don't you see Jimmy was full of emotion?" she appealed to him

"I actually thought he was begging you to go with him." This was disastrous, but he couldn't stop.

"So it's not a marriage made in heaven—" her voice

rang with pain "—but we've got to give it every chance."

He could only marvel at her stricken look. "So what does this involve?" he taunted her. "Do you plan to move out of their lives?"

She looked at him aghast. "Melinda and I are very close. We were reared as sisters."

"But Tyler fell in love with *you* first?" Anyone would.

"Tyler never fell in love with me at all." She shook her head in a kind of desperation.

"Are you sure of that?" The disbelief was thick in his voice.

"Where and when did you learn differently?" she challenged, her eyes sparkling brilliantly, a pulse in her throat at full throttle.

He shifted his gaze unwilling to admit he, too, felt her power. "You must know it shocked a lot of people seeing Tyler reach for you?"

"He wanted comfort." She dropped her head in seeming defeat, but on pure reflex he tilted her chin.

"My dear girl, he had just married your cousin. A very sweet girl. I think *now* Tyler was on the rebound from you. Melinda did tell us he was spellbound by your beauty. I don't know whether you realise it, but your cousin has a problem with you. Sibling rivalry it's called."

"And you'd know a great deal about that yourself." She pushed his hand away, anger lilting out of her voice. "As much as I care about Melinda, she talks a great deal of nonsense at times."

"You don't mind her going off with Tyler?" Better, far better, he shut up, but he couldn't.

"All I want for them is to be happy."

"Well, *good*," was his sardonic answer. "I don't want to have to worry about you, to tell the truth."

"Worry about *me?*" She spun so the long flowing skirt of her dress flared out around her.

It came to him with amazement his own emotions were surging dangerously. "You must see it will be better for you to get on with your life."

Again her face flamed. "If I weren't stuck in the middle of the Never-Never I'd be out of here in a second."

"Forgive me." He could hear the ringing arrogance in his apology. "You are a guest in my home."

"And you're a very powerful and dangerous man," she said, looking out at him accusingly from her great dark eyes. "It hasn't just occurred to me. I've listened to everything Jimmy has said about you."

His downward stare was more daunting than he knew. "Tyler loves me as I love him," he said coldly. "I know he has his hangups—who doesn't?—but he knows he can always count on my support."

"Surely that's to be expected of a brother?" Her scorn was genuine.

"And what can be expected of cousins?" he countered harshly. "Cousins as close as *sisters?*"

Her slender body fairly danced with fury mixed up with a kind of anguish that showed in her eyes. He saw the bright flash in them, like a flame set to oil, then she brought up her hand incredibly to strike him. He couldn't for the life of him think why, but it made him want to laugh. He hadn't seen such spirit for ages. He caught her hand in mid-flight, his own blood aflame, then for one extraordinary never-to-be-repeated moment swept her into his arms, covering her romantic soft mouth in a kiss so raw and ruthless it later filled him with a kind of horror and self-contempt. For all her beauty and female allure she was little more than a schoolgirl.

She didn't speak afterwards, as shocked as he was and close to tears. He knew he had to keep hold of her all

the time he was apologising, his senses swimming and
his veins continuing to run lava. He knew she would
never forgive him and God knows he had his own intense forebodings about her. Certain women because of
their female power and seductiveness could bring de-
struction to a family.

Ainslie's long distinguished face was distorted with
grief. Dana's heart ached for her but she knew from the
outset Ainslie wanted no words of sympathy from her.

"That dreadful girl," Ainslie moaned, her fine skin
mottled with red. "I knew the moment I laid eyes on
her she would bring grief to this family."

What matter now? Dana had thought it herself. Still
she tried to defend her cousin, so ingrained with the
habit. "Ainslie, Melinda is bereft. We're full of anguish.
It's so dreadfully, dreadfully tragic."

"Ah don't defend her, Dana," Ainslie admonished
her. "No more. We women can't fool one another.
There's something twisted about my daughter-in-law.
Look how she is with poor little Alice. She never loved
my son, either. Why couldn't *you* have been the one?"

Dana couldn't hide her shock. "But it wasn't that
way, Ainslie. Jimmy had no romantic feelings towards
me."

"Tyler *loved* you," Ainslie said, sounding utterly
convinced.

Dana laboured hard to correct her. "As a friend. A
good friend."

"No, my dear." Ainslie gave her a small, sad smile.
"He told me he loved you."

"Jimmy did?" Dana's shock was total.

Ainslie sighed heavily, patting Dana's hand. "Please
don't call him Jimmy in my presence, dear."

Dana flushed with dismay. "Forgive me but it's
what—Tyler called himself. The very last thing I want

to do is upset you, Ainslie. What Tyler *meant* was, he loved me as family. Alice's godmother.''

Ainslie looked obliquely at her, drying her deeply shadowed eyes. ''You're much too intelligent and intuitive a young woman to say that. Tyler admired as well as loved you. Surely you know Melinda was sick with jealousy?''

Dana set her jaw against her sudden anger. Anyone who knew Melinda knew she habitually lied. ''That's not possible, Ainslie.'' Dana felt like she was drowning in deception. ''Believe me on this terrible day when I say there was nothing between Tyler and me but a deep friendship. I was his confidante when—''

''When things got bad with Melinda,'' Ainslie interrupted. ''I know. Tyler told me. In those early days I prayed and prayed the marriage would work. But I hadn't reckoned on what Melinda was really like. She planned her pregnancy to trap my son.''

''But we have Alice, don't we?'' Dana pointed out with great gentleness.

''Yes, we have Alice.'' Ainslie gave a shuddering sigh. ''We have no choice but to go on, but I don't want to be near Melinda today, Dana. I don't think anyone else does, either. It's sad, but that's life. She has always pretended to be so quiet and sweet, yet all the time she's been causing trouble. The marriage would have worked had she really been what she pretended, instead Tyler's gone and we're all punished.''

Sandra was less restrained, off balance with grief and swollen-eyed.

''This is a house of mourning, Dana,'' she cried, her hazel eyes clouded with her inner rage. ''It's a good thing Melinda has chosen to hide away upstairs. I knew last night she was in a panic about fronting up. *You* had to do that for her. I know she's your cousin, but I really think you shouldn't bother with your loyalty anymore. She depends on you, I know, but she's not your friend.''

Hold the presses, Dana thought dismally. It was no news. "Sandra, don't compound all this grief," she warned, leaning forward to kiss Sandra's cheek.

"I'm sorry, Dana, I can't seem to stop. What we should have stopped was the wedding. It was never destined to work out. Look at Alice, the sheer misery of that little girl. You don't think Logan's going to let Melinda take her out of our lives? A cat's a better mother. A cat is kinder.''

Dana took Sandra's hand between her own and rubbed it. It was icy cold. "Melinda doesn't want to do that. You're Alice's family.''

"We are," Sandra replied fiercely, "so we can't desert her. Melinda has never found a place in her life for Alice. Anyone would think Alice was thrust upon her instead of…''

"Alice is very important to me, as well." Dana led the tormented Sandra farther away from the other mourners.

"She loves you. She adores you." Sandra nodded her head frantically. "She wants to belong to you. So did Tyler.''

Dana wanted to protest the truth from the rooftops. "Sandy, why are you saying this? It makes me sick with dismay. Tyler and I were friends. That was the extent of our relationship. Why are you speaking out like this now? Why the sudden doubts?''

"And Melinda *dreamed* up all the rest?" Sandra gave a broken laugh.

"I don't want to have to say this, but I must." Dana looked back at the other woman very directly. "Melinda has a gift for twisting the truth.''

"We learned that," Sandra confirmed bleakly. "She was born to breed trouble. I don't think badly of you,

Dana. I can't. You're too honourable and decent. If Tyler loved you, I do, too.''

The crushing burden of misunderstanding was too much for Dana to bear. She withdrew at the first opportunity and went upstairs to Melinda's bedroom, shutting the door behind her and moving over to the huge four-poster bed where her cousin lay her golden head pressed into a mound of pillows.

''Is it *too* ghastly?'' Melinda asked in a sympathetic tone.

Dana felt a powerful tide of revulsion. ''Ghastly, why *wouldn't* it be ghastly? I keep seeing Jimmy striding along the beach holding Alice on his shoulders, both of them laughing. Jimmy, my God, my God, he was only twenty-eight. The family is devastated.''

''That's it. Ignore *me*.''

Dana heard the tremble in Melinda's voice and tried desperately to rein herself in. ''I know your suffering in your way, Melinda.''

''Don't think for a moment I'm not,'' Melinda retorted, admonishing her. She sat up, plumping the pillows behind her. ''And what about you? You look wonderful in black, darling. As though you didn't know,'' she added archly.

Dana shook her head slowly. ''I simply don't understand you, Melinda, and the things you say.''

''Oh, yes, you do.'' Melinda gave a brittle laugh. ''I've never been able to fool you, from day one. Worst of all, in some subtle way you've become my enemy.''

''Ah, cut the act,'' Dana snapped. ''I don't want to listen to your nonsense anymore.''

''It's not an act, I mean it,'' Melinda shouted. ''I bet they all hate me downstairs.''

''Well, you haven't tried very hard, have you?'' Dana all but abandoned herself to her disgust.

"I never did have Jimmy completely to myself, did I?" Melinda said, her voice hard and sullen.

"I know there were other women," Dana said heavily, forced to agree.

"Other women?" Melinda sneered. "The only one who counted was *you*."

"So this is how you mean to play it." Finally Dana saw the light. "Are you never going to stop playing fast and loose with the truth?"

"I'm not going to change," Melinda confirmed. "I saw the way he looked at you. The innocent temptress in our midst."

The colour drained entirely from Dana's face. "Spread that lie and I don't see how you can live with yourself. It's a bid for sympathy, isn't it? You want the family to forgive you. Let you back in. I'm to be the scapegoat. The marriage couldn't work because *I* came between you both. It won't wash, Melinda. *You* know it. *I* know it. The only feeling I had for Jimmy was friendship."

Melinda gave a bitter laugh. "You've always been too good to be true. I really can't help what anyone else thinks. They didn't get it from me. Jimmy was the stupid one. He opened his big mouth. You know Logan hates you."

Dana pulled back from the bed like it had caught fire. "He does not. We mightn't be compatible but he doesn't hate me."

"He does, too," Melinda confirmed as though she'd just heard it straight from Logan's mouth. "I'm amazed you refuse to believe it. Logan's ten times the man Jimmy was, but *you* couldn't catch him in a million light-years." There was a glitter of pure malice in Melinda's blue eyes.

Dana's breath came so hard she nearly choked.

"Catch him? Aren't you mixing me up with someone else?"

At that, Melinda's cheeks burned. "You've been dying to say that all these years, haven't you?"

"It would never have helped anyone to have said it," Dana answered bluntly. "Be warned, I'm not going to allow you to make up lies about me, Melinda. And about Jimmy. I can't help what Logan thinks. You must be some sort of a monster. I've done everything I could to support you since we were kids."

"I know. You're a bred-in-the-bone do-gooder," Melinda replied almost cheerfully with her odd capacity to confound. "Logan thinks it was good old you who first captured Jimmy's heart. Which you did. But it was *later,* and all unaware. I used to watch the two of you together and enjoy a good laugh. Jimmy knew you would never look at him. Then you got engaged to your precious Gerard. What a swathe you two cut. You so blond, he so dark. Both of you so damned clever. You never did tell me what happened there."

"I couldn't love Gerard in the way he wanted," Dana said in a voice as quiet as possible. "I realise now it wasn't love. It was deep affection. Gerard deserved the lovely girl he has since married."

"And you're all friends," Melinda crowed. "That's the really funny part. Your lovely friend Lucy is a bit of an idiot if you ask me."

"You can't hurt her, Melinda," Dana said. "You can't hurt Gerard and you can't hurt me, though you've tried often enough."

Melinda's shoulders against the pillows went rigid. "I'm scared, Dana," she suddenly confessed. "I'm so terrified I'm shaking inside. What if Jimmy changed his will?"

Dana caught the panic in her cousin's voice. "You think he did?"

"Well, he didn't love me, darling." Melinda was back to mockery.

"He might have had you given him a chance. He never mentioned anything about changing his will to me. You are his widow."

"And Alice was his dear little changeling. How she ever got to be so plain I'll never know. I've been complimented on my looks all my life. Jimmy was very good-looking. Not like Logan, of course, but then, who the hell is?"

"Alice will come into her own as she matures," Dana said sharply, her condemnation of Melinda spilling out. "Ainslie is a distinguished-looking woman. Alice takes after her grandmother."

"With a face like a horse," Melinda said waspishly.

"A *thoroughbred,* that's the thing. It's terrible what you're doing to Alice, Melinda. One day you're going to bitterly regret it. You're starving her of your love."

"I am not and I never have been. I just don't pander to her like you do. In many ways she's a big disappointment to me. You might think of that while you're ticking me off. She's difficult, she's plain, and she doesn't know how to *behave.* I've had to put up with her tantrums for years on end. I've had no life. I lost all that when I married Jimmy. I thought we were going to travel the world staying in the best hotels. But he had to stay close to you and his adored family. Well close enough. No way anyone could expect me to live out here. It's like another planet. Maybe Mars."

"Until it turns into the biggest garden on earth. I must go back, Melinda," Dana said tiredly. It was impossible to get through to her cousin.

"Do that," Melinda called after her bitterly. "Don't forget to give them all my love. I'm sure you've been answering queries about the bereaved widow around the clock."

*   *   *

By late afternoon everyone had left except two elderly relatives who couldn't face the return journey and had elected to retire with a light supper to be served later in their rooms. Ainslie was at the end of her tether and had retired, as well, taking a sedative at the behest of her doctor. Sandra, wishing to escape for a few hours and openly hostile to Melinda, had flown out for the night with her boyfriend, Jack Cordell, and his family. The Cordells owned Jindaroo Station on Mara's north-east border, some sixty miles away. Alice, tired out by her accumulated tears and fears, had for once climbed quietly into her bed and instantly fell into a deep sleep from which she was not to wake until dawn the following morning.

Left to her own devices, Dana sat on the veranda looking over the extraordinary sweeping vista of Mara's home gardens. It never failed to move her how the early settlers through their sense of nostalgia had tried to re-create something of "home" in a landscape as remote from the misty beauty of the British Isles as the far side of the moon, yet the Dangerfields had succeeded to a remarkable degree. Every last mistress of Mara had been a passionate gardener, but it took Ainslie to begin the long task of replacing exotics extremely difficult to get to flourish with the wonderful natives that abounded but had hitherto been considered too "strange."

Dana would never forget her first visit to Mara. Nothing could have prepared her for the heart-stopping sight of a magnificent green oasis in the middle of a red desert. The splendid homestead was sheltered by magnificent old trees planted to mark the birth of each child through the generations. For one family to have established all this was inspiring. Even more incredulous was the garden's dimensions. Fed by underground bores, it included its own huge informal lake with its colony of black swans and wealth of water plants. There were sunken rose gardens with long beds of massed plantings and wonderful old statuary brought out from England, native gardens, fruit gardens and vegetable gardens all tended by a small army of groundsmen under a Mr. Aitkinson who had been with the family since forever and was a horticulturist of some note. Great sheaves of flowers from Mara's gardens had covered Jimmy's casket.

At the memory, tears rushed into Dana's eyes and she stood up, twisting her body as though trying to shake off a great burden of sadness. She couldn't fully take in what the family was saying about her and Jimmy. She would have to make a great effort to remember to call him Tyler. Certainly they had grown close over the years, their love and concern for Alice their common bond, but to suggest Jimmy had loved her in any romantic sense simply wasn't true. He had never shown a hint of it in his behaviour. Indeed he had treated her more like a sister with a tender affection. Was it possible she had been blinded by her own immunity? Had she failed to divine his true feelings?

It was an unhappy fact Jimmy had turned to other women for comfort and sexual release. Melinda, so eager for his lovemaking before their marriage, had inexplicably turned off physical intimacy after the birth of their child. Or so Jimmy had thought. Dana knew her cousin better. Even as a child Melinda, behind the soft smiles, had been a cold and manipulative little person. ''Grasping'' one of Dana's friends had called her. A charge that had upset Dana at the time but one she was later forced to admit was impossible to defend. The same friend had suggested to Dana that her cousin's ''love'' for her contained an element of deep resentment.

In her heart Dana knew it. There had been many little betrayals through the years. It was Melinda who had planted the seed. To cause doubt in them all. To lessen

Dana's standing in the eyes of the family. She was the third person in a doomed relationship. Whatever Melinda's purpose, the strategy had succeeded. Dana had won over Ainslie and Sandra, all three of them naturally compatible, but as for Logan? Logan had distrusted her from day one.

Logan, too, had a failed engagement. Dana had met Phillipa Wrightsman on several occasions although she had not attended the engagement party nor had she been invited. Phillipa, as a member of the landed gentry, was eminently suitable to succeed Ainslie as mistress of Mara. But the engagement hadn't worked. No one seemed to know why. Logan never spoke about it other than to say the decision was mutual. The family wouldn't have it any girl in her right mind would reject Logan. In fact Dana, with her excellent eye, had taken note this very day Phillipa was still in love with her ex-fiancé. Logan had driven Phillipa and her family down to the airstrip some twenty minutes before with Phillipa holding on to Logan's arm. Phillipa had tried to be friendly but Dana knew she would never be regarded as anyone else but Melinda's cousin. Melinda was deeply disliked, although the extended family had tried hard to disguise it in the name of good manners. Melinda's blond curls and big blue eyes had rarely seduced her own sex, either.

Even as Dana stood at the balcony, her hands gripping the wrought-iron railing, a jeep swept through the open gates of the main compound. Logan returning. There was no time to retreat. He brought the jeep to a halt near the central three-tiered fountain, swung out, slammed the door and took the short flight of stone steps to the homestead in two lopes.

If Dana had been asked to sum up Logan Dangerfield with one word it would have been: *electric*. He radiated power. It crackled and flew in the very air around him.

She had never in her life met anyone who could equal
Logan for sheer impact and she had met many high-
profile people in the course of her work as a professional
photographer. Though he would be amazed and not too
pleased to hear it, she had a framed photograph of him
in her apartment. She had taken it herself, an action shot
of him on horseback, controlling his favourite stallion,
Ebony King, spooked by a visitor's flyaway hat. It was
a great shot. All her girlfriends who saw it thought she
had to be madly in love with him. Not really believing
her when she said all that had ever been between her
and Logan was a kind of cold war. Nothing but that
unspeakable, unbanishable kiss. Not a kiss. A punishment.

"You look terribly on edge," Logan now said, his
brilliant eyes moving over her with extraordinary intensity yet that curious reserve.

"So do you," she responded tightly, taking a chair.

"God, why not? On this horrendous day." He had
removed his suit jacket sometime earlier, now he jerked
at his black tie, pulling it off and throwing it over the
back of one of the wicker armchairs. "Where's everyone?" He unloosened the top button of his shirt then
another, exposing the strong brown column of his throat.

"Ainslie has retired," she told him quietly.

"Poor Ainslie!" His voice was deep with sympathy.
"For a mother to lose her son and in such a way. Uncle
George and Aunt Patricia? What about them?"

"They're played out. They're having a light supper in
their room. Alice is asleep, as well. She's worn out by
her tears. It's been a terrible day for her."

"I know." Under his dark copper tan was a distinct
pallor. "And Melinda? I have to tell you, Dana, I hope
I'm not seeing her tonight. I just couldn't take it."

"She's staying in her room." Dana's voice firmed.

"She said to tell you she'll be taking the plane out in the morning."

"After the will reading, I bet. What about you?" He shot her a quick look. A recent assignment on the Great Barrier Reef had gilded her skin. It glowed like a pale golden pearl against the sombre black of her two-piece suit.

"I'll be going, as well, of course." She looked back at him in consternation.

"I thought you might think of family for once," he replied bitingly. "Ainslie and Sandra. They could do with your company."

"I can't stay here without Melinda, Logan. Surely you see that?"

"No, I *don't*," he clipped off. "The best thing you could do, Dana, is get shot of your cousin."

"And what about Alice?" she retaliated, her own brown eyes suddenly blazing. It was always like this with Logan.

He pulled out a chair and slumped into it moodily. "Yes, yes. Poor little Alice. My heart bleeds for that child. At least when Tyler was there…" He broke off in grief and anger.

"*I'm* here, Logan." Her eyes welled with tears and she turned away abruptly so he couldn't see.

His laugh was discordant. "And we're very grateful for that. Why don't you and Alice stay on for a few days? I'm sure Melinda won't mind. She's let you take care of Alice often enough."

Dana turned, feeling a queer stab of regret. One part of her would have loved to stay but as a fellowship-winning photographer and currently "hot" property on the art scene, she had numerous commitments. "Logan, I'd do what I could," she said, "but I have assignments and a set of pictures for a Sydney showing due in.

Besides, when have you ever wanted me around the place?''

His eyes were as hot and stormy as the electric blue sky. "Don't be so bloody ridiculous," he rasped.

"I'm not being ridiculous at all," she retorted, stung by his long-held attitudes. "You've never liked me, Logan, any more than I like you."

"So what do you want from me?" he taunted, deliberately trying to stir her. "What you're used to? Men who worship the ground you walk upon?"

"If that were true, we'd have an awful lot in common," she flared. "Phillipa is still in love with you.

He looked back dispassionately. "Like most women, Phillipa doesn't want to let go. She'll meet someone soon."

"I hope so, for her sake," Dana answered, suddenly sounding very cool, though it cost her dearly. "It's been three years."

"Really?" He shifted position abruptly so he could stare at her. Face to face. "I didn't realise you kept such tabs on me."

Before she could prevent herself she arched back in her chair, her two hands gripped together. It was a significant move, one he appreciated from the mocking look on his face. "How could I not know what was happening in your life. I saw Jimmy—"

Logan winced, dangerously close to breaking loose. "Can't you say Tyler?"

"Of course I can." She took a deep breath, trying to hold on to her own escalating emotions. "But it will take time. Tyler was Jimmy to us. I suppose he was trying for a new life." She stopped abruptly, continued in a gentler tone. "He used to love to talk about you. About Mara. When you were boys. He had such great love for you, Logan. Such respect and admiration."

His knuckles gripped until they gleamed bone white.

"But I wasn't able to help him at the end?" There was a whole world of regret in it.

"He was a grown man," Dana offered in the spirit of reconciliation, though every nerve in her body was on edge. This had been such a terrible day for everybody. She could see the depth of Logan's grief.

"And he had the great misfortune to marry Melinda. Just about any other girl would have made a go of it." It was said not in anger, more a point of fact.

Dana sighed, a sad and haunted look in her eyes. "Tragically they weren't suited to each other at all." She put back a hand, lifted her long hair away from her hot nape, unaware a beam of sunlight was streaming through it turning it to a waterfall of ash gold. When she looked back at Logan, some expression in his eyes made her heart pound. It wasn't anger or even the sexual hostility that often flared between them, but something more primitive and dangerous. "Is something wrong?" she asked, a betraying tremor in her voice.

He shoved back his chair, stood up, all six foot three, flexing the muscles in his back. No one better than Logan to throw a long shadow. "Sometimes I can't take your feminine wiles," he growled.

She stared up at him in amazement. "I've never met anyone in my life who fires up like you do," she protested. "*What* feminine wiles?"

He shot her a sharp, potent glance. "Hell, every time I see you, you've got a new one. I guess you're the sort of woman a man would do anything to have." There was condemnation mixed up with the grudging admiration.

"Well, I haven't made my mark on you." Dana, in her turn, jumped up from her chair. What *was* this between her and Logan? A kind of love-hate? Nothing else came to mind.

"On the contrary, you made your mark," he said

moodily. "You were dangerous as little more than a schoolgirl," he brooded. "Now you're a woman and ten times more alluring. Ah, what the hell! Let's get away from the house," he said with a kind of urgency. "Change your clothes. We'll ride. I feel like galloping to the very edge of the earth."

CHAPTER THREE

AND gallop he did, with the kind of desperate anguish Dana shared. Though an excellent rider, well mounted, she couldn't hope to match him, but she drove her beautiful spirited mare until her aching head started to clear and the awesome splendour of the sky entered her blood.

A storm was coming. The very air sizzled with the build up of electricity. On the western horizon huge mushrooming clouds of purple and silver were shot with flame as the slanting rays of the sun cut a great swathe through them. Even the sandhills on the desert border glowed like furnaces against the eerie, super-charged sky. It was a barbaric scene and, despite her grief, Dana felt a rising wave of excitement.

Birds, great flights of them, were coming from all points of the compass, splitting the air with their cries. They passed overhead at lightning speed, homing into the shadowy sanctuary of swamps, billabongs and lagoons that crisscrossed the vast landscape. The air vibrated with the whirr of a million brilliantly coloured wings. Often such spectacular atmospheric effects came to nothing or little more than a fine beading of raindrops, but Dana could tell from the violent and acid-green streaks in the heatwaves this was going to be big. She believed wholeheartedly the storm was sent to mark Tyler's passing.

Logan thought so, too. She could see it in his face, dark, brooding, despairing.

"We'd better take shelter," he shouted to her, lifting his voice as the first clap of thunder rolled across the

heavens. Even as they turned the horses towards the line
of shallow caves the aboriginals called Yamacootra, a
jagged spear of lightning flashed through the low canopy
of clouds. The caves right in the heart of Mara were
prehistoric sites, hallowed ground inhabited by
Dreamtime spirits, the largest of them pitched high at
the dome allowing easy access to a man as tall as Logan.
It was there they headed. Incandescent light seething
around them as they galloped up the slope. Once a pair
of brolgas shot up from a huge clump of cane grass,
causing Dana's mare to rear in sudden fright. So strong
was the tension in the atmosphere she thought she would
be thrown but Logan closed in on her, grabbing at the
reins and subduing the mare with his superior strength.

When they arrived at the entrance Logan settled the
excited, sweating horses in an overhang partially
screened by high tangled vegetation and a spindly ghost
gum growing out of rock. A bank of flowering lantana
all but blocked the mouth of the cave but Logan ripped
it aside as the driving wind turned the fallen leaves into
a whirlwind of green and purple. Temporarily blinded
by the whirling cloud Dana lurched over a half-hidden
rock, clawing at Logan's shirt to keep her balance.

"Here, steady, I've got you." His strong arm whipped
around her and he muffled a violent oath as a disturbed
goanna, fully six feet in length, shot out of the cave
opening like a projectile, hissing at them hoarsely.

Dana held a hand over her face for protection. Her
heart was thudding behind her ribs. Logan was holding
her so painfully close she had to grit her teeth against a
whole range of electrifying sensations.

Logan shouted at the giant lizard, watching it race
down the slope. "Go on, get. I just hope he hasn't got
a mate." Shielding her body with his own, Logan entered the cave, his eyes darting swiftly around the inte-

rior. There was plenty of light now as brilliant spears of lightning forked down the sky. The ancient stone walls glowed with ochres, red, yellow, burnt orange, black and white and charcoal.

Moving very quietly, Dana moved back into the cave, further unnerved by the presence of little lizards that dashed across the sand at her feet. This wasn't the first time she had been inside the cave. Logan had permitted her access several times, but for once she felt threatened by the forces that were at work all around them. The cave was eerie, hushed, dim except for the brilliant flashes of light. There was hardly an inch of wall and roof space that wasn't covered in drawings of totemic beings and creatures. Like the great undulating coils of the Rainbow Snake executed on ochres, stark white and charcoal. As the lightning flashed, the snake seemed to move, causing Dana an irrational spasm of fear. She continued to move about, trying to cover her agitated state of mind though it must have been obvious to Logan. A great crocodile was incised and painted on the wall, its broad primeval snout peering out of what appeared to be a clump of reeds. A crocodile in the desert? Either the aboriginal artist was a nomad or the drawing dated back to the inland sea of prehistory. In a sort of desperation she stopped and focused on it, murmuring more to herself than Logan who was standing at the entrance of the cave staring out at the brilliant pyrotechnics.

"I'd love to photograph all this. It would sell like hot cakes."

"The answer is no," he threw over his shoulder.

"I understand why."

"That's why you've been allowed in."

"No need to snap my head off." Damn, his tone of voice wasn't the problem. It was being alone with him. Both of them usually took care it didn't happen. He was standing quite still but his whole aura told her he was on full alert. Would she ever find an answer to the mystery that was Logan Dangerfield? The rain was coming down harder now, falling in a solid silver sheet from the overhang. They might have been sealed in some ancient temple.

For the first time she noticed Logan's tanned skin, taut over his chiselled bones, was sheened with rain. His blue-black hair was damp, as well, curling over the collar of his denim shirt. He always wore his thick waving hair full and a little long, not wasting much time looking for hairdressers. He didn't have to. Most women would give anything to have hair like that. Once or twice she had seen him with a beard when he'd been away for weeks on end visiting the outstations. The sight of him *wild* with his blue eyes blazing had all but dried up her mouth. She realised now she had always revelled in his arrogance and splendid male beauty even as she buried it in the wary banter they indulged in.

Another bolt of thunder flashed across the heavens, then a flash of lightning so harsh it was almost withering, filled the cave.

Dana in sheer reaction fell to her knees holding both hands across her ears.

"It's okay." Logan tried to comfort her though he spoke between his clenched teeth. He crossed to her, easing himself down on his haunches. "Dana?"

She didn't answer, her ash-blond head down between her arms. He took a thick silky fistful of hair, lifting her face to him. He had never seen her eyes so huge, so dark, pools of an answering tension. Her body might have been wired it was so electric to his touch. "No need to panic. You've seen a storm before." Even as he spoke his words were almost drowned out by the violent crack of thunder that crashed like a giant drum. There were massive thunder-heads backlit by flashes that rivalled the brilliance of the sun. If the rain kept coming, all the gullies would be overflowing, bringing precious water to the eternally thirsty land. A strong wind had blown up outside the cave, parting the silver curtain of rain so that it flew into the mouth of the cave. They were forced to pull back into the interior. Logan, with one arm, half dragged her across the sand.

Today of all days he thought he could just lose his last hold on control, do something both of them would regret all their lives. But his feeling for her ran contrary to his will. It was an urgent pulse drumming deep inside of him. Desire that had been buried deep since the first time he had taken her in his arms. "Damn you, Dana," he said explosively.

"And damn you, too," Dana answered with equal fervour, trying to break his strong grip. "I can't bear to be with you, Logan."

The knowledge tore at him. "So what are you waiting for?" He jerked her to her feet, overcome by sexual hostility that fairly crackled and spat. "This isn't the biggest storm I've ever seen. In a minute or so it will be all over. You can ride."

That sent her wild. "Why do you hate me?" she hurled at him. "Melinda told me you did but I wouldn't believe it. But it's *true*. You're so cruel. Then I see another side of you. You're so bloody charming, so bloody *perverse!*"

His blue eyes blazed an ominous warning. "I don't hate you, Dana. Far from it. But my heart and mind are locked and barred against you."

"Why?" She cursed herself for asking but she was obsessed with knowing. "Can't you tell me *why?*"

"You've known since the day I met you," he returned harshly. "For what happened between you and Tyler.

Melinda wasn't alone in this disaster. *Your* hold on Tyler was too powerful for him to break.''

Any sense of balance disappeared entirely. She closed her eyes, shuttering them with her lashes. ''What you're saying is terrible. It's so ugly.''

''Yes, it *is*,'' he agreed with terrible irony. ''You may not have broken any code of honour but there were consequences, Dana. Consequences for us all. You were forbidden to Tyler, just as you're forbidden to me.''

Forbidden? Was that the awful truth? ''You're crazy,'' Dana said in dull despair.

''He told me you were the best thing in his life,'' Logan said just as bleakly.

''The best thing in his life was *Alice*.'' Her voice picked up power. ''My only role was *friend*. Can't you get that through your fool head?'' A dull roaring had begun in her ears. Fool? Logan Dangerfield. What was she saying?

''I don't give a damn for words, Dana.''

''You're calling me a liar? I don't like that.''

His blue eyes *burned*. ''Then how come Tyler spoke so lovingly of you to us all? Ainslie, Sandra, me. Even Alice. You were in all his letters. I can show them to you. Hell, Dana. He was my brother. I understood him.''

''He couldn't have said we were *lovers*. He could never have said that,'' Dana waivered, wondering if she had ever known Jimmy at all.

''*Were* you?'' Logan caught her face between his hands, forced her to look at him.

''I would swear on his grave.'' She was trembling so violently she thought she might fall.

''Do you mean that?'' He shook her as though unable to deal with his anger.

''Of course I mean it. Why are you trying to ruin my

life? Why are you trying to force this role of seductress on me?''

''Because I have to *know*.''

''Why is it so terribly important to you?'' she demanded. ''You act as if you can't stand it.'' In another minute she knew she'd either cry or lunge at him.

''Maybe I *can't*.'' His voice was very bitter. ''I knew the minute you stopped my breath with your beauty you would know how to wreck lives.''

She felt ravaged, full of pain. What he was saying was monstrous.

''I want to leave.'' Dana held up her hand as if to ward off danger.

''I'm not going to stop you,'' he rasped.

''Because you're afraid. The great Logan Dangerfield, master of all he surveys, is afraid. Afraid of a woman.'' Hostility flooded her, an aching desire to punish him as he punished her. ''You know in your heart there was nothing between Jimmy and me, but you have to tear at me anyway. You know why? Because you don't want to answer to your own desires. It must be really bad for you to want a woman you profess to despise.''

It was a moment of such tremendous tension Dana feared a dizzy spell. What was happening was more powerful than either of them. Adrenaline coursed through her overheated veins, so her body flushed. She turned on her heel, determined to rush out into the driving storm, but he came after her, locking a steely arm around her, staring down into her face framed by the blond turbulence of her hair.

''Don't be a damned fool,'' he said, feeling on this day of all days just touching her would set off a landslide.

''Better the storm than you,'' Dana cried tempestuously, feeling all the air was being sucked out of her body. Didn't he know his long fingers were cupping her breast?

"Dana, don't do this. *Don't.*" His nerves were so jangled his hands were rough, but she continued to struggle as if she didn't care, more invited it. Her struggles and the high soft moans that went with it like a keening bird, only served to inflame him.

Finally he lost it. Lost whatever had held him in check all these years. Furiously, a driven man, he spun her into his arms, his mouth moving with insatiable hunger all over her face, her temples, her eyes, her cheeks, her breathtaking mouth, her high arched throat, bending her backwards until he could taste the sweet satin swell of her breast. He knew he shouldn't give in to this but the whole catastrophe of the day had shattered him. She was Dana. She was Woman. She was Fantasy. A liberation from the black well of grief. He wanted her even if she detested him.

But Dana, too, was in the relentless grip of passion. She had always known this man could break her heart. Hadn't their relationship always been fraught with intensities? She knew she would bitterly regret this. But for now…for now… In his way he was an irresistible force. Her body was responding to him like it responded to nobody else and never would. She realised in a moment of terrible truth she loved him. That all the emotional ambiguities had nothing to do with her deepest driven secret. She wanted him as badly as he wanted her, both of them wholly dependant on the other to reaffirm Life.

His mouth and the questing urgency of his hands left her breathless, half crazed. For all they had tried, what was about to happen could not be averted. It was even a release to get it out into the open, the dream after midnight become reality.

She was lying on the sand, feeling its coolness against

her heated skin. She saw Logan bending over her, his dynamic dark face all taut planes and angles, his blue eyes blazing like the jewels in some primitive mask. Hadn't she known in her heart of hearts this was going to happen? She had hidden from the danger, now she was mad to embrace it.

But it was all *wordless*. Only the air thrummed with the electricity their bodies generated and the soft sound of the moans that bordered on anguish. As a lover he was extraordinary, more extraordinary than in all the little fantasies she had kept to herself.

When his mouth found her nipple it set off an avalanche of pleasure. She had to gasp aloud. Excitement was building so rapidly she could hardly remember to breathe. This was the perfect way of blotting out pain and grief. But at such a risk! Her stubborn resistance to him and the power he projected had been her perfect camouflage. Now this headlong surrender. The *enormity* of it. The intense fear and the rapture. Sensation was obscuring everything. Any need for caution. All she was aware of was her overpowering hunger for him. With a few sweeping motions he removed the rest of her clothing. His blue eyes burned at the sight of her body so perfectly designed for a man's loving. They moved over her so intensely he might have been memorising every inch of her, the fine pores of her skin.

Then he was making love to her with such passion yet a curious underlying tenderness that left her dazed with wonder. Both of them had dropped all form of pretence; the masks they had kept in place for so long.

While the rain continued to drum down on the parched earth and the cave was filled with white-hot flashes of intermittent light, the fire that was inside of them burst into a conflagration that finally gave expression to the bewildering pain/pleasure that had plagued them for so long.

This was ecstasy even if they had lost all sense of the morrow.

Another secret.

It was Dana's first waking thought. Around her was silence and the grey pearly light of pre-dawn. As the light brightened the birds would begin to sing in their trillions but for now the silence rang like a hammer on her heart.

Impossible to describe her night. It had been full of fragmentary-coherent dreams and heart-stopping moments when she awoke with a convulsive gasp thinking Logan's hands were caressing her. Her face flushed with colour at the memory and she turned sideways burying her head in the mound of pillows that smelled so beautifully of the native boronia that perfumed the linen press.

Yesterday had been the most traumatic day of her life. It had started so grimly with Jimmy's funeral yet ended in a dazzling ecstasy that redefined life. Two separate momentous experiences. She wasn't a virgin. She and Gerard had shared a warm, caring relationship which she gradually came to understand was not the passionate overwhelming love she really craved. It was she who had broken off the engagement knowing in her heart the right person was out there for both of them. And so it had turned out. Gerard had found his Lucy, but the man who held her under his spell was already in her life. A man who until yesterday had been armoured in discipline, authority, control.

And after the bubble burst and they came back to cold reality?

Neither of them seemed ready to handle what had happened, accepting no amount of mind power could ever wipe it out. For as long as their lovemaking had lasted, both of them had lost all thought of anything but one another. They had breached the iron rule. To keep their physical and psychological distance.

What now?

So deeply was Dana immersed in her thoughts it took a little time for her to register a small voice was calling her name.

Alice.

Dana sprang up from the bed, pulling on her robe as she went.

"Why, darling girl, whatever's the matter?"

Alice stood just outside the door dressed in one of the pretty pin-tucked batiste nighties Dana had bought for her as a balance to the "sensible" apparel Melinda favoured. Her dear plain little face was streaked with tears and her light brown hair free of its plait stuck out in a tangled nimbus around her head. She went straight into Dana's arms, hugging her.

"I went into Mummy's room but she told me to go away. It isn't time to get up. She said she's sick of me and my silly fears. She's not going to look after me anymore."

Shockingly, it was something Melinda said often. Neither Dana nor Jimmy had been able to stop her.

"Mummy doesn't mean it, darling," Dana soothed. "I expect she's still very tired and sad. This is a bad time for all of us."

"It's worse for Daddy." Alice's voice broke on a sob. "Why did he have to die? I'll never forgive him."

Gently Dana drew the child through the door and shut it after her, feeling the grief and frustration that was in the child's small frame.

"It was a terrible accident, Ally. Daddy had no control over what happened to him.'' Which sadly wasn't strictly true. ''He would never have left you. He loved you.''

''Then why didn't he stay? Now I'll be more different than ever. I won't have a Daddy.''

Dana couldn't answer that. Although she hadn't the slightest doubt Melinda would remarry soon. Melinda had never felt secure on her own. ''Hop in with me,'' Dana invited. ''I'll give you a cuddle.''

Alice expelled a soft shuddery sigh. ''That will be lovely. There was a beastie in my room.''

Assorted beasties and bogeymen had long plagued Alice during the hours of darkness. She was a sensitive, imaginative child and, it had to be faced, emotionally disturbed.

''Wasn't your night-light on?'' Dana asked, pulling up the covers and settling the little girl against the pillows.

''Mummy doesn't like me to have the night-light, Dana. You know that. She always scolds me. She said it was all your fault filling my head with silly stories.''

Dana stroked the fringe from Alice's eyes. ''Don't worry, darling, I'll speak to Mummy about it. She doesn't quite realise how much imagination you've got. Lots of children don't like the dark. It's always been part of childhood. A lot of adults don't like it, either. It's nothing to be worried about.''

''I like the light on,'' Alice insisted, already snuggling down. ''Dana, do you think I could come to live with you instead of just for a visit?''

Dana tried to cover up her sadness. This was a terrible state of affairs.

''Darling, how could I deprive Mummy of her little girl?''

Alice gave her a very grave adult stare. ''She wouldn't

miss me. She said she might put me in a boarding school while she travels the world.''

This was entirely new to Dana. "When did she say this?"

She got into bed beside Alice while Alice moved into the crook of her shoulder. "Yesterday. She said I was part of the problem with her marriage."

"Oh, rubbish!" Dana couldn't help herself. It just burst out. Melinda depended on her for many things. She would have to flex what little muscle she had for Alice's sake.

"You're really funny when you get mad," Alice giggled. "Daddy said to me once, if I'm not around, find Dana."

"Well, I am your godmother," Dana answered finally.

"And you love me." Alice gave a great sigh of belonging. "Sometimes I really am scared of Mummy. Even the kids at school think she's awful."

Dana pondered on that. "Awful when she's so young and pretty?"

Alice squirmed. "Miss Eldred said, 'It's just awful what she's doing to that child.'"

It was amazing how she caught the teacher's tones. "Surely she wasn't talking about Mummy?"

Alice shot her another look. "Some days when Mummy picks me up she's in a really bad mood."

"Why on earth didn't you tell me?" Dana was appalled.

"You might be so angry at Mummy you might never come to see her and she wouldn't let me see you," Alice answered in her extraordinary way.

"Alice, I would never desert your mother. Or you," Dana said fervently. "You must believe that. Your mother and I have been together since we were little girls. She's almost my sister."

"Then why does she tell you so many lies?"

The skin on Dana's head actually prickled. "Whatever do you mean?"

Alice looked back in genuine puzzlement. "Daddy said she did. Didn't he tell you?"

Dana took her time replying. "Listen, cherub, I hate to say this but too many people have been doing too much talking in front of you. Why don't you curl up now and close your eyes. It's going to be a long, tiring day, I'm afraid. You'll need your sleep."

"Can't I stay awake and listen to the birds? They're so beautiful."

Dana felt a great rush of affection. "The birds will sing for you another day, sweetheart. Get your rest now. We have a lot of travelling to do."

Alice obediently composed herself, giving an exhausted little yawn. "I hope I'll be as beautiful as you are, Dana, when I grow up."

Dana gave the little girl a hug. "Darling, you're going to be a lovely person to be with."

"I want to have a light about me, like you," Alice breathed, her lashes coming down to rest on her cheeks. "Like the picture of an angel."

"That's lovely, darling." Dana was touched.

"Daddy said about the light, but I know exactly what he meant." Alice suddenly opened her eyes and turned her head along the pillow. "Take care of me, Dana?"

"I'll take care of you as long as I live," Dana said staunchly.

"Swear you'll live a long, long time." There was a sudden rush of tears into Alice's big brown eyes.

"You don't have to worry about that." Dana fought to keep her voice steady. "I'm going to live until I'm a hundred and I get a telegram from the Queen."

"Does she really send a telegram?" Alice giggled.

"Yes, she does," Dana said very softly into the little girl's ear.

"Thank you, Dana," Alice answered simply, and almost immediately fell asleep.

Alice was still sleeping when Dana went down to find herself a cup of coffee. The house was quiet, but Mrs. Buchan, the housekeeper, was in the kitchen making preparations for the day.

"So, can I get you a cup of tea, Dana?" she asked as Dana came quietly through the door.

"A cup of coffee would be lovely. Here, let me get it." Dana put a gentle hand on the older woman's shoulder, hearing the uncontrollable tremor of grief in the housekeeper's voice. Mrs. Buchan, in her mid-fifties, had been in the family's employ since she was a girl. Her husband, Manny, Logan's overseer, had started his working life on the station as a young jackeroo. Both of them had watched Tyler grow up.

"Toast, dear?" Mrs. Buchan breathed deeply to calm herself.

"No, I think I'll go for a little walk."

"How about Alice?"

"Don't worry. She'll sleep for a while yet. She woke up early and came into me."

"You tell me where that little girl would be without you." Mrs. Buchan shook her head sadly.

Outside in the brilliant early morning sunshine, Dana walked down the drive, feeling the crunch of gravel beneath her shoes. There wasn't a single cloud in the sky. It was a deep vivid blue. A sense of foreboding hung over her, the feeling that life was rushing out of her control. She had an acute sense, too, of her own sensuality. Not so long ago she thought she had discovered love with Gerard, but compared to what she had experienced in that explosive storm it now appeared very quiet and safe. Logan had taught her more about her own body than she had learned in a lifetime. She had discovered herself as he had discovered her, unlocking all her closely held secrets. For that time in the cave there hadn't been one tiny part of her that hadn't responded to his touch. Passion at that level was stupendous. It was also perilous. How, for instance, was she going to live without it?

CHAPTER FOUR

RESTLESSLY, Dana veered off towards the lake. She could see the exquisite black swans sailing across its glassy green surface with a flotilla of ducks and other waterfowl in attendance. The dense green perimeter of reeds was illuminated by large stands of day lilies, strap-leafed iris and the water-loving arum lilies with their handsome velvety white spathes. It all looked so peaceful, so beautiful, *eternal,* when Jimmy was gone. He had paid a terrible penalty.

She couldn't fathom why he had told his family of a depth of feeling for her, which he had never shown. Of necessity because of their common bond of love and protectiveness for Alice, they had been drawn closely together. Both had tried very hard to shield Alice from a mother who was cold to her.

Trying to find some defence for Melinda, Dana had come to the conclusion Melinda had been emotionally crippled by the early loss of her parents. Dana had once heard her own mother say Melinda was incapable of showing affection. But she was bonded to Dana. Their kinship made Dana unique and Dana had always made allowances for her cousin. They all had. Perhaps in retrospect it had been a mistake. A little toughening up might have made Melinda a more complete person.

Jimmy's death had precipitated a crisis. Alice had lost the loving, caring parent. It was a bruising reality Melinda could and would not show Alice the affection every child needed. Such coldness and Alice's obvious unhappiness troubled every sensitive person who came into their orbit. Dana herself couldn't count the number

49

of times she had felt its chilling effect. Melinda was such a very difficult person. It was because of this Dana had felt compelled to build up a supportive relationship not only for Alice but for Jimmy, who had suffered in his own way. Perhaps her best efforts had complicated things terribly. Without Jimmy to explain his precise emotional attachment, the family might always believe she had deliberately allowed his feelings for her to develop. Truly it looked a hopeless dilemma.

She didn't hear Logan's approach until he was almost up to her, then she turned, her velvety brown eyes almost black with intensity. It came to her with anguish that she wanted him to gather her into his arms, but from the expression on his face, yesterday might never have happened.

"Have you decided what you're going to do?" he asked tautly.

Even the set of his body had a daunting authority. She looked away across the lake, her heart beating painfully. "If I could stay, Logan, I would."

"So what's so damned important to take you off?"

They were caught in the old minefield of antagonism. "I have a career. A successful career, but I don't have a fortune behind me. Not like you."

"I'll take care of that," he said curtly.

"I know you would, but nothing could persuade me to take money from you, Logan."

"Dana, please." He took hold of her shoulders, turned her to him. "Ainslie is desperately in need of comfort. Sandra, too. You can help."

"I know that." Dana's eyes filled with tears. "And I'm so terribly sad. Please don't be angry with me, Logan. I'm so upset myself, I feel I want someone to take care of *me*."

"I'll take care of you until the cows come home," he

clipped off. "God, Dana, if I let you, you'd have me eating out of your hands."

Incredulously she heard his words, assimilating them through every cell of her body. "But you can't handle that?" she questioned. What was power without love?

His brilliant gaze was the distillation of his passionate nature. "You're running, too, Dana," he told her bluntly. "Hell, you can't wait to get away. But neither of us is going to forget what happened."

"Knowing you, Logan, you'll give it your best shot." She couldn't prevent the upsurge of bitterness.

He let out a sigh that seemed filled with terrible doubts. "It's going to be a long time before I can part you in my mind from Tyler."

"You've just got to be Number One," she said in a low, weary tone.

"So what are you telling me?" he challenged her fiercely.

"I'm telling you *nothing*. You've already decided what you want to believe."

Her eyes were so dark, so beautiful, they could hide many secrets. He wanted desperately to know them all.

She half turned as her voice broke, hair and skin gleaming in the vivid shimmering light. She could taste the pain it was so intense.

"Dana." He came after her immediately, catching hold of her bare arm. "I'm sorry. God, I'm sorry. I don't even know what I'm saying. We're all hurting. I'm only asking you to use your gift."

"Gift, what gift?" She wasn't comforted by his touch. She was on fire. Both of them were still on the thin edge of control.

"People want to talk to you, Dana," he said, his eyes searching her face. "They want to confide in you. I suppose it's called healing."

"But it's Alice who's most in need of me now."

"And how are any of us going to find a way around Melinda? No court will take a child off its mother unless the charges are very serious. Melinda may be damned awful to Alice, but it's emotional abuse and it's mostly hidden. How the hell did you have such a ghastly cousin anyway?"

Dana didn't allow herself to consider she had asked herself the same question. "You've always been rough on her," she accused him.

"I agree." His tone was unapologetic. "I don't seem capable of hiding my dislike. Melinda wrecked my brother's life. She tried to wreck this family. She's turning my little niece into a real mess. Frankly, I find that very hard to stomach. What's more, I'm sick to death of listening to you defend her."

"And I'm sick of listening to you." Dana stopped abruptly, afraid she was about to crumble.

"Then isn't it hell for us to want one another so badly?" he retaliated. "I couldn't bear the thought of you out of my life, yet I don't know how to reach you. You're very valuable to us, Dana. We just can't do without you."

"Valuable? I don't deserve that." His words stirred her so much, her heart pounded in her chest. He was alternatively sharp then seductive. No wonder she was in such a state of constant emotional flux. "I know I'm the intermediary between Melinda and the family."

His expression softened. "Alice is in trouble, Dana. You know that, don't you?"

"Of course I do." She bit her lip.

"I can't walk softly around Melinda. Alice is my brother's child, my niece, a Dangerfield. I'm going to make sure she has a good life."

"And I'm going to help you, Logan," Dana responded with fervour. "I promise you I'll have a serious talk with Melinda."

He groaned, his eyes fierce. "I've heard all about your serious talks. I know how much you love Alice, how much she loves you, but in the end all the talk turns out to be a monologue. When has Melinda ever *listened?*"

It was true. "So *you* talk to her." Dana's voice rose. "You're all powerful."

"I intend to," he said decisively. "Melinda will be financially secure for the rest of her life, but she's not getting what she may have counted on. I've seen to that."

"How?" Dana was completely thrown off stride.

"I had a damned good talk to Tyler last time he was home," Logan told her tersely. "As a family we haven't been wasting our time all these years. We've worked hard to hold on to all we've got. The bulk of the money will be held in trust for Alice. I administer that trust, as you know."

"So there's a new will?"

"There is, my lady. I don't mind your knowing. If Melinda is smart, she'll accept it. It will advantage her nothing going out on the attack. I should tell you, too, so you won't get too emotional. Tyler left a legacy to you."

The shock of it almost sent her reeling. *"No."*

"You didn't know about it?" He smiled tightly, like a tiger.

Her face flamed and she was sorely tempted to hit him. "God, Logan, I hate you."

His handsome mouth twitched in bleak humour. "Sometimes that's the way I feel about you. It's rather a lot of money," he added.

"I don't want it." Her turbulent emotions matched his exactly.

"Maybe you could even quit work," he suggested.

"Go on. Have your hateful fun," she cried.

"It would be the only fun I could have at a time like

this," he pointed out grimly. "I don't think Melinda is going to like it."

"Melinda can think what she damned well likes." Dana was so angry she fairly trembled. "She does anyway. I don't want to say this, but she lies."

"No kidding."

"Why are we fighting, Logan?" she asked bleakly.

"It seemed like the best solution up until now." It sounded unbearably cynical but at that moment he wanted her so badly he clenched his fists until his knuckles whitened. His brother's death was a terrible tragedy and Dana was his good and beautiful friend.

At the look in his eyes, the half-expected rejection, something seemed to die in her. "I'm going back to the house, Logan," she said.

"That's just what I'm doing," he said.

"Then why don't you take another route?" Her voice was cold and dismissive.

He reached for her, holding her still without any physical effort. "Are you telling me what I can do on my own land?"

She tried to pull away. "I sure am. You're like one of those feudal barons, aren't you?"

"Not that I'm aware," he said coolly, but his blue eyes burned.

"Oh, yes, the whole persona fits you perfectly, just like a second skin."

"Then surely I can demand anything of any beautiful woman who passes my way?" he suggested with the powerful urge to fold her in his arms.

"It's part of it, yes," she hit back.

"Like yesterday?" He was so angry, for a moment his grip tightened painfully.

"I suppose now you think you can have me anytime you want." She was shocked at herself but determined to say it.

"Leave it there, Dana," he warned, his eyes fixed on her.

"It may be years before I have another opportunity," she retorted in bitter irony.

"All right, then." Like yesterday, his strong will fled him, leaving only the desperate hunger he believed nothing else could fill. He swept her into his arms, silencing her lovely mouth with a kiss that was without a skerrick of tenderness, holding the kiss powerfully until her furious resistance yielded in sheer surrender and her own needs were utterly betrayed. When he released her, her face was flaming and her dark eyes sheened with tears.

"You brute!" When she had let herself fall fathoms into that kiss.

"Tell me something I don't know," he said with a kind of self-contempt. "I've always wanted to make love to you, Dana. Didn't you know? Stretching right back to the day when you simply burst into my life like some exotic flower."

Want? What was want when she needed so much more from him? "Nevertheless you made sure you kept me at a great distance."

"I know I *attempted* to." His voice was suddenly wry.

"And succeeded rather well. You even got yourself engaged to Phillipa."

"And I'm very fond of her, but it wasn't the classic love at first sight. Maybe it even had something to do with the fact you were marrying your...Jeremy, wasn't it?"

"Gerard, as you very well know." A sudden wind tore at her hair skeined out around her face, causing her to turn away.

"So both of us made a mistake."

"I like that, Logan. You making a mistake," she said in response.

"I don't mean to make another."

She had begun walking, now she turned on her heel. "Does that hold some message for me?" she asked, her face lit by pride.

"You're welcome to see one in it if you like."

She made a sound of distress and shook her head. "We can never be together five minutes without this happening."

It was perfectly true, and under the truth a very good reason. He closed the short space between them. "And I apologise. Most of it is my fault. But it's just as I told you, I have warring feelings about you, Dana."

"It's damned hard to live with," she said bitterly.

"For you and for me." He caught her hand, raised it to his mouth in one of his totally disconcerting gestures. "I didn't want to upset you. I want you to stay."

"As Alice's comforter, or your mistress?" she asked, unable to resist it, but dazed at the thought.

"Well…both."

Some note in his voice made her look up at him sharply, only to find him smiling at her, that rare, charm-the-birds-out-of-the-trees smile that so illuminated his dark face.

"You're insufferable." She was losing the battle to fight his strong aura.

"I know." He tipped up her chin, kissed her briefly but with a haunting sympathy that stayed with her for the rest of the day.

The will reading went badly. Melinda sat white-faced with bitter resentment as Logan read through the four page document, mute until the moment when Logan announced in dispassionate tones Dana's legacy. Then hell broke loose. Melinda rose so swiftly from her chair that if it hadn't been for its substantial weight she would have sent it flying. As it was, her leather armchair rolled back on its casters, scraping the parquet around the Persian rug.

"I don't believe this." For the first time Melinda showed the anger and hostility she usually kept so carefully under wraps.

"All of us are aware Tyler thought very highly of Dana," Logan said, his handsome face without expression.

"Felt highly of her! Is that what it was?" Melinda was totally unable to accept she was not the main beneficiary let alone Dana had been left a considerable sum of money.

"Please sit down, Melinda," Dana begged. "I won't, of course, be accepting it."

"Of course you *will*," Logan cast her a brief glance. "Tyler counted on you for a great deal."

"He was in love with her!" Inexplicably Melinda laughed as if at a joke. "He revelled in her company, the warmth he wouldn't let me give him. I never counted on my own cousin ruining my marriage."

While Dana drew a sharp breath preparatory to answering, Ainslie burst in. "I think you took care of that yourself, Melinda."

"I did not!" Melinda was too far gone to care. "She was always around us. I can still hear their laughter in my ears. Do you think I'd speak like this if it weren't true?"

"Yes," Dana answered without hesitation. "I've always supported you, Melinda, but I'm not prepared to let you destroy my good name. Stop this unforgivable offence right now. I want to be cleared fully. Jimmy—" She corrected herself immediately. "*Tyler* and I were friends. Our common bond was Alice."

"Before God it's true," Melinda announced ringingly. "I even caught you one time."

A deep unstoppable anger took hold of Dana. She felt

she could protest her innocence forever and never be believed. She shot out of her chair like an avenging angel, grasping her cousin's upper arms tightly. "You'll never drag me down, Melly," she promised. "I'll never understand why you want to."

"If you hadn't been around he would have come back to me," Melinda exclaimed with a high moral tone.

"Well, you had to make sure we all knew," Logan said in a harsh voice. "Now that you've got that off your chest, would you mind resuming your seat, Melinda? There's more to get through. Despite your disappointment I'm sure you're going to be very comfortable with five million. Tyler's main concern was for Alice."

"I can't see why she needs all that money when she has you to look after her," Melinda retorted, her pale blue eyes almost colourless with anger. "I know I can fight this."

"I would advise you not to," Logan looked at her for a space of time. "I want it on record we'll continue to exercise our rights as Alice's family. We'll want to see her and have a say in her education."

"Please, Melinda," Ainslie implored as Melinda's expression slid into one of regained bargaining power. "We must all co-operate for Alice's sake. My little granddaughter is all that is left to me of Tyler. I did love him so."

"He wasn't the husband I imagined he was going to be," Melinda continued in the flat ugly tone she had always kept from the family. "As for your rights with Alice? Well, we'll see. I'm not dependent on you Dangerfields anymore. You never wanted me from day one when you were always so affable to Dana. You should have thrown her out."

"For having a heart, Melinda?" Logan challenged, and his voice reverberated around the room. "Her loving manner with Alice alone would have endeared her to us. You're so anxious to belittle your cousin when she has always been so loyal to you. Why *is* that?''

''She betrayed me.'' Melinda's voice cracked with emotion. ''She took everything I ever wanted.''

''No, Melly.'' Dana let out a long, terrible sigh, at that moment she could have killed Melinda for the lie. ''It was always the other way about. Everything was given to *you*. We all did it. It was a way of compensating for what you'd suffered.''

''Well, you don't have to worry about me now,'' Melinda said in a strange singsong voice. ''I've got enough money to live my own life. I bet you're happy with your little sum. You must have planned it all along.''

There was total silence in the room, then Logan rose from behind the massive mahogany desk with detached disgust. ''Our business is concluded here. Your plane is due in just over thirty minutes, Melinda. I'll drive you down to the airstrip. I'd like to say goodbye to Alice there. May I wish you a safe journey. This has been a terrible time for all of us. I know none of us wants to compound the grief with disharmony in the family. We want the very best for Alice.''

Outside in the hallway, Melinda stalked up the central staircase the very picture of outrage, while Ainslie, looking paper white and suddenly frail, clutched at Dana's arm.

''Surely you can't go back with her now, dear?''

Dana was almost at the point of abandoning her commitments but she couldn't. ''I must, Ainslie,'' she said regretfully. ''I know Melinda. She says many things she doesn't mean. She really needs me. Alice, too.''

Ainslie's expression went wry. ''It's wonderful you can feel for your cousin like you do. Today she was absolutely ghastly.''

"I apologise for her," Dana said. "I think you should be in your bed. You're in shock. When is Sandra due home?"

"Shortly. Jack is bringing her." Ainslie sighed heavily. "If we hadn't lost Tyler I think they were coming around to announcing their engagement. They've always been very happy in one another's company."

"Yes," Dana murmured. "Here, let me take you upstairs." She slipped an arm around Ainslie's waist, leading the older woman towards the stairs. "I have a number of commitments I must honour, but can't you come to me for a little while. A change of scene. I don't have a mansion but I do have a very comfortable guest room. We could talk and I could bring Alice to see you. Melinda won't mind. Sandra could come, too, if she liked. We could manage."

For the first time Ainslie smiled. "You're very kind, Dana. One can see it in those great dark eyes. I'm tottering today but I just might take you up on your offer. I need solace a million more times now."

Upstairs Dana knocked on Melinda's door then opened it without waiting for an answer. Melinda was standing in the centre of the room vigorously brushing her short blond hair away from her face.

"God, Melly, you must want to hurt me badly to have said all that. What gets into you?"

"Nobody puts any value on me," Melinda explained in a shaking voice. "Sometimes I find the way everyone loves you utterly insupportable. If I had to be born again it would be as *you*. Even my own daughter doesn't love me like she loves you." Melinda threw down the brush and collapsed into a chair. "I'm going to find someone who really cares about me."

"I understand how you feel, Melly," Dana said, wishing her cousin had just a little more iron in her soul. "But you have to learn how to *give*."

Suddenly Melinda's face changed. "Be mad at me, Dana," she said. "You have a right."

Dana sighed. "Be mad at me" had always been her cousin's way of showing shame or remorse. "I'll go and get Alice ready. I'm all packed. Put your luggage at the door. One of the men will take care of it."

At the airstrip with the charter plane waiting to take them to the nearest domestic terminal, Alice, high in Logan's arms, threw her arms around his neck, burrowing into it, crying with the pain of departure.

"Please, Uncle Logan, don't forget me."

"Miss Dangerfield," he said in a mock-stern voice, "would you mind repeating that?" He lifted her chin so that Alice staring into his eyes saw only love and a devotion that would last a lifetime. Her uncle Logan represented safety and comfort. He was so tall and strong and though he didn't look like Daddy, his voice it suddenly occurred to her was like Daddy's only darker or deeper and more definite somehow. "You could have me back for the holidays," she ventured.

"We could indeed." Logan kissed her cheek lightly then set her down, resting his hand on the top of her head. Alice was wearing a yellow dress that gave off a bright glow, but her smile was small and sad. "Be a good girl, sweetheart. Grandma might be coming to Sydney to stay with Dana for a while so you have that to look forward to, then the Christmas holidays. We'll fix something up with Mummy."

Instantly Alice's cheeks took on a little bloom.

"Goodbye, then, Logan," Melinda said stiffly. "I don't imagine I would be included in the invitation. I've had no refuge here."

"That was one of your choices, Melinda," Logan answered in quiet somewhat weary tones.

Melinda grabbed for Alice's hand and began to walk

towards the waiting Cessna, leaving Dana to say her goodbyes.

"It doesn't exactly sound good," Logan murmured ruefully.

"I'll speak to her, Logan," Dana promised. "Things will work out."

"Is that the prognosis for us?" His eyes were jewels; his words so disturbing she put a hand that suddenly trembled to her breast. "*Is* there an us?" She felt the fire run through her, the tremendous swell of desire. Just to stand near was like being trapped in a magnetic field.

"You're very bright, Dana. Very intelligent. There always was an us and always some reason for hiding it. When Ainslie wants to come to you, I'll fly her in. You might find some time for me. In the meantime so you won't find it quite so easy to block me from your mind…"

As his voice trailed off he took her by the shoulders. The next moment she felt his mouth close over hers, its sensuous contours warm, alive, her soft face revelling in the slight rasp of his shaved skin. He kissed her, not gently but matching perfectly the emotion of the moment so her lips yielded beneath his, every inch of her body sensitized and sheened with excitement. Griefs ebbed away as the kiss lengthened, searing her in golden heat.

Logan's brand, she thought. She would never be free of it. At the same time it gave her great energy and the strength to go on.

CHAPTER FIVE

THE next couple of weeks were a mixed bag so far as Dana was concerned. On the one hand she was thrilled and delighted to win a prestigious award for excellence in Children's Portrait Photography, further enhancing her career; on the other, trying to be there for Melinda and Alice proved harrowing.

The loss of one's husband is an enormous crisis in a woman's life and although the marriage had not been a happy one with neither partner making the right moves to improve it, Melinda had fallen into a depression that involved either venting her feelings very forcibly or bouts of sobbing that bordered on hysteria.

Alice, suffering in her own way, had gone back to school, but it was Dana in the main who collected her after school or when Alice's own tantrums became too overwhelming for her teacher and fellow pupils to cope with. The fact Alice's behaviour had been tolerated so long was due to her attendance at a small private school where the teachers had the necessary time to try and establish a good relationship with her and help her over an extremely difficult period in her young life. A school psychologist had even been called in to observe Alice but when Alice had refused in no uncertain terms to have her near, the young woman had thrown up her hands in defeat. Alice's main temper tantrums occurred when the teachers tried to get her to do something she didn't want, as in group activities or when it was time to go home, unless Dana was to collect her. Finally when everyone had done their best and the other parents were beginning to voice their complaints, the headmistress requested an interview with Melinda.

"I'm not going," Melinda told Dana flatly.

"Melly, you'll have to." Dana sat with her arm around Alice's shivering frame. Almost a half hour had gone by since Dana had arrived home with Alice in tow. Alice had pushed another little girl so hard the child had fallen back against a desk and sustained a bruise to the temple. Not only that, the child's grandmother was on the board of trustees. Melinda hadn't answered her phone, so the school had rung Dana who at this stage was well known to them.

"I don't have to do anything," Melinda said, oblivious to Dana's ongoing hassles. "There's something wrong with Alice. It has to be in the Dangerfield's history. There's absolutely nothing wrong with me. When did I ever give trouble at school?"

"Quite often as I recall," Dana pointed out dryly. Melinda right through primary and secondary school had been a controversial little person with a habit of fabricating stories. A kind of payback to classmates out of favour.

"I hardly expect you to stick up for me," Melinda said bitterly. "Everyone seems to think so highly of you, *you* front up to Mrs. Forster. I'm in no condition to sit through interviews."

Mrs. Forster, a handsome woman in her early fifties, received Dana very graciously, listening quietly while Dana explained why Melinda was unable to attend the interview.

"I understand completely." Mrs. Forster's shrewd grey eyes were fixed sympathetically on Dana's face. "We were all shocked by the tragedy. It explains so much of Alice's behaviour. On the other hand…"

For the next twenty minutes Dana sat patiently

through a stream of constant concerns. Alice was highly intelligent but did her level best to hide it. On her good days she was very endearing. She was good with little Samantha Richards, for instance. Samantha had a mild form of cerebral palsy. Alice's gentle kindness at least was judged admirable. But with the others... Here Mrs. Forster threw up her hands. Alice's behaviour was very uneven. She was either aggressive or withdrawn. She wanted to sit in a corner and read books all day, telling everyone to keep away, including her teacher.

Finally it was suggested it might be better for Alice to take time off school while she tried to cope with her obvious unhappiness.

Against Melinda's strenuous protest the school was shirking its responsibilities, Alice had her enforced holiday with Dana, taking her goddaughter at the weekend. To "give me a break," Melinda's own words. It curtailed Dana's social life but she wasn't concerned. Alice was very important to her and in great need of emotional support. How it was all going to end, however, she didn't know.

Ainslie's visit considerably eased the burden. In her grief Ainslie found great comfort in the very nearness of her little granddaughter. Because it suited her, Melinda had offered no objection beyond the mandatory bitter comments to Alice's staying over, and Alice, for her part, sensitive, intelligent little girl that she was, realised her being there was very important to her grandmother. Alice, the school rebel with a history of causing trouble, was markedly different when it came to "hurt people." Just as she took special care with her little friend, Samantha, at school, Alice showed the utmost concern for her grandmother's well-being.

To Dana's mind they moved closer every day, taking walks in the park together, sharing an ice cream, visiting the beach and going for drives. In this way Dana was free to keep up with most of her commitments although she curtailed her hours so she could be home for Ainslie and Alice. Despite Ainslie's obvious delight in her granddaughter, Dana realised it was tiring for Ainslie to keep going when she was physically and mentally laid low. Still, by the time the fortnight was over Ainslie was showing a heartening recovery.

"I feel exactly the same as you, Granny," Alice told her gently, putting a comforting arm around her grandmother. "We're sad for Daddy, but us two can stick together."

"Yes, darling, we can," Ainslie replied, smiling through her tears. "*Us two*. That is as it should be. Us two from now on."

Logan couldn't accompany Ainslie to Sydney for her stay. Pressure of business had allowed him only enough time to fly her to the nearest domestic airport. Mara was going in for organic beef in a big way and there were many meetings and discussions about this, but Logan had rung to say his schedule was fine for picking Ainslie up for the return flight. Ainslie even suggested she might be able to take Alice back with her, but here Melinda put her foot down.

"I can't begin to contemplate it," she told Dana. "Too far away. And Ainslie knows it. No, Dana, don't bother trying to win me over," she warned, catching sight of Dana's expression. "Alice stays. I have you to help me and I don't want to lose control to the Dangerfields. To hell with them all!"

Dana felt a mounting excitement not unmixed with trepidation as the morning of Logan's arrival approached. Much as some elements in their relationship disturbed her, by the Friday afternoon she felt like a bonfire blazing away merrily.

"You won't find it so easy to block me from your

mind," Logan had said. Easy? It had proved impossible. She still heard his voice in her head, still trembled at his remembered touch. She thought she had had a good idea of what it was like to be in love. She had been a little bit in love with all her boyfriends since she had started dating. She thought she had loved Gerard, had become engaged to him, but nothing had prepared her for the enormous heart-stopping pleasure she took in Logan. It was infinitely greater than any pleasure she had ever known. Pleasure, a certain apprehension, the melting heat of excitement. She couldn't wait for him to arrive. The anticipatory glow almost made up for the grinding disappointment she had experienced when he had been unable to accompany Ainslie on her arrival.

She arrived home a little later than she had hoped Friday afternoon, apologising to Ainslie who met her at the front door.

"Darling girl, come in and relax," Ainslie said, drawing her in. "You're much too pressured. I feel a lot of it is due to me."

"Not at all. I love having you here." Dana deposited her things on a chair. "Where's Alice?" she asked.

"She's changing her shoes for joggers." Ainslie laughed, her cheeks pink. "We're going for a walk in the park. She just loves the fountain, the way the sun makes those little rainbows in the spray."

"Excellent! I can have my shower." Dana slipped out of her linen jacket. "It's been one long hot day. A shower will feel fantastic. What say we have a nice family dinner at Ecco." She referred to one of the small superb restaurants in the area, specialising in Italian food as the name would imply. Alice adored "Italian."

"Lovely." Ainslie stretched out a hand to pat Dana's soft cheek. "Logan will be here tomorrow, but I want to tell you now how much I've appreciated being here this fortnight, Dana. I've loved having your company, enjoying little Alice. It's not a feeling of visiting. It's a feeling of being *home*."

Standing outside the door of Dana's apartment, Logan hesitated for a moment thinking up an excuse for why he hadn't let them know he was arriving a day early. Alice enjoyed surprises? Ainslie would greet him as she always did with arms out-thrown. But Dana? He had to confront the fact he had arrived early because he felt maddened to see her. It all came of making love to her. The unbearable involuntary longing. This from a man who had prided himself on his self-sufficiency, his content with his own company. No more. The longing came as a severe jolt. Every day it seemed to get worse. He could hear music coming from inside. A violin. Not classical. Something modern, elegant, distinctive. Probably Nigel Kennedy, he guessed. He pressed the buzzer, gave it a few moments, suddenly aware of a charge of adrenaline. What exactly would happen if Dana came to the door? Would he suddenly grab her? Draw her into an impassioned embrace? Hell, he felt wild enough.

But no one came. The music played on.

Exploratively he put his hand on the doorknob expecting to encounter resistance from the lock, only the knob turned. That was decidedly odd.

He stepped inside, feeling a surge of anxiety. The apartment looked wonderful. Like Dana. The combination of colours of fabrics, of ornamentation, the beautiful flowers.

"Dana?" he called, his tone urgent. "Anyone at home?" Surely in this day and age when security was paramount, she would think to lock her front door.

Beyond the seductively haunting sound of the violin another sound reached his ears. Running water. Someone was home. Maybe Ainslie. Dana and Alice could be out.

It was getting on for late afternoon even if the sun was full of blazing sparkle.

"Hello?" He moved farther into the apartment, experiencing a tightening anxiety until someone appeared. He moved past the empty guest bedroom, the sliding-glass door open to the balcony incandescent with massed pink and white daisies in blue-glazed pots.

He found her in the master bedroom, or rather in the shower of the ensuite, eyes closed, head tilted back as the water ran in rivers over her exquisite woman's body. He knew he had to, but he couldn't. He could not look away. His very breath caught in his throat. She was creamy pale to her toes. Swan's throat, delicate shoulders, a tilt to her breasts with their pointed rose nipples, the long curve of her back, the small perfectly shaped buttocks, the slender straight legs. He wished he could draw. He wished he was a gifted painter who could seize the moment, capture it on canvas, so he could look at it forever. But then she reached forward, making an effort with her eyes closed to turn off the faucets. Only a few moments, yet it had been timeless delight. But not for the world would he embarrass her. He moved back soundlessly, deciding the best thing he could do was start all over again.

The doorbell. Dana heard it just as she reached for a towel. Surely they weren't back already? These little walks usually spun out to an hour. Perhaps it was too hot. Hastily she put on her robe, careless of the fact her wet body was leaving sprinkles of damp all over the short pink satin gown. Walking back through the hallway, she shook her long hair free of its coil, feeling its bulk and softness against her nape.

The door wasn't locked, causing her a frisson of anxiety. She hadn't thought to check it after Ainslie and Alice had left, which was a mistake. Usually Ainslie snibbed the lock and pulled the door after her. Better to say nothing however.

"You're early…" she cried, sweeping the door open to confront them. Instead of Ainslie and Alice, Logan was staring down at her with open fascination, his gaze so deep she thought she could drown in that radiant blueness.

"You're right. By a day. And you look so… delectable." In fact she held him utterly. He could smell the perfume of whatever she had used in the shower. Gardenia? The sweet freshness of her skin. Beads of moisture like dewdrops ran from the base of her throat down the shadowed valley between the lapels of her robe. For a moment he thought he would bend his head and tongue up those drops. He badly wanted to. He even stepped forward, his features tautening.

"Welcome," Dana breathed. Her blood was racing as the sensuality that was in him communicated itself powerfully to her. This complex intimacy. She had never known anything like it.

"No kiss for me?" he mocked, desperate now for the taste of her mouth.

"Maybe a gentle one." She stood on tiptoe, shut her eyes and presented her mouth, every pulse throbbing, every nerve tingling and alive.

Just to touch her was to realise the depth of his hunger. He gathered her close to him with one arm, amused yet on fire with the way she had jokingly made her full rounded mouth even more pouty. Her body against his. Her beautiful naked body beneath the soft satin robe. A gentle one? Hell, he wasn't a boy. He was a man racked with hunger.

The kiss lasted a long time as their defences unfurled and fell away.

"God, I've missed you," he groaned, his hands cruising with controlled yearning over her body. This wasn't the time to act on his feelings. He was already living dangerously. He'd totally flipped his cool over this one, velvet-eyed woman.

"I've missed you, too," she murmured, seduced at every level.

"You can't invite me into your bedroom, I suppose?" To kiss her was to want it all.

"No," she said regretfully, her body alight.

"Damn!" He tried to joke, even gave a little laugh, when he was thoroughly aroused. "You're obviously not as reckless as I am." And what a glorious risk! He bent his head, kissed her again, feeling with a hard jolt of pleasure the tip of her tongue mating with his.

"Ainslie and Alice will be home soon," she warned him shakily, trying to fight down her own tempestuous sensations. "They've only gone for a walk."

"Hell, when I want you so very very much." Another kiss. This time a little rough. He let his hand skim her back, feeling the slick satin warmth from her body. He urged her closer, closer so he could feel her breasts crushed against him, the thud of her heart.

"Logan!" There was a little flutter of panic in her soft cry. Panic and acknowledged desire to surrender.

"You're right to be scared," he rasped, moving her hair away from her ear so he could nibble the succulent lobe. "I could kiss you until hell freezes over."

"And it's fabulous." She had to swallow hard on all the emotion that was in her. "But I should get dressed." Any moment Ainslie and Alice could return.

His eyes were electric. "I think *no* clothes work better," he drawled. "Oh, all right." He relented, dropping his hands before he arrived at a point neither of them could handle. "Go, then. Put on something pretty, though you look great in anything. I've a mind to take us all to dinner."

* * *

Melinda chose the following morning to pay a courtesy call. A gesture so phony, Dana was disgusted.

"Just so they don't decide to whisk Alice away," she mouthed at Dana the moment she stepped in the front door.

As soon as Alice saw her mother, her voice quavered and she looked like she was about to cry. "Hello, Mummy," she said anxiously.

"Hello, Alice." Melinda barely looked at her daughter. She walked to the hall mirror and fluffed up her hair. "Logan arrived yet? A lot of traffic from the Hilton." She continued to study her makeup intently.

The seemingly offhand remark had the crack of a whip. "How did you know he was staying at the Hilton?" Dana stared at the cousin she knew so well. And didn't know at all.

"I'm not dumb." Melinda glanced away from her reflection. "He usually stays there, doesn't he?"

"But he wasn't supposed to arrive until this morning. I told you that on the phone."

"I know." Melinda shrugged carelessly. "But it just so happens a friend saw you all dining out last night and passed it on. Silly to think I might have been invited. Anyway, I gave Logan a call just before I popped over."

Dismay caused Dana to react forcibly. "Whatever for?" Once Melinda started talking to Logan everything went wrong.

Patches of red stood out on Melinda's cheekbones, the only indication she was flurried. "Don't be difficult, Dee. Just keeping in touch. I would like you to remember I'm the Dangerfield around here."

"That's funny. I thought you'd forgotten it entirely," Dana retaliated, sickness stirring.

"How you love to have your little digs," Melinda responded with venom. "You don't have what it takes to land a Dangerfield. No way. Logan has a dark side to him.''

''You and he both,'' Dana burst out feelingly. ''You didn't make any trouble for me, did you?''

Melinda's blue eyes were wide and guileless. ''Good heavens, no. All I did was say hello. I wish you all the good things in life a million times over.'' She smiled at Dana as she said it, but Dana was unhappily aware of the jaggedness that was in her. Melinda, she had come to realise, revelled in sowing the seeds of discord. It was almost a sport to her. She had also developed a compulsion to destroy the blossoming relationship between Dana and Logan.

Dana was sure of it the minute Logan arrived. One glance at his hard handsome face revealed the difference. One exchanged greeting. The formality was back in place. The ease and warmth of the previous evening had just as suddenly been reversed. They were back to their familiar *distance*. Only Ainslie's gentle presence as Dana drove them to the light aircraft terminal saved the situation. The constraints were on. Dana was positive now it had something to do with Melinda.

Melinda, of course, denied it. ''Would I do anything to upset you when I desperately need your help?'' She had rounded on Dana as she and Alice left to go home.

''I'm sure you would,'' Dana had replied, feeling defeated and betrayed. Melinda shifted moods so often she might have suffered from multiple personalities.

With Ainslie and Logan safely back on Mara, things continued as before. Alice came to Dana at the weekend, unchallenged because Dana simply couldn't bear to let the little girl languish. Something had to bring it to a head, but not in a way Dana had ever contemplated. One Sunday evening when Dana returned Alice to her mother's care they found the house was empty and a

letter addressed to Dana in Melinda's handwriting
propped up on the mantelpiece. Childlike, Alice was intrigued more than worried. She ran through the house,
room after room, checking her mother wasn't simply
hiding. Her mother's behaviour was often strange.
Meanwhile Dana read through the letter thinking she
would never forget the contents.

Melinda had gone away to find herself. She had in
fact taken a Qantas flight to London that very day. She
made it sound like a harmless joy flight. Obviously she
had been planning the whole operation for some time,
Dana thought dazedly. Melinda intended to travel the
world. She was going to stay in the best hotels, treat
herself to some really beautiful clothes. Furthermore she
intended to marry just as soon as she found the right
man. A man who would cherish her and appreciate all
she had to offer. She stressed she needed her freedom.
She could not be "shackled with a child." Alice was in
good hands. As an heiress she had a secure future.

And to hell with the emotional well-being! Dana
leaned back in her chair momentarily staring sightlessly
at the ceiling.

"I'm going to get out from under your shadow,
Dana," Melinda concluded. "And about time, too. Life
has been so damned disappointing. Never what I hoped
for. Maybe things would have been different if my
mother and father had lived. Anyway now I've got sole
control of the money, I'm going to make my dreams
come true. Bright and beautiful as you are, you'll never
land that lord of all creation, Logan. He'll never forgive
or forget the role you played in Jimmy's life. Logan's
woman would have to be *perfect*. And he has already
decided you're not."

With your help, Melly, Dana thought bleakly, afraid
now to contact him.

But despite the pressure of her work, the difficulties

of adjustment, despite *everything,* Dana was able to manage. What held her and Alice together was the love they had for each other. On some occasions Dana was able to take Alice along on location, other times she was forced to employ an agency nanny. That was the worst part. Dana ran herself ragged but whenever she arrived home it was to Alice begging her never to leave her again. Much as the kind and competent nanny tried to soothe and please, Alice remained intractable. Eventually Dana had to face the truth. She couldn't cope on her own. Someone had to be on hand full-time to combat Alice's profound sense of loss and abandonment. Alice needed her family around her. She had taken overlong to work up the courage to contact Logan and Ainslie. The reason being her sensed estrangement from Logan the day they had parted. Now the moment had arrived. She could put it off no longer.

"How do you feel about going to visit Grandma and Uncle Logan?" Dana asked one evening, watching Alice put a quite difficult jigsaw puzzle Dana had just bought her together.

Alice who had been hunched over her project sat up straight, a beaming smile on her face. "Oh, that would be lovely! I adore it on Mara. You'll have to come, too."

Dana confronted the issue head-on. "I'll have to stay here, Alice, while I get an important project under way. I have a solo showing early December."

"But after that?" Alice began to look less happy.

"If it's all right with Uncle Logan I'll come later," Dana said, anxious not to disappoint her.

That settled it for Alice. "Uncle Logan will be all for it." She grinned. "Let's go to Mara. It'll be fun."

Dana should have acted there and then but decided to wait until the next day when Alice wasn't around to put through a call. It would be agonising to have to explain Melinda's defection and not in front of the child.

Morning, like most mornings, proved hectic. She was out of the studio for most of the time on a fashion shoot checking in with Becky her seventeen-year-old assistant and apprentice who fielded all her calls. Dana had first seen Becky on a T.V. programme about youth unemployment and felt constrained to offer a job to the tough, valiant little Becky who wanted ''to make something of herself.'' A snap decision that had worked very happily.

''You've had a visitor,'' Becky told her on the last call-in. ''Best-lookin' guy I've ever seen. Tall, dark and handsome with brilliant blue eyes. High flyer. *Very*. Moves in all the best circles, I'd say.''

''He didn't leave a name?'' As if he *had* to with that excellent description of Logan.

''And he gave me such a smile,'' Becky crowed. ''Said he'd be back. I told him you'd be free for lunch. You're such a terrific compassionate person you're not gettin' to enjoy yourself.''

Nerves on edge, Dana took a taxi, thankful she was wearing a favourite sand-coloured Armani suit, an expensive badge of confidence. On a lot of assignments she opted for casual clothes but this had been a high-fashion shoot, something of an occasion. The clothes had been wonderful, especially a red lace evening dress she took quite a fancy to. Christmas was coming up. Lots of parties she realised she wouldn't be attending. Alice was her first priority.

When she arrived back at the studio it was to find Logan looking the picture of cool, hard elegance, wearing a beautiful city suit, his enviable hair gleaming blue-black, shorter, the deep wave controlled with excellent barbering.

''Haven't you led me a merry dance?'' he drawled, lifting himself out of one of the leather armchairs and rising to his impressive six-three.

''For once in my life I was hoping you wouldn't hurry

up.'' Becky grinned cheekily. ''Logan has been telling me the most marvellous stories about life in the Outback.'' Too young to hide her enthrallment, Becky's pert, animated little face glowed.

''I'm pleased.'' Dana inclined her cheek as Logan barely brushed it with his lips. ''This is such a surprise, Logan,'' she said in a poised voice when the familiar charge of electricity was kicking in. ''Are you in town on business?''

''One all-important appointment late afternoon,'' he told her. ''It's been set up for some time, otherwise I'm free. Perhaps we could have lunch. Becky has already shown me your appointment book.''

''That would be lovely,'' Dana murmured carefully. ''Just give me a few minutes to freshen up. It's been quite a morning.''

''Which you handled beautifully I'm sure.'' Mocking, angry, loving. It was the most seductive voice she had ever heard.

''Dana can cope with anything,'' Becky piped up loyally. ''Even little kids.''

It was absolutely *crucial* Becky said no more. Dana shot her a swift quelling look, which Becky, needle-sharp, caught.

''How is Alice?'' Logan asked. ''I've brought her a present. I'd like to give it to her in person.''

''I'm sure you will.'' Dana felt another wave of guilt and anxiety. Why hadn't she contacted him last night? She was angry at herself. She deserved what was coming. Logan hated being kept in the dark.

They lunched in a riverside restaurant on baby lobster with a piquant lime sauce followed by coral trout. It was delicious but Dana was so nervous she left most of hers.

''What's the matter?'' Logan asked with raised brows. He let his eyes move over her, feeling the pull of attraction, too deep, too threatening. Still he had called on her, never managing to keep his emotions under control. He loved the sleek simplicity of her pale suit, the beautiful silk blouse beneath. He had always admired her dress sense. He had never seen her look anything less than stylish in whatever clothes she wore. But it wasn't simply her beauty that gripped him, it was the slender grace of her body, the way she sat and stood, the colours she wore, the meticulous grooming. She radiated a quiet confidence. Today she looked the successful professional woman she was, but a weight loss was apparent and her lustrous skin had a transparent look, as though she was working herself too hard.

"I'm not all that hungry, I'm sorry," she apologised.

"Are you sure all this dedication to your career is worth it?" he asked dryly.

He would have to know sometime. "It's not exactly my career, Logan." Dana raised her eyes to his, met them fully. "There's been a whole chapter of disasters lately."

"Meaning what?" His answer came swift and clipped, just as she expected.

"I'll tell you, but please don't lose your temper."

Narrow-eyed, he sat back. "It's something to do with Melinda, of course. Has she been giving you and Alice a hard time?"

Now her sense of being in the wrong swelled to huge proportions. "There's no easy way to put it, I'm afraid. Melinda's gone."

"Gone?" His tone bit.

"As in, took off," Dana explained with grim humour.

"Don't tell me with Alice?" Logan asked through clenched teeth.

A waiter approached them, took note of their expressions and immediately backed off.

Dana reached for her wineglass, took a long, calming sip. "No. Melinda left for London all by herself."

"I think you'd better tell me the whole story," Logan suggested in a tone that made her wince, "and don't leave anything out. I knew from the look of you something has been weighing pretty heavily on your shoulders."

"I don't think we should discuss it in the restaurant." Dana's eyes made a quick circuit of the luxuriously appointed room. Several women were staring at Logan with undisguised interest.

"So where would you suggest?" He lifted an arm, signalled the hovering waiter for the bill.

"I want your promise you won't get angry."

"That may be tricky."

"Logan, you look dangerous!" she said, and meant it.

"I might be if you don't get around to telling me," he warned. "Where is Alice? At school?"

Dana could see what was in store for her. "She's staying with a friend of mine. A lovely person. Alice is in good hands."

"Let's get out of here," he said with exasperation.

They went to her apartment to have their long overdue discussion.

"Would you like some coffee?" Dana stalled as they entered the living room.

He whirled her around, compelled her to face him. "Don't act as though you're frightened of me. That's not you, Dana."

His closeness totally rattled her. He was a passionate man. The tight self-control was more a necessity. "I'm ashamed to say I'm in awe of you, Logan. I always have been."

He made a sound of disgust. "Let's talk. We can have coffee later."

So the whole story came out. Logan listened in silence, making a visible effort not to intervene, though anger showed in his eyes.

"Aren't you feeling a little ashamed of yourself?" he asked finally.

She nodded. "I wanted to ring a dozen times but something always got in the way. We didn't exactly part the best of friends. I'm not such a fool I didn't know that. I've been thoroughly occupied trying to keep up with my commitments and looking after Alice." She couldn't mask her hurt.

His handsome mouth twisted and he stood up, pacing to the doorway that gave onto the balcony. "Whatever is between us shouldn't have stopped you. You only had to make one call and we'd have given you all the help you needed. Taken Alice off your hands. If she needs some counselling it can be arranged. There are no obstacles that can't be overcome."

"No, but there's a whole lot of disarray while you set about tackling the problem. Please sit down again, Logan. You remind me of a prowling tiger."

"Good," he said shortly. "Now you just might walk more carefully around me."

"Surely I've always done that?"

"That's interesting." He turned on her. "Tread carefully yet lure me on at the same time?"

"Is that how it looks to you?" Dana spread her hands, looked down at her ringless fingers.

His eyes gleamed. "Damn right! Only I'm not good at playing games."

"Really?" Their fragile truce was splitting wide open. "You don't hesitate to step over the edge."

"Only with you, Dana," he said very quietly. Too quietly. He moved with coiled energy to where she sat, coming behind her as she sat on the sofa, letting his lean strong hands encircle her slender throat. "I want so badly to believe in you," he said with a curious mixture of sadness and hostility.

"Haven't you ever heard of an act of faith?" She shuddered convulsively as his hands slid down over her shoulders to her silk-covered breasts.

"Maybe I'm too suspicious a man." There was pain now in wanting her. Real pain. The force of it shocked him.

"You would rather allow your doubts to warp you rather than follow your instincts?"

"If I followed my instincts right now, you know what would happen." His voice registered a hot sensuality.

"Oh, I do," she said bitterly, and sprang up, her skin flushed, her eyes deep and dark. "Whatever you want you get."

"You played your part, as well," he charged her, his voice hard now. He wanted to pull her to him, fold her in his arms. He wanted to connect with her at the deepest level, but he heard Melinda's voice in his head, too. Even despising her she had only said what his own family believed. The spectre of Tyler would always be there to haunt them.

Watching him, Dana smiled grimly, suddenly feeling humiliated. "I can't bear much more of this," she confessed. "Perhaps we shouldn't see one another at all."

"Did you switch on for Tyler, Dana?" he flared.

She threw up her hands. "That's it. The big question! Nothing I could say would convince you otherwise. If you'd like a cup of coffee I'll make it. God forbid, I should keep you from your appointment."

In the kitchen Dana moved quickly, even though her hands were trembling with emotion. To be alone with Logan in this mood was enough to drive her frantic. She was pouring near boiling water over the fresh coffee grounds when Logan moved into the kitchen, instantly charging the atmosphere. It was like all the overhead lights had been switched on.

"Black?" she said stormily when she knew perfectly well. Black. Two sugars.

"I'm sure you know the answer to that." He curled his fingers into his palm, exercising the tight control he had long used around her.

Her lashes were low, sweeping her cheeks. Her hands, like his, weren't quite steady. Next thing he knew the glass coffeepot was skidding along the counter and Dana was crying out.

"Ouch!" Hot coffee had splashed over her hand, causing an instant red stain. Quickly he grabbed her, propelling her towards the sink where he turned on the cold water.

"That must have hurt."

His concern, the sudden tenderness in his voice, quite undid her. "It's all my fault. So stupid." She was trembling all over.

"No, damn it, it's mine. I've upset you. God, I'm a brute." He continued to hold her hand under the cold running water. "Most of it has gone over the bench. It could have been a lot worse. Poor baby."

Why these lightning transformations from accuser to lover? They were nearly destroying her.

"Dana." He put his mouth to the sensitive skin behind her ear, moving her back closer so they were body to body. "Want me to kiss you?"

Desire. The warm oblivion of it. "No." Her denial was pathetic, little more than a whisper.

"Liar." He lowered his dark head, his mouth trailing gently down her cheek.

She lost herself in sensation. Her head fell back against his shoulder and though she kept her arm extended as though on automatic, she lost all sense of injury and the running water.

"I can't help but want you," he murmured, desire and a kind of despair deep in his voice. Maybe some things in life were best left alone. Past relationships. His arms wrapped her completely now, his mouth moving over hers with incredible hunger, capturing it, claiming it for him alone.

She was so physically vulnerable to him. Sheer ecstasy shot through her. Rapture to glory in. She hadn't thought it possible to need a man so much; hadn't thought it possible the depth and abandonment of her own response. Her will was so fragile, melting under the force of his. How had he ever learned so much about her? How had he arrived at such a level of intimacy as though he knew her body as well as his own?

Her head was beginning to swim as passion drove deep. Only a kiss, and her sensuous nature was released. The longer his mouth held that kiss, the more her body yearned. She wanted his hands and his mouth all over her. She wanted that matchless passion even as she realised she might never have his love. These moments for him were a form of imposed blindness.

His long lean fingers were laced into her hair, his body almost supporting hers as she leaned into him, helpless to deny conquest.

"What do you do to me?" he muttered against her throat. "I'm crazy about you. Want it or not."

That element of male hostility had her struggling away from him. "Chemistry I think it's called." Even to her own ears she spoke raggedly.

"And an awful lot of it. Maybe too much for a man to handle. I don't just want to *kiss* you, Dana. I can tell you that." He leant forward, turned off the tap. "Here, show me your hand. I hate to see those red marks on your beautiful skin."

"Don't fuss," she almost shouted, no longer able to act normally.

There was a faint pallor beneath his dark copper skin.
"All right. Take it easy." He spoke soothingly, as
though women were as fractious as horses. "I don't want
you hurt, Dana," he said, his dark timbered voice deep
and serious. "I don't want to be hurt, either."

CHAPTER SIX

IN THE following weeks Dana was overtaken by a recurring sense of emptiness and loss. It was almost like a darkness had fallen on her. The urgency of her work propelled her along, nevertheless she was terribly aware something altogether vital was missing from her life. She and the Dangerfields were bound together. She missed Alice greatly. She had become very used to having her little goddaughter under her wing, but through all her thoughts, flamelike, ran Logan. The tragedy was she had allowed that flame to burn her. She had even begun to fantasize about having him for a husband. Logan to share her days. Logan to share her bed.

For the first time in her life she was having trouble sleeping, and even when she did, it was only to have that impossible, unattainable man stalk her dreams. Why had she ever allowed him to make love to her? It had so profoundly changed everything. Logan's lovemaking was all she seemed to think about. Even when she closed her eyes his image moved like pictures behind her closed lids. To lose him now would cut her to the heart. Jimmy and Melinda between the two of them had cost her Logan's trust. Logan thought a great deal of trust. He would demand it totally of the woman he loved. She truly knew what it was to be the innocent victim and it made her ache.

Ainslie rang weekly to keep in touch, always allowing Alice to speak, Alice's words tumbling over each other with her excitement. No reproaches from Ainslie. Dana had brought her granddaughter closer. Nevertheless Ainslie told her privately Alice had reverted to a few difficult moods and the occasional tantrum which rather shattered the overall harmony. Only when Logan was at home could the household be assured of no discord. Alice's emotions were not yet in balance. She seesawed between sunny periods and days of wilful behaviour that required a lot of love and patience. She was missing Dana dreadfully, Ainslie said. Dana was a pivotal part of Alice's life.

"We're all looking forward to having your company, Dana," Ainslie told her warmly. "I'd love it if you could see your way to coming to us *before* Christmas. Some days I desperately need your support. Sandra spends so much of her time with Jack. My disciplining skills have blunted over the years, I'm afraid. My heart aches so for Alice, I should be a little firmer. Logan, of course, charms her. She's a little angel with him."

Dana could believe that perfectly. Though Sandra often took over the phone for a chat, Dana had no contact with Logan. It was Sandra who gave her the news Phillipa had taken to dropping in at Mara. She was piloting her own plane now, a single-engine Cessna, a magnificent birthday present from her wealthy pastoralist father.

"I think she's dying to start up with Logan again," Sandra confided. "There's no other man in her life and there's been no other serious relationship for Logan. I don't know how he feels about Phillipa now but I can tell you for a fact she's still in love with him."

Just hearing it made Dana's blood run cold. It was never clear to her why Logan and Phillipa had split up in the first place. Any man would be happy to marry Phillipa, she thought. Everything about her was calm, confident, controlled. She was good-looking in a healthy, athletic way, not glamorous like most of Logan's ex-girlfriends, but well turned out, attractive, a fine companion for the owner of a grand station. She could just bring it off, Dana thought. Phillipa was far closer to what Logan really wanted than she could ever be. Phillipa could never be accused of having had an affair with the tragic Tyler, either.

In the end Dana didn't send Logan an invitation to her solo showing. In one way she desperately wanted him to see her work, admire her artistry and professionalism, in the other she was unwilling to put herself through the torture. So emotionally buffeted she had taken shelter in the calm waters of isolation. Encounter could only bring ecstasy and anguish. The sense of loss would go on forever. How to survive without Logan was going to prove one huge ongoing problem she had brought on herself.

On the evening of her showing, which took up a whole floor of the prestigious Stanford Gallery, Dana dressed to the nines. This was going to be a very social evening. One couldn't do without the "glitz crowd," not that they ever bought anything, but their very presence added glamour and excitement to the occasion. The serious people from her own world would be there and art collectors looking to wider fields. Colin Stanford, the gallery owner, had rung her earlier in the day to tell her two representatives from overseas galleries had flown in especially after the gratifying reception of her work at the Venice Biennale. Both representatives were from commercial galleries like the Stanford, one in Berlin, the other in New York. It would pay her to impress not only with her artistry but her personal presentation. As one of her colleagues put it laughingly, "the whole package."

Tonight she wore a short slip dress of dark chocolate taffeta covered with exquisite black lace. She always looked good in black. It went well with her hair and skin and the gleam of the taffeta gave the whole outfit an additional lustre. Because the dress called attention to her legs she had invested in a pair of beautiful Italian evening shoes worn with the sheerest of black stockings; gold and jet drop earrings, an antique shop find, her hair a long ash-blond slide. Always light-handed with her makeup she set to a little extra colouring and sculpting so in the end she thought she looked rather exotic. Certainly glamorous enough to fit in with the ultra-chic crowd.

When she arrived the gallery was already so crowded Dana thought anyone who was seriously interested in her work would have to come back the next day when the gallery would be near empty. Colin Stanford rushed forward to greet her, delighted she was looking so absolutely "smashing," something he couldn't take for granted with a lot of his artists. Taking Dana by the arm, he introduced her around, beaming fondly while she was offered a whole lot of compliments. The men were delighted to meet her, blondes always were the centre of attention; the women, either envious or impressed, seemed more interested in what she had on than the wide range of photographs expertly placed around the walls. The showing had a name: "Journey of Life." It featured images from the moment of birth, through childhood, adolescence, the courting years, marriage, midlife, old age, on one's own or in nursing homes, the inevitable images of dying and death. It was a serious body of work. Dana had put her heart and soul into it.

While the champagne and finger food were being circulated and the hum of conversation had reached such a high level the air itself was turned to noise, she was approached in turn by the two overseas representatives who seemed genuinely excited by her work.

"So young to know so much about the human condition," the gentleman from Berlin murmured, seizing her arm to discuss a booking.

The American in the next ten minutes, not to be

beaten, offered to "buy up the whole showing." "Australia's too small my dear," he told her. "You have to exhibit in the States."

It sounded as though she was quite a success.

Long-time friends swelled the ranks, people she had known since college days when she had studied film-making and had even made a couple of documentaries and a short film that had received quite a bit of attention. Gerard and Lucy arrived, delighted at the brilliant showing, hugging and kissing her.

"I always knew you'd make the big time," Gerard told her with pride and pleasure. Though he loved his Lucy dearly, Dana would always have a place in his heart. Everyone knows about first love. One never entirely gets over it.

Logan, who had waited for an invitation and deemed it perhaps unwise to accept, found himself reacting badly when one didn't arrive. This was throwing down the gauntlet indeed. And how it stung him! The past month he had found himself toiling through his days with a lack of enthusiasm that was entirely new to him. He had managed his life so much better before he had allowed a woman to slip into his bloodstream exposing his all-too-apparent vulnerability. His life up to a point had been rife with good-looking girls. He had even become engaged to Phillipa whom he had known all his life.

Phillipa was bright and attractive, suitable in every way. She understood thoroughly his way of life and enjoyed it, but he had learned the hard way Phillipa could be as disloyal as the next one. While he had been away on a trade mission to South-East Asia, Phillipa had spent the weekend with an old boyfriend who was still crazy for her. She had claimed later, weeping copiously, it had been just "one of those things." They'd been to a rock concert. She'd had too much to drink. But loyalty shaped his life. He didn't want a woman who could fall into bed so easily. He also became uncomfortably aware he had never loved Phillipa in the first place. Maybe it was all his fault. Phillipa had become aware of his true feelings and sought comfort where she could. In any event, they agreed to break off the engagement. A mutual decision. He didn't want to be taken over by love. He had far too many responsibilities.

His strong feelings for Dana Barry had always disconcerted him. Not only was she extraordinarily beautiful, she was extraordinarily gifted with a warm, giving nature. She aroused such sensations in him, strange hungers that gnawed at him long after she left and Mara was his own again. The relationship seesawed constantly before the sharp winds of doubt. A kind of self-sabotage and mostly on his part. Never a man to waiver, he wasn't doing too well now. The trouble was, he could never reconcile himself to a reality of Dana with Tyler. He has always thought her, for all their complex dealings, absolutely straight. He hated himself for even suspecting her, but he couldn't unload the burden of evidence.

Except for that time in the cave. There all the barriers had been swept aside as their bodies reached a sublime harmony. She had been perfect to make love to, filling him with such pleasure, such a sense of wholeness, he felt the Bible was right. She was his Eve, his missing rib. Was this intense passion something to be seized on rather than cause alarm? It was the end of peace. He knew that. The end of his peace of mind. When there was important, even dangerous work to be done, the image of Dana got between him and the project. In a way it was like leaving one's borders undefended. Maybe this was the way Tyler had felt. Captive and confused. Dana Barry was a crisis in both their lives.

No one challenged him when he arrived at the gallery. He wasn't asked to show his invitation. He simply walked through the door, not stopping to think his whole aura assured him of automatic entry. Why would a man who looked like that ever have to gatecrash anything? One or two even stopped him, trying to gather him into their circle, but he smiled and said he was anxious to view the collection. A futile pursuit, he thought, when the crowd was so huge. Were any of these people genuine buyers or were they simply being seen before going on to the theatre or dinner.

In the end he stood back, as much away from the crowd as possible, seeking out Dana. He knew she was successful, of course. He knew she was very good. Over the years he had seen quite a lot of her work, which was becoming far more meaningful as she matured. His interest was genuine.

"Super stuff!" a distinguished man said as he walked past. American, from the accent.

A small section of the crowd moved suddenly, heading en masse towards the photographs which were beautifully lit and displayed. It was then he saw Dana and something like elation rose in him on a wild wave. Their coming together the way they had, had opened up the floodgates so his whole world looked different and he found himself moving in a strange new landscape. He continued to stare at her, spellbound.

She was the most wonderful-looking creature he had ever seen, beautiful as were others, but so full of life, of sparkle. The laughing, chattering crowd moved around him but he felt compelled to stand and stare at her. She was looking highly polished and sophisticated in a way he had never seen her. Tall on her high heels, beautiful black-sheened legs. The dress was exquisite. Suddenly melancholy, he remembered how well black suited her. The black suit she had worn the day of the funeral. She was laughing at something an attractive young woman said as she hugged her, obviously a friend, adjusting her gilded waterfall of hair before a young man captured her, kissing her cheek soundly then holding her by the shoulders, looking down smilingly into her face.

Hell, the guy was in love with her. Their whole body language was far from casual. They knew one another well. For an instant he felt an unprecedented surge of pure jealousy, which only abated as he saw Dana move back, her expression full of an affection which embraced the young woman, as well.

So he was wrong after all. Just as he could be very wrong about Dana and Tyler. The seeds of doubt once sown spread tenacious tentacles.

A moment later he felt a touch on his arm, dissolving a moment of anguished struggle.

"Good Lord, Logan, what are you doing here? I thought you'd be back on Mara, pulling your weight for the country."

"Good evening, Sir William." Logan turned, smiling to acknowledge the handsome, elderly man at his side. "Actually I know Dana Barry very well. Have known her for some years. Her cousin Melinda was married to my late brother."

"Terrible business." High Court Judge, Sir William Hardy, shook his pure white head. "I'm so sorry, Logan. It must have been a great blow to the family."

The two men stood in conversation for a few more minutes before a colleague sought the judge out. Much as he liked and admired Sir William, Logan had kept his eyes trained on Dana all the while as she spoke to the changing crowd clustered around her. She was obviously very popular with the kind of vibrancy that drew men and women to her. She was very gifted, as well. Now he could see the photographs more clearly as some of the crowd left to go on with their evening. Another twenty minutes or so and he would be free to study the collection in detail.

And then she saw him, her colour deepening with a rush of astonishment, excitement, whatever. It didn't take her long to reach him. "Logan!" she said quickly, almost breathlessly, presenting her perfect cheek for his kiss that wasn't social at all. "Why do you always confound me?"

"It's nothing really," he drawled, blue eyes blazing. He wanted to pick her up in his arms there and then. Carry her away to the quiet opulence of his hotel suite. Make love to her until she lay rosy and satiated in his arms.

"I'm absolutely delighted you've come!"

He heard the warmth and excitement in her voice, revelled in the transparent joy in her face.

"How could I refuse your personally worded invitation?" He smiled with that part of him that mocked.

"I did *want* to but I was afraid of... Oh, I don't know—" She broke off. "Anyway, you're here and I'm absolutely thrilled."

How could he doubt it when her beautiful eyes, tender and velvety as a doe's, sparkled with pleasure?

She took his hand, her tumultuous feelings for him gathering force, introducing him around with great pride. Everything about him made her heart beat faster, made her feel more alive such was the power and vibrancy he generated. Others felt it, as well. She saw it clearly stamped on their faces.

"You must come and meet two very dear friends of mine," she invited him, brushing her long gleaming hair out away from her creamy neck. It was a trick that tantalised him, making him want to put his mouth to her satiny skin.

Lucy and Gerard Brosnan.

Gerard. The name cut through him. The ex-fiancé. Now he had it. His instincts were never far out. The young woman, his wife, was pretty, with short dark hair, vibrant green eyes, and a pair of engaging dimples in her cheeks. An attractive creature but no Dana.

"They all love you, don't they?" he murmured as eventually they moved off.

"I'm a very lovable person," she joked, a little thrown by his tone. She knew, none better, Logan was a man of strong passions, but she had never seen him exhibit the faintest trace of jealousy.

"One wonders what you saw in Gerard as pleasant as he undoubtedly is." He bent to her ear.

"Perhaps it had something to do with the fact he's not in the least like you. Phillipa, too, has moved on." She felt a strong desire to add, "It appears now she's back," but that would be giving Sandra away. Better by far to keep that inside information to herself.

"Will you let me stay with you tonight?" he asked abruptly in an extremely taut tone.

She had to remind herself forcibly she was on full view of the crowd. Even then her whole body trembled as though she was on the verge of a high fever.

"We both know, Logan, that would be a mistake."

"I want to touch you. I want to make you shiver with ecstasy. I can't seem to get the last time out of my head."

His voice was so sensuous, so rich and deep, it was almost like being made love to. She could feel her whole body quickening, the shooting, piercing little thrills, the startling tightening of her nipples.

"Logan, stop," she whispered.

He took her hand, brushing her with delight. "Don't close me out."

It was the nearest Logan Dangerfield would ever come to begging. She was so excited. On top of the world yet full of confusion that flowed around her like floodwater. She knew the sting of his mocking tongue. She knew

the whole range of emotions she incited in him. The
underlying hostilities. The deeply implanted doubts.

"Please come and look at the collection," she said,
and gave a little involuntary shiver. "I don't know that
I can cope with any more than that."

He laughed deep in his throat, so vividly, vividly
alive. There was never any doubt for either of them
about what would happen.

The day before she was due to fly to Mara, a long letter
arrived from Melinda. Dana sat in her living room for a
long while turning it over before opening it. Something
about it made her feel physically and emotionally
drained. She had done far too much trying to fit all her
commitments in before taking off. Now this. Finally she
sighed and, using a small silver letter opener, slit the
envelope neatly.

A whole store of memories of Melinda came back to
her. None of them pleasant. When Melinda had abandoned her child, Dana felt her days of covering up for
her cousin were over. There were few surprises. Melinda
wrote endlessly of herself. How these days she was looking so good she was turning heads. She had met a lot
of very nice people who had "taken her over," showing
her a good time. She was wearing her hair differently
now. Several lines to describe this. She was wavering
about cosmetic surgery. No matter her weight loss she
still had a trace of a teeny double chin. In fact she had
had one since childhood. A negligible thing. Not even
unattractive. She had met someone very interesting only
that week. A lot older but someone rich and cultivated.
Someone high up in the city, a stockbroker.

Just as Dana was beginning to wonder if Melinda
would ever mention her daughter, Melinda advised she
had sent early Christmas messages off to the family. A
letter each for Logan and Ainslie. A very expensive card

for Sandra, "Never did like her, looking down her long
nose at me." A magnificent life-size doll for Alice when
Alice wasn't a doll child at all. Surely Melinda knew
that. "Max and I picked it together." Melinda was just
beginning to find herself, fighting out of the trauma of
her disastrous first marriage. Obviously this meant she
contemplated a second. "A door has closed behind me,
Dana," she wrote. "I'm starting a whole new chapter in
my life. Maybe I can find time for Alice later. I do love
her, you know, but there's so much of the Dangerfields
in her."

Thank God, Dana thought.

She didn't want to read any more but felt she had to.
"I hope you've forgotten about Logan," Melinda added
a warning. "He's the type to find second-hand goods
distasteful."

Dana flinched. *Second-hand goods?* Did anyone say
things like that anymore? Truth and lies. Melinda didn't
know the difference.

Dana rose with a passion, tearing her cousin's letter
into shreds. Why had it taken her so long to realise
Melinda had never wanted her to find happiness?
Perhaps it was a kind of madness? Melinda had coveted
everything she ever had. She remembered that now. For
the first time in her life Dana began to seriously contemplate a child might be better off without a certain kind
of mother. A mother utterly insensitive to her child's
needs.

CHAPTER SEVEN

THE charter pilot was brisk, businesslike, directing her to one of the rear seats of the Cherokee Six. There were four other passengers, twin boys of around fourteen, old hands at air flights, on their way home for the long Christmas vacation, a very tense elderly man with a clipped moustache who was visiting his sons, and a middle-aged woman with an attractive friendly face returning to Teparri Station where her husband was head stockman. This was after a two-week visit to her sister in the Big Smoke which was still the Outback name for beautiful, bustling, cosmopolitan Sydney. They all began talking to each other in easy Outback fashion except for the elderly gentleman Dana had privately labelled ''The Major.'' The pilot made another quick round of external checks then shut the baggage doors hard. A moment more and he climbed into his seat, glancing over the flight plan.

''Wow, aren't you lucky!'' the boys said when they found out she was en route to Mara. ''Dad took us there once to watch a polo match. Mr. Dangerfield's team won, of course. He's a great player,'' Chris, the elder boy by ten minutes, told her, ''the homestead is out of this world. Compared to Mara, Dad said our place is a tin shed.''

''I bet you love it all the same,'' Dana smiled.

''It's home.'' Chris sighed in a happy holiday-time voice. ''Can't wait to get there.''

Mara was the last stop, the most remote. On Teparri the Cherokee taxied along the strip towards the hangar, braking to a stop just before a boundary fence. Mrs.

97

Harrison disembarked and waved. Now Dana was on her own. It had been an uneventful trip, clear blue skies, no rogue air currents to lift the aircraft up and down like a yo-yo, which sometimes happened, but tiring. Logan was to have come for her, picking her up at the domestic terminal but at the last minute had to change plans to make an urgent visit to one of Mara's outstations.

Dana was dozing lightly when the pilot's voice reached her, calm but very decisive. "Listen, I want to put down. There's no need to be alarmed. It's just a precautionary check."

Dana jerked forward so suddenly her seat belt cut into her. "There's nothing wrong, is there?" As used as she was to light aircraft, indeed enjoyed flying, she was perfectly aware there was always an element of trouble and danger.

"Just something I don't think I should ignore. Call it instinct. I can't actually see anything wrong. All the needles are pointing the right way. It's just a feeling. I'm very sorry, Miss Barry, but it's best to err on the side of caution. The plane's a bit sluggish."

"Well, you're the boss," Dana said doubtfully. "Where are we?"

"Our exact position is twenty-five miles south-west of Teparri Station. I'm sending a message now to Flight Service to announce my intention to land," the pilot said. "If I *have* to, I'll arrange for our engineer to be flown in. If we flew straight on we'd be over Mara in about forty-five minutes. With any luck at all there should only be a shortish delay. One of the wires might have come off the pulleys. Or—" He broke off, by this time almost talking to himself. "It's the oil pressure. The gauge is dropping."

It was on sunset before Logan flew into Mara, asking his overseer, Manny Buchan, who was waiting for him, if Miss Barry had arrived.

"Not as yet, Boss," Manny answered in his usual drawl.

"What?" Logan, who had begun walking to the waiting jeep, turned back on him sharply.

"What time was she supposed to be here?" Manny asked, surprised by the boss's reaction. He looked shocked and then anxious.

"I would have thought four o'clock. Run me up to the house, Manny. There may be a message."

"Hop in." Manny took the wheel with alacrity. He'd been caught up most of the day supervising a muster so although he knew Miss Barry was due to arrive that afternoon, he hadn't heard when.

At the homestead, Ainslie came out to greet him, her expression matching his own. "Dana hasn't arrived as yet. I'm starting to get worried."

"Did you get onto State Aviation?" Logan referred to the charter service.

"I was just about to when I heard the jeep. You do it, dear." Ainslie's voice sounded strangled in her throat. In truth she was seized by a panic that had never left her. She had lost her husband, Logan's father, to a fatal plane crash over which she was still agonising. Flying was a way of life in the vast Outback but it was never without its fatalities nor would it be.

Logan more than anyone knew the dangers. His father had been a very experienced pilot, as he was himself, but that hadn't helped with mechanical failure. In his study he got through to the charter service who at that point didn't know the plane was overdue. It took ten minutes before they were notified by Flight Service in Brisbane the pilot had advised them of his intention to land but there had been no subsequent confirmation the aircraft had landed safely. A search flight would have to be organised.

It wasn't enough for Logan. Fierce anxiety rushed through him. Never a man to panic, he realised his heart was thudding. His strong features drew together, giving him a very daunting demeanour. The fellow at the other end kept talking, explaining the situation, but he found himself chopping him off, telling him as an experienced pilot he intended to start the search himself. The only remaining passenger on the Cherokee was a member of the Dangerfield family which was to say close to God in that part of the world. The thought of Dana out there in the desert was tearing at his insides. It was too soon to think of anything else.

At that point Alice, who had broken away from Ainslie, ran into the study causing him to almost jump at her high-pitched yell.

"Where's Dana? Where's Dana? Is she going to be killed?"

Logan slammed down the phone, caught the child and lifted her in his arms. "Alice you'll have to quit that racket. Where did you get that idea?"

"I heard Retta tell one of the girls the plane was long overdue," Alice choked.

"Well, you can stop worrying right now," he told her firmly. "The pilot had to put down. Just a precaution. That means he was being very careful. He radioed his position, south-west of Teparri Station. You know Teparri Station. It's not all that far from here. I'm going out to find them now."

"Really? Aren't you wonderful. Can I come?"

"No, you have to stay with Grandma and I don't want any fuss," Logan said. "I'm going to bring Dana home."

"I can't help being frightened, Uncle Logan."

"I know, sweetheart." He kissed her cheek. "If you like you can wait up, though it might take a while."

"Oh, yes, *please*," Alice breathed in a fervent little voice. "I couldn't sleep anyway. I can't even remember a time when I didn't love Dana. Do you believe in God, Uncle Logan?" she asked, her child's gaze very direct.

He nodded, keeping control over his own apprehension. "I believe in a Divine Being, yes."

"He wouldn't let Dana get lost," Alice said.

He was airborne just after dusk, flying into a night sky already peppered with stars. Mercifully he knew this part of the world, vast as it was, like the back of his hand. He had the charter flight's last recorded position. The pilot had notified Flight Services he would let them know when he had landed safely. No further transmission had come through but that didn't necessarily mean a crash. He had to hold on to that. There was another scenario. The pilot couldn't contact Flight Services on his VHF on the ground. He would be out of range and he mightn't have checked his high frequency radio before take off. He prayed to the God Alice so staunchly believed in that was the case.

Dana. She was never off his mind. Why hadn't he gone for her? It had been the plan. Now he wished with all his heart he had put the outstation's problems on hold. In a blaze of new knowledge he realised he loved her. Had loved her for some time even when he was crippled by doubt. An image of her slipped into his mind. The image when she was last in his arms. Her beautiful eyes full of magic, her mouth curving, her long gleaming hair spread out over the pillow, her body so warm, so sweet, so silken, desire tightened in him even then. Dana had transformed his life, now the thought of her mortality cut through him like a knife. On odd occasions in the past he had thought himself a man of stone so controlled were his emotions. It was a measure, in a way, of how he had been brought up. Responsibilities, a big heritage, the untimely death of his father, the disaster of Tyler's marriage, then the terrible news that had brought a hard lump into his throat. Men didn't cry. They were trained not to. It was only underneath they took the full brunt of their losses.

Losses?

God, what if...?

When he saw the lights of the charter flight he cried aloud with relief. Shouted at the top of his voice. No crash. His entire body relaxed and his formidable strength flowed back. How strange and extraordinary to find these feelings in himself. The crazy thought that without her he would most likely die? Him? Whose whole life was duties and commitments? No wonder the immense power of these feelings made him fearful.

He landed the Beech Baron on a track baked so hard it was almost as good as a landing strip.

Dana swooped to him, arms wide open like wings. "Oh, Logan!"

He gathered her to him, held her painfully fiercely close, struggling not to kiss her senseless. "What the hell do you think you've been up to, frightening the life out of me?" he demanded, feigning exasperation.

"All I can say is you've found me." She lay her silky head along his chest, feeling the texture of his khaki bush shirt against her skin, her ear attuned to the strong beat of his heart. "Not hurt, either."

"Thank God." His voice was deep and quiet. "Hello, there. Dangerfield," he introduced himself to the pilot who approached hand outstretched.

"I remember your dad well." They shook hands. "Never had the pleasure of meeting you. It's damned good of you to come." The pilot taciturn, but always polite, began to open up to another man. "Trouble with low oil pressure,'' he said. ''Tried to get a message out when we landed. No problem with that, but my H.F. isn't working. My fault, I'm afraid.''

While the two men walked back to the Cherokee still in conversation, Dana walked over to Logan's Beech Baron which was resting like some giant wide-winged bird on the desert track. She had known, of course, they would be rescued but she hadn't fancied a night under the stars with a complete stranger, correct as he was. Now Logan had come for her. He really was a knight in shining armour. In *some* ways, she smiled to herself, when he wasn't the impatient, impossible oh-so-arrogant autocrat laying down the law. Just the sight of him made her radiant. Logan Dangerfield in action was a glorious sight.

Dana lifted her head to look up at the stars, marvelling at their infinite numbers, their unique brilliance. The desert air was so pure nothing got between her and them. A series of images like snapshots flashed across her brain. She had camped out under the stars only once. That was when Jimmy was alive and as a special treat he and Logan had allowed Alice, with Dana for company, to experience how wonderful it was to spend a night around the camp fire; sleeping out in the wild bush, along the bend of a billabong. She still remembered the moment when Logan had bent over to check on her sleeping bag, asking her if the ground wasn't too hard. Just an ordinary thing yet as his hand briefly touched her, her heart had leapt like a fish to the lure. She had never managed to keep her calm around Logan but at least her imprisoned heart had kept its secret.

Almost immediately, Logan got a fire going, brewed up coffee he had on the plane to make them feel better. He hadn't stopped to pick up food, but he had a few bars of chocolate and some fruit, which he offered to the pilot. He'd already offered to fly him back to Mara but the pilot made the decision to stay with his plane, apologising again his high frequency radio hadn't been in order. Logan had already transmitted the message the Cherokee had been found with all on board safe. He advised further he would be flying Miss Barry on to Mara Station, her original destination. "How do you feel about a night in the desert?" he asked the pilot, who only grinned.

"The desert is my kind of place. I'm a bit of a loner. Anyway another plane will be here in the morning."

"Just stay put," Logan advised.

On the flight back to Mara, Logan said surprisingly little, wanting to keep the force of his emotions tamed. He expected he'd go crazy but he had promised her once there he would keep his needs under iron control. One hell of a promise when he wanted to claim her this very night. Even the thought of it made him groan aloud.

"What's the matter?" She turned her head, seeking the reason for that sort of pain.

"What do *you* think?" His brilliant eyes flashed.

"Logan, I don't know." She touched his arm.

"I'm thinking of laying you out on my bed. I'm thinking of unbuttoning that silk blouse. No hurry. Nice and slow. Then the jeans. I'm thinking of feeling your satiny woman's flesh under my hand, only it's business as usual. Wasn't that the deal?"

She laughed at the brisk change of tone. "I'm almost sorry we made it."

"*Almost?* Even in this light I can see the blush."

"I have to look to my position," she said. "Your position."

"True. You're Alice's godmother. I'm her uncle. Both positions are sacred."

"Have you ever thought of marrying me?" she asked as she meant to, satirically.

He laughed deep in his throat. "I've thought of it dozens of times."

"And?"

"I'm damned if I know how it would turn out," he drawled. That wasn't fair. "We live in different worlds. Your last exhibition really opened my eyes to your artistry. You're still young. You could have the art world beating a path to your door. How could you turn your back on all that?"

"If you're making excuses, Logan, they're working," she replied dryly.

"I mean how could we make the transition from *family* to husband and wife?"

"I never understood how we made the transition to lovers," she retorted sharply, lying through her teeth.

"I'm going to die of wanting you," he said.

Their arrival back at the homestead turned into a celebration, with station staff coming to the door to check all was well. The word had gone out and everyone was anxious. Mara had had enough tragedies. Though long past her bedtime, Alice ran around ecstatic with joy. Finally she sank with sheer exhaustion to the floor, her feet perched on a footstool, her head on a cushion. "Next time I'm going with you, Uncle Logan."

"Next time?" Logan threw back the last of his single malt Scotch, and set the glass on a side table.

"Next time you have to rescue Dana."

"I don't know that I like the idea of *next* time," Logan said feelingly. "Once is enough."

"But wasn't it romantic?" Alice queried happily. "Did you kiss her?"

"Heck, Alice, I didn't have a chance to." He smiled, his beautiful white teeth in stunning contrast to his dark tan. "I hugged her. That's a start."

Ainslie, who was sitting on a sofa, caught Dana's eyes. "Dear girl, could you pour me just a little more champagne? I really want to unwind. I'm no good with worry anymore.''

Logan moved first, on his feet as smooth as a big cat. ''I'll do it, Dana. And you're for bed, young lady,'' he told the excited, yawning Alice, large eyes overbright.

''No thanks. I can't get up. I might sleep here.''

''No way.''

''Carry me,'' Alice cajoled. ''Some nights it seems like half a mile to my room.''

''You will live in a mansion, darling,'' Dana smiled.

''You have to come, too, Dana.'' Alice rose, a little wobbly on her feet, going to her grandmother, kissing her soundly. ''One of these days, Grandma, I'm going to have a little sip of champagne.''

''Happy times ahead,'' Logan joked, swooping his niece up. ''Are you turning in, Ainslie?'' he asked, his eyes on his stepmother's pale face. To his sorrow Ainslie seemed to have aged dramatically since Tyler's death.

''Yes, dear,'' she murmured, followed by a tired little laugh. ''Dana, give me a hand up. I don't think I've ever been so pleased to see anyone in my life.''

After Dana had seen Ainslie to her room, she walked along the wide corridor hung with paintings, to Alice's room. Logan was there, tucking her in.

''Uncle Logan and I are good buddies,'' Alice informed her. ''I like that. Good buddies. And he believes in God, Dana. He told me.''

''You were having a very serious conversation, were you?'' Dana moved to the opposite side of the bed, smiling down at the little girl.

''I was terribly frightened when you didn't arrive.'' Remembering, Alice's eyes filled with tears.

''Oh, darling, that's awful.'' Dana's heart smote her. She bent down and hugged her. There had been too many traumas for Alice.

"Uncle Logan kept my hopes up. He told me I could stay up and wait for you."

"I'm safe. I'm home. And your eyes are drooping," Dana said soothingly. "You get your sleep and tomorrow we can talk all you want. I've got books and games for you and a little camera. I'm going to show you how to use it."

"What about now?" Instantly Alice sat upright.

"Not a chance," Logan said in a firm tone. "I hate the idea of you girls going without your beauty sleep."

That made Alice laugh. She snuggled down obediently, and fell asleep wondering what her first picture would be. Maybe one day she would be as famous as Dana and have her own exhibition.

Out in the corridor once more, Logan caught her hand, determination in his fire-blue eyes. "Let's go for a walk," he suggested. "I want to clear my head."

Excitement soared, looped like a bird. Still she said from behind her perpetual shield, "But what's the time?"

He laughed, a sound so attractive it made her senses swim. "What an idiotic question. Whatever the time, it doesn't matter."

As they walked through the moonlit garden their feet crunching on the fallen leaves, they were serenaded by a solitary bird.

"He's singing his heart out for us," Dana murmured. "Sweet and silvery and sad."

"Then it just has to be a song of love," Logan responded, lifting an overhanging branch out of her way. "Love's an agony after all."

"You really think that?"

A gentle breeze was blowing full of the scent of flowers and the wild bush. "I've had a taste of its power," he returned very dryly.

"Is it something you're going to share with me?"

"I think you're perfectly capable of working it out yourself."

"Well I'm not," she said honestly, breaking off a gardenia and twirling it under her nose.

His voice was crisp and very slightly edged. "I think it's transparently clear I'm in love with you."

The thrill of hearing him say it swept through her like a fire. "But you don't trust me?" she said, a great sadness in her eyes.

"In some ways I'd trust you with my life," he admitted.

"But you can't stop thinking about me with Jimmy?"

"I thought you were going to try to say Tyler?" he responded in the same slightly edged voice.

"Jimmy is how I remember him, Logan. I hope that doesn't upset you too much."

"You know it does. I can't exactly say why. I don't blame Tyler for loving you, Dana. You're awfully easy to love."

"We *are* at war, aren't we?" she said quietly, glad of the fragrant blackness to hide the sorrow of her expression.

"It's like something we can't help. But I'm never going to let you get away."

She took a few moments to speak. "Are you going to allow me to marry or are you going to lay down another one of Logan's laws?"

"Why, do you have anyone in mind?" He sounded utterly certain she didn't.

"I'm twenty-six, you know. I want what every woman wants. I want a husband who loves me as much as I love him, children we can both adore, a home to share. I want a purpose in life. I want to push the boundaries of my self-development as a woman, a human being."

He bent his head, kissed her briefly, a mocking gesture. "I think you're doing very nicely. I've said it before, but you have a considerable gift with your photographic images. You're a true artist."

"I hope to be," she answered gravely. "I have other needs, as well."

"You think I don't?"

"Beyond your basic instincts?"

"That's a low blow. Do you seriously believe what I feel for you is *lust?*"

She shrugged, realising it wasn't. "I know some part of you finds me taboo."

He made a sound of frustration. "Surely it doesn't require much understanding to know I have difficulty dissociating you from Tyler in my mind."

"When all you have to go on is Melinda's lies?" She stopped short and turned to him, raising her face.

"Melinda?" He gave a bitter laugh. "We'll come to her later. I had a letter from her. So did Ainslie."

Dana felt her heart sink. "She wrote me about it. What did she have to say?"

"A whole lot of garbage," he answered bluntly. "I really enjoyed hearing about how she's enjoying herself in London, how she's met a new man. I'd be beside myself only Alice is taking her defection unnervingly well. I thought the disappearance of one's mother, even a bad mother, would cause a lot of trauma."

"Children get on with life," Dana said a little awkwardly. "I had thought she'd be more upset myself."

"But she's confounded us all. Her grief is for her father and she was fretting about you."

"Her father was able to demonstrate his love."

"Melinda's your enemy, you know," he said with deep conviction.

"That's an odd word for a cousin."

"I know it hurts." He brushed her words aside. "For some reason Melinda is flawed. She sent me another warning about you. Of course that's what the letter was all about.''

''All you have to do is ignore it.''

''I did tear it up,'' he said shortly. ''Ainslie made a little bonfire of hers. Ainslie has just lost her son and Melinda can't wait to tell her about her new man. She really needs help.''

''I'm sorry, Logan. There's nothing more I can do about Melinda. Having one's parents is central to development. Melinda lost hers early. Obviously all we tried to do for her was unappreciated and unwanted.''

''One would have to feel sorry for—what's his name?''

''Max. Maybe she's a different person without her stresses.''

''Without her child, you mean,'' he said incredulously. ''In the last analysis, Dana, she wants to hurt you.''

''That's becoming increasingly clear,'' Dana said bleakly. ''I'm a little tired, Logan. Can we go back?''

''Why don't we just move into the summerhouse?'' His voice was both intense and ironic. ''I want to make love to you.''

''When I don't have your respect?'' she challenged.

''Dana, I never said *that*.''

''And I believe I said I'd never be your mistress.''

She went to turn away from him, suddenly deeply emotional, but he gathered her to him. ''Lust corrupts, Dana. What I feel for you is entirely different.''

''Then why do you have to punish me for it?'' She was truly bewildered.

''Because you make me so damned *miserable* when you're away from me,'' he protested, his expression for a moment touched with male outrage. ''You get between me and my work. What kind of a thing is *that*? I'm supposed to be entirely focused and all I can see is your beautiful face. It's clear to me that's obsession.''

"Well, it must be a real change for you," she said tartly. "You never did tell me what happened between you and Phillipa. Was she giving you a bad time, too?''

"I didn't worry about Phillipa when I wasn't with her," he said.

"Have a care, Logan. I think you're admitting you got engaged to someone you didn't really want.''

He laughed shortly. "You aren't going to tell me you didn't? Anyway that's all in the past.''

"Are you quite sure?" She was afraid now of losing control.

"What's that supposed to mean?''

"I think Phillipa's heart is still in your hands," she retorted fiercely.

"Dana, our relationship is over. Why on earth are you mentioning it?''

"Maybe Phillipa doesn't believe it. Something about you puts women in a frenzy." She stopped abruptly, starting to crumble. Her emotions were more fragile than she thought and she'd had a glass too many of champagne.

"Don't you dare cry." He looked down at her intensely.

"Who said anything about crying?" She heard the rising note in her voice.

"Because if you do... if you do, my God, you'll be lost to me.''

"We can't do this," she pleaded, but her voice was no more than a whisper on the wind.

"There's nothing in the world I want more.''

"Wanting isn't the same as getting." Even when she was trembling in his arms she employed her defence weapons.

"Is it not?" He turned up her chin, allowing the moon

to shine down on her face and reveal the liquid glitter of her eyes. There was such a vulnerable innocence about her. Despite the dreadful letter that had made his heart twist inside him, he wanted to believe in her. So *badly.* ''I'm not going to let you go without a kiss.''

Though she yearned for him, she resisted. But only for a moment. In the end she could deny him nothing. He knew it. She knew it. So when he released her her heart was hammering and her body was profoundly aroused.

''I guess you're lucky I'm a man of my word,'' he said, anguish in his harsh tone.

To be together now on Mara. On his own land. And so many barriers still left between them.

CHAPTER EIGHT

IT TOOK Phillipa less than a day to find out Dana Barry was in residence at Mara. The following day she obeyed the compulsion to fly in, the very picture of friendliness. As far as Phillipa was concerned, her love story wasn't over. She wasn't such a fool she didn't know Logan had never been *mad* about her, but she was in love with him, had always been in love with him and he had been very fond of her.

Logan was the most dynamic man she had ever known, the sexiest, the best-looking, the smartest, the richest, a star of the first magnitude. The same hero he had always been in her mind. That little episode with Steve, nothing really, and she was not promiscuous, had cost her dearly. She had lost Logan's respect though there was nothing cheap or shabby about Steve. Steve did love her and he had asked her many times to marry him. In one way she had always known it was wiser to look to Steve as a life's companion. Steve wasn't complex like Logan, neither was he terribly exciting. Logan was incredibly so and very glamorous however much he would deride the term.

Now Dana Barry with her beautiful face and well-documented talents had moved in. Phillipa had always found her very pleasant, well-informed and interesting to talk to, but she was increasingly disturbed by the thought Dana could present a problem just when she and Logan had made up their quarrel and she was once more in his good books. Of course Logan had never told anyone of her little ''slip.'' She didn't expect he ever would, which was her great good fortune.

Once or twice in the past Phillipa had thought she had
discerned a very curious tension between Logan and
"the cousin," which was how most of them knew Dana.
Nothing very obvious or important. Logan and Dana
were both very correct with each other, but a certain
atmosphere prevailed so that on hearing the news
Phillipa and her mother decided immediately Phillipa
had best get over to Mara and size up the situation.
Phillipa's mother had been planning their marriage since
childhood. The breaking off of the engagement had upset
her dreadfully. "How could you have lost him?" There
was no doubt in Phillipa's mother's mind Phillipa had
done all the losing but Logan was still unattached, lend-
ing weight to her theory Phillipa and Logan were destined for each other.

Logan was out on the job when Phillipa flew in, but
the women greeted her with a genuine warmth. They all
sat out on the veranda enjoying morning tea, with Alice
sitting close by reading one of the beautifully illustrated
children's books Dana had brought her.

"I thought it was high time we got to know each other
better," Phillipa said amiably, leaning back in her com-
fortably upholstered wicker armchair, watching a couple
of groundsmen move around the many-acred garden,
bringing down yellowing fronds on the tall palms. It always gave her enormous pleasure to visit Mara, one of
the great historic homesteads and such a wonderful
showcase. The Dangerfields were vast landowners but
Mara was the flagship. It was a compelling enough reason to marry Logan even if he hadn't been every
woman's dream.

Mistress of Mara!

Phillipa very nearly cried aloud at her loss. Instead
she asked, "How long do you plan on staying, Dana?
Long enough to come visit us, I hope?" Phillipa's fami-

ly, the Wrightsmans, owned Arrolla Station some two hundred miles to the north-east.

"I'd like that, Phillipa," Dana responded lightly. "I'm here until around mid-January."

"No you're not," Alice said, briefly lifting her head. "You're going to stay with me forever."

"But surely, dear, you'll be going back to school?" Phillipa laughed uncertainly, looking towards Ainslie whose expression looked vaguely embarrassed. "And how is Melinda? I expect she'll be joining you for Christmas."

Dana remained silent, waiting for Ainslie to deal with it, but Alice as was her wont, burst in, "Mummy took off. She's over in London now. That's the capital of England where the Queen lives. She's not my mother now. She doesn't want me."

"Alice, darling, would you mind popping into the kitchen and asking Mrs. Buchan for fresh tea?" Ainslie asked.

"Sure, Grandma." Alice put down her book at once. "I expect you want to tell Phillipa all about it."

Ainslie's mouth pulled down. "Thank you, darling."

A brief look of shock passed across Phillipa's cool good-looking face. "Is there a problem?"

"No problem," came Dana's reply, intercepting Ainslie's agonised look. "As I'm sure you'll understand, Melinda is going through a bad time." Dana made it sound convincing. "She wants some quiet time to herself. Somewhere far away."

"Yes, of course," Phillipa murmured, her agreement tentative. Whoever heard of a mother leaving without her child? Of course the marriage had been a disaster. Everyone knew that. "So does this mean Alice will be living here for a while?"

"She's looking on it as a great adventure," Dana said. "And she desperately needs her family."

"You, too, by the sounds of it." Phillipa's gaze shifted constantly from Ainslie to Dana as though looking for some break in a united front.

"Well, we're family, too. Alice is my goddaughter as well as my second cousin. I've been looking after her for a long time."

"She's a dear little thing," Phillipa murmured when she didn't think so at all. She had seen Alice in one of her tantrums with no one in the house outside Logan able to handle her. Ainslie, always a robust woman, was looking almost frail, obviously grieving for Tyler. She wasn't up to looking after a difficult small child, Phillipa thought. Sandra was spending more and more time with the Cordells. In-laws one day. "I haven't seen any of your photographs, Dana, but I read in one of the papers your recent showing was a great success."

"Yes, it was." Dana smiled at the memory. "I'm really thrilled at the public response."

"And she's had wonderful offers from overseas galleries," Ainslie said proudly. "Logan was telling me all about it. He was immensely impressed."

"Logan?" Phillipa showed a glimpse of shock.

"He went to see it, of course," Ainslie said.

"When was this?" Phillipa's lightly tanned skin took on a rosy hue.

Here we go again, Dana thought. "He came to the gala opening," Dana informed her.

"Really? Well, he kept that a secret."

"Was he supposed to have told you?" Dana smiled slightly.

"It probably slipped out of his mind," Phillipa said, shrugging a straight shoulder. "I'm envious, of course. I never can take a decent photograph. Don't have the time really."

"I intend to take hundreds while I'm here," Dana said, excited at the prospect. "I want to make my own contribution to recording this unique environment.'' She didn't mention some of her best photographs had been used in a conservation battle.

"But surely—'' Phillipa gave a little smile ''—with all due respect, Dana, there are scores of books on the Australian wilderness? Mumma has dozens. All the coffee table variety.''

"But I have my own way of looking at things, Phillipa. That's the point. The photographer's individuality. Great photographers are great artists. I want to make my way.''

"I'm sure you will,'' Phillipa hurried to say. "I know Serena wants someone really good for her wedding but I expect she would be fixed up by now.''

"Thanks, Retta,'' Ainslie said in a rather tired, sweet voice as an aboriginal girl, as graceful and small-boned as a bird, moved out onto the veranda bearing a tray.

"I'd love to do a series of pictures on our aboriginal women,'' Dana said, making room for the tray, and greatly taken by the beauty of Retta's hands.

"I can help you there, Miss Dana,'' Retta said.

"I'm counting on that, Retta.'' Dana smiled.

In the end Phillipa stayed all day and was invited to spend the night just as she expected. It was the routine. Dinner would furnish her with the opportunity of observing Logan and Dana together. Dana appeared to be genuinely devoted to the child, spending the afternoon entertaining her with lessons on how to use a camera, while Phillipa herself went in search of Logan, finding him rounding up clean skins at Cudgee Creek. This was Phillipa's world. She had been born and raised on a large station that ran both sheep and cattle and she was very knowledgeable about all aspects of station life. A prerequisite she had always thought for becoming mistress of Mara. Logan might have a great eye for beauty but he was very hard-headed when it came to making the big decisions. And marriage was the biggest. Dana Barry with her extraordinary silver-gilt hair and contrasting velvety brown eyes was essentially a creature of the big cities. Maybe she might even make the move to the United States if she was that interested in furthering her career.

As it happened, Sandra returned home early, before lunch, with Jack Cordell in tow, throwing her arms around Dana and hugging her. Something that Phillipa found a mite disturbing. Although she and Sandra, who was several years younger, always got on, they had always stopped short of demonstrations of affection.

They had finished a highly enjoyable shooting session with Alice's brand new Olympus MJU, a compact and robust little camera, basically point and click but with excellent results. Now they were resting under a beautiful old ghost gum on a hilltop that looked down on a panorama of flower-strewn slopes and flats, the results of one of the late afternoon storms that worked up with great thunderclouds and little passing rain just a short week before. The flower displays that after good rains could turn into blinding displays of pink and white paper daisies were a vision that could never be forgotten, but the Spring rains had been unpredictable with only isolated falls. Songs and prayer chants had already begun for the longed-for rainy season linked to the northern monsoon when the desert wilderness turned into the greatest garden on earth. Still Alice was happy to photograph the bush that she loved, a goanna resting on a log too lazy to move, three brolgas standing in deep conversation beside the silver bend of a billabong, an obliging aboriginal stockman leaning against a gate holding his horse by the rein, and a desolate pile of rubbish and mortar that long-ago sheltered stockmen touched some artistic nerve in her.

"Thank you, Dana," Alice said, softly touching her godmother's cheek. "I love my camera."

"I'm so glad, darling." Dana was indeed pleased with Alice's vision, enthusiasm and quickness of mind. "I'm hoping this might be the start of a lifetime interest. I started very young." She leaned back and opened the picnic basket they had brought with them. "Fancy a sandwich?"

"Yes, please." Alice accepted one gratefully. "I'll have my drink now, as well."

"This is marvellous, isn't it?" Dana sighed with contentment, leaning back on a cushion. "A glorious place if you have an eye for the wild, vast, open spaces under a perpetual cobalt sky."

"It's our home," Alice said. "Mine and yours."

"And Uncle Logan's." Dana laughed. "He's the boss, so we can't forget him."

"It was Uncle Logan who said it." Alice sipped her home-made lemonade through a pink and white straw. "I think that was lovely of him."

"I agree." Dana's heart melted. "I didn't think he would include me."

"Well, he did. He likes you a whole lot better than you think," Alice pronounced owlishly. "Phillipa doesn't have to come here anymore, does she?"

Dana broke off part of a cookie and put it in her mouth. "Why's that, darling? The family have known her since she was a little girl, just like you."

"Is that why she and Uncle Logan got engaged?" Alice leaned over and plucked an iridescent little beetle from Dana's collar, admiring it then placing it gently on a leaf.

"He may have loved her perchance," Dana tried to joke.

"I don't think so." Sometimes Alice was given to enunciating very clearly, just like her grandmother.

"And what would you know, young lady?"

Alice rolled her eyes. "Give me a break. If you love someone so much, why do you have to hide it?"

"Meaning?" Dana turned to her, startled.

"Kissing and stuff. Hugging. When Uncle Logan speaks to her, he just sounds kind. I thought he might be in love with you."

"Oh, man," Dana sighed. "How did you figure that out?"

"Simple." Alice put out her hand for another sandwich. "His eyes light up. They go all blue and sparkly like Grandma's big sapphire. And he *sounds* different."

"You're really smart."

"Yes," Alice agreed complacently. "Kids are a lot smarter than grown-up people think. I don't think Phillipa likes me."

"I'm sure she does," Dana responded instantly. She didn't like Alice to be hurt. "Some people are better with children than others, that's all."

"No, she doesn't like me, Dana," Alice repeated. "It's all right. I don't akshly like her. I heard her asking Mrs. Buchan once if I was the naughtiest girl in the world?"

"And what did Mrs. Buchan say?" Dana looked into the big, gold-flecked hazel eyes.

"You bet!"

At that they both broke up.

Because the afternoon was so hot they drove to one of the many beautiful lagoons that formed a network all over the station, leaving the open jeep on the plain and walking down the narrow, winding slope to the moon-shaped pool. Here the calm cabochon waters glinted with a million sequins, with islands of deep pink lotus lilies glowing like sculptures on the sea of green floating pads. Hundreds of golden bottlebrushes and wild gardenias grew close by, spreading their delicious scent over the entire area and filling their lungs. Anticipating just such a swim, both of them had worn their swimsuits beneath their clothes losing no time peeling them off and folding them in a neat pile on the back seat of the vehicle.

Just as they were about to enter the water, Alice caught at Dana's fingers. "Don't go into the deep, Dana," she said, a little catch in her voice.

"Of course I won't." Dana, busy plaiting her hair, stopped to reassure her. "I would never do anything to upset you. You know that."

Alice nodded, brushing her fringe off her face. "Mummy thinks its terrible I can't swim properly. After all, I'm nearly seven."

"Darling, you'll be able to swim a whole lot better by the end of the holiday," Dana promised. "Mummy was expecting a little too much of you."

"She's terribly good, isn't she? Almost as good as you."

"We had our own pool at home, Alice, and my father coached us a lot. I'll give you some lessons in Mara's swimming pool. Now we're going to have fun."

They sported without incident for the best part of an hour, revelling in the open air and pure cold water on their heated skin. This was a timeless place, an oasis of quiet calm, sustaining a wide spectrum of birdlife. Above them a black falcon soared majestically, wings outstretched forever in the search for prey and, undisturbed by their presence, a pair of brolgas began to wade out to the succulent waterlilies on their lofty, stick-like legs.

Afterwards they spread their towels on the honey-coloured sand, their bodies protected for the most part by overhanging green boughs.

"Do you miss Mummy, darling?" Dana asked, concerned despite all that had happened Alice didn't appear to be missing her mother at all or perhaps was bottling up her grief.

"I do sometimes," Alice confided, turning to look steadily into Dana's eyes. "She's Mummy even when I know she doesn't want me."

So small and so brave. So much the victim of Melinda's lack of love and understanding. Sometimes Alice broke her heart. Dana tried to find the right words. "We have to remember, like you, Mummy was frightened and lonely after Daddy died. She needs time to find herself, to adjust to a new life."

Alice sighed deeply. "But she told Daddy she hated him. They had a big fight. It was *terrible*."

Almost moaning in her grief, Dana reached over and took the little girl's hand. "I'm so very sorry you had to hear that, Alice. But I'd like you to think of this. Sometimes when they're upset and angry, people say things they don't mean. I know you will understand that!"

"You mean, my tantrums?" Alice said immediately in her intelligent way.

"I mean when you're upset and confused. When we sob and rage, it's a protest about something. It means you're not satisfied. Probably Daddy had done something Mummy didn't like. Telling him she hated him was just a reaction, like you tell people you hate them and want them to go away."

Alice frowned, remembering. "I've never said that to *you*, Dana."

"Oh, yes, you have, my girl. Lots of times." Dana tickled her.

"I never ever meant it. You're always lovely to me, Dana. So different from Mummy."

Dana's feeling of regret was enormous. "We'll have a long talk about it, darling, when Mummy returns."

If she *ever* returns, she thought dismally. It was a good

thing most women weren't so woefully deficient when it came to loving kindness.

"So this is how some people spend their day?" a familiar voice, pitched loud enough to reach them, called.

Alice stared back, then jumped up excitedly.

"Uncle Logan, Uncle Logan."

"Hi, sweetheart." He flashed her a white smile.

Now another figure emerged. Phillipa, looking a little bit hot and bothered. Logan reached back a hand to her and in another few moments they were down on the sand.

"Are you going to have a swim, too?" Alice asked, so put out by Phillipa's unexpected appearance her voice held a trace of wrath.

Phillipa laughed sharply. "Not today, I think. I don't have a swimsuit."

Her cheeks began to burn. Oh, this was upsetting indeed! And it had only taken one look. One look to turn a pleasant acquaintance into rivalry. When had Logan ever looked at her like that, his blue eyes blazing? It was like a blow to the stomach. Not that she could ever look as good as that in a purple bikini. Not given to envy, Phillipa felt a great wave of it.

Dana, not unaware, came to her feet, her long ash-blond hair sliding out of its loose plait and cascading over one shoulder. Emotions were palpitating in the air like actual heartbeats. "That's a pity," she managed lightly. "It's absolutely beautiful in. The water's surprisingly cold." She, too, had caught Logan's look, the blue-fire eyes, the slight flaring of his finely cut nostrils. She realised, too, Phillipa was disturbed, and no wonder! Logan wasn't supposed to look at her like that, but for once his reaction had been unguarded or maybe he didn't care.

Alice came to their rescue, grasping her uncle's hand.

"I'll have all these great photos to show you, Uncle Logan."

He smiled down at her, pleased she was looking so much better than when she had arrived pale and pinched. "So Dana's started you off already?" he asked

"Aren't you glad she did?"

"I sure am. Anything that makes you happy makes me happy. It was very nice of Dana to buy you a camera. I wish I'd thought of it."

"But surely she's too small to use one properly?" For an instant, cool, confident Phillipa couldn't contain a sudden flair of hostility. Something that really shocked her.

"Not at all," Dana answered smilingly. "The one I bought her is excellent for a beginner. Alice is very intelligent and she has a very good 'eye.' I'm very pleased with her. What have you two been doing?" Dana only glanced at Logan, wishing she had at least brought her pink cotton shirt down with her. Never a self-conscious person she now felt extraordinarily aware of her own body and the amount of cleavage her bikini top was showing.

"Doing the rounds, the usual old thing," Logan offered casually, blue gaze flowing over her. "Pip always shows a great interest in Mara."

"It's my favourite place," Phillipa gushed, pleased Logan had reverted to her old nickname.

"Don't you like your own place better?" Alice asked in a vaguely belligerent voice.

"Of course I love it!" Phillipa glanced down at this horrid little girl. "But bless me, it's not Mara. I don't know anything to equal Mara."

"Someone should take you to Kinjarra, or Main Royal, or Bahl Bahla," Logan mocked.

"The devil's in you, Logan," Phillipa said.

"Thanks a lot."

"It only makes you more attractive."

Dana privately agreed. "So, will we go on home, Alice?" she asked. "Sandra will want to see you."

"Nah, not with Jack around," Alice said, startling them all. "They're sort of mad about each other, aren't they?"

"One is supposed to be when one intends to get married," Phillipa began rather piously only to then blush a bright red.

"One day you'll meet one special guy," Logan told Alice lightly, taking her hand.

"Will I really?" Alice looked thrilled.

"Count on it. I'd say you're going to make one heck of a woman"

"Like Dana." Alice smiled.

Phillipa moved off, striding it out. Half an hour ago she'd been happy. Now she was down in the doldrums, wishing Dana would go back to where she came from.

Dana tried to keep up, but she wasn't wearing shoes and her city feet were very tender. Logan and Alice were a little distance behind her, Alice straggling to protect her bare feet, as well. The track was harder to negotiate going up than down, the sandy earth covered with leaves and twigs and seed pods, abundant little scurrying insects and isolated masses of delicate yellow wildflowers.

"Why don't I carry you?" Logan suggested to Alice.

"Not unless you want to break your back," Alice chortled. "No, I'm okay, Uncle Logan."

"How's it going, Dana?" Logan called, wanting to trap her in his arms. The light was dancing over her beautiful skin. She moved like she was dancing. She had a dancer's lovely strong but delicate legs. That neat little butt just made for a bikini. He could see the slight swing of her small perfect breasts as she bent suddenly, putting her hand down as if to steady herself.

"Ouch!"

They all heard the little sound of pain.

"Dana?" He left Alice's side, moving swiftly, efficiently, up the slope. "What is it?" He grasped her around her bare, narrow waist, bringing her upright.

"Damn. After such a delightful day I think something has stung me."

"Hang on one minute. Just one minute." He moved back to Alice, swinging her into his arms and carrying her to the top of the slope.

"It's probably nothing, Logan." Phillipa frowned, for a moment considering. "A bull ant." When had he ever acted so concerned about her?

"Dana doesn't normally react like that," he answered a little shortly.

"I don't think it's a bull ant, either," Alice said.

"Okay. So what is it? She'd know if it had been a snake."

"It can't be a snake," Alice said with great intensity.

"Next time you'll remember to wear your shoes," Phillipa responded with faint censure.

Alice glared at her but had the sense to keep silent.

Logan reached Dana in half the time it took him to ascent. "Here, hold on to me while I take a look. Where is it, your foot?"

"Yes, the soft part underneath." She was speaking calmly but her foot had started stinging badly.

"You really should have worn shoes. It's always best to take precautions."

"I know, I'm sorry." She laughed a little shakily, reacting to the closeness of his body, his warmth and his strength. "It could have been Alice."

"That must be painful." He held her slender foot in his hand. "A bee sting probably. All the bottlebrushes are in flower. The bees love the nectar. You trod on one or a couple by the look of the swelling. Only other thing is a spider. It's certainly not snakebite."

"I'm pleased about that." Dana's tone was dry.

"There's not a damn thing I can do about it until we get you back to the house."

"I'll survive." She fought down the instinct to reach out to him. Instead she tried to put her foot down.

"What the hell!" Logan stared at her for a long moment then lifted her as easily as he had Alice, into his arms. "You're one lovely creature, Dana Barry. I could carry you for miles."

"The trouble is, I need my clothes."

"Not by me." He gave a provoking little laugh. "That's what comes of being a hot-blooded male."

"Oh, yes?"

"Shall I prove it?"

"Not with *Pip* around."

"Why don't I just kiss you and be done with it?" His gaze touched her, sizzled.

"That seems monstrously cruel."

"Maybe," he agreed.

"Are you alright, Dana?" Alice called anxiously.

"Of course she's alright." Phillipa was dismayed by her own grumpy voice. "Don't worry, dear, Uncle Logan to the rescue."

"He practically loves Dana," Alice said.

For an instant Phillipa felt close to screaming. A remarkable thing for her.

"That is a shame," she clucked sympathetically when Dana showed them the fiercely red, swollen area. "As I've just said to Alice, it's wise to wear shoes, but then, you haven't spent a great deal of time in the Outback have you, Dana?"

"Nonsense, she's been coming out here for years," Logan clipped off. "Listen we'll all go back in the one jeep. I'll send someone back for the other. Dana needs some tea tree oil on that sting and a painkiller."

"Oh, my, what's the fuss!" Phillipa laughed lightly,

watching Dana shoulder into a pink shirt, buttoning it
modestly over the creamy swell of her breasts. "I rode
in a cross-country race once with a broken collarbone."

Dinner made Phillipa even more uneasy. Because there
were only six of them, they used the informal dining
room which flowed on from the breakfast room adjoining the kitchen. Not that there was anything too informal
about it, Phillipa had always thought; a large dark-
panelled room illuminated by day with tall leaded
windows, a Venetian glass chandelier by night, a huge
tapestry on one wall, a matching pair of consoles with
mirrors above them on the other, a long refectory-style
English oak table with two magnificent oak carvers at
either end and eight chairs. Because there were guests
there were a series of silver candlesticks with tall lighted
tapers down the centre of the table, with a low crystal
bowl of yellow roses in the middle.

   The Dangerfields were used to living grandly so much
so it was bizarre to think just outside the main compound
was a great wilderness, as savage as it was splendid and
beyond that the Simpson Desert spreading its vast in-
timidating presence over an area of 15000 square kilo-
metres. Sandra, though she was still grieving deeply over
the loss of her brother, had picked up, Phillipa thought,
and with Jack to stay, joined in the conversation that
ranged over a wide area: local news, the political situation, various hotly debated issues and Dana's highly successful show.

   "It must be so exciting for you, Dana, to be invited
to New York?" Sandra smiled across the table, looking
for a moment so much like Jimmy, Dana had to look
down quickly so as not to show her feelings. "You'll
go?"

   "Of course she will!" Phillipa interjected, wanting

nothing more. "It would be so exciting, no artistic person would think of giving up the chance."

"And all the showing sold." Sandra showed her genuine delight. "Now I can boast about you to all my friends. Fancy having an international audience for your work."

Think about that, Logan cautioned himself, his eyes on Dana in her exquisitely soft green dress. Was there no colour she couldn't wear? He knew, first-hand, dealers had been vying to get hold of her work. She had sold every last photograph that evening, in the end to the American dealer because he intended to keep the entire show together.

"After all, you can only go so far here," Phillipa was saying. Almost like a prompt.

Dana twisted the stem of her wineglass, knowing what Phillipa was about. In a way, feeling sorry for her. "My work is really about being an Australian, Phillipa. It's *my* country and *my* way of looking at things."

Phillipa had to force a smile. "I think you'll change your mind once you get to New York."

New York, Logan thought. A world away. Almost another planet. What did an Outback cattleman have in common with a photographic artist on her upward climb to the top? Her talent would get her there. Her beauty, like a lily in bloom, would assure her of a public image. The whole world admired beauty and talent.

Jack Cordell, who had a secret desire to beat Logan at billiards at least once, dragged him off for a game. Logan had tried to cry off but in the end gave in goodnaturedly. He had plenty of paperwork to get through and a proposal from a pastoralist colleague to consider a partnership venture, but he always tried to get in some relaxation and he liked Jack. He had known the Cordells all his life and he approved of Jack as a husband for Sandra. Jack was a fine young man from a well-

respected family and he was always on hand to give
Sandra the kind of comfort and support she needed.

Once the men departed, the women retired to Ainslie's
large sitting room. It was a beautiful ''blue'' room with
an entrancing painting of a tree in a green field against
a densely blue sky above the mantelpiece. The painting
alone was so real it transported the viewer to the green
meadow. Dana loved it and the combination of sofas,
armchairs, fabrics, a few wonderful antiques and the tall
bronze lamps. It was a room as distinguished and restful
as Ainslie herself.

They chatted for some time, listened to Ainslie's classical CD's, then Dana excused herself saying there were
a number of things involving her studio she still had to
attend to. Although she had worked intensive hours to
clear her commitments she still had letters on hold which
she would now send by fax.

''You'll look in on Alice, would you, dear?'' Ainslie
said. ''It took her such a long time to go off.''

''Excitement.'' Dana smiled. ''Don't worry, Ainslie,
I'll attend to it.''

''I've been no help.'' Sandra apologised for her ab-
sence. ''I've needed to be with Jack but I'm going to
get closer to my little niece now she's here. I must say
she seems a lot happier than I supposed under the circumstances.''

''When did you last have word of Melinda?'' Phillipa
came a little too near to demanding.

It was Ainslie who answered, slowly, reluctantly,
acutely aware of Phillipa's disapproval. ''Just recently.
You must remember, Phillipa, Melinda is a woman in
shock.''

''She's the most selfish woman in the world, you
mean,'' Sandra burst out, then, catching Dana's eye,
apologised. ''Sorry, Dana. I know Melinda is your

cousin, but she makes me furious. I can't understand how she can do this to Alice.''

''Please let's drop it, dear,'' Ainslie begged, unwilling to discuss family matters in front of Phillipa. Though she had always liked Phillipa, liked the way she was so active in community matters, she had never found her particularly tolerant of failings in others, and her mother, though a bright energetic woman, was a great gossip. Time had to go by before any of them would know exactly what Melinda's plans were for the future.

In her room, Dana drafted a few letters, took her shower, put on her nightclothes then padded down the corridor to Alice's room. Alice was lying quietly, two hands locked beneath pink cheeks, her breathing easy. She looked fine, lightly tanned and healthy. Dana moved the night-light a little further away from the bed. The light was very soft but it was falling across Alice's eyes. She resisted the impulse to kiss the little girl's cheek in case she woke her up, going to the French doors that led onto the upper balcony and catching the gently swaying curtain back into its silk rope.

The night sky was blazing with stars, the sky itself tinted a marvellous dark purple. She ventured out onto the veranda exulting in the warm darkness, the wonderful scents of the bush that rose over and above the more familiar perfumes of the garden. Mara was an incredible place. It had been her first experience of a great Outback station and one that would never leave her. All this was Logan's. Had been his from birth. In a way it was like being born a prince. And tragic Jimmy! To have died so young and so far from home. Now he would never leave.

Dana was just about to turn away from the door when a woman's voice, low-pitched but urgent, reached her from the terrace below.

''How much punishment must I take?'' It was

Phillipa, and she sounded deeply upset. "I told you it meant nothing. A mad moment. I'm sick with shame."

It was no surprise when Logan responded, "Why are you bringing all this up, Phillipa? It's over."

It was time to move yet Dana was rooted to the spot, her better judgement way off.

"I can't accept that. How can I?" Phillipa, so cool and contained, responded passionately. "It seems to me with a little forgiveness on your part we could get back to what we had before."

"*Were* we so happily engaged?" Logan asked, and his voice sounded dismayingly cool.

"You know we were," Phillipa protested. "We were meant for each other from the outset."

Logan's laugh was brief and cynical. "So as soon as I turned my back you fell into Steven's bed?"

At this point Dana moved back, in the process stubbing her bare toes against a sandstone pot containing a lush golden cane. Shock acted as an anaesthetic. She couldn't believe the impeccable Phillipa with her holier-than-thou manner, had taken such a wrong turn. It would have been funny only the consequences had been disastrous, dashing Phillipa's hopes and dreams.

"You've heard this a hundred times before," Phillipa pleaded. "It was a mistake. We both had too much to drink. God, Logan haven't you ever made a mistake?" she cried.

"Plenty of them." His tone was hard. "But I'm a great believer in fidelity. Anyway, it doesn't matter anymore."

"But you haven't found anyone else." Renewed hope sounded in Phillipa's voice. "Tell me, Logan, I have to know."

Logan was silent for a few fraught seconds as though measuring her claim. "I don't see it that way at all."

"It's not Dana, is it?" Jealousy distorted Phillipa's normally attractive tones.

"Why would you say that?"

On the veranda above, Dana's face flamed.

"She's very beautiful," Phillipa said wretchedly. "I know how much you prize beautiful things."

"Surely you don't think that's all there is to Dana?" he asked. "Beauty?"

"All right, she's interesting." Phillipa considered shortly. "I've always liked her, unlike that ferocious little pussy cat of a cousin. But Dana Barry isn't the right woman to have by your side," Phillipa said with strong conviction. "On her own admission she's a career woman. She belongs in a different world, not out here."

Logan sounded so taut it was nothing short of hostile. "I appreciate that, Phillipa."

I can't bear this, Dana thought, her frozen limbs unlocking. She began to back slowly, stealthily, towards the French doors, not wanting her movements to be heard nor to wake Alice up.

"It would be awful if you allowed her to disrupt your life." But Phillipa was so upset she was forgetting to keep her voice down. Almost at the door, Dana stood stock-still, desperate to hear Logan's reply.

"I hope I can handle that myself, Pip, with no help from you," he said curtly.

"But I love you. I loved you long before she came into our lives." Phillipa's voice was less audible. "Doesn't that mean anything anymore?"

"This is insane, Pip." Logan's tone was final. "Insane, and I wish you'd stop."

If only Phillipa had, but she was clutching at anything. Things she wouldn't normally have said. Taboo things. "How can I when I feel so *betrayed*," she cried. "I'm not the first woman to lose her man to Dana Barry."

The air started to shimmer before Dana's eyes. She

felt dizzy, disoriented. It was all her own fault. In listening had she really believed she would resolve her own dilemmas? What was coming would be worse by far. She knew it in her bones.

"What about her relationship with Tyler?" Phillipa challenged in a burning rush.

"I beg your pardon?" Most people would have shrunk from Logan's tone but Phillipa gave a distraught laugh.

"We all knew the marriage wasn't perfect. How could it be with someone like Dana in the background? Why she showed her cousin up at every turn."

"So?" Logan's rasp cut her off.

"A blind person could see Tyler was in love with her." Phillipa's voice was unnaturally clear. "I was a guest here at different times."

What is happening to me? Dana thought.

"You're not so different from your mother, are you?" Logan accused cruelly. "Endlessly in search of gossip."

"I'm clearer eyed than you," Phillipa burst out just as fiercely, her nerves frayed. "My only interest is *you.*"

Dana felt a desire to cry out her innocence, but who would listen? She moved back into the bedroom, standing shaken beside Alice's bed. It was just as well children slept so soundly, so clearly had the voices floated upwards. She was nearly weeping herself with pain and frustration, causing her to put a hand against her mouth, swallowing down hard against the tears. All the hoping and praying in the world weren't going to change the fact they all believed in a terrible triangular relationship between her, Melinda and Jimmy. Jimmy could have put things right, but Jimmy hideously was dead. Melinda *knew* the truth, but Melinda these days was filled with a terrible desire to hurt people. For any young woman to marry Logan Dangerfield would be considered a triumph, a splendid match. Melinda was going to make certain that didn't happen to Dana.

It all went back to sibling rivalry on a scale Dana had never dreamt of.

In a flash of recall Dana remembered her cousin as a child, pretty as a porcelain doll with her apple blossom skin, blond curls and big blue eyes. She remembered clearly, keenly, how her heart had gone out to that little cousin so tragically bereft. It seemed to her now she had fallen over backwards all her life trying to make excuses for Melinda, yet she remembered the times they had cried together locked in one another's arms, their tears mingling. Some subterranean part of Melinda did love her. It had showed itself from time to time. So how could she have ever imagined Melinda could turn on her with such venom?

When she finally moved out into the corridor Dana had to stop abruptly, heart hammering, as she saw a lean, powerful figure silhouetted against the pool of light from an open doorway.

"Dana?"

She wrapped her arms around herself in a futile attempt to protect herself from the overwhelming magnetism that never failed to grab her.

"I was just checking on Alice." She flushed, attempting a matter-of-fact tone and failing dismally.

"So what are you shivering for? It's a hot night," he challenged.

Strongly, purposefully, like a panther on the prowl, he began walking towards her. "How much did you hear?"

No mercy from Logan. "I don't know what you're talking about." Absurdly she lied.

"The hell you don't. You were on the veranda weren't you?" He looked down at her, a hard excitement spiralling up in him at the sight of her. How huge were her beautiful eyes, glittering as if on the verge of tears. How pale that lovely face. Desire jabbed at him so painfully it was like a knife point at the heart.

She scented the wildness in him. "Please, Logan. It's late. I want to go to bed."

"No, Dana. I'd rather you talked to me." He pulled her back against the wall. "I knew you had to be there. I could *feel* you. I could even pick up your scent."

"I'm sorry." There was nothing more she could say. "I was looking in on Alice. I had no idea anyone was on the terrace."

"But once you heard us you stayed?"

"I made that mistake, yes." Her chin came up. He had never seemed so formidable or so tall. "I didn't want to, but I couldn't move."

"And I bet you're sorry?" His laugh was low and harsh.

"Don't you think it best if I went to bed?"

"And which bed do you belong in?" he asked.

She didn't think. She didn't repress her blind anger. She was swamped by it. Logan's sardonic tongue laced with honey or gall. She struck out at him, breathing hard and furious, her fists clenched, the force of her emotions staggering in their intensity. So this is what it was like to love? To hate? Their mutual sexual hostility was never far beneath the surface.

"You want to hit me. Go on. Don't bottle it up." He taunted her, letting her flail at him, the blows landing with a satisfying thud on his wide shoulders or the hard wall of his chest. "I could use some kind of fight. Only you're hardly a match, are you?" Then his arms were pining her, his hands moving restlessly, ruthlessly, over her lightly clad body. "How do you think I can hold tight to promises when I feel like this?" he rasped.

"I don't know," she answered bitterly. "Since when did you have time for fallen angels anyway?" She tried desperately to keep her traitorous body under control but it was too avid for his.

"Twenty four hours a day, Dana," he gritted. "That's a helluva lot."

She continued to struggle, fighting down her own weakness.

"What? Didn't Phillipa convince you?" she shot at him, ramming her fists against his chest, trying to put distance between them only she might as well have tried to push back a brick wall.

"What made you do it? I mean...God, Dana." Stifling a violent oath, he grasped a fistful of her silky hair, dragging her head back so his mouth could plunge over hers. Whatever she had done the sheer power of his passion undermined his will, sending it spinning away into space. This wasn't the magic they had known in the cave, or that night they had spent at her apartment. This was treacherous, overwhelming, threatening desire. He could stand no more, his jagged emotions sweeping over him like a flash flood.

She was trembling so badly she thought her knees would buckle. She was shrinking from him yet wild for his touch. She was two people. The woman who loved him, and the woman who couldn't bear his disbelief in her. A disbelief impossible to fight. Only as he took her mouth with such all-conquering passion, the woman in love found supremacy, the other Dana, the victim, moaning with the pain of it all.

He placed his hands on both her breasts, cupping them in his palms, then he bent, lowered his body so he was kneeling, drawing her to him so he could kiss her through the layers of filmy fabric, plunging his face against her, breathing in her body scents.

The excitement of it was so tremendous, her body felt incandescent. Finally she could no longer stand. She pitched forward overcome by ungovernable sensation, her blood in a ferment, her nerves frenetic.

He rose to his feet, lifting her so she slumped over his shoulder, like a rag doll he was holding.

"Logan...Logan..." was all she could say, her voice in an agonised whisper of sorrow, of protest, of an answering compulsive desire. She had to stop him. This one time at least.

Only Logan came to his senses. "I'm going to beat this," he said, and his strong voice shook. For once she was entirely in his power, but it gave him no satisfaction. Holding her captive like some pirate of old, he carried her to her room, throwing her down on the bed so tempestuously her body and mind whirred with reaction and her hair flew wildly around her head in a silver-gilt cloud.

"I won't hurt you if I can help it," he gritted from behind clenched teeth.

She grabbed for his hand and struggled to keep hold of it. "Then start believing in me," she begged, a pulse pounding away in her throat.

"I'm not the damn fool you think I am," he said angrily, pulling his hand away, his eyes in the lamplight blazing like sapphires.

"Okay," she said miserably, feeling utterly defeated. "I'm leaving. I mean that."

His dynamic face hardened to granite. "If I don't want you to leave, Dana, you *don't*."

"You think you can keep me a prisoner?" she said bitterly, trying to sit up.

"You know I can."

And so he could. "I've always been afraid of you, Logan," she said, feeling the cold steel of him.

"I guess I've always been afraid of you, too. With good reason." He bent, kissed her again, so hard it pushed her head right back to the mattress. "Anyway, Alice needs you. Don't you remember? Her beautiful angelic Dana. Not the Dana who inflames men.'' With a violent movement he pulled away from her, away from the sight of her, her skin flushed, her eyes so dark and disturbed, her light robe that seemed to have lost its sash thrown back from her body, covered in a mere wisp of some creamy silk material. She looked so delicate, so mesmerizing, her nipples erect against the feather lightness of her nightgown, the long skirt of which had wrapped itself around her, pulling taut across her body, exposing her beautiful slender legs the sun had flushed with gold.

He was hideously humiliatingly aware of his own driving hunger. It bordered on agony but he forced himself to control it, tightly coiling his fingers into the calloused palms of his hands. He had never felt so smothered by desire. So smothered by a woman. And the worst part of all. The worst part…

With one galvanic movement Logan moved back from the canopied bed a fine beading of sweat breaking out on his dark copper skin. He could master it. He could master it. He was his own man.

"I can't stand the thought of another day with you," Dana cried, sick with love of him.

"Ditto, my lady." He had recovered sufficiently to manage a hard sardonic drawl. "This just isn't the right time to do anything about it, though, is it? Christmas is coming, remember? The season of peace on earth and good will to men. Everyone is enjoying having you here with the possible exception of yours truly, but then you're not making things exactly easy. Tomorrow I thought we might put up the Christmas tree. For Alice, of course. At least we both love *her*.''

CHAPTER NINE

THE next morning Dana, unwilling to face the day, tried to sink back into sleep but it was too late. She was awake. Early morning sun washed across the room in a wave of bright golden light and bird calls were ringing again and again, carolling across the many species of beautiful native eucalypts that grew in the garden. She lay still on her back feeling the emotions of the night before pressing down on her. How could she carry off the rest of this holiday with Logan feeling the way he did? And all because she had tried to be there for Jimmy when Alice was the real object of her love and attention. She had done everything she could to deny it but there seemed no way to counter the damage. She might even have difficulty trying to explain the situation to an outsider. Where there was smoke there was fire, they would probably say. It was a classic example of mud-sticking.

Dana threw back the bedclothes, moving through the small dressing room to the pretty adjacent bathroom with its Wedgwood blue and white tiles. She was still shocked by Phillipa's admission she had slept with another man when engaged to Logan. Phillipa had claimed alcohol as an excuse and there was no doubt when under its influence the little devils got to work but the excuse hadn't worked. Had she really thought it would with Logan? Probably Phillipa had thought he would never know, when Logan had tabs on everyone even when he was out of the country.

Poor Phillipa! She shouldn't really be feeling sorry for her but she did. Phillipa was a woman who would use every weapon when under threat. Phillipa's words came back to her. "A blind person could see Tyler was in love with her." What had made her say that? Jealousy, of course. But had she *really* believed it or was it a wild charge born of desperation? But where had she got the idea? Sandra? Sandra had been so shocked and lost at Jimmy's funeral, her usual sense of discretion hadn't been working. Had Sandra said something for Phillipa to catch on to? I don't really need another person to condemn me, Dana thought.

When she walked out into the hallway, dressed in yellow cotton jeans and a white tank top, her long hair pulled back into a cool knot, Phillipa chose exactly that time to emerge from her room.

Dana felt like bolting, making a return rush for her room but Phillipa had already seen her. She, too, was dressed in jeans and a pink shirt, dragging on a packed bag and leaving it just outside her door.

"I always said there was a great deal more to you than met the eye." Phillipa lost no time addressing Dana directly.

"Good morning, Phillipa," Dana responded. Keep calm. Keep cool. Phillipa is leaving. "Is there a problem?"

"I'm not sure it matters anymore," Phillipa answered in a bitter tone. "I never realised it before, but you and your cousin are two of a kind." She strode up to where Dana was standing, her eyes pink and puffy as though she'd been weeping.

"Are you going to explain that?" Dana asked quietly, thinking this time she'd have to put Phillipa straight.

"I'd be happy to." Phillipa gave a discordant little laugh. "Both of you went after the Dangerfield men. Your cousin caught Tyler by getting herself pregnant. It shouldn't take you long to achieve the same objective."

There was a sudden chill in Dana's voice. "You're getting very personal, aren't you, Phillipa? Offensive, too. I can see you're very upset but I'm not prepared to listen to this kind of thing. Your engagement to Logan is long over, so you're getting into something that isn't even your business.''

''Of course!'' Phillipa seemed to be trying to hold herself together but failing. ''You don't cheat on Logan Dangerfield. No, sir. If you do you end up in Outer Mongolia.''

''I'm sorry, Phillipa,'' Dana said, dipping her head, trying to balance pity and anger.

''*You're* sorry?'' Now it was Phillipa's turn to stare. There was obvious sincerity in Dana's voice.

''I know what the pain of rejection is like.'' After all, she had been rejected last night.

''Well, well,'' Phillipa mocked. ''I appreciate your concern, but only for *you* Logan might have come back to me. Then you had to arrive with your sparkly hair and your big brown eyes. You're as dangerous to my happiness as you ever were to your cousin's.''

It was a monument to Dana's control she didn't cry aloud. ''You're talking *scandal,* Phillipa,'' she warned. ''You're talking character assassination. Mine as well as Jimmy's.''

Phillipa's gaze went cold and triumphant. ''I never said anything about Tyler. *You* did.''

''I didn't intend to overhear you and Logan talking last night, either,'' Dana flashed back.

''An eavesdropper. Was it worth your while?'' Phillipa asked contemptuously.

''I didn't know about Steve. That would be Steven Mitchell? One of the elite circle.'' Dana thought she deserved it.

Phillipa flushed violently. ''I'm hoping you won't pass that on,'' she said stiffly, totally ignoring the fact she herself was into trading insults.

''No, I won't. I don't have any time for people who

pass on hurtful gossip. I can only tell you this, Phillipa, and I want you to believe it, Jimmy and I *did not* have an affair. The thought never crossed my mind. Not ever. He was married to my cousin. End of story.''

''But there's what Tyler said himself.'' Phillipa shook her head, brooding seriously.

''He never said anything about an *affair*. My God, Jimmy wasn't a liar. A destroyer. Maybe he had deep feelings for me and told his family, but when I think about it, why not? In so many ways he was a lost soul. He was doomed right from the start to walk in Logan's shadow. He never had a proper sense of himself, his own worth. He squandered his gifts and his money. But he was really only looking for love and fulfilment. I grieve to say Melinda didn't offer it to him.''

Phillipa frowned severely. ''We all knew about Melinda. But are you sure you didn't offer comfort?''

''Look at me, Phillipa,'' Dana urged. ''Look right at me. Do you really think I did?''

Instead of looking at her, Phillipa looked off. ''I'm not usually like this, you know,'' she said bleakly.

''There's a lot of pain in you.''

Phillipa gave a wry laugh. ''I guess.'' She reached out spontaneously and touched Dana's shoulder. ''You can have Logan if you want, Dana. Have a great life.''

''Except Logan doesn't want me,'' Dana was driven to say. ''You see, Phillipa, I don't have the necessary qualifications. Like most women, I can't live up to perfection.''

Midmorning hours, after Phillipa had flown out, three of the station hands brought the Christmas tree into the house. It was a specially grown-for-the-occasion casuarina, an annual thing, with the tree to be planted out after. Care had been taken to train the tree as it grew, now the slender grey-green pendulous branches, which naturally mimicked a conifer, showed a pyramid form. A huge sandstone pot had been placed to the right of the staircase in the entrance hall, now the men lofted the earth-balled tree into position.

"Up, up and away!" Alice cried excitedly. She stood within the circle of Dana's arms, her gold-flecked hazel eyes filled with joy. "Doesn't it look marvellous!"

"Wait until we decorate it." Dana hugged her. "Grandma has the most wonderful ornaments. They've been in the family for generations."

"This suit you, Miss," one of the men, the ginger-haired Bluey, called, willing to put it wherever Dana wanted. The top of the stairs if need be.

"That's fine, Bluey. Thank you. It's been beautifully grown. So much a part of this desert environment."

"No spruce's here, Miss." Bluey laughed. "Smells great, too. Want me to bring the stepladder in?"

"If you wouldn't mind, Bluey," Dana said. "We're going to start decorating it right away."

When Logan returned to the house he found the women happily engaged in setting up the tree. Already its slender branches were hung with a glittering array of silver, gold, scarlet and green orbs, baubles and ornaments of all kinds, things Ainslie had collected over the years. It came to him he had great affection for the woman his father had married when he was only four. Ainslie had never tried to mother him. Something in him must have held out against it. God knows why. Maybe his soul dwelt with his own mother. The beautiful creature who had died giving him birth. Said to be the image of his father, his father had always told him from the near-empty well of pain, "You have your mother's eyes. Her beautiful, beautiful sapphire eyes. Otherwise, you're a Dangerfield."

Ainslie had come to her marriage knowing she was a kind of rebound, a marriage of convenience, fearing her husband would never truly love her and her stepson would never accept her. Neither had happened. Ainslie was a woman who gave with all her heart, creating her own special place in the Dangerfield family. A position cemented when the children came. Tyler, then Alexandra. Logan remembered he had been ecstatic when his father told him there was going to be an addition to the family. An addition who turned out to be Tyler. He had loved Tyler from the beginning, proud of being big brother, longing for the day when the baby would be old enough for them both to go adventuring in the bush.

Only he and Tyler had been opposites.

And they had both fallen in love with the same woman.

There she was, beautiful, intelligent, gifted Dana, for all of that unassuming, no conceit in any form, full of the social graces. Both Ainslie and Sandra had almost from the start treated her like family. Tyler should have married someone like Dana, he thought grimly. Dana would have understood him, been firm enough, demanding enough to insist Tyler live up to his potential. Tyler had always been capable of so much better. It was their own father who had never understood him, forever holding up Logan as some impossible role model. It was a wonder they had remained as close as they had, Logan thought with deep regret.

Alice, turning, saw him, cried out, "Uncle Logan, come and see the tree. We've only got a few things more to put on. Grandma's little angels. They're all playing instruments."

"And we must be careful how we handle them, darling." Ainslie smiled. "They're quite precious."

"I know." Alice took a bisque porcelain angel very

carefully into her hands. "Look at this one. He's playing the violin. I think I'd like to learn a musical instrument."

"That can be arranged." Logan trod across the parqueted floor, covered with a beautiful antique Persian rug, in his riding boots. "How are you, Dana?" he asked suavely. He'd been out since dawn so this was the first time they'd met up. "Sleep well?"

"Like a top," Dana responded just as pleasantly. "You're just in time to place the Star of Bethlehem at the top. None of us can match you for height."

Alice squealed with merriment. "Ladies don't grow *that* tall."

"You should see Bert Bonner's mother," Logan joked. "I practically have to look up to her."

"Really?" Alice asked, wide-eyed.

"Bert says he has to get up on a box to talk to her. Right, Dana, you can pass me the star." Logan put out his hand, catching her fingers briefly as she tried to hand it to him without actually touching him.

Her fingers tingled with electricity.

"Oh, this is so beautiful!" Alice breathed when the glistening silver Star of Bethlehem was in place. "Can we turn on the lights?"

"Go right ahead." Logan stepped down from the ladder, looking up at the tree that almost lofted to the upstairs gallery. Even in daylight the multicoloured lights were a bright illumination, reflecting each sparkling ornament, throwing a kaleidoscope of colour outward in a halo.

"Perhaps a little more tinsel," Dana mused. "That's if we've got any left."

"Plenty of everything in the attic, dear." Ainslie smiled, then inevitably grew sad. "Year after year we've had a tree since the children were babies, but this is the first time we've had it in the hall. I'm glad you came up with that idea, Dana. It makes a lovely change."

Feeling her grief, Logan bent and kissed the side of his stepmother's cheek. "You're the centre of this house, Ainslie. You've been since the day you came into it."

Ainslie caught her breath. Logan had always had the capacity to surprise her with the perfectly beautiful things he said. For a moment she let her head rest against his shoulder. "It's time to tell you, too, my dear, you've been a wonderful stepson to me. A wonderful brother to my children."

It was an emotional moment that could have turned to tears, but Logan saved it, bowing from the waist, an exaggeratedly formal gesture he managed to pull off with considerable natural grace. "Thank you, Mamma."

Alice came to hold his hand, staring up into his face. "I'm glad I'm here, Uncle Logan. I feel safe."

She, too, seemed on the point of tears. "Your darn right you are!" He picked her up, whirling her around. "I tell you what that tree really needs."

"What?" Alice stared adoringly at him.

"Lots and lots of wonderful presents all around it."

As the countdown to Christmas began, Mara was host to an influx of visitors, younger members of the extended Dangerfield family with their children, friends from all over the Outback popping in and out on private flights, business people from the Outback towns, all wanting to convey their best wishes and enjoy Mara's legendary hospitality at the same time.

The Christmas tree in the entrance hall was now surrounded by a great pile of beautifully wrapped and beribboned presents chosen with care, the papers luxurious, most in the festive colours of Christmas: gleaming silver with ruby, rich gold and emerald, Santa Claus and mistletoe and berries, reindeers, winged angels in flight, all casting their own special glow. The children who came to call found the sight irresistible and Alice for once was in her element playing the small hostess and leader.

Christmas is such a wonderful time of the year it softens everyone's heart and Alice had discovered peace and sunshine in her life. Her "bad moments" when she couldn't cope with the pressures were becoming far less frequent now. There was more understanding in her life, more happy experiences, more encouragement to learn things and build up her own feelings of confidence and inner strength.

Reared in an increasingly unhappy household with her father too little there and her mother not bothering to mask her own unhappiness and frustrations, Alice had not been allowed to grow and blossom. In her new environment she was developing overnight, secure in the love and stability of her family around her. Not that there wasn't the occasional storm, but when it wasn't getting much attention it quickly passed. The thing that most impressed the family was the way Alice was now relating to her own age group, the previous big problem.

"It's not the same as school," she told Dana. "These kids all like me."

Dana took her by the shoulders so she could get Alice's full attention. "So help me they'll *all* like you at school if you're the friendly little person you are here. I'll even go beyond that, Alice, you have the capacity for leadership. It's all up to you, darling, isn't it? You can be anything you want to be. You're clever. You're full of ideas. You're a sensitive little soul. You can afford to take pride in yourself."

"That's right," Alice confirmed with a big smile on her face.

Little trips were organised to entertain, picnics beside the billabongs, where the children looped ropes around the tree and swung out into the water. Even Alice, once a little fearful, tried it, full of life and joy. Her swimming lessons had been progressing and in any case the younger children weren't allowed into the deep.

"You're such a good example to Alice," Sandra told Dana one day as they lazed against cushions watching Alice and the visiting cousins swoop shrieking across the glittering water.

"It's a wonder for her to be within the magic circle." Dana smiled. "Not like school with the other children poking fun at her. Alice loves these children and more wonderfully they love her. Just look at her now."

"Dana, Sandy, watch me, I'm going to let go," she yelled, and fell without a moment's hesitation or fright into the sparkling water where the other children were sporting like small dolphins.

"I do admire the way you handle her." Sandra sighed. "She's changed so much she's almost a different child."

"Well, she had a tough time of it, don't forget. It was a very bad experience for her seeing her parents fighting. She's escaped all that. She feels loved and secure."

"Until the day her mother wants her back," Sandra warned, waving at little Katy. "It's all up to Melinda really. She's the mother, right or wrong."

There was no need to tell Dana. She never stopped worrying about it.

Around this time she also began regular photographic sessions, her mind constantly turning over ideas and possibilities, which, as she moved freely around Mara, seemed to be endless. She had worked a number of times with a well-known travel author and journalist mostly in tropical North Queensland's sugar lands, glorious country, and the wonder of the Great Barrier Reef, which had to be paradise on earth, but nowhere she found so compelling so challenging as the vast Timeless Land. One of the world's harshest environments, it was frighteningly lonely, savage in drought, yet capable of turning on heart-stopping displays of beauty.

When the time was right, she had seen and photographed Mara literally covered in flower. Miles and miles of fragrant flowering annuals that spread in all directions as far as the eye could see. The wildflowers were remarkable but so was the prolific bird life, the vast spinifex plains, the great flat-topped mesas, the crystal-clear spring-fed pools, the gibber plains that glittered like a giant mosaic and the magnificent albeit terrifying sight of the Simpson Desert, the Wild Heart.

More and more she was filled with the invigorating ambition to capture on camera the very essence of this mirage-stalked country, to bring it to people who might never have a chance to see it for themselves. She was in a unique position to do that with her ties to Mara. It seemed to her, too, she would like to do her own writing, convey her own feelings and reactions as she explored this remote part of the world. Perhaps she could inspire her readers as she was inspired herself. It gave her lots to think about. She was grateful, too, for her technical expertise, though it hadn't come overnight. It was the result of years of highly specialised training.

Returning one afternoon from one of her treks she came on a mustering party driving a herd of cleanskins, cattle as yet unbranded, into one of the holding yards. Red dust rose in a whirlwind so she parked some little distance off enjoying the spectacle framed in the dancing gold-shot blue light. Vivid green butterfly trees grew in clumps all round the area still heavy in white and mauve blossom, the earth a bright red ocre, the sky a vivid cloudless blue. It really was a scene for the cinema screen, she thought. There were even sound effects. Cattle lowing, stockmen riding in among them, whips cracking harmlessly in the air, urging the beasts into the yard. Every few minutes one would try to make a break

with no success until a young red bull decided it was
high time to leave the mob and head back for the hills.

Through the wall of men came a rider, darting his
horse in and out, nosing the errant animal back into the
enclosure. Both man and horse were lightning quick in
their movements, a pleasure to watch. Dana took up a
position with her Hasselblad, aiming it at the tall lean
cowboy, pearl grey akubra rakishly angled on his dark
head, sitting his bright chestnut horse with easy mastery.

She shot off a half a dozen frames before she became
aware of him riding towards her and holding up his
hand.

"What are you up to?"

She lay the camera down. "Does it require an explanation? I'm taking pictures of you."

"Whatever for?" He seemed genuinely puzzled.

"Because your so damned colourful. You look like
the guy in the old Marlboro commercials, only better,"
she said.

"At least I have the sense not to smoke."

"Pretty well everyone has these days. Why don't you
let me take a few more for my girlfriends," she taunted
him. "Most of them fell in love with you on the strength
of that one photo on my bookcase. You're every
woman's idea of an Outback hero."

"That's me." He smiled with lazy satire. "God, it's
hot!" He took off his hat and ran a hand through his
thick hair. His hands were beautifully shaped. She remembered the feel of them on her body. How she found
their faint callousing and strength so exciting.

"If it's not too personal a question," she asked, "are
we likely to see Phillipa again before Christmas?"

He bent the full force of his brilliant gaze on her.
"Phillipa is past caring about me."

"So that's a no?" With Phillipa, anything was possible. She might have got her second wind.

"More or less." This with a slight edge. "Her parents might turn up. They won't want to cut themselves off from us in any way."

"I guess not," she agreed laconically.

"Where's Alice?" Deliberately, he changed the subject. "The two of you are always together."

"She's having fun with the children. The last time I saw them they were dressing up in the attic. Someone is going to have to put all the stuff they've pulled out of the old trunks away."

"Don't *you* bother about it," he told her. "Now that you're here, why don't we go for a ride?"

For a moment she couldn't think of anything at all to say. They had been well and truly keeping their distance for just on a week now.

"Is there something wrong?" he challenged with the old tantalising mockery.

"Friendly today, are we?"

He gave a brief laugh. "Dana, you're my pain and my delight. Besides, even my iron control doesn't work all the time."

"Then I'd love to." Just for a second she smiled at him. "You'll have to come with me. I haven't got a horse."

"Mine will take both of us."

"You're joking?" Her eyes widened.

"Dana, I mean everything I say. You're a featherweight, that's okay. Or are you frightened of coming up before me?"

His amusement restored her cool. "It works for Alice. I don't know about me."

"So let's try it."

"What about the jeep, my equipment?" She looked around. "It's valuable."

"Don't fret. Who's here to steal it? Cover it with something. Zack can run the jeep back to the house."

She was fiercely tempted even when her wounded feelings were barely healed over.

"Make up your mind," he said, directing a challenging look into her eyes.

"I can't believe I'm doing this." Dana moved to take care of her camera and equipment, covering it with a light rug. Meanwhile Logan rode back a little distance having a short conversation with Zack, his leading hand. She had one last chance to cry off and drive home, only she was too damned excited. This was the sort of man Logan was. All electricity and excitement, and just to prove it while her mind was in arrears, he reached down for her like a stuntman doing tricks and lofted her into the saddle before him. His enveloping arm was an inch from her breasts, his breath fanning her cheek. She scarcely heard the men's applause. She didn't even remember riding out of the camp. They were heading for the crossing fording it at the shallowest point then galloping up the incline to the sheltered valley beyond.

It was a madly heady feeling galloping across the desert flats, the wild bush around them, the wind tearing at her hair, a great flight of budgerigar, the phenomenon of the Outback joyfully joining in the chase, winging in an emerald green and gold V-shaped formation, as though spurring them on. Logan's face was hunkered down over hers, his left arm locked around her upper body, the tips of his fingers pressing into the swelling flesh at the side of her breast. Just to have physical contact was to feel enormously energised. She thought she could have cheerfully ridden to the ends of the earth with him so infinitely spell-binding was his influence over her. Almost unknown to her, her own hands were caressing the length of his bare arm, moving up and down, stroking the light tracery of hair, holding his arm even closer to her so he had to feel her quickening pulses, the primitive throb of her heart. It was almost as though someone had started up a small drum. Over the flats they went until finally they reached the point where their bodies were burning. Not from the heat that rose in waves from the red sun-baked earth, but the heat within. The great all-pervading flames neither of them could put out. This was part of the sorcery of love, the recklessness, the anguish, the ferocious need for physical fulfilment.

Finally, Logan rode down on a spring-fed pool, clear cool water oozing up from the sandy bed, the pool lined by long reeds the area totally surrounded by stands of desert oaks. He dismounted swiftly, seized Dana, pulled her from the saddle and into his waiting arms. He was mad for her, even dangerous, he thought. In truth he was trying to get a hold on himself, hating the sense of going out of control, but he wanted this woman too much. He could never have foreseen how terribly he would want her.

Forgetful of his strength, he almost lifted her off her feet to kiss her, pushing her head back into his shoulder, covering her mouth passionately as if kissing her was as necessary to him as the air he breathed or the precious water without which a man would die. He kissed her over and over as if this was his one and only chance, his hand moving, moving, deeply massaging her spine, moulding her body ever closer. Her mouth tasted of apricots, her skin smelled like wildflowers after rain. He knew she was breathless, panting in his arms, but she wasn't struggling away. The more he wanted, the more her body gave. He plunged his hand into the open neck of her soft shirt, breaking a button, but anything to get to her exquisite naked breast. Now he understood fully how that one woman could change a man's life. He didn't want an affair. An affair would be wrong. He wanted this woman to love all the days of his life. He wanted to be free of the torment. He wasn't good at giving up the things he wanted.

She hadn't been wearing her hair loose but the wind had whipped it free of its ribbon. Now he grasped a handful of this beautiful long hair he loved, turning her head to the side so he could kiss her lovely neck. She was quivering in his arms. Burying her face against his shoulder, moaning a little as though her heart was breaking.

He drew a breath so sharp it hurt his ribs. "Let me love you," he urged. "I would never force you. But let me love you."

Her eyes were so dark yet at the centre was a leaping flame. She began to laugh, a soft wild little sound, no mirth in it but a kind of acknowledged abandonment. "We said we wouldn't."

"I know." His face was full of urgent hungers, a desire that raged. "You want it though, Dana, don't you?"

Want? She was ravenous. She let her head fall back, stretching her throat. "Ah…*yes!*" She wasn't a woman who had ever expected to be totally dominated by a man yet nonetheless she was. Logan consumed her. It was that simple.

CHAPTER TEN

THREE days before Christmas the peace of the household was shattered when Melinda flew in unannounced and alone. Logan, who saw the four-seater Cessna fly in, doubled back to the landing strip in the four-wheel drive, his eyes focused on the charter flight that was just coming in to land. He felt absolutely no warning. Visitors had been flying in and out for most of December. Usually, though, they always rang ahead to say they were coming. He was familiar with the charter plane. It was one of Westaway's. Ray Westaway was a good friend. It was probably Ray come to say hello and pay his respects to Ainslie. By the time he drove the vehicle to the strip, the plane had landed and the pilot was on the strip, handing down a young woman.

Melinda.

Dismay welled up in him, a fierce sense of protectiveness for his family, Alice in particular. Whatever Melinda was doing here it could only spell trouble. A harsh judgement to some but he knew her too well.

The pilot came towards him, smiling like he was among friends, carrying his passenger's two pieces of luggage. "Hi, there, Mr. Dangerfield. One passenger delivered safely." He turned to include the very pretty blonde who was showing for the first time an unexpected uneasiness? Wariness? Whatever. Dangerfield wasn't smiling. To the pilot's mind he looked positively formidable. This was his reputation anyway. A powerful man who had stepped very neatly into his father's shoes. And he was angry. Quite angry. He had never seen such a blaze in a man's eyes before.

A few minutes later the pilot flew off, feeling molli-
fied Dangerfield had greeted him pleasantly, giving him
a message to convey to his boss. He remembered now
they were good friends.

On the ground, Logan settled Melinda in the front
passenger seat then went around to the other side, opening up the door and climbing behind the wheel. "You're
full of surprises, Melinda," he said, trying to view the
arrival calmly. "I understood you were enjoying yourself in London?"

Melinda touch a hand to her short, pretty hair. She
was doing it a new way and she looked older and more
sophisticated than he had ever seen her. "Max hates the
cold. He has great friends in Sydney. We're staying with
them."

"So it's serious, then, with Max?" What exactly had
Tyler meant in his wife's life? he thought with a heavy
heart, asking, "What's Max's other name?"

"He's the man I'm probably going to marry,"
Melinda evaded. "It doesn't matter his name."

"I'm afraid it does, Melinda, as you're Alice's
mother."

"I've learned to keep a few things to myself," she
said, "for the time being anyway."

"You could have let us know you were coming."

"Don't be awkward, Logan. It was a spur-of-the-
moment thing. I wanted to give you all a big surprise."

"Then I have to say I find your idea of a big surprise
pretty bizarre. You can't expect us to feel overjoyed
about it."

"Well, it was never your way, was it?" Melinda gave
him her kittenish triangular smile.

They were even more shocked at the house. The moment Melinda set foot in the entrance hall exclaiming at
the Christmas tree, the pervading tranquillity seemed to
fly out the door.

"Melinda!" Ainslie tried her level best for courtesy and calm. "This is indeed a surprise. We didn't expect you back so soon."

"Only a flying visit. A week or two to miss the Winter. "Dana!" Melinda held out her arms as Dana for a few moments transfixed started down the stairs. "My very *favourite* cousin."

"Good God, Melinda," Dana responded in a heartfelt groan. "Couldn't you have let us know you were coming?"

"Why, Dee. Don't you like surprising people? I'm here with Max, actually. We're staying with friends of his, right on the Harbour. An absolute mansion. The Goddards. You must have heard of them." She named a well-known racing family then stopped abruptly as though she had given away too much. "I slipped away for a time. I hope you don't mind, but I have a few things to straighten out."

"Of course," Ainslie answered, still shocked. "You're staying overnight surely?"

"I'd like that." Melinda smiled. "I can't be away from Max's side for any longer than that. And Alice, where is she?"

Logan couldn't help the cynical laugh that broke from him. "I was wondering when you were going to mention your daughter." He gestured towards the formal drawing room. "Let's go in and sit down, shall we?" He turned his head briefly to speak to Dana. "Would you mind finding Alice, please, Dana. You could prepare her by telling her her mother is here."

Dana sprang into action almost running through the house. What did Melinda's sudden appearance mean? Was it possible Melinda was becoming more human? Did she intend to resume her God-given role and take Alice back with her? If so, they would miss Alice dreadfully. And what of Alice's feelings? And who was this

Max? How serious was the relationship? Was he the sort of man who would be prepared to love another man's child? And *Jimmy!* Had he really meant so little to Melinda she had already put him out of her life?

She came bursting out of the house, finding Alice sitting beside Retta on the grass. They were spreading out drawings, things Alice had completed with Retta acting as teacher. Retta was a very talented artist, both in the traditional aboriginal way and the Western culture. She had already shown Alice an easy way to draw animals.

"There you are!" Dana breathed.

They both turned at the tight, constricted sound in Dana's normally warm melodious tones.

"I've got a good little pupil here." Retta smiled, then with her enviable sensitivity picked up on Dana's agitated feelings. "Everything okay, Miss Dana?"

Pray God it was. "Yes, fine, Retta." Dana tried for a smile that didn't quite come off. "Thank you so much for looking after Alice, but she has to come into the house now."

"Ah, Dana, I'm having a nice time," Alice complained.

"Yes, I know you are, darling, but something has happened. I want to tell you all about it."

"You're not upset about it, are you?" Alice rose immediately to her feet, staring into Dana's face.

"No, dear." Dana turned to address Retta who was standing quietly nearby. "Perhaps you could collect the drawings, Retta. I'd love to see them later."

"No trouble. Go along now, Alice. We can take a walk together later."

Inside the house, Dana drew Alice into the kitchen storeroom. "Listen, darling, a very big surprise. Mummy is here. She wants to see you."

For answer, Alice reached out, picked up a small can of baked beans and threw it violently against the wall.

"If this means I have to go back with her I'm not coming."

"Alice," Dana came close to wailing, taking the child into her arms. "This is *Mummy*. She's been missing you."

"Well, I haven't been missing her." Alice frowned ferociously, twisting away. "I don't want her anymore, Dana. I like things the way they are."

"But will you always, Alice," she pleaded. "Your mother has hurt you, but give her a chance. She's come all this way out here to make amends."

"You take care of me, Dana," Alice said, her light brown head dropping. "Mummy is mean to me. She doesn't like me. She doesn't want me around."

"Alice, please, why don't you let her tell you how sorry she is? Please give her another chance. Mummy was hurt, too."

Alice looked up into Dana's eyes. "You really want this, Dana. You're not punishing me?"

Dana almost reeled back in shock. "Punishing you. Lord, sweetheart, would I ever do that? Would I ever do anything to make you unhappy?"

"Daddy said you didn't know about Mummy."

"Daddy had his own problems. Mummy and I grew up together. We've been together all our lives."

"And what does Uncle Logan and Grandma say?" Alice looked her straight in the eye.

"We're all trying to understand our feelings, darling. Maybe we all can't be together nice and friendly like your cousins and the children, but we have to learn how to cope with what's going on in our lives. You're growing up now, Alice. You're a serious little person. I only want you to greet your mother and listen to what she has to say. Parents must be treated with dignity and respect."

"Kids have to be treated with respect, too," Alice

burst out, giving vent to all her pent-up feelings of hurt and rejection.

"You should be happy Mummy's here," Dana said sorrowfully.

"Well, I'm not." Alice reached out and grasped Dana's hand. "This is important to you, Dana, isn't it?"

"Important to you, too, darling." Dana squeezed her small hand, praying and praying Melinda would come into her own and express loving maternal feelings. She had changed a good deal in appearance. Indeed she was looking stunning. With the grace of God she would make up for the hurt she had inflicted on her child.

When they went into the drawing room, Melinda, sitting alone on a Victorian settee, jumped up, a radiant smile on her face. "Alice, sweetie, don't you look well. The prettiest I've ever seen you. Come to Mummy and give me a great big hug."

Alice hesitated a moment, turned and looked at Dana, then walked towards her mother.

"Hello, Mummy," she said composedly. "Didn't you like London?"

"I loved it! I can't wait to go back." Melinda bent over Alice and kissed the cheek her daughter presented. "This is what is called a flying visit."

"Why?" Alice asked.

"Why what?"

"Why did you come?" Alice asked. "It's a long trip just to see me."

"That's right, and I am a little tired. Aren't you pleased to see me?" Melinda's blue eyes looked hurt.

"You look very pretty," Alice commented.

Melinda brightened. "Well, I know I can never be a genuine beauty like Dee but I can turn a few heads. Why don't you come up to my room while I have a little rest? We can talk. Is that all right, Ainslie?" Melinda turned her blond head.

"Of course, Melinda," Ainslie answered quietly. "I'm hoping when you're feeling refreshed you can tell us your plans."

"Oh, I will." Melinda took hold of Alice's hand. "I've lots to catch up on with my daughter."

"Come with us, Dana," Alice begged.

"Not now, Alice." Melinda gave a little smile. "I know you love Dana, but I'm hoping you can spare a little time for your mother."

"Dear God!" Logan said slowly and deliberately after they had gone. "What does all this mean?"

"I couldn't bear to lose Alice now," Ainslie said piteously. "To take her away to another country! Don't grandparents lose out."

"Who said anything about her wanting to take Alice away?" Logan asked, a vertical frown between his black brows. "It's a good thing Sandy isn't here or we could have a fight on our hands."

"Give her a chance, Logan," Dana implored.

"You *want* her to take Alice?"

"No, no." Dana slumped dejectedly into an armchair. "But she is Alice's mother."

"Of course she is," Ainslie agreed wretchedly. "If only she was a real mother. A real person. I don't think she's changed."

Dinner was a quiet meal with a kind of unbearable tension beneath the superficial conversation. Alice had been allowed to stay up, now she sat beside her mother, wrapped in a blanket of silence.

"Everything all right, my little love?" Ainslie asked, her pale face showing her anxiety. "You're not eating."

"I have a headache, Grandma," Alice said quietly.

"Naturally she's wanting me to stay on," Melinda said.

"I imagine she might, as you're her mother," Logan

clipped off. It was driving him wild Melinda just sitting there saying nothing. He had the dismal feeling she was toying with them, playing some preconceived game.

Alice spoke again. "I don't care if Mummy goes." From the expression on her face there could be no doubt she meant it.

"That's not very nice, sweetie," Melinda said.

"It's what I want," Alice exclaimed.

Melinda reached for her wineglass and picked it up. "I can see you've all been doing your best to turn my child against me," she said acidly.

Dana looked directly at her cousin with angry eyes, then she pushed back her chair and stood up. "If you have a headache, Alice, why don't I take you up to your room?"

"I want her to stay," Melinda said.

"I think not." Logan gestured to Dana to go. "This conversation is obviously for the grown-ups."

In her bedroom Alice slumped down dejectedly on the bed. "I belong to Mummy. Is that right, Dana?"

"Pretty well, darling, until you're older."

"So she can take me at any time?"

Yes, Dana thought. "If you want that, darling."

"Well, I don't." There was rebellion in Alice's voice. "I want to stay here. I don't want to go away. I would miss you terribly. I would miss Grandma and Uncle Logan and Sandy. I would miss all the kids when they come to visit. I'd miss Mrs. Buchan. Retta, too. She's so sweet to me. Mara is a wonderful happy place."

This was a dilemma and it was tearing at Dana's heartstrings. "Don't you think you could be happy with Mummy?"

"Not the way I want to be," Alice said slowly.

"Did Mummy say she was going to take you?" Dana didn't like to question Alice too closely but they had to know.

"She was talking mostly about you," Alice surprised her by saying.

"Me?"

"You and Uncle Logan." Alice nodded her head. "She asked how you were getting on."

"And what did you say?"

"I said Uncle Logan loves you and you love him. I can feel it deep inside." Alice clasped her small hands together and pressed them to her heart. "I've been praying you'd get married then I could be your child."

"Oh, Alice." Dana sat down on the bed and caught the little girl to her. "Oh, Alice," she moaned, "this is so very very hard for all of us. I'm your godmother. I'll always be your godmother. I'll always be there for you."

"I'm afraid," Alice said.

It took Dana close on half an hour to settle the child for bed, so when she returned downstairs she found the family had adjourned to the library.

"Alice is asleep at last," she said as she walked into the room, acutely aware of the tension that clouded the atmosphere.

"You've quite taken her over, haven't you, Dee?" Melinda said, not troubling to hide her disdain.

"You didn't seem too concerned about doing the job," Logan reminded her very abruptly. "You've obviously come to tell us of your intentions, so we'd appreciate it if you would. Alice has had a very disruptive life. She's only now settling down."

"Why this endless talk of Alice?" Melinda fumed. "She's had a pretty good life. Anyone would think she was suffering some abuse."

Logan stared at her from his position behind the massive mahogany desk. Behind him, above the mantelpiece hung a portrait of his grandfather, a sternly handsome man with a look of power and achievement. It was obvious they were cut from the same cloth. "Ever heard of emotional deprivation," he said.

"It seems to me I know more about it than you do," Melinda retorted. "I'm the original deprived child."

"That's right, the never-ending story," Dana burst out. "Deprived of your parents certainly, Melinda, but not of plenty of love and attention. You've never been gracious enough to acknowledge that. Anyway I would have thought your own emotional deprivation would have made you more understanding. More determined to see Alice would have a good life."

"It's a great relief then, isn't it, she's an heiress," Melinda countered. "Which brings me to my proposition," she went on calmly. "I'm willing to sign papers relating to *your* guardianship of Alice, Logan, if that's what you all want. You don't seem to be able to hide it. There is, however, a price."

"Really?" Logan's voice was marvellously ironical. "How did I know that was coming."

Melinda flushed and stood up abruptly, beginning to pace the far end of the spacious room. A pretty, petite figure in a short, gold-embroidered navy dress. "Max is a wealthy man, but I have no intention of being dependent on him like I was on Jimmy."

"You have a not considerable inheritance from my son," Ainslie pointed out bleakly, glad Sandra wasn't there to hear this.

"I want more," Melinda said flatly. "A lot more. You've got it."

"What sort of money are we talking about here?" Logan demanded, his handsome mouth thinning.

"Another five million," Melinda said as though that was more than fair. "It doesn't seem much for a child and you Dangerfields always figure in the Rich List."

She didn't have long to wait for Logan's answer. "I'm

terribly sorry, Melinda,'' he said very quietly, ''but it's not on.''

''Logan!'' Ainslie stared at her stepson as if to measure the wisdom of his words. What was money compared to the happiness and well-being of her granddaughter?

''See, Ainslie agrees!'' Melinda turned on him in triumph. ''What about you, Dana? You know how important your opinion is to Logan,'' she said, with sly meaning.

''I'm not believing this,'' Dana said, a slight betraying tremor in her voice. ''Are you saying you're prepared to *sell* your child?''

Melinda shrugged. ''Well, I'd certainly like to see her from time to time. Don't look so damned righteous. You've always told me I'm a poor mother.''

''Even so, I'm not handing over another penny,'' Logan cut across them, rising to his daunting six-three. ''So what are the other options, Melinda?'' he asked, watching her pretty kitten face suddenly look pinched.

''I'll collect her after Christmas. You won't have her, I'll see to that.''

''And Max is in agreement with all this?'' Logan looked suave.

''Anything I do is fine with Max,'' Melinda said shortly. ''He's madly in love with me.''

''Poor devil! He's happy to take on a ready-made child, is he?'' Logan continued.

''He certainly is!'' Melinda huffed.

''Then why not take her now before Christmas?'' Logan suggested, quite reasonably. ''I see no reason to wait. You're Alice's mother. No one can deny that. You want her. Well and good. You can't expect us to keep looking after her. I say take her tomorrow. We have all her clothes ready.''

For the first time Melinda appeared aghast and she

wasn't the only one. Ainslie covered her face with her hands and Dana sprang up, velvety brown eyes flashing fire. "You can't mean this, Logan. You can't," she cried, knowing Logan had a ruthless streak.

"Indeed I do," he said harshly. "I won't be black-mailed."

"It's Alice's whole life that's at stake." She went closer to him, caught hold of his arm.

"I thought you were the one who was telling us all to give Melinda a chance." He looked down at her. "Something miraculous was to happen and she'd turn over a new leaf."

"Please, Logan," she begged. "Won't you consider it? She can have what money Jimmy left me. I haven't touched it."

"You're not seeing this clearly, Dana," he told her, his blue eyes cold. "I'm the head of this household and I say, *no.* Melinda has received more than enough and I have no intention of getting into a legal battle. If she's going to marry this Max and he is quite happy about assuming the responsibilities of a stepfather, I say Melinda should cut all the anguish short and take Alice now."

"Excuse me, dear. I'm going to bed," Ainslie said, rising a little unsteadily to her feet. "You must do as you think best."

"Let me take you up." Logan moved swiftly to support his stepmother. "I'm sure you and Dana have things to say to each other, Melinda," he threw over his shoulder. "I won't be long."

Both young women were silent until long after the sounds of footsteps had died away, then Melinda launched into a plea, a well-remembered febrile look in her light blue eyes. "Talk to him. Convince him this is the best way to do it."

"What makes you think I could possibly sway Logan," Dana demanded. "He's a law unto himself."

"Come on, Dee." Melinda flashed her a look. "You two have something going, haven't you? You've always been in love with him only you were too stupid to see it."

Dana ignored that. "I'm telling you, once Logan has made up his mind, no one on earth could change it for him."

"But you must *try,*" Melinda insisted with extreme intensity. "Invite him into your bed, that's if you haven't done it already. I bet he's one hell of a lover, too. All that fire! But underneath, he's cruel. He professed to love Alice yet he's prepared to let her go."

Dana, too, was unprepared for his reaction. "What did you expect him to do?" she said wretchedly. "Pay up just like that. Who could ever trust you anyway?"

"You can trust me *easily,*" Melinda maintained.

"How's that? You've been a liar all your life. You've lied about me."

"And enjoyed it," Melinda clipped off, crisply decisive.

"Why would you want to hurt me, Melinda? Hurt Jimmy's memory?" Dana asked very seriously.

"I've buried Jimmy," Melinda flashed back. "He was unfaithful to me God knows how many times. If you weren't one of his women it was only because his feeling for you was all tenderness. Dear sweet Dana, the embodiment of all that is good."

"So why did you write to Logan telling him Jimmy and I had an affair?" Dana asked heavily.

"Oh, jealousy I suppose," Melinda cried in exasperation. "What kind of an idiot are you? I've always been jealous of you. Even your friends told you that. Why should you have a man crazy about you? I never had."

"What about this Max?" Dana rushed in, frowning.

"What's the big secret about his last name? Does he even *exist?*"

"It's Max De Winter, if you must know," Melinda joked. Then, "No, it's Max Ferguson. No need to tell Logan, I don't want him checking up on me. Max is a lot older than I am, as I told you, but he's an impressive-looking man and he can give me the life I've always wanted."

"And he wants a child?" Dana was starting to wonder.

"Exactly. A ready-made one. He won't want me to fall pregnant. We'll be doing a lot of travelling together. Entertaining. He has a lot of business interests across the Atlantic and here. I could see Alice when we're in the country."

"Gee, that's big of you." Dana shook her head sadly. "I just don't understand you, Melly."

"When did you ever?" Melinda retaliated, sweeping out of the room and up the staircase to her bedroom, where she locked it.

Dam all the Dangerfields to hell! Especially Logan.

Dana waited quite a while for Logan to return. She stood by the window looking sightlessly out over the moonlit garden, desperately trying to keep herself together. Could Logan really bring himself to pass Alice over at this time? At Christmas, when Alice was the happiest she had ever been?

She could understand his anger at Melinda's demands for money. A great fortune to most people but not people like the Dangerfields, the establishment since pioneering days. She'd had to face, much as she regretted it, Melinda would never become the person she had hoped. Melinda was a bitter disappointment, with little capacity for parenthood. So why then, if she didn't get the money, was she going to take Alice? Because the current pivotal person in her life, Max, wanted it? Would a middle-aged businessman who travelled extensively want a small child? Was Alice to be shunted to a boarding school? Why didn't Logan just pay the money? Let her have it. Could he see the loss of her grandchild would shatter Ainslie's life? Let alone hers. Hadn't she sworn to Alice she would never abandon her?

By the time Logan did return, Dana, for all her efforts, had worked herself into an emotional state. It showed in the line of her body, her flushed skin and the glitter in her dark eyes.

"We won't stop here," Logan said in his command-ing way, taking her arm and ushering her out onto the colonnaded terrace. "Let's get away from the house. I take it Melinda has gone up to bed?"

"Yes." Her response was brittle but it was the best she could do. "She's beside herself her little scheme mightn't work."

He tried to restrain the abrasiveness that was in him but failed. "So you've finally got your eyes open?"

That stung her. "I'm not like you, Logan, I'm sorry," she answered in a jagged voice. "You have a rare talent for being able to categorise people on sight. I like to give them a chance."

"Well, you must be feeling you've made one hell of a mistake tonight." He tossed her a tight smile. "Your cousin is what's known as a gold digger."

"It certainly looks like it. But she's dealing with the wrong person, isn't she? The toughest negotiator for miles."

"I wouldn't last long if I weren't and I've had a lot more exposure than you to the underside of human na-ture. Let's walk."

"Anything you say, Logan." She meant to mock him, instead it echoed the pain in her heart. She let him lead her down the short flight of steps onto the circular drive with the lights from the house playing over the three-tier fountain. "Is Ainslie all right?" she asked, looking up into his face. A handsome face. A proud face. "It worries me to see her so upset."

"You surprise me, Dana." He used the sleek tone she knew so well. "Don't you think I can look after my stepmother?"

"I'm certain you *mean* to."

"You can't expect me to adopt your sweet girlish ways. Ainslie's willing to let me handle this situation. Unlike *you.*"

She tried unsuccessfully to hold on to her temper. "That's really weird. Ainslie must know all about your ruthless streak."

"Oddly she regards me as the perfect stepson. What's so ruthless about what I'm doing, anyway?" he countered.

They had begun walking, now she stopped in the semi-darkness of the trees and faced him. "You're prepared to let Alice go?"

"You mean I'm not doing what Melinda is asking," he corrected, his voice hard.

"I can't bear to think about it." Dana began to move on, agitation racing through her blood. How could she love Logan when he tied her in knots?

He caught her up easily, whirling her around. "It might pay you to use your mind and not your emotions. You're tearing yourself to pieces. That's not a man's way."

"Hell no!" She reacted with unconcealed hostility, pushing against his strong hands but he only tightened his grip on her. "Why would the all powerful cattle baron accept blackmail?"

"It's not going to come to that."

"Why? What are you going to do to stop it?" Even

when they were arguing her pulses were all aglitter, her heartbeats racing.

"I'm going to call Melinda's bluff. Pulling stunts doesn't sit well with me and that's what's she's doing. It would be great if it could come off. An extra five million to get on with her life." He stared down into her face, shifting her a little so she was caught in the full moon's copper radiance. "You don't really think she wants Alice, do you, or are you still wallowing in all those cousinly marshmallow feelings?"

"You hate women, don't you?" she accused him.

He seemed amused. "Only one of you can drive me nuts and I'm looking at her."

She tried desperately to interpret every nuance in his voice. "I'm scared of what she'll do, Logan. Can't you understand that?"

"Of course I can." He released one hand to cup her nape. "You've had too much trouble dealing with your cousin. Now you have to leave her to me. Are you prepared to do that?"

"I don't have much choice." She moved her head against his hand, unable to resist the basic sensual pleasure.

"No, you don't," he agreed. "But you could have some faith. While you've been thinking of ways to kill me, I've been calling in a few favours."

That would explain his time away. "Good heavens!" Dana stared up at him in surprise. "You should be running the country."

"No thanks, but we now have the lowdown on Max. Max Ferguson is his name. Melinda let slip she was staying with the Goddards. I don't know them personally, but I have plenty of connections who do. One's Eve Goddard's brother."

Frantically she considered the ramifications. "Could this damage Melinda?"

He tilted her chin. "Do you care?"

"I can't help caring, Logan. It's the way I am."

"Sure." His voice softened. "Anyway, Max is over fifty. He already has a grown up family."

Dana's eyes widened. "You can't mean he's married?" She felt shocked.

"Not exactly. He's divorced."

"Good grief!" She had to steady herself against him and he drew her right into his arms. "The word is out and it's all very confidential, Max would be highly unlikely to want to start another family. He has one and he's a very busy man. The whisper is Melinda is part of a package. She's young, she's blond. Max has always preferred blondes, and she has a nice little nest egg of her own."

"Most people would call it a lot. Does your friend know if he means to marry her?" Dana asked, wondering if Melinda had made yet another mistake.

"Apparently she's just what Max needs in his life."

"And Mrs. Goddard won't say a word?"

Logan shook his head. "She swears she won't mention the phone call to another soul. I don't know that I can see her doing that in the fullness of time but by then Melinda and Max should be out of the country."

"Without Alice?"

"That's what we're counting on," Logan said a little grimly.

"I know you keep a perfect picture of motherhood in your head, but you'll have to accept all Melinda thinks about is herself."

"So she was lying?"

"Isn't it something she does all the time?" He took a skein of her hair and twisted it around his arm.

"One of her lies was pretty effective with you."

"Especially when everyone else was saying the same thing."

Her eyes were sad. "You're going to break my heart, Logan, if you don't believe me."

She looked so perfect, a moon maiden, with her lustrous skin and long gilded hair. Her skin was warm to the touch, almost feverish like below the surface there were sparks in her blood. It drove him to straining her to him, the slender, almost fragile body he couldn't get enough of.

"Could I?" he asked.

"You know the answer to that."

"I thought it was my heart on the line?" His voice was deep, caressing, heavy with desire. As his dark head came down, Dana lowered her eyes, feeling the exquisite crush of his mouth over hers, the fierce strength of his arms that excited her so intensely. She knew he was in love with her, perhaps in his heart of hearts *loved* her, but she had gotten to the point where she believed there could be no future for them if she couldn't have Logan's trust.

Dana was never to forget the early part of the next morning. Despite Logan's assurances, his insistence that calling Melinda's bluff would save the day, Melinda was full of qualms. Melinda was a parent who didn't hesitate to project her own conflicts on her child. She had even done her best to cause Dana harm. At some deep psychological level Melinda was a person full of resentments and frustrations. The family was trying desperately to recover from Jimmy's death yet Melinda seemed hellbent on causing them more pain with her actions. It all added up to the fact Melinda was a loose cannon.

When Dana very quietly entered Alice's room to check that the little girl was all right, instead of a sleeping child she encountered an empty bed. Already suffused with anxieties she checked the bathroom, the veranda outside Alice's room. No sign of her. Next she hurried down to Melinda's room, tapped on it briefly, then finding the door unlocked pushed it open and went in. It was still early. Not quite seven o'clock. She remembered now Melinda hated being woken out of a sleep but her concerns about Alice were making her jumpy.

Melinda had her narrow back to her, curled up in sleep, but there was no Alice beside her.

"Melinda?" Dana didn't hesitate to call urgently. "Wake up."

"What?" Melinda stirred, muttering very crossly. She turned on her back, her blond curls a halo around her small face, one strap of her luxurious nightgown falling off her white shoulder. "What the heck is going on, Dee? Are you throwing me out or what?"

"I can't find Alice," Dana answered, holding her hands together tightly.

"Great!" Melinda groaned. "She'll be around some place."

"She should be in her bed," Dana said worriedly.

"Kids get up early. You know that. What's the matter with you? You're like some poor old mother hen."

"What did you say to her, Melly?" Dana advanced on the bed, such a fire in her eyes Melinda sat up straight.

"Nothing!" Melinda snapped.

"You didn't tell her you wanted to take her back to Sydney with you?"

"It's Logan who decided she has to go," Melinda reminded her angrily. "Always set himself up as the wonderful uncle, too. Now he can't wait to get rid of her."

Dana decided to strike while the iron was hot. "Then you've accepted he won't pay up?"

"You're sure of it, too?" Melinda searched her cousin's face. Dana would never lie to her.

"You know Logan, Melly," Dana said, as if that were sufficient explanation. "He's as hard as nails."

Melinda nodded, biting her lip. "Like that Getty? Remember when he wouldn't pay up for his grandson?"

"That's right, so you might as well forget your little scheme. We'll have Alice ready for you by the time you leave."

"Oh, God." Melinda closed her eyes tightly then she stripped back the bedclothes and stood up, a pocket venus in her peach satin nightdress. She had lost quite a bit of weight and she looked little more than the young girl Dana remembered. "You have to wonder about some people," she said, reaching for her matching robe and putting it on. "I thought you loved Alice?"

"I do." Dana nodded, in one way not wanting to do this but she had no choice. "But you're Alice's mother. We must all focus on that."

"But damn it all, I don't want her!" Frustration distorted Melinda's voice. "I *can't* want her. Max knows I have a daughter who lives with her grandmother. I explained Alice is quite difficult and needs special attention. He understands that, but he doesn't want or need a small child to disrupt his world."

Dana forced her voice to remain even. "Let me get this straight. You've come out here trying to extort money? Is that it?"

"Bunkum. It's justice, Dee. Haven't you ever heard of justice? Alice is the heiress not me."

"And Max is prepared to marry you only if Alice remains with her family?"

"Can you blame him," Melinda retorted, as if Dana was stating the obvious.

"I expect he has a family of his own tucked away some place?" Dana said grimly. "Are you sure he's not married?"

Melinda stood stock-still, suddenly uneasy. "He's *divorced.*"

"I guess Logan could talk to him," Dana suggested. "Establish you're not without family."

Evidently that was the last thing Melinda wanted. "Leave Logan out of this," she cried. "I don't want him interfering in my affairs."

"Then I suggest you come clean with your intentions, Melly," Dana said shortly. "Get it over. He'll be as mad as hell but it probably won't go any further. Alice has to have stability in her life. Make Logan her legal guardian. You need have no fears. He'll look after her and he won't deny you access to your own child."

Melinda began to drum her fingers on a small marquetry table. "You're absolutely sure I couldn't break him down?" She glanced at Dana, who shrugged.

"*Convinced.* Logan means what he says. I should have known but it shocked me nevertheless." Hurriedly she turned to the door. "I'll get back to you, Melly. I'm going downstairs. With any luck Alice might be with Mrs. Buchan eating breakfast."

Mrs. Buchan was surprised. "I haven't laid eyes on her, Dana. She doesn't come downstairs until around eight o'clock, as you know." She stepped closer, speaking in a confidential murmur. "You don't think she could be hiding? She's done it before. In the old days when life got too much for her."

"*Hiding?*" Given that Alice was very upset it was more than likely. But where? There were a million wild acres out there. Even the house was huge. "Where's Mr. Dangerfield?" she asked, feeling she needed Logan beside her.

Mrs. Buchan considered. "I fed him breakfast at six. He wanted to be at the Four Mile when the men came in. Other than that I can't say."

"We'll have to search the house from top to bottom,"

Dana said. "Someone has to go for Logan. Alice could have headed out into the bush."

The search began in earnest and a short time after Logan strode through the front door. "Why didn't I consider this is what she might do?" he said, his eyes flashing. "Alice has always been full of action."

"You don't think she's in danger?" Dana's pale face was showing her anxiety.

"I'll bet my riding boots she's just hiding out." Logan went to her, pulled her into his arms, let her head rest against him as her support.

"My, isn't that a touching scene!" Melinda called, coming daintily down the stairs. "I always knew you two would get together at some point."

"So that made you tell all your lies," Logan confronted bluntly.

"Well, you did get hooked for a time." Melinda looked completely undisturbed. "Jimmy may have hankered after Dee but even for him she was the princess in the tower. You know, *inaccessible*,"

"But you decided to hang it on him all the same." Logan shook his head, feeling a vast shame and anger. In doubting Dana he deserved to lose her.

"Jimmy ripped my heart out with his infidelities," Melinda retorted. "I owe him nothing. Dana and I have been together since childhood. I love her, I guess. I don't really mind hurting her, either, from time to time. And while you're all knocking yourselves out searching for Alice as though no one else matters, I should tell you she's given to this sort of behaviour. Just her way of looking for attention. I'd advise you to get on with what you're doing and the little devil will come home. She'll be hiding out until she figures it's safe."

"Safe?" Dana asked the question, sounding appalled.

"Until I'm gone," Melinda explained. "The moment

she hears the plane take off she'll come out of her hiding place.''

''Very likely,'' Logan agreed, his voice quiet. ''But surely you feel some anxiety?''

''Do you?'' Melinda countered. ''That child's a Dangerfield. I've said it all along.''

Melinda flew out at ten o'clock sharp, convinced there was no remote cause for worry and that's exactly how it turned out, though the search continued unabated, spreading out into the bush. It was Dana who found her, given a clue by one of the drawings Alice had made with Retta the day before. It was a picture of the Dangerfield stone chapel, an excellent drawing for a child, showing its Gothic features and the tall spire. Even an attempt had been made at drawing the intricate design on the beautiful wrought-iron gates that enclosed the grounds. A church. A chapel. Historically, a safe haven.

Alice was nowhere to be seen inside but when Dana called her name, trying to communicate all the love and protectiveness that was in her, Alice suddenly emerged from behind the altar, rising a little stiffly from her cramped position.

''It's all right, I'm here. Were you worried?'' She stared at Dana with big over-bright eyes.

''Oh, darling, you mustn't do that again,'' Dana said when they were through hugging one another. ''We're only looking to do what's best for you.''

''Not if you mean to send me back with Mummy,'' Alice maintained stubbornly. ''If you hadn't found me I'd probably have stayed here until I heard the plane.''

''But you understand, don't you, Grandma has suffered enough grief? She's not young anymore. We mustn't worry her.''

''I'm sorry.'' Alice hung her head, shrinking from the vision of her grandmother's sad face. ''I love Grandma,

I love you all. I even love Mummy if she'll only leave me alone.''

"We must go back to the house," Dana said decisively, holding out her hand.

"I'm not," Alice cried passionately, backing away. "Mummy does what she likes. She doesn't care how anyone feels."

"She's not taking you back to Sydney, Alice, I promise."

"Are you sure?" Alice watched Dana closely.

"I'm certain. I probably shouldn't be discussing this with you now but it might put your mind to rest. Mummy has decided Uncle Logan can be your legal guardian. You'll be able to see Mummy anytime you like but you'll be living here.'' Where you belong, Dana thought.

Alice held out her hand, obviously imitating her Uncle Logan. "Will we shake on that."

"I'm pleased to.'' They shook hands. "Can we go up to the house now?" Dana asked. "I want everyone to know you're safe."

"I bet Uncle Logan wasn't worried." Alice grinned.

"He knows all about your bolting."

"What did Mummy say?" Alice gave her an intense stare.

"Mummy is worried, like the rest of us. Even Uncle Logan is under some strain. You could have wandered off into the wild."

"No way!" Alice snapped off. "I could have got lost."

Dana went to take the little girl's hand, anxious to return to the house, but Alice escaped, entering a pew and ramming her small frame into the corner. "As soon as I hear the plane." Her voice was still wary. "You can go and whisper to Grandma I'm all right, if you like.''

Dana sighed, lifted her wrist and stared down at her watch. There wasn't much longer to go before Melinda's flight. She moved into the pew, reached for Alice, who fell sideways into her lap.

On Christmas another contingent of Dangerfield relatives arrived to spend Christmas Day and Boxing Day on the station. It was a yearly ritual with different members of the extended family taking turns. This year because Alice was in residence, younger members had been invited to bring their small children to join in all the fun.

Another Dangerfield ritual was the Christmas Eve party. Not only for the family, but for everyone on the station. It was set in the Great Hall, built almost twenty years before to accommodate large gatherings. Now the whole family, children, as well, had worked to decorate it and make it beautiful for the party. When Dana looked in, Jack Cordell and Sandra were perched on stepladders busy hanging Christmas swags with glossy green foliage and dozens of gold and scarlet baubles. Even the dais where the band would be playing was decorated with a semicircle of ''snow''-tipped Christmas trees in pots flashing tiny white lights. Like so many stars. Everything that could be tied with a big gold-trimmed ribbon was tied. The children loved it; all the Christmas songs were played constantly, they hugged one another exuberantly, thrilled they would be allowed to stay up until nine-thirty. No later. They had to be in bed and fast asleep before Santa Claus began patrolling the station.

Dana chose a beautiful gold dress to wear to the party. Actually it was her bridesmaids dress from a friend's wedding. She had brought it with her thinking it was suitable for the Christmas ritual. The bodice was gold lace, the calf-length full skirt lustrous taffeta. She even had a small jewelled headpiece to catch up her hair at the crown. She had debated arranging her hair in a coil

then decided to leave it out. She couldn't fail to be aware
Logan found her long hair exciting. Searing relief still
washed over her at the memory of Melinda's "confes-
sion." Maybe it was Melinda's peculiar way of letting
her know she loved her. And it vindicated Jimmy who
could have lived such a different life.

Dana was almost ready to go downstairs and join the
others when someone came to her door. Almost certainly
Ainslie. Alice, she knew was with the children, every
last one of them radiant with happiness and excitement.

"Logan!" She stared up at him, her limbs melting,
almost literally because she had to hold on to the door-
jamb. "You look wonderful." It wasn't as much a com-
pliment as a plain statement of fact. He was wearing a
white dinner jacket with his black dress trousers, a white
pin-tucked shirt adorned by a blue silk tie.

He smiled at her, his handsome face a little taut.
"Thank you. A man does his best, but no one will be
able to match you. You look breathtaking." His blue
eyes moved over her with an almost unbearable pleasure.
"May I come in for a moment?"

"Of course." She took a deep breath, held it, convinced from the underlying seriousness of his demeanour
matters between them would come to a head. She heard
herself asking, almost shakily, "Everything's all right,
isn't it?"

"Fine." He seemed to come out of a slight reverie.
He was standing in the centre of the room, now he turned
to face her directly. "I have something to give you before we go down. I hope you'll honour me and wear it
tonight. But first I wanted to thank you from the bottom
of my heart for everything you've done for my family."

Dana pressed her hands together, fighting an irresistible impulse to weep. "Oh, Logan, you don't have
to say this," she implored.

"I do." His reply was harsh, self-judgemental. "I

want to thank you for your great loving kindness to Alice. For the way you have supported Ainslie and Sandra. The way you tried to help Tyler through the difficult times. I even admire your loyalty to Melinda even when we both know she doesn't deserve it. You've been strong through the tragedy that has engulfed us all."

"Please, Logan," Dana begged. "You needn't say any more. Alice and I are blood kin. I've had all my efforts rewarded. I have love and I have enduring friendships."

"You must let me finish, Dana," he said inexorably. "I want you to forgive me. I want you to forgive me for ever having doubted you. No matter what I've *said,* I knew you wouldn't fly in the face of honour. I knew you would never betray anyone. Even before Melinda's conscience attack, I *knew.*" He paused, admitting, "I do have a hard streak at times. Put it down to the fact I'm not a man who finds it easy to hand over his heart. And yet I have. I love you." His blue eyes blazed. "I love you body and soul." He reached out and very tenderly stroked her cheek. "You fill me with the most beautiful feelings I've ever known. You bring me sweetness and character, dazzling joy. Even when you wring my emotions dry, you're my shining hope. I just can't go on like this. I need a resolution."

"Oh, so do I!" Dana responded. It came out like a vow. "You're everything to me, Logan. I don't *have* a life unless we're together."

"But your career?" He cupped her face between his hands, held it still. "I can't let you go off and leave me. I couldn't bear it."

"Not even for a short time?" she asked in a profoundly happy voice.

His mouth twisted into a wry smile. "How much time are we talking exactly?"

Dana smiled, linked her slender arms behind his neck. "What's wrong with coming with me sometimes? We would manage. I have a lifetime's work out here. A thousand ideas. Anyway, you have some explaining to do. You haven't actually asked me to marry you."

"Okay." He moved her in very close. "Marry me, Dana Barry." He bent to drop multiple kisses on her lips, feather-light so as not to disturb her make-up, the tip of his tongue just entering her mouth. "You know you've always loved me."

All of a sudden she *was* crying, though her heart was filled with boundless joy. This was one of the great moments of life.

"Darling, please don't." His voice was a mixture of amusement, dismay and indulgence. "You simply have no idea what it does to me. And we have to go downstairs."

"I just *need* to…" Dana made a valiant effort to blink back teardrops.

"Here." He removed a beautiful monogrammed handkerchief from his pocket and dabbed very gently at her cheeks. "I can't tell you how much *I* need to give you everything you want." His vibrant voice rang with a passionate seductiveness. "Dana, darling," he warned, "if you don't stop we might have to forget the party altogether."

"No… No… " She lifted her head, paused, inhaled a long deep breath. "Do I look all right?" She stared up so sweetly into his face. Glorious, radiant, she brought a lump to his throat.

"Perfect."

A great sense of peace was moving over him. An intensely felt joy. This was Christmas Eve. He had asked the woman he loved to marry him. Now he reached into his breast pocket and produced a diamond ring so exquisite Dana gasped.

"This is for you, my love," he murmured, gently, so gently, taking her hand. "It belonged to my mother. It was her engagement ring and it's one of my greatest treasures. My father gave me all my mother's jewellery when I was only a boy. 'This is for *your* wife, Logan,' he said to me, and there were tears in my proud father's eyes. 'This is bonding us all together. Past and future. This is keeping our heritage alive.' I've never offered this ring to anyone but you, Dana. I believe now that was the forces of destiny at work. If you would like something else, something of your own choice, you have only to say."

The light in his eyes brought back the tears. She felt for a moment there were other presences in the room. Loving presences who gave them their blessing. "Put it on my finger, Logan," she invited with absolute reverence. "Put it where it belongs."

BUSH DOCTOR'S BRIDE

MARION LENNOX

CHAPTER ONE

IT WAS Dr Lynton's aim to photograph a koala—not to squash one.

Tyres squealed and gravel flew as Sophie Lynton hit the brakes. Her hired car slewed sideways. The car finally ceased its skid at a ninety-degree angle to the road, headlights beaming uselessly into the bush.

Had she hit it or not?

What was the creature doing sitting in the middle of the road on a blind bend anyway? Sophie's fingers gripped hard on the wheel and she closed eyes, reacting to her fright. She'd spent hours searching tourist trails for koalas, found none and made herself late searching. The guesthouse she'd arranged to stay at tonight didn't seem anywhere down this dirt track, it was dark, she was lost, and now...

Now somewhere under her car was a koala. Now she had to emerge from the car and look.

'Don't let it be dead!' With the silent plea echoing in her head, Sophie gingerly opened her car door and stepped out onto gravel.

The koala was straight in front of her headlights.

The huddled fur-ball didn't move as Sophie knelt over it. The koala was crouched less than a foot from the bumper bar, terror-filled eyes reflecting the lights from the car. Sophie's heart twisted in pity.

'Oh, you poppet! I've scared you even more than you scared me.'

The koala appeared unmarked, but it stayed motionless. Its eyes looked blank and stunned.

With the koala where it was, Sophie couldn't move the

car. She'd have to shift the animal. How did one shift a koala?

Sophie ran a hand through her dishevelled curls and bit her lip. Having just completed two years in the casualty department of St Joseph's, handling emergencies was supposed to be Sophie's forte—but this was a smaller and fluffier emergency than she was used to.

The koala wasn't much larger than a toy—and it looked just as cuddly. Surely she could move it?

'OK, koala,' she said softly. 'You can't sit there all night waiting for my car or something else to squash you. I'll lift you off to the side of the road.' Decision made, Sophie grasped it firmly around its midriff from behind.

Mistake! The small creature slashed back with one savage swipe, slicing Sophie's arm from elbow to wrist.

Pain shot upward in an agonising lance. The koala was released as Sophie gazed at blood welling from a deep and jagged tear.

This wasn't in the tourist brochures. Sophie was in Australia, land of sun, wilderness and cuddly koalas... And dreadful roads, and obscure road maps and loneliness and stupid koalas who tore the arm trying to save them.

'I think...' Sophie said unsteadily to the darkness around her, 'I think I want to go home.'

Home...

London, England. Two thousand miles, or was it three...?

'Some honeymoon,' she whispered as blood from her injured arm dripped steadily down onto gravel. 'I'm not even married, and Kevin's still in England and I'm lost and you've cut my arm to the bone, you stupid koala, and I don't know how to shift you. If you keep sitting there I can't move my car without squashing you...'

It was too much. Sophie gave a desperate sniff and let an unaccustomed tear trickle down her cheek.

It was the first time Sophie Lynton had cried for years.

Sophie scorned tears. Her mother cried to manipulate all around her, and Sophie had sworn never to follow her example. Here, though... Here there was only the koala, and the koala wasn't about to be manipulated by weeping.

She was wrong. There wasn't just the koala. As Sophie reached into the car for a towel to wrap her arm she caught the sound of an approaching vehicle. By the time she'd wrapped the gash, the sound was a rattling roar—some sort of vehicle was approaching with the sedateness and rattle of age.

It was just as well it was sedate. Sophie's car was blocking a blind bend and a fast car could have careered straight into hers. As it was, the approaching truck clattered round the corner, the driver slammed on the brakes and it came to a halt with ten feet to spare.

Sophie leaned back against her car. The pain from her arm was making her feel nauseous and the darkness and loneliness of the place was making her just plain scared. To be stuck in the dark in a strange country on a road that seemed in the middle of absolutely nowhere...

What she wanted was a capable middle-aged couple to emerge from the truck—people able to tell her she was safe, move the koala, direct her to her guest-house and maybe throw in some sympathy for good measure.

This was no middle-aged couple. It was a lone man, and at first sight he wasn't in the least reassuring.

Sophie's car was lighting the road, and the man emerging from the truck left his lights on as well. He stood by his ancient vehicle as he surveyed Sophie and koala, and Sophie felt the fear within her swell even more.

The man was filthy. He was in his thirties, large, lean and rugged. Tanned, muscled arms emerged from a sleeveless shirt, he wore faded jeans and battered leather boots, and a couple of days' stubble obscured his strongly boned face. Sophie couldn't see the man's eyes. Underneath the wide brim of an ancient hat they were hooded shadows.

Instinctively Sophie took a step back, frighteningly conscious of the isolation of this place—and the man's size.

'This isn't the most sensible place to park, lady.' The man's voice was deep and harsh. He clearly wasn't wasting time on pleasantries.

'The koala was on the road…' Sophie's response came out a nervous whisper and the man threw her a curious look before striding across to the front of her car. His easy, long-legged gait spoke of country rearing—a man at home in this setting.

'You hit it?'

'I…I don't think so.' Sophie flinched. Why wouldn't her voice work properly?

The stranger ignored her, kneeling down by the koala and slowly running his eyes over the frightened creature. Then, once again, his hooded eyes looked up at Sophie.

'You're a tourist?' His voice implied what he thought of the species.

'Y…yes.'

'Well, for once there's no damage.' He ran his gaze thoughtfully over the position of her car. 'Though you could have killed yourself as well as the koala. You'd be a damned fool to be travelling at speed on these roads at night.'

'I wasn't…' To Sophie's dismay there were tears in her voice. Drat the man. 'If…if I was travelling too fast I would have hit it. But I can't…I can't get the koala to move.'

'You could try turning your headlights off. How do you expect a wild animal to move when he's effectively blinded?' The man sighed, not expecting an answer from one so patently stupid; then with one fluid movement he effortlessly lifted the small grey and white furred creature. One strong hand grasped the scruff of the koala's neck, the other its rump, and he lifted and carried the koala out well before him to evade the slashing of terrified claws.

As the man reached the grass verge with his furry burden the koala let his opinion of proceedings be known, emptying his bladder in a long, steady stream.

'I agree. Tourists!' Incredibly, the man's deep voice was laced with laughter.

Ignoring the koala's waterworks, the stranger lifted the little creature into a fork of a gum tree and then stood back and watched as the animal clawed its way to safety. Finally he turned back to Sophie.

'You can turn your car now,' the man said dismissively, clearly glad to be shot of her.

'Thank…thank you.'

Something in her voice reached him. The man pushed his hat back from his face to reveal a mass of dark hair, and his deep-set eyes narrowed.

'Is there something else wrong?'

'No…' Sophie turned and fumbled with the door of her car but the man was fast, covering the distance between them in three long strides. As her car door swung open his hand was reaching out to stop her. He grasped her injured arm through the towel and she gave an involuntary whimper of protest.

Her sound of pain made him release her. He drew back, but not far enough to let her climb into the car. He was so close…

'What the…?' He stared down at his hand and his square, work-soiled palm showed red with Sophie's blood. His eyes widened in understanding. 'You tried to lift the koala?'

'It scratched me.' Sophie attempted to shove her way into the car but his body blocked hers. He stood like immovable iron. 'Please…' she whispered. 'Just let me go…'

'That's some scratch.' Ignoring her protest, the man reached once more for her arm, holding her this time by her fingers and pulling back the towel to expose the wound.

For a long moment there was silence and then the stranger gave a soundless whistle. 'This is going to need stitching.'

'I know.' Sophie pulled her arm back but her effort was futile. 'I'll get it seen to when I get where I'm going.' The culmination of fear and shock was making her voice tremble.

'Look, I'm not planning to rape you, lady.' The harshness was back in the man's voice and the eyes staring down at Sophie were filled with self-mockery. 'This is nasty. I'll drive you back to my place and—'

'No!' There was no disguising the fear in Sophie's voice.

He sighed. Pulling off his hat, the man ran a hand through jet-black hair and his voice gentled. 'Lady, I'm the local doctor. Five minutes from here I've a surgery with all I need to stitch this arm.'

'A doctor!' Sophie's eyes widened in incredulity. 'You expect me to believe that?'

'Yeah.' The man's eyes met hers, and the self-mockery was again plain. 'Strange as it may seem, I do, and there's no other doctor within fifty miles of this place. Like it or not, you're going to have to trust me. Now, let's shift your car off the road and get you somewhere I can work.'

'No!' Sophie's voice again rose on a desperate sob of fear, and it checked the stranger.

There was a long silence while Sophie's breath came too fast into the silence. Finally the man lifted a hand to her shoulder and the touch made her flinch.

'Hey, I really am a doctor.'

The man's rough voice gentled still more, seductive in its comfort, and it was close to Sophie's undoing. She was scared, she was dead tired and she was confused. How dared he make her want to weep still more…?

'I don't…I don't care,' she faltered. 'Please…I'm supposed to be at Mrs Sanderson's. She runs a guest-house and according to my map it's supposed to be near here. I've been looking, but the map's useless. It has roads where no roads exist...'

'Maybe it's because our roads aren't bitumen highways,' he suggested. 'You must have missed the sign. It's about half a mile back on the last turn-off.' The stranger's hand was still on her shoulder and his touch was doing strange things to Sophie's body. She badly wanted to sit down.

She swallowed desperately, pulling away from his hand. 'Then, if you don't mind... Will you let me go? Mrs Sanderson will organise me medical help when I get there.'

'You mean organise a nice clean doctor—maybe a nurse or two in white uniforms standing in attendance? Hey, how about a full-blown casualty department with the odd consultant surgeon?' The ironic laughter was back.

'Look, just stop playing games.' Sophie's voice shook with fear and pain. 'I appreciate your help, but Mrs Sanderson was expecting me hours ago.'

The man was silent. In the absolute stillness of the bush night they could hear the scratching made by Sophie's koala as it made its way up into the heights of its gum tree. There was nothing else.

He was too near. The man was less than a foot from Sophie, his body blocking her from her car. He was six inches taller than Sophie. If he wanted to hurt her...

He hadn't made a move to hurt her. Why was he so frightening?

It was because he was so darned male. He even smelled male, Sophie acknowledged—the strong smell of a man who'd been doing hard physical labour for hours. Some doctor...

'You can't drive.' He was watching her face, and his voice was still gentle.

'I can,' she said defiantly. 'If you get out of my way I'll show you.'

'And if I don't…'

'Then… I'll…'

'Scream?' Once again that mocking smile, twisting the corners of his wide mouth. His teeth flashed white in the darkness. 'And our friend koala will dash down to the rescue…'

'Please…' There were the remains of tears in her voice and Sophie despised herself for it. He mustn't hear it.

It seemed he had. After an endless moment he finally stood aside.

'I guess, if I offered to drive you, you'd refuse?'

'Yes.' What did he expect? That she would get in that ramshackle vehicle with him…or he would drive her car…? He had to be kidding!

The wide mouth twisted again. Once more he reached for her hand, taking her fingers in his strong grasp.

'Is there any numbness?'

'No,' she snapped. 'I've checked. I haven't damaged the flexor tendon or nerve.'

'Oho…' His look of amusement deepened. 'So you'll play nurse to my doctor?'

'Don't be stupid.' She pulled back again and he released her arm. 'I know what I'm talking about. I can drive and I don't need your help.'

His dark eyebrows lifted. 'So gracious a maiden in distress! Give me koalas any day.' He shrugged. 'OK, lady. Turn back and take the left fork. Moira Sanderson's place is half a mile along on the left. You'll drive at no more than five miles an hour, and I'll be travelling straight behind. My place isn't much further on and I'm damned if I can reconcile my conscience with leaving you to faint through blood loss. If you so much as think about putting your foot on the accelerator I'll run you off the road, and if you feel dizzy then you stop and I'll drive you.'

Sophie stood back, slightly stunned and very confused. 'Th…thank you.'

'I don't want your thanks. In one sentence you infer I'm intending rape and in the next you thank me nicely. You're not making sense. So just move, lady. It seems I have work to do tonight, and the sooner we get on with it the better.'

On which enigmatic statement he wheeled abruptly away and climbed back into his truck. Without another word he started his engine, then idled the truck in neutral while he waited for Sophie to get in her car and do the same.

What on earth...?

Panic welled within her. She didn't know where on earth she was. He could be directing her anywhere...

'Stop it, Sophie,' she told herself on an hysterical sob. 'You're letting your imagination run riot.'

'Why did he say he was a doctor?' she then demanded of the darkness.

'Don't think about that. Maybe you misunderstood and he's done some first-aid course. You don't have a choice, Sophie, but to do what he says. Police stations and hospitals are hardly thick on the ground around here.'

She had no choice.

With a sob of disbelief at the mess she was in, Sophie finally climbed into her car. She steered her car back onto the road, and the stranger's truck moved into place behind her. Wherever she was going, the stranger was clearly following.

CHAPTER TWO

IT SEEMED the man's intentions were honourable.

The house was where he had said it was. Half a mile down the side-road was the sign she'd been looking for for two hours. SANDERSON'S GUEST-HOUSE. Sophie turned into the driveway with a gasp of relief.

And she was suddenly alone. Behind her, the truck's horn blared and it rattled on. Duty done, it seemed the stranger was leaving her to her own devices. He had no ill intentions after all.

The relief made her feel dizzy.

As the lights of the ancient truck disappeared into the distance Sophie felt the first twinge of conscience. She'd sounded dreadful—exactly the sort of tourist he so obviously thought she was. He'd helped her and she'd been so frightened that she'd been obnoxious. She was in a strange country—she'd expected the worst and she'd made her distrust obvious.

He hadn't helped, though. The man must be some sort of simpleton, telling her he was a doctor...trying to persuade her to go to his 'surgery'...

She couldn't think about it. Her arm was throbbing with a grinding ache and it was still sluggishly bleeding. She pulled to a halt and laid her weary head on the wheel in a gesture of pure relief to have finally arrived.

Despite her pain and confusion, the stranger's dark eyes still mocked her. The truck lights were gone, but the image of the man stayed with her.

It was fright that had left such an impression, she thought wearily. It had to be.

There were stirrings from within the guest-house. Lights

14

were being flung on, and a middle-aged lady came hurrying down from the veranda.

'Dr Lynton... Oh, my dear, is that you? I've been so worried. You were supposed to be here hours ago.'

Sophie climbed wearily from the car and looked around her. This was the place she and Kevin had dreamed of—or rather she had dreamed of and Kevin had nodded and agreed and thought of something else.

The house looked just like the pictures in the brochures she had read back in London—a massive white weatherboard house with wide verandas and rambling roses growing in profusion everywhere, their heady scent mingling with the eucalyptus from the gums encircling the house. The mountains loomed behind, black and forbidding against the night sky, and the sound of running water nearby reminded Sophie of the clear streams and waterfalls to be explored in the morning.

'I nearly called the police.' Moira Sanderson's wispy bun bobbed back and forth in a gesture of decision. 'When you called and said you'd be coming alone instead of with a new husband—and then you didn't come at all...'

'You thought I might have driven off a cliff in a moment of suicidal madness.' Sophie gave a wry smile as she collected her suitcase from the luggage compartment. 'It's not that bad, Mrs Sanderson. Kevin's still coming and we still are getting married.'

'Any man who lets urgent business interfere with his marriage sounds a worry to me, dear,' Moira said roundly. 'Can I help with the suitcase?' Then she gave a horrified gasp as Sophie moved under the veranda lights. 'Oh, my dear... What on earth have you done to yourself?'

What indeed...?

She must look like something out of a horror movie, Sophie though ruefully. Her jeans and white blouse were liberally smeared with her blood. The car wasn't air-conditioned, so Sophie had driven with the window open

to escape the heat—and her shoulder-length chestnut curls
were caked with dust from the dirt roads. She still had the
odd tear stain on her face, she guessed, and she'd touched
her face with her injured arm, leaving a streak of blood
drying down the length of her cheek.

Looking the way she did, it would hardly be surprising
if Moira Sanderson ran inside and closed the door in her
face. The landlady, however, was made of sterner stuff.

Moira Sanderson grasped Sophie's suitcase from her in
an instant and placed an arm around her waist. 'You look
about to drop,' she said soundly. 'What happened?'

'A… There was a koala on the road…'

'A koala.' Moira shook her head, needing, it seemed, to
know no more. 'Oh, dear. They look so cute, but when
they're frightened they certainly know how to defend
themselves.' She looked down at Sophie's arm. 'And you
tried to pick him up? They'll do that every time.'

'I didn't know they scratched…'

'They're wild creatures, dear, despite their cuddly appearance. Ugh. It'll infect too if that's from his claws.
There should be a sign on every tourist brochure saying
"The Health Department Warns Koalas Can Be Injurious
To Your Health". Like on the cigarette packets. Well, I
guess it's too late to warn you now. A bath, something to
eat and a doctor I think…'

A doctor…

It seemed, despite what the stranger had told her, that
there was a doctor in the valley. Moira Sanderson was
reassuring.

'Inyabarra's tiny. The town consists of one general
store, one pub and a consolidated school because our children can't make that awful bus trip across the mountains
each day—but we do also have a doctor,' she told Sophie
proudly.

Sophie had been firmly ushered into a bath, and it had

been all Sophie could do not to prevent the kindly landlady drying and dressing her herself. Now Sophie sat in the kitchen in Moira's all-enveloping dressing-gown, sipping hot sweet tea and trying to block out the pain in her arm.

'Dr Kenrick's been here for the last five years,' Moira continued, 'and where we'd be without him I don't know. He looked after my Patrick all through his last illness—and without him Patrick would have died in hospital fifty miles from the place he loved.' Moira sniffed. 'Enough. You don't want to hear my life story. I rang Dr Kenrick while you were in the bath. He'll be right over.'

'Maybe…maybe I can drive to him—if the surgery's not too far away.'

She didn't want to. Sophie's voice sounded doubtful even to her. If she was her own patient she wouldn't advise driving—and as for finding her way back into the tiny township and back again…

'No.' There was no thought of her trying, it seemed. Moira was shaking her head with decision. 'Dr Kenrick said he'd be right over—and if I'm not mistaken that'll be him now.'

There was certainly a vehicle approaching.

A vehicle…

Sophie sat bolt upright, her tea splashing onto the table before her. The sound was unmistakable. There couldn't be two such decrepit vehicles in the valley.

'Does…does Dr Kenrick drive a truck?' she managed. 'An old one…?'

'Yes, dear. We tease him that he should drive a Mercedes but he says on these roads he's better with something that's already been jolted to bits and has nowhere left to jolt.' The landlady had crossed to the kitchen door and was standing with it open, waiting for whoever was arriving to walk in out of the night.

Sophie took a deep breath, a silent prayer echoing in her head. Let it not be him…

Of course it was him. The man had transformed himself, but Sophie would have recognized her rescuer anywhere.

A shower, shave and clean clothes had turned the man into a possibility of a doctor, but it had done nothing to conceal the sheer, rugged maleness of the man. He was wearing clean trousers and a neat open-necked shirt, his strongly boned face was clean shaven and all Sophie could see were those mocking, deep-set eyes…

'Well, well,' he said, standing at the door and surveying the seated, dressing-gowned Sophie with a mocking smile. 'What have we here, then? A dose of flu?'

Sophie flushed crimson.

'Dr Kenrick, this is my guest, Sophie Lynton.' Moira Sanderson was looking a little confused. 'I thought I told you on the phone she'd had some trouble with a koala.'

Sophie stayed speechless. The man's eyebrows rose in mock astonishment.

'You don't say? They're getting more vicious all the time. There used to be a myth that koalas just eat euca-lypts—but how many tourists were eaten last year, Moira?'

'Very funny,' Sophie whispered, shaking herself out of her daze. 'Are you…are you really a doctor?'

'Of course Dr Kenrick's a doctor!' Moira Sanderson was shocked.

'A real one, I mean?' Sophie was struggling through a fog of confusion.

'My degrees are on the wall at my surgery,' the man told her. 'As you'd have seen if you came to my surgery when I invited you.' He walked across and lifted her throbbing arm. 'I'm Dr Reith Kenrick, lady. M.B.,B.S. from Melbourne University. Graduated seven years ago, fol-lowed by two years internship and then country practice for the last five years. Satisfied?'

'But you looked so…so…'

'Dirty?' The wide mouth flashed in a grin. 'Maybe doc-tors are allowed to get dirty once in a while.'

'Dr Kenrick, Sophie's a doctor as well,' Sophie's land-lady announced, clearly at a loss as to what was going on. 'She's come all the way from England.'

'A doctor...' Reith Kenrick was carefully examining Sophie's wound and hardly seemed interested. 'Doctor of what? Cartology?'

Cartology... The study of map-drawing. Sophie's breath drew in on an indignant hiss. 'Now who's being insulting?' she asked.

Reith nodded absently, his mind once again clearly on his work rather than her, and Sophie felt herself strangely at a loss. He saw her as a cut arm rather than a person—and she didn't like the sensation.

She looked up at him as he inspected her arm and her impression of distance deepened. It wasn't just that he was uninterested in her. Reith Kenrick seemed a person apart. Even as he'd smiled at Moira Sanderson in greeting, there had been something in his eyes that suggested a deep and constant reserve.

'Let's check the hand.'

'I told you,' Sophie managed, unnerved and totally out of her depth, 'there's no tendon or nerve damage.'

'I'm not intending to sew a cut I haven't checked—so co-operate or find yourself another doctor.' Reith Kenrick raised his mobile eyebrows again. 'Or stitch it yourself.'

It was her right arm. To stitch her own right arm...

She looked up into those dark, mocking eyes and felt a surge of helpless anger.

For heaven's sake... He was a doctor. He was here to help her and, like it or not, she needed help. Somehow she found the resources to summon a smile.

'I'm...I'm sorry.'

'Very good.' Once more he switched into professional, absent mode. He lifted her fingers. 'Tell me what you feel?' One after the other he tested sensation on each fin-gertip, examined her movement and finally nodded.

'You've been lucky.'

'It's my lucky day,' Sophie said through gritted teeth. 'My lucky week.'

'Dr Lynton's supposed to be here on her honeymoon,' Mrs Sanderson offered helpfully. 'But her fiancé had to stay behind in England.'

'Maybe he ran out of clean shirts,' Reith said drily. He turned toward his bag to fill a syringe with local anaesthetic, avoiding Sophie's glare of pure hatred. He turned back, his attention solely on her arm. 'This will sting a bit. Try and be brave.'

Sophie's fingers curled. She gritted her teeth, but not with pain. This man was impossible.

Her anger carried her nicely through the next few unpleasant moments. Reith Kenrick was a skilful operator. He cleaned the wound with meticulous care, and then sutured it closed with tiny, neat stitches.

'You'll have a hairline scar,' he told her as he tied off the last stitch. 'Unavoidable, I'm afraid.'

Sophie looked down at her stitched arm. It was a skilful piece of work. In fact, she had been lucky. There were many doctors who couldn't have done as neat a job as this.

With an effort she pushed her anger to the back of her mind. Sure, this man was unlike any colleague she had ever met—but he had helped her. He had not only rescued her from the roadside but he had come out on a house call to someone who had been blatantly rude to him.

'I really am grateful,' she said softly. 'Dr Kenrick, you've been very patient...'

He straightened from adjusting the dressing and looked down at her. Clean-shaven, tanned and immaculately dressed in well-tailored trousers and linen shirt, the man was impossibly handsome. Impossibly... If Sophie hadn't been happily engaged to her Kevin...

What on earth was she thinking of? Sophie gave herself an angry mental shake.

'It's my job to be patient,' he said drily. His deep eyes mocked her, as though he guessed what she was thinking, and to her fury Sophie felt a tinge of colour surge across her face. 'So…if you're not into cartology, are you really a doctor of medicine?'

'I can't display my certificates on my surgery wall,' she told him, managing an apologetic smile with an effort. 'But I really am.'

'A general practitioner?' He was filling a syringe with antibiotic.

'I guess that's what you'd call me. I qualified three years ago and have been working in Accident and Emergency since then. Now—'

'Now you're supposed to be being married,' Moira broke in. 'Of all the inconsiderate males—'

'Kevin didn't mean to let me down.' Sophie shook her head, her fingers touching the stark white dressing on her arm. 'He's still coming. He's supposed to be here on Friday. This way…well, we'll just have the honeymoon before the wedding.'

'That's not how it was done in my day,' Moira said darkly. She peered down at Sophie. 'Eh, my dear, you look done in, doesn't she, Dr Kenrick?'

'She does.'

Sophie was struggling to rise but the effects of the night's events and loss of blood were taking their toll. Her legs felt unsteady under her, and her head spun sickeningly.

'I'll…I'll be OK. If I can just go to bed…'

'Her bedroom's the first at the top of the stairs, Dr Kenrick,' Moira said firmly, and there was no mistaking her message.

'No!'

'Yes.' Reith Kenrick's low growl was an order, and Sophie was no match for it. She could hardly fight him off. He injected antibiotic with clinical efficiency, then, before she could try to rise, his arms came around to lift her to him. In an instant she was cradled against his hard, muscular chest.

'Put...put me down!' Her voice was hardly a squeak.

'I'll put you down in your bed.' Ignoring her protest, Reith was striding out of the kitchen toward the stairs. 'Put the kettle on, will you, Moira?' he called back to Sophie's landlady. 'I'll be down for a cup of tea after I dump this.'

This...

She really was an object. He saw her as a patient to be rid of as soon as possible. Reith strode up the stairs with long, easy strides and Sophie knew he might just as well be carrying a sack of potatoes. So...so there was no reason why her heart should be doing crazy backflips.

It was just that she was unused to being held by a man.

Kevin holds you, she told herself savagely, but the thought of Kevin was a dim, faint memory. All that was real was the warmth and hardness of this male body and the strength of his hands...

She looked up and found his eyes on her, his mouth twisting into a quizzical grin.

'Enjoying the sensation, Dr Lynton?'

'N-no!' It was an indignant gasp.

'Well, well...' His eyes mocked her as he pushed open her bedroom door with his foot. 'A cold lady. My sympathies to the absent Kevin.'

'I don't mind when it's Kevin—' Sophie bit her tongue in horror. What was she saying? She had no need to defend her relationship with her fiancé to this man.

'You don't mind if Kevin touches you?' His eyebrows rose. 'Lucky Kevin.'

Moira had pulled the bedding back on the double bed while Sophie was in the bath. Now Reith Kenrick lowered Sophie with exaggerated care and Sophie grabbed the sheet and hauled it up to her neck. Moira's huge dressing-gown was concealing but not concealing enough. What was it about this man that made her feel so exposed?

'Thank you,' she said stiffly. 'Now...now will you please go away?'

He didn't. Reith Kenrick stood looking down at her, his face a curious mixture of derision and pity.

'You're not having a very good time, are you, Dr Lynton?'

'Of course I am. I'm having a terrific time. I like coming on my honeymoon on my own. I like getting lost for hours on end in the middle of nowhere and being savaged by koalas. I especially like being laughed at by country doctors who haven't washed for days and who mock me and make me feel...' Her voice rose and to Sophie's horror she choked on an almost hysterical sob. She put her hand to her face in horrified dismay but Reith Kenrick was before her.

His long, lean fingers touched her face—lightly—in a feather touch of reassurance and comfort.

'You're exhausted,' he said softly. 'I'll give you something to let you sleep.'

'I don't want anything.'

'I'm sure you do. When the local anaesthetic wears off that arm will hurt, and there's nothing like a sleepless night in pain to make things worse.'

He moved swiftly from the bedside and out of the door, but in moments he was back, a syringe in his fingers.

'Pethidine, Dr Lynton? You know you need it.'

'OK,' she said ungraciously and then flinched at the sound of her voice. She looked up at the man standing before her, and found his eyes gentle with understanding. The desire to weep was almost overwhelming.

'Very wise,' he said softly and carefully inserted the needle. The tiny pinprick in her arm hardly hurt at all.

'I'll drop in tomorrow morning to check on my handiwork,' he told her.

'There's no need.'

'If it's going to infect I should be able to tell by then.'

'I can check it myself.'

'I check my own work.'

'So what do you charge for home visits?'

Oh, for heaven's sake… Why on earth had she said that? This man was bringing out the worst in her. Out on the roadside in the dark she had thought it was fear that was making her react as she was. Now here…

There was the same sense of fear, but it wasn't a fear of physical danger. It was fear of what her body was doing to her—of how she was reacting to this aloof, contemptuous colleague.

There was a long, long silence. For a moment Sophie thought he would wheel away from her bedside and leave her to her bad manners. Instead that mocking smile finally returned.

'You'll get my bill,' he said softly, and his eyes locked on hers and held. 'I'll let you know what you owe me. And maybe you're right to be worried…'

The drug Reith Kenrick gave her made Sophie sleep like a baby. She'd spent thirty-six hours travelling from England to Australia, and then another twelve in an unfamiliar car in a strange country, culminating in the koala incident. Now her body demanded its due, and it was past midday when she stirred.

The curtains were still closed but the windows behind them were open, and the soft linen folds were stirring gently in the warm breeze.

For a moment Sophie was confused and then the events of the previous two days came back in a distressing flood.

There was a pergola outside her bedroom window roofed with lush greenery and brilliant red flowers, the like of which Sophie had never seen before. The sun was dappling through as the curtains shifted with the breeze. So-

phie lay back on her pillows and let the events of the past
few days settle themselves from crazy kaleidoscope into
some sort of pattern.

First there had been the telephone call from Kevin saying he was caught up in Belgium and wouldn't make it to
their wedding.

Fine. It wasn't as though it was a grand occasion anyway. They'd booked the register office and let a couple of
Sophie's best friends know—so it was a simple matter to
cancel.

'Go on to Australia without me,' Kevin had laughed
over the telephone. 'It seems a shame to waste a perfectly
good honeymoon.'

'I'll wait for you.'

'Sweetheart, I don't know how long this will take. It
could be days. It could be a week. If you leave tomorrow
I'll try to be there by Friday.'

As he'd put the phone down Sophie had imagined she
had heard the sound of a woman's voice in the background, softly laughing.

Kevin…

He was a high-flyer. He always would be, Sophie knew.

They'd been at university together—coupled at a time
when Sophie desperately wanted to be a couple. She
wanted to be a family more than anything else.

She didn't have a family of her own. Heaven knew
where Sophie's father was—Sophie certainly didn't. Her
mother was a cold, manipulative woman who moved from
man to man with an eye for the main chance. There had
never been anyone for Sophie—and what Kevin offered
seemed too good to be true.

What did Kevin offer? Security. Admiration. A linking
to someone—a sense of belonging…

She and Kevin had started going together when Sophie
was seventeen—and that sense of belonging was so important that she couldn't end it.

But I will if he doesn't come on Friday, she told herself harshly, twisting the extravagant diamond on her third finger. Kevin…

Curiously, though, the desolation she was feeling wasn't for the man himself. It was for that sense of belonging that was so important to her. She'd be alone again…

'Completely alone,' she murmured. 'I was mad to come to Australia. Mad!'

There was the sound of voices below stairs and then a heavy tread, taking the polished stairs two at a time. A firm knock on the door…

'Y-yes.'

It wasn't Moira. She should know that step. It was as distinctive as the man's decrepit truck. Maybe it was his truck that had wakened her.

Reith Kenrick's head came around the door—and then his whole body.

'Well, well,' he smiled as he strode across to the bed. 'The lady's awake. Had enough beauty sleep, then, have we?'

'I told you I didn't need you to come,' Sophie said crossly, pulling herself into a sitting position and lifting her knees to her chin in a gesture of defence. Her sheet stayed tucked under her chin.

'Do people always follow your orders?' Reith asked politely. He crossed to the window and flung the curtains wide, letting the dappled sun pour into the room. 'Does Kevin?'

'That's none of your business.'

'No.' He grinned. 'I don't suppose it is.' He strode to the bed and perched beside her. 'Let's see your arm.'

She cast him a suspicious glare and thrust her arm out in front of her. To her disgust, he laughed.

'You'd like me to take your arm somewhere else and inspect it?' he asked and raised his dark eyebrows at her.

Sophie took a deep breath, and suddenly found she was

smiling back at him. Those eyes were compelling—and when they were filled with laughter...

'I'm sorry,' she told him, lowering her arm into his hands. 'I behaved... Yesterday I behaved...'

'Like a scared kid,' he smiled, and his eyes were warm with compassion. 'I know. Things got out of control. When did you arrive in Australia?'

'Yesterday morning.'

His brows snapped down. 'So you came straight from the airport here—and then got yourself lost? It's a six-hour drive from Tullamarine when you know the road.'

'I wanted to make the most of my holiday,' she said stiffly. How to confess she'd been hurt and confused by Kevin? and to stay still and think about it seemed the worst thing she could do.

'Mmm.' He was unwrapping her arm, and the sight of the wound reassured him. 'Great. No sign of infection. You've been lucky.'

'I... Maybe I have,' she said stiffly. An apology was certainly warranted and she had to make it in full. 'You...you've been really good to me and I didn't deserve it. If I were you I would have driven off and left me to my koala.'

That surprised him. The mobile eyebrows arched upward and his face stilled.

'I wouldn't do that.'

'No.' She met that look. 'I know you wouldn't.'

The sudden frisson of electricity between them shocked them both into silence. A butcher bird was cackling away to itself in the bottle brush somewhere in the garden, and the remaining silence seemed endless.

Reith rewrapped her arm in silence and then stood up.

'I have a suggestion,' he said at last, and his voice was hesitant.

'A suggestion?'

'About that account you owe.'

Sophie licked her suddenly dry lips. She looked down at her bandaged arm. Now what?

'Just…just tell me what I owe.'

'A day's work.'

'A day's…' Sophie shook her head. 'I don't understand.'

Reith shrugged. 'Easy. I need a doctor for a day.' He spread his wide hands. 'Sophie, have you heard of Chlamydia?'

The use of her first name disturbed her. She struggled to concentrate on the question. 'Chlamydia?' Sophie frowned. 'Yes. It affects the eyes—or there's a strain that's a venereal disease…'

'Yeah. Well, there's also a strain that's present in koalas.'

'Koalas. You mean…you mean the koalas here?'

'Mmm.' Reith ran a hand through his hair in a gesture Sophie was starting to recognise. 'Chlamydia's latent in the breed, but overcrowding brings it out. The animals here have multiplied vastly since we turned the district into national park and rid ourselves of the koala's predators—like domestic dogs.'

'So what does Chlamydia do to koalas?' Despite her discomfort in the situation, Sophie found she was interested. She was also interested in the way Reith's voice became deeper and his eyes darkened as he forgot her presence and talked of something he was interested in.

'They have the same symptoms as humans. It affects their eyes, and in extreme cases it causes blindness. It makes the animal listless and apathetic. Their coat becomes matted and dull, and generally loses condition. Sometimes their weakness kills them, but mostly the worst thing it does is makes the animal sterile.'

'And…and it's curable?'

'Yes. Remove the overcrowding and with a good diet

the koalas pick up like magic—but the sterility is irreversible.'

'I see.' Sophie's knees were still tucked up under her chin but, unnoticed, her sheet had slipped so that she was only covered by her soft cotton nightdress. It no longer seemed to matter. 'What do you want me to do, then?'

'Get yourself rested first.' Reith grinned and Sophie managed a return smile. 'But today's Monday and you're here until at least Friday without your appendage fiancé.'

Your appendage fiancé... Sophie gave a soft chuckle, thinking how much Kevin would hate the description. That was how Kevin thought of Sophie, though... An appendage, to be discarded at will...

'S-so?' Her smile had slipped but Reith didn't seem to notice.

'The conservation and wildlife boys are having a drive to get as many koalas as they can out of the district in the next few weeks. They're shifting them to an area north of here where the koala population was decimated by bushfire a few years back. By next month, one of the main sources of koalas' food—the manna gum—starts giving off a toxin and the koalas have to change to alternative eucalyptus. The overcrowding problem becomes worse by a hundredfold.'

'So?'

'So I'm good with koalas. I act as the local vet when need arises, and I know how to handle them. It's too hot to transport animals today and tomorrow but we'll be working again on Wednesday, and we want to get a couple of hundred moved by the end of the week.'

'In case you hadn't noticed,' Sophie said mildly. 'I'm not all that dab a hand at catching koalas and putting them in boxes.'

'No.' Reith's wide mouth twisted into a grin and Sophie found herself responding to the humour in the depths of his dark eyes. 'I am, though. I spent most of yesterday in the bush and I want to be back there on Wednesday.'

'And?'

'And I wondered…' He shrugged. 'I run a quiet medical practice. I'm on call as needed, basically, but I found yesterday it didn't work. I was raised in the bush and I'm better than most at scaling eucalypts and bringing koalas down—much better than some of the conservation guys— but while I'm up in the heights they're busy falling out of trees and they want me on the ground where I can minister to their broken bones and bruised egos. So…'

'So you'd like me to help?'

'I only help with their koala collection in the mornings mid-week, but I'm finding even that hard without medical help. And it's a great way to see all the koalas you'll ever want to see.'

Sophie gave a rueful smile. 'I've seen one koala and I'm starting to think that's enough.'

'You mean you won't help?'

Sophie took a deep breath. She looked up into those dark eyes, and for a moment was silent.

The eyes stayed watchful. This man was an enigma— an unknown. He was expecting her to refuse. She could see it in the set look of his mouth. He was expecting…

Nothing. The impression caught and stayed as her view of him shifted imperceptibly.

This man expected nothing of anyone. He was a loner. The gauntness of his finely boned face deepened her impression of solitude. Of solitude and rejection…

This man had been hurt somewhere along the way, Sophie thought suddenly—and badly hurt at that. He expected nothing of anyone. He expected her to be a selfish little brat—and something deep inside her cried out to reverse that impression. She felt an almost overwhelming need to reach out and touch the forbidding face.

'Of course I'll help,' she said softly and watched the expression in his eyes change to wary surprise.

He collected himself in the same instant.

'Great. I'll collect you at six.'

'Six…' Sophie squeaked her dismay. 'Six in the morning, you mean?'

'Six in the morning.' He grinned. 'We work until ten and then call it quits. What do they say, Dr Lynton? "Mad dogs and Englishmen go out in the mid-day sun…" You might brave the heat to climb gum trees, Union Jack waving from your pith helmet, but koalas and yours truly have more sense. Medical emergencies permitting, we sleep in the shade.'

'Very sensible,' Sophie snapped and Reith grinned.

'That's us colonials for you. Always take the easy option and let you colonisers take the hard course.' He touched her face lightly with his finger and the touch set a tremor through Sophie's body that he must almost have been able to see. 'Will I see you on Wednesday, Dr Lynton?'

'I—'

'Great.' One more brush of those long, strong fingers and a heart-wrenching twist of the mouth. 'Goodbye until then, Dr Lynton. Take care.'

CHAPTER THREE

THE next day and a half passed in a lazy blur. Sophie slept, took gentle walks along the stream running behind the house, swam in the waterhole and generally let her exhausted mind slip into neutral.

It was too hard to think...

Neutral? Who was she kidding? It was too hard not to think of Reith Kenrick...

Kevin and the unknown woman laughing behind him on the telephone were somehow much easier to banish from her thoughts. As Sophie lay on the lawns under the canopy of eucalyptus, the pages of the book before her kept reflecting Reith Kenrick's shadowed face. Over and over...

On Tuesday evening as she sat on the veranda and helped Moira shell peas for dinner Sophie's tongue finally revealed her almost overwhelming curiosity.

'Moira, will you tell me about Reith Kenrick?'

She had meant not to ask. Her mouth came out with the request all by itself. She could have bitten her dratted tongue right off.

Moira was smiling.

'I wondered how long it would take you to ask.'

'It's just...I mean, with him being a doctor...'

'Curiosity's natural,' Moira beamed. 'And healthy too, I'd say. Your dratted Kevin...'

'Kevin couldn't help being delayed,' Sophie said firmly, but Moira just shook her head and kept podding peas. She'd demurred at Sophie's offer of assistance, but, as Sophie was the only guest, the two were fast becoming friends.

'Reith Kenrick's a loner,' Moira told her, peas shooting into her basin with speed, and Sophie nodded.

'I can see that.'

'Yeah, well, life's given him some kicks.'

Silence. Having asked the initial question Sophie couldn't ask more. She wasn't supposed to be interested in the man.

'I've known him since he was a baby,' Moira said finally. She was talking to her peas, her mind obviously wandering from Sophie—wandering back thirty-odd years to when Reith Kenrick was a child. 'Reith's mother and I were much the same age. We married at the same time, but she wouldn't have a thing to do with me. She thought she was too good for this valley—and maybe she was at that.'

'So why did she come here?'

Moira shrugged. 'Reith's dad was an artist—a good one—and he lived in the bush not far from here. I personally think his paintings are appalling—all tortured skeletons and staring eyes. Nightmare stuff. He made a mint, though, and was critically acclaimed throughout the world. Heidi was a model—and I wouldn't mind betting Heidi wasn't her true name, but she never let us call her different. She married Reith's dad in a blaze of publicity. Married for money and position, folks said, but a fat lot of good it did her. Reith's dad hated people. He lived a hermit's existence, and he abused alcohol and pills… He was violent too. Heaven knows the real reason Heidi married him—but she did and then found she was pregnant. In those days it wasn't easy to end a pregnancy—or you can bet Reith wouldn't be alive now. He sure as heck wasn't wanted.'

'But…they stayed married?'

Moira shrugged. 'I don't think Heidi's career as a model was exactly lucrative—and Reith's dad made a fortune. She'd leave every now again but flitted back when she ran out of money. Reith was left alone with the old man—and he was old. Nearly seventy when Reith was born.'

'And he looked after Reith?'

Moira snorted. 'If you can call it that. He put a roof over the boy's head. There was money for food and if Reith disturbed his father he was beaten. I know Social Welfare took Reith away for a bit—but the old man had pride and contacts in high places, so managed to get him back. Reith ran wild in the bush—growing more and more into himself. Then, in his teens, he suddenly got a bee in his bonnet that he'd be a doctor. He started going to school regularly and worked himself to the bone. His mum had disappeared completely by this stage—married an actor, I hear—and the old man died just as Reith qualified for medical school. Reith left and we thought we'd seen the end of him.'

'But he came back?'

'How could a boy used to a life of complete solitude become accustomed to the city? He said it drove him crazy. Reith Kenrick needs no one. He's learned not to need, and he's at home only in the bush. Now no one comes near him emotionally and he likes it that way. He's modernised his father's farmlet, turned it into a surgery, and it makes him enough to live on—though he inherited a fortune from his father's art. He doesn't need to work, but we hope he always will because he's a blessing for this place. Inyabarra's too isolated to attract either doctor or vet—and Reith Kenrick acts as both. We pray he'll never leave—though it condemns him forever to his hermit life. It seems, though, that that's what he wants.'

Maybe.

Sophie thought about that gaunt, hungry face and wasn't sure. An unloved child… A man who wore cynicism like a second skin…

She thought back to her own childhood, and her heart reached out to him. They had hoed the same lonely row—

and maybe Reith had reaped the more bitter harvest. Sophie hadn't been ill-treated as a child. She had just been ignored, and she knew how soul-destroying that could be.

Reith collected her right on six the next morning. Despite her protests, Moira had risen and given Sophie breakfast, preparing a vast morning tea for her while Sophie tackled coffee and toast.

'I'll never eat all that,' Sophie had protested but Moira had shaken her head.

'It's not just for you, dear. Reith will bring nothing— see if I'm right. If you know how much I've longed to get a good feed into that man... This way you can say you have too much and offer to share.'

Sophie grinned. 'He just might suspect your motives. I can hardly be expected to eat four rounds of salad sandwiches and a whole chocolate cake...'

She walked out to Reith's truck as it rattled into the yard, absurdly self-conscious in the cool morning light. It felt almost a betrayal of Kevin to be going.

For heaven's sake... Kevin was in Belgium with a woman she didn't know and didn't want to know. What possible harm was there in doing as Reith Kenrick suggested?

'Planning on staying a week?'

Reith climbed from his truck and took Sophie's basket from her. He was dressed again in his disreputable clothes, and, although he was now clean, the same frisson of electricity quivered through Sophie. Why did he make her feel like this?

'Pardon?'

He held up the basket. 'Provisions for an army.'

'Moira's organising.' She smiled, her heart doing silly jumps in her chest. She lifted her shoulders. 'My landlady seems to think you need feeding up and sees this as a glorious opportunity.'

He grinned, swung the basket into the truck and then held the passenger door open.

'I'll try to oblige. Ready for work, Dr Lynton?'

'I'm ready,' Sophie said steadily and didn't feel ready at all.

They didn't travel far. Two miles from Moira's house, Reith brought the truck to a halt in a clearing a little off the road, on the banks of the same creek that ran through the Sanderson guest-house grounds.

There were already people there, most in khaki uniform indicating wildlife officers, with a few civilians interspersed.

'Like me, they're the ones who can climb trees,' Reith grinned. 'And who know enough of koalas not to trap animals already severely affected by Chlamydia.'

He introduced Sophie briefly and she was greeted with easy friendliness.

'Another doctor? What'd you do to get another medico here, Reith?' they demanded. 'Kidnap her?'

'Can we keep her?' one of the officers asked and they all laughed. Sophie's slim figure in her tight jeans and soft blouse brought general approval.

'There's a fiancé coming on Friday,' Reith growled drily. 'Hands off, boys.'

'So what's he doing letting you come out to the Antipodes on your own, Doc?' the same officer grinned at Sophie. His eyes were warm with admiration. In this predominantly male group she was causing a considerable stir. 'He must have a few kangaroos loose in his top paddock, I'd reckon, letting you come this far on your own.'

They left her laughing, a trace of unease running behind Sophie's smile. What *was* Kevin doing?

The men started efficiently preparing the individual cages, with little time for pleasantries. There was work to be done, and they wanted it done as fast as possible.

'If we get our quota done this morning then we won't be driving late tonight for release,' the man in charge told Sophie as they worked. He looked a question at Reith. 'We can call on Dr Lynton for any medical problem?' His doubt was clear. Sophie hardly looked a competent medical practitioner in her denim. Sophie drew in her breath in an indignant gasp.

'I know you'd like a nice antiseptic doctor in a white coat,' she managed. 'But I dressed according to what I perceived local custom required.' She cast a meaningful glance at Reith. 'And at least I don't stand in need of a shave.'

Her crack brought a shout of laughter from the men, and Reith was subjected to good-natured teasing as they scattered into the trees. He took it in good part, Sophie noticed, but there was still that aloof air about him—he held himself back.

Sufficient unto himself. He had to be. He'd learned the hard way.

To begin with she had little to do. She sat on a fallen log by the creek and watched the men near to her work.

The technique was simple enough. The men raised long, extendable poles into the trees, a red flag on the end. This flag they positioned over the koala's head. Frightened, the koala moved downward, the red flag inexorably following, driving it still further toward the ground.

It worked fine until the man on the ground became more of a threat than the red flag, but that was usually not until the koala was fifteen or twenty feet above ground. Then the koala headed out on the nearest branch and stayed there.

That was the end of the easy part. The final capture was effected by the hunter climbing the tree, positioning himself in a fork and working with another pole. This pole had a noose on the end. The noose slipped over the koala's head and tightened as it was released from the pole. Then the animal was jerked back from its hold on the branch and lowered fast to a waiting captor on the ground.

Simple! Except there was no way she was going to try it, Sophie thought, mindful of those dreadful claws. These men made it look easy—and it wasn't the least bit easy.

Her first patient appeared after half an hour. The man had loosened his hold a fraction of a second too early as he placed a koala in its cage—and was savagely scratched for his efforts. Reith's bag was well-equipped for such a wound and twenty minutes later the man's wound was cleaned, dressed and he was back in a tree.

'Most scratches don't need stitching,' Reith had told Sophie. 'These guys know what they're handling—and when they see those claws coming back at them they take evasive action.'

Nevertheless there were two gashes that did require stitching and Sophie could see what Reith meant when he said he hadn't been able to help with the koalas when he was needed medically. If he'd had to clean up every time he needed to inspect a cut, he'd get nothing done.

As it was, Reith moved with twice the speed of the other men, capturing koalas with an ease the conservation officers could only envy. They used him too to check animals they were unsure could withstand the move. If there was the least doubt, Reith did a fast examination when he brought his own koala back to the group of cages.

'We should have a veterinary officer on site,' the man in charge told Sophie. 'But there's another group of us ten miles south and the vet's there. Doc Kenrick's every bit as competent—or more so—at telling us whether a koala is fit or not. He seems to have some sort of sixth sense...'

A sixth sense. She wouldn't doubt it. Reith Kenrick seemed almost fey. He worked swiftly and silently, and the more Sophie watched him the more intrigued she became. Wilderness doctor...

A blaring horn made her turn toward the road, breaking

her train of thought. She'd been left alone for the moment, the men working further and further from base as the koalas nearest the clearing were captured.

A family sedan, coated with dust from the gravel road, was pulling fast into the clearing, and the driver's hand was hard on the horn. Instinctively Sophie stood and hurried toward it, sensing the same urgency in the way she'd seen people arrive at Casualty.

'Dr Kenrick! Please...I need Dr Kenrick...' A woman in her early twenties, her face stained with dust and tears and eyes huge with fright, tumbled from the car. She was staring wildly round the clearing and there was only Sophie in view. 'Is he here? Oh, for God's sake, is he here?'

The woman made to run straight past Sophie but Sophie's hands came out to catch and hold her.

'Reith Kenrick's in the bush. I'm a doctor. How can I help you?'

'A doctor?' The girl cast Sophie a wild, disbelieving look and then stared frantically past her, willing Reith to appear. 'Dear God...'

'What's wrong?' Sophie raised her voice to a curt, authoritative command, the voice she had perfected in the years she had spent trying to calm hysterical relatives.

The girl's long blonde hair was falling over her eyes. She pushed it away, swiping at her tears. 'My...my baby.'

'He's in the car?'

'She... I... Oh, God, I don't know what to do.'

Sophie released her and moved the ten steps to the car with lightning speed. A fast glance through the rear window and she was hauling open the door, and lifting a baby from a capsule in the back seat.

The infant—a little one of maybe four or five months— was limp in Sophie's grasp and it didn't take a medical degree to know what was wrong. Sophie put a hand on the child's face and flinched at the feel of fever. The child's temperature must be forty-two or -three—and she was still swaddled in blankets.

Almost in the same movement she had used to lift the child Sophie hauled the blankets away, sinking to crouch in the dust so she could rest the child on her knees.

'What…what are you doing? Are you really a doctor? Oh, why doesn't Dr Kenrick come?' The girl stared hopelessly down at her child.

'I'm really a doctor,' Sophie snapped. 'How long has she been fitting?'

'Fitting?'

'How long has she been limp like this?'

'About…maybe about fifteen minutes or a bit more. She's got a cold but Dr Kenrick told me she didn't need antibiotics. This morning her cold seemed a bit better but I was feeding her and she just sort of rolled her eyes back in her head and went stiff. Then…I don't know…I thought she was dying and I shook her—and she went all limp.'

'How hard did you shake her?' Sophie demanded, her heart sinking. Shaking on its own could cause a cerebral bleed in a little one this age.

'Not…not hard. Just a couple of gentle shakes. Then…I knew Doc Kenrick was working out here, so I just wrapped her in her blankets and drove like fury. Oh, God, do you think she's dying?'

Sophie didn't answer. Her mind was racing and she had no time to find words of comfort.

The baby had been convulsing for fifteen minutes. The blankets were off the child now, but how on earth to get her cool fast? Instead of cooling the feverish child, the woman had heated her still further, wrapping her in blankets and placing her in a sun-drenched car. After fifteen minutes of continuous fitting there was a major risk of brain damage. They had to get her cool.

There was only one fast way.

'Come with me,' Sophie ordered and ran, not looking behind to see if the young mother followed.

The girl did.

A hundred yards away the creek bed dropped steeply away from the level ground. It was a four-foot drop to the water, with sheer, sandy sides. Sophie stared down at the sluggishly moving stream. How deep?

There was only one way to tell. She handed the child back to her mother and slid, feet first, down into the water.

The water hit her body in a chilling shock, cool and clear from the mountains above, and no more than waist-deep. Sophie steadied, then hauled herself up on the narrow bank, and held her hands up for the baby.

'Give her to me,' she demanded. 'Fast.'

'What…what are you going to do?' Fear was still trembling through the woman's voice. Clearly she thought she was dealing with a mad woman—and she wasn't about to hand her precious baby over.

Sophie took a deep breath, willing her voice to be calm and for her to sound as if she knew what she was doing.

'Your baby is fitting because she's running a temperature and has overheated,' she told the woman. 'This is the only way to get her temperature down fast.'

'But—'

'Give her to me,' Sophie demanded harshly. She was balancing precariously just out of the water. 'I know what I'm doing. You have to believe me.'

The girl cast a wild look round, still willing Reith to appear, but there was no one—only this mad, English-accented girl standing knee-deep in water and demanding her baby. She cast a scared look down at her child's lifeless face, and reluctantly handed down the baby. Two seconds later Sophie had slid back into the water and was lowering the baby slowly down against her chest.

This was less than ideal. In a hospital setting, Sophie would undress the baby and bathe her gently in water slightly less than skin temperature. The next alternative was to wash the child down with wet towels—but here, where there was no ledge on which to stand and work beside the water, to waste time undressing the child and trying to get wet cloths up and down the bank was to court disaster. After fifteen minutes there could still be permanent damage anyway. She just had to hope that the shock of immersion into cool water could be tolerated without further damage.

The limpness ended almost immediately. Sophie felt the baby's tiny body tense as the water soaked through her clothes. Good grief... The baby was dressed in a little woollen dress, with singlet underneath, by the look of it, and tightly buttoned matiné jacket. There were buttons and ribbons everywhere. It would have taken five precious minutes to undress her. Cute little woollen booties were on her feet and a little knitted cap was on her head. Adorable—but totally impractical in today's heat, and with blankets as well...

They'd shrink now, Sophie thought grimly, and the baby would be better off for its ruined clothes. Summer heat was hardly layette territory. Even if the child was well, she should be wearing little more than a nappy.

'OK, sweetheart...' The layers of wool were letting the cold seep in gradually, giving some buffer from the shock of cold on hot skin, but by now the clothes were thoroughly wet. Sophie managed to flick off the useless bonnet from the little one's head and lowered her so the back of her neck and head were in the water.

'Come on, little one,' she murmured, watching the rolling eyes. 'Come back to us.'

On the bank above, the young mother stared down with desperate hope. She had to trust Sophie, but Sophie could see in the way she stared down that she thought she was crazy to do so.

'Is she...?'

'Give her time,' Sophie said, softly splashing water onto the little face. 'It'll take time to get her core temperature down—'

'I want Dr Kenrick!' It was a heartfelt wail, and as if in answer to the plea Reith was suddenly on the bank, staring down at Sophie and baby.

'Dr Kenrick…' The young woman grabbed him as if she were clutching a lifeline. 'Stephanie…she's gone all funny and this woman says she's a doctor and she's going to drown her…'

Reith put her gently aside. In one lithe movement he swung himself over the embankment and slid down into the water beside Sophie.

'What seems to be the trouble, Dr Lynton?'

Sophie ignored him. Her eyes were only on Stephanie. Was she imagining it?

She wasn't. The focusless eyes were changing, fixing, staring up at Sophie with shock. Sophie felt the shift in the way the baby lay in her arms. Stephanie was back in charge of her body, and she writhed in indignation and fear.

Another tiny wriggle, and then the rosebud mouth dropped open. The child's eyes narrowed, and she let out a feeble wail.

It was one of the sweetest sounds Sophie had heard. She looked up at Reith and her eyes laughed with sheer joy.

'She's back with us.'

'So I see.' Reith looked down at the child in Sophie's arms. 'After fairly drastic treatment, wouldn't you say?'

Sophie flushed crimson, her delight in the child's recovery somewhat abating. Then she looked down at the angry little furrow on the baby's brow and the intelligence glaring up at her and her delight returned. There seemed little possibility of brain damage here.

'I dare say there's diazepam in your car that I could have searched for and injected her with to stop the convulsion, Dr Kenrick—or a bucket somewhere I could use to fetch water to wash her down with,' she said softly. She was trying to unbutton the baby's matiné jacket as she spoke and Reith moved to help her. To hold a writhing baby and undress her at the same time was no easy task. 'But it would have taken time, Dr Kenrick, and I figured after fifteen minutes of convulsions what we didn't have was time. What would you have done in the circumstances?'

Her voice held a trace of defiance. Reith cast a swift glance up at her and then concentrated again on the fiddly buttons. His long, surgeon fingers unfastened them much more swiftly than Sophie's could.

'I would have done exactly what you did, Dr Lynton,' he said at last. 'Well done.'

The crimson flush didn't fade one bit. Small praise for a simple procedure, but it was enough to make the cool of the water she was standing in fade to insignificance. Sophie warmed from the inside out.

The warmth grew. Reith concentrated on the buttons. It was crazily intimate, to be standing waist-deep in water with the baby between them. Their fingers touched as the baby's clothes slipped away and the strange feeling Reith engendered in Sophie took a stronger hold. He was so darned competent... He was so darned male!

Finally the baby was undressed, only her sodden nappy remaining. By now her crying had become a furious frenzy, small fists pummelling uselessly in the air.

'No damage at all, it seems.' Reith smiled, his hands reaching out to steady Sophie as she pushed herself through the water toward the bank. Where his hands touched her, the warmth was heat.

Men had appeared above them on the creek bank, drawn by the unaccustomed sound of a baby's cry. Reith took Stephanie firmly from Sophie and handed the baby up to waiting arms.

'Jenny, I'd sit down under the gum trees and feed her,' Reith told the anxious young mum. 'She won't settle until she's on the breast, and she'll make herself hot again screaming.'

'I'll just dress her again first,' the young mother started as Reith hauled himself up the bank and turned to pull Sophie after him.

'No.' Sophie and Reith spoke in unison and Reith grinned.

'It seems we have medical unity,' he told the small group of onlookers, steadying Sophie on her feet and casting a quick, concerned glance down at her arm. Traces of blood were showing through the drenched dressing. He touched it lightly, looked a query up at Sophie and she shook her head. She was fine.

Reith nodded, accepting her need for him not to fuss. He crossed to where the young mother stood. Jenny's face was ashen and the hands holding her dripping baby were shaking.

'Jenny, it's heat that made Stephanie convulse,' he told her gently. 'I know you're proud of Stephanie's beautiful clothes but you just can't use them except on cool days. Feed her in her wet nappy and leave her in that until she needs a fresh nappy—and then leave her in nothing more than a singlet and nappy until the temperature drops under seventy degrees. That's an order, Jenny.'

Jenny looked up at him, her face uncertain and unhappy. 'That's what you said yesterday, but my mum-in-law says you're wrong. She says you should have given her antibiotics and she says you have to keep her warm if she's got a cold...'

There was silence among the group of onlookers. The men shifted uneasily, aware that Reith was being challenged, and Sophie stood silent. A first-time mother, and a very young one at that, had all sorts of pressures on her, and it was hard to withstand the pressures of a dominant mother-in-law.

'Do you think I'm wrong, Jenny?' Reith asked, his dark eyes fixing the frightened girl. His tone was gentle, as if he understood her conflict.

'N-no. Not now.'

'Would it help if I talked to your mother-in-law?' Reith asked and the girl's face cleared like magic.

'Could you? I mean…I know you're busy, but you see, Mum Lee knitted the clothes. She's been at me and at me for not using them and she was coming for lunch today, so I had to use them. And I've six full woollen layettes she knitted that Stephanie won't fit into by winter…'

She ended on a hiccup of a sob to match Stephanie's, and Reith smiled.

'Hey, Jen, settle down and feed Stephanie. I'll talk to your mum-in-law. Stephanie's her first grandchild but there are three more daughters and daughters-in-law to produce little layette-wearers. I'll settle her. I promise.' He turned to the men. 'Drama's over, boys. We've only fifty more koalas to go and we can call it quits for the day. Reckon we can make it?'

There were murmurs of agreement and the men moved off. Sophie expected Reith to go too but he came purposefully back over to her.

'Let's check your arm, Dr Lynton. It looks as if you might have broken your stitches.'

'I can check it myself,' she told him. 'Your koalas need you.'

'You need me first,' he told her firmly. 'I don't intend to let that arm get infected. It seems to me, Dr Lynton, that you could be very useful to me. You're one tourist worth looking after.'

Sophie stared up at him, her tongue for once bewilderingly at a loss. There was no reason at all for the warmth to build and spread over such a simple accolade. No reason at all...

An hour later the koala collection was complete. Sophie hadn't been needed again and, as Reith had needed to retie a couple of torn stitches, she was grateful to rest. She'd sat under the gums watching Jenny feed her baby, noting in satisfaction how the child drifted into sound, healthy sleep after the feed.

'You'd think she'd be cold in a wet nappy here in the shade,' Jenny said wonderingly, and Sophie shook her head.

'She's suffering from an infection that's putting her temperature up. By keeping her cool you're giving her body a better chance to fight the infection.'

Jenny cast her a shy look. 'You...you really are a doctor?'

'I am,' Sophie smiled. 'Trained in England, so I guess I'm not quite up to the standard of you colonials, but I'm a real doctor none the less.'

Jenny didn't return her smile. She clearly had something important on her mind.

'Would you...would you have given Stephanie antibiotics?' she asked. 'My mum-in-law will say that's why she had a convulsion. She says I should have demanded them yesterday when I took Stephanie to Dr Kenrick for her cold. She'll say now that Dr Kenrick was negligent not to give them.'

'Was there anything wrong other than a simple cold?' Sophie asked.

Jenny shook her head. 'No. Just a runny nose and a fever for the last couple of days.'

'Then I definitely wouldn't have given her antibiotics,' Sophie said firmly. 'A cold in the head is a virus, and antibiotic doesn't cure or even help a virus. If the virus causes an infection—for instance an infected ear—then there are bacteria the antibiotic can fight. Otherwise antibiotics are worse than useless.'

'Worse...'

'If you give antibiotic for every trivial illness then there's the chance that if Stephanie suffers a major infection the antibiotic will be less efficient. That's why Dr Kenrick wouldn't give it to her when you asked.'

'That's...that's what Dr Kenrick said.'

'Then your second opinion backs him up all the way,' Sophie smiled.

'How very supportive.' The deep voice behind Sophie made her jump six inches.

Sophie hadn't heard Reith approach. The man moved with the stealth of a cat. He smiled easily down at Jenny and her baby and his wide, easy smile encompassed Sophie and made her catch her breath. 'Satisfied, Jenny?'

'I... Yes...it's just...I didn't mean to doubt you. It's just that my mum-in-law made me feel like a bad mother for following your advice.'

'It's hard to know who to believe.' Reith nodded, his eyes gentle with understanding. 'But you're intelligent, Jenny. You need to trust your intelligence. Listen to what people say, make up your own mind—and then have the strength to stick to your guns.'

'I'll try.' Jenny smiled shyly. 'But you will...you will speak to Mum Lee this time...'

'I'll speak to your mum-in-law,' Reith promised. 'You said she was coming to your place for lunch?'

'Yes...' Jenny gasped, looking down at her watch, and then sighed in relief. 'It's only eleven...'

'I'll drop in at your place this afternoon,' Reith promised as Jenny rose with the sleeping baby. He raised his eyebrows at Sophie. 'In fact we might visit Mrs Lee with a deputation. Dr Lynton supports me nicely, don't you think, Jenny? We'll come together.'

'But...' Sophie shook her head '...I'm not—'

'Having lunch with me?' Reith lifted his mobile brows. 'It's too late for morning tea, and you try keeping Mrs Sanderson's chocolate cake to yourself, Dr Lynton, and I'll get in my truck and drive off with the lot. Now, we have all the koalas we need for the duration. I intend to take you back to Mrs Sanderson, make you respectable for home visiting and then take you and your basket of food with me on my rounds. I'll show you what country medicine is all about.'

'Make me respectable?' Sophie frowned and then looked down at herself. As she did she gasped. The water had made her blouse almost transparent. She wasn't wearing a bra, and as it had dried the soft fabric had clung to her nipples, moulding their shape. Sophie drew in an indignant breath and folded her arms across her breasts.

'Too late, wouldn't you say?' Reith grinned. 'I think it's very fetching but I doubt Jenny's mum-in-law will approve. So…let's make you decent.'

'You can leave me at Mrs Sanderson's,' Sophie said stiffly. 'If you don't need me again today…'

'Oh, I need you.' Reith smiled. 'Chocolate cake excluded, I'm beginning to think you have all sorts of possibilities.'

CHAPTER FOUR

ANY illusions Sophie had that Reith Kenrick was taking pleasure in her company were dashed well before lunch. Her desirability, it seemed, was purely medical.

'I jumped at the chance to introduce to you Margaret Lee,' he confessed as they left Mrs Sanderson's. Sophie was demurely dressed in a loose cotton frock and decent bra. She'd done the front opening up to the highest button on her throat—a stupid gesture, she acknowledged as she climbed back into the awful truck, since Reith didn't seem to notice. He didn't seem to notice her as anything more than a tool.

'Margaret Lee... Jenny's mother-in-law?'

'Yes.' Reith drummed his long fingers on the steering wheel, staring straight out at the dusty track. Sophie had the feeling, though, that he was seeing more than the dirt road. 'She's behaving as if she hates me.'

'I can't imagine why,' Sophie tried drily and Reith's dark eyes creased in appreciation.

'Yeah, well, strange as it may seem, Dr Lynton, the lady has been a faithful patient for the last few years. Now, though...I haven't seen her medically for six months and as far as I know she's not using anyone else but she's sending hate vibes all around the community. I don't know how many of the locals she's badmouthed me to—and I can't figure out why.'

'And you want me to find out?'

'That's the idea.'

'So why is Mrs Lee more likely to tell me than she is to tell you?' Sophie asked dubiously.

'Because you're a woman.'

'It doesn't endow me with any magical powers.'

Reith's mouth twisted in a half-grin. 'No. I guess not. But if I can leave you alone together maybe she'll give you a run-down on me—and just maybe she'll tell you enough to figure out what's going on.'

'She's ruining your practice?' Sophie asked caustically and Reith's eyes darkened in surprise.

'I don't know whether you're taking much of the local situation in, Dr Lynton, but the people here are stuck with me. If they have the time and ability to get themselves to the city to see an alternative then good luck to them. I don't worry about losing patients.'

'Then why...?'

'Why worry about Margaret Lee? Because I have a gut feeling she's running scared. Jenny and her husband are worrying about her. They say she's grumpy and withdrawn, and she seems to be losing weight. See what you think, Dr Lynton. I look forward to your professional opinion.'

Jenny Lee lived on the outskirts of the tiny town of Inyabarra, high on a ridge with a view of the town and mountains beyond.

'Jenny's husband's the local schoolteacher,' Reith told Sophie as they climbed the steps to the front door. 'Another Inyabarra boy who couldn't bear to leave the place forever.'

'I can understand why,' Sophie said softly, looking out over the spectacular view as they waited for Jenny to answer the door. 'This place is fantastic.'

'That's what all the tourists say.'

'And you don't believe it?' she threw at him and Reith shrugged.

'It's home.'

Before he could say more the door swung open, to reveal a shy, smiling Jenny. She was clearly nervous.

'Jenny? Who is it?' A querulous voice sounded from inside and Jenny grimaced.

'It's Dr Kenrick, Mum,' she called back to her mother-in-law. 'And Dr...'

Reith's hand caught Jenny's, stopping her short with the last word only half uttered.

'Not "Doctor",' he whispered urgently. 'Unless you've already told her what Sophie does, introduce her as Sophie.'

'But why not?' Jenny talked back in a half-whisper, her eyes puzzled.

'Because your mum doesn't like doctors at the moment and I want her to like Sophie.'

His smile of encouragement brought a conspiratorial gleam to Jenny's eyes. She grinned and led them through to the sitting-room.

Mrs Lee rose to meet them. She was a short, wiry woman, lean to the point of emaciation, with sharp, piercing eyes that missed nothing.

'I don't know why the heck you're here,' she said bluntly to Reith after casting an uninterested glance at Sophie. 'You've done enough damage already.'

'Meaning?' Reith surveyed the hostile woman with lazy interest, as though the last thing he would do was become offended by her words.

'I told Jenny to get penicillin for the baby's cold. You refused to give it to her. You'll kill my only grandchild...'

'Stephanie didn't need penicillin,' Reith said.

'Then why did she convulse?'

'Because she was overheated,' Reith said bluntly. 'Mrs Lee, I've told Jenny that Stephanie is not to wear anything more than a nappy and singlet from now on, until the temperature drops at least ten degrees. That's an absolute medical imperative and if she disobeys she'll be risking her baby's life. If you persuade her to go against my advice then it's you that's putting Stephanie's life at risk.'

'I won't do it, Mum,' Jenny said softly. 'I'm sorry. But I think Dr Kenrick's right.'

Mrs Lee's mouth twisted in a narrow line of disgust. 'You doctors. You don't know anything.' She cast a look of abhorrence at Reith and Sophie flinched. What had happened to make her hate him so?

Fear him so…

The thought flew into Sophie's mind so swiftly that she was sure she was right. This hate… She had seen it before when she'd had to tell a relative that someone they loved was dying. It was a way of rejecting truth—to hate the bearer of such tidings.

Reith had turned to the crib at the other side of the room where Stephanie lay in untroubled sleep. She was only in her nappy. Reith touched her forehead and gave a grunt of satisfaction.

'She'll do, Jenny. Ring me if you have any trouble but I doubt if you will now.'

'Thank you,' Jenny said gratefully. She looked over at the lunch table and then doubtfully at her mother-in-law. 'I don't suppose you'd like to stay for lunch?' she asked Reith and Sophie.

Reith shook his head and glanced at his watch. 'We've lunch with us, thanks, Jenny. We'll have it on the road.' He grimaced across at Sophie and lowered his voice, speaking to Jenny and her mother-in-law in a tone that Sophie could just hear but wasn't certain she was meant to. 'This dratted woman expects to be shown all the tourist sights—as if I haven't better things to do!'

Sophie cast Reith a look of astonishment and then looked quickly away at the message in his eyes. He was firmly telling her to shut up and play along. OK…

'Well, I haven't much time here…' Sophie said, and made her voice sound a little sulky. She wasn't sure what was going on but she wouldn't interfere with his game plan.

'Where are you from, dear?' Mrs Lee asked with interest and her look said it all. Anyone Reith didn't like was OK with her.

'England, of course,' Reith said in a bored drawl. 'Where else do you get that plum-in-the-mouth accent? And she's a dratted royalist...'

'There's nothing wrong with our royal family,' Mrs Lee said stoutly. She cast Reith a look of venom—as if she suspected him of being anarchist to the core—and then beamed her very nicest smile at Sophie. 'I'm English too,' she told Sophie. 'I came out here as a tourist, met my husband and stayed forever. But what...?' Another darkling look at Reith. 'What on earth are you doing with Dr Kenrick?'

Jenny was silent. She knew why Sophie was with Reith but Reith's eyes were telling her messages too and she was a smart young woman.

'Dr Kenrick's one of only two people I know around here,' Sophie said slowly. 'Yourselves excepted now, of course. I'm staying at the Sanderson guest house until my fiancé arrives...'

'Well, you must come to lunch with me,' Mrs Lee told her firmly. 'Tomorrow? I can show you my scrapbooks of the royal family—and if you're lucky there's sometimes a koala in my backyard.'

'So...why exactly am I going to Mrs Lee's for lunch?' Sophie asked cautiously as Reith ushered her once more into the truck.

'Because I'm worried about her, her family's worried about her and she won't let me near. You're the sacrificial lamb. Go in and ask questions, don't take no for an answer and find out what's going on.'

'Act as a nosy, rude tourist, you mean?'

'If that's the only way. You've nothing to lose. Margaret Lee cooks a great roast dinner.'

'Roast dinner! In this heat?'

'Yep,' Reith grinned. 'Speaking of dinner…'

They ate lunch back at Reith's surgery. His place was on the same meandering creek that ran through Moira Sanderson's, but higher on the ridge. The creek fell away below the house over a series of rocky falls, tumbling to the bush-filled valley below.

It was the perfect place for an artist, Sophie thought as she settled herself under the gums and stared appreciatively out at the view. Hardly an ideal place for a doctor's surgery, though.

'You look disapproving.' Reith emerged from the house, a blanket and wine glasses in his hands. He spread the rug and looked speculatively at Mrs Sanderson's basket. 'I'll provide wine.'

'Wine in the middle of a working day?' Sophie said in astonishment, and Reith grinned.

'One glass of wine and then a sleep, lady. Very civilised.'

'But if you get called—'

'One glass of wine isn't going to make any difference to my capacity to treat.'

Most unprofessional. Sophie gave a small, disapproving sniff and caught Reith's eyes gleaming laughter. Dratted man! She unpacked the salad rolls as Reith produced ice-cold moselle and poured. 'So…so when do you run clinic? You do run a clinic, I presume?' This was the most unusual medical practice she had ever encountered.

'Sure do. I run it in the evenings at this time of year. Clinic from five to nine, unless something crops up. It pays in a place like this to be flexible. The bush telegraph works pretty well if I'm called out and people understand. Next week it might be them who fall out of a tree and need all my attention when I should be running clinic. Most people around here are grateful that there's any sort of medical service at all.'

'And in emergencies? If anyone needs an anaesthetic—or you have more than one urgent case at a time?'

Reith shrugged. 'We cope. Anaesthetic cases get taken thirty miles to the nearest hospital—though there's been the odd time I've acted surgeon anaesthetist in one.'

'You're kidding!'

'I had a lady last year—a city hippy with ideas that she'd like her baby born in the bush. She and her partner took a tent high up in the hills behind Mount Ranree and sat down to commune with nature until junior appeared. Unfortunately undiagnosed pre-eclampsia turned to full-scale eclampsia. She hadn't been near a doctor for her pregnancy. By the time her partner hiked down here to call for help and we got men and four-wheel-drives up there she was too far gone to move. Somehow we managed the most unantiseptic Caesarian on record—and ended up with two live patients. Bloody miracle!'

Sophie closed her eyes. The stuff nightmares were made of!

'You didn't try to settle her first…' With eclampsia, drugs could often settle the mother, giving time to transport her to hospital.

'Whatever was happening was affecting the baby. The foetal distress was marked. I had to make an impossible decision. As it happened…well, she's suffered severe renal failure. There'll never be another baby—so maybe my choice was the right one.'

'As you say…an impossible decision,' Sophie said grimly.

'Something you don't get to face in inner-city London.' Reith lifted a salad sandwich. 'Here's to city practice and my escape from it. I wish you joy of it, Dr Lynton.'

'You didn't like it?'

'I hated it.' His face closed.

'Too many people.'

'As you say.'

They ate the rest of their meal in silence. It was an odd sort of silence, Sophie thought. Her mind was full of questions she was aching to ask, and yet there was a reserve about him that prevented intrusion. It was a reserve that demanded respect.

The silence drifted on. The midday heat had become a soporific blanket, casting a deep laziness over them. Sophie's eyes drooped downward. She pulled her head up with a jerk and found Reith smiling at her. Rather than unsettling her, it only deepened her sense of peace.

Of belonging. As if she was growing into the place.

Weird, total falsehood. How could she possibly think that?

'Go to sleep,' Reith said gently, taking her shoulders between his hands and pressing her toward the waiting blanket.

'I'm not going to sleep with...' she murmured and then her eyes widened as she heard what she had said.

'Not going to sleep with me?' Reith smiled, a gleam of laughter in the depths of his eyes. 'Very prudent, Dr Lynton. What would the absent Kevin think of that?' He released her and stretched out fully on the blanket beside her, his disreputable Akubra falling forward to shade his face. 'But sleep by me, Dr Lynton? That's a very sensible thing to do. In fact, until I choose to drive you home, it seems the only thing to do—in the circumstances.'

To her amazement, Sophie slept. She'd never done such a thing since childhood. It seemed the height of indulgence—to sleep in the midday sun—and yet here, with this man, it felt entirely natural. It was a deep sleep that was the most untroubled she had had since arriving.

Since...

Since when? Not for years had she woken like this, to languorous contentment, as if the world had somehow righted itself on its tilting axis and the way ahead was different...

It wasn't different at all. Nothing had changed. She blinked twice and then looked up as a shadow fell over her face.

'Lemonade, ma'am?' Reith Kenrick was holding two glasses filled with pale yellow, clinking ice cubes and sprigs of mint. 'Homemade.'

She struggled to a sitting position. 'What…what time is it?'

'Four o'clock. I've been out and done two house calls but it seemed a shame to wake you.' He grinned. 'You make a nice garden ornament.'

'Better than a concrete gnome.' Sophie smiled, accepting his proffered drink with gratitude. She looked up at him, suddenly shy. 'Th—thank you.'

He stood looking down at her for a long moment, his face shadowed. 'No trouble,' he said at last. He glanced at his watch. 'I'd better run you back to Mrs Sanderson's now, though. My clinic starts in an hour.'

'Could I…could I see your clinic first?' For some reason Sophie felt reluctant to leave. There was little reason for her to see this man again. On Friday Kevin would be here and then…

Friday seemed suddenly inexplicably bleak. She wasn't even sure if Kevin would come. That must be why the shiver of desolation crept through her.

'Sure.' Reith put his hand down to help her to her feet. His hand in hers made the shiver of desolation turn to something else.

For heavens' sake, Sophie Lynton… What on earth are you thinking of?

She was thinking of this lean, solitary man smiling down at her with a smile that committed nothing—that said he was pleasant and courteous and that was all. He wanted nothing. Totally self-sufficient…

Why did that trouble her so much? Reith Kenrick was nothing to her. Or was he?

He was looking down at her, his dark eyes creasing in swift concern.

'Is something wrong?'

She gave herself a swift mental shake and withdrew her hand from his grasp. 'No. Nothing, thank you.' She gave him her brightest smile and bent to lift the rug she'd been sleeping on. 'Lead on…'

He showed her through the clinic with the same detached courtesy and noncommittal friendliness she was learning to expect. He expected neither interest nor praise in his beautifully set-up little surgery, and his eyebrows rose in a cynical question as she gave it.

'You've seen better set-up surgeries than this in London.'

'Yes, I have,' Sophie agreed. 'And I've also seen worse ones. What I haven't seen is such a well-equipped situation for one doctor.' His tiny theatre was set up with the latest technical equipment. It glittered with clinical cleanliness, and Sophie blinked at the situations he was obviously prepared for. 'Surely it's not cost efficient?'

'To have equipment such as X-ray machines for one doctor?' Reith queried and shook his head. 'No, it's not cost efficient. Try telling that to the next farmer who comes in here with a broken arm and neither the time nor the money to go to the city for treatment.'

'The farmers round here aren't prosperous?' Sophie queried.

'You could say that,' Reith said drily. 'We get a lot of alternative lifestylers who come to me as a last resort and can pay very little—and there are the few who are struggling to keep old family farms going. The land round here's been marginal for farming for years. The farmers used crown land for grazing, but now the place is national park the cattle can't be grazed on government land and it's sending a lot of our people to the wall.'

Our people…

Did Reith think of the locals as his people?

'Why did you come back here?' she asked softly. 'Was it the place—or the people?'

'The place,' he said bluntly. 'I don't need people.'

'No one?' It was such a blank statement that Sophie was startled.

'I don't think anyone does. Where does involvement with people get you, Dr Lynton? Where does attachment to the absent Kevin get you?'

'It just might get me a family and children and warmth and laughter…'

'Or a whole heap of heartache.'

'That's cynical.'

'Honest.'

'So what about Mrs Sanderson?' Sophie said stoutly. 'She and Patrick had thirty years…'

'And then?'

'He died,' Sophie agreed. 'But surely those thirty years were worth something?'

Reith shrugged. Not to him, they weren't, his shrug said, and he looked at his watch. 'How the hell can I judge? I just know that I'm not buying into emotional baggage. I'll show you my father's studio if you like, then I'll have to take you home.'

A dismissal. She had earned as much from probing. Emotional baggage… Sophie bit her lip as she crossed through the door Reith was holding open.

The room he led her into took her breath away.

It was all window, with an almost circular view of the forest outside. The creek swept downward over rocks just outside the window and the huge plate glass swept upward so high that Sophie felt her eyes being drawn to the mountains in the distance.

It was no longer being used as a studio. Easels were still set up but they held finished paintings—and good ones at that.

This was a room Reith lived in, it seemed. There was a massive settee, its ancient leather upholstery softened and splitting with age, a vast Persian rug over the floor and books scattered in low bookshelves along the edge of the huge windows.

Sophie drew in her breath. She had never been in such a place. A swift glance behind at Reith and she wasn't all that sure that he wanted her to be here. His face was closed and empty. He was a courteous host showing a darned nuisance of a tourist the sights before getting rid of her.

She wouldn't be hurried. She couldn't. He had shown her this place of his own free will and she was going to look. He hadn't been compelled to show her.

She walked slowly from painting to painting. Many were the tortured abstracts Mrs Sanderson had described— all skeleton and harsh, tortured lines— but there were others...soft water-colours whose brilliance screamed out from the easel and whose contents reflected a pain she was starting to know. Like father, like son...

There was one...

Sophie stood before a small water-colour and looked at it for a long, long time. It was a bush scene, a mirror-still lake with a woman's face reflected through the trees. The face was superimposed on the scene as though part of it and yet apart—as if the woman was staring down, asking questions of her reflection. The woman looked out through the trees as if the forest were the bars of a cage.

There was something familiar about the woman's face. Sophie glanced back to Reith. The same fine bone structure... The same...

What?

The same closed look. This woman too had shut herself off. The forest was closing in on her and she wanted no part of it. Its beauty was all around her and yet she was closing it out, allowing it not to touch her even though she was part of it. The eyes were brooding and aloof as though she was planning—yearning to escape. There was a bleakness about her, though, that said escape was impossible.

A tiny label across the bottom said *Bush Bride*.

'Your mother?' Sophie said tentatively and Reith nodded. 'She didn't like the bush?'

'My father never should have brought her here. It's no place for a woman.'

'There are women here who are happy.'

'If they're born here maybe.'

'So if you marry—'

'I won't marry.' Reith's eyes flashed ice and Sophie grimaced. She was really stepping where angels feared to tread here. And yet... The solitude in this man's eyes was almost pain, and Sophie had never been one to ignore pain.

'Because your parents might have been unhappy is no reason—'

'Do you mind?' he snapped. 'What do you think this is, Dr Lynton? A counselling session? I don't ask your advice. If you want to sort out a marriage try concentrating on your own. Your nice, convenient boyfriend who's going to supply you with family and children...'

'Kevin's not convenient.'

'No. He's twelve thousand miles away. And you're hardly breaking your heart over him, now, are you?'

'That's none of your—'

'Business,' he finished for her. 'Now who's talking? But that's all marriage is, isn't it, Dr Lynton? Business. A nice, convenient hot-water bottle. Security for your old age.'

'Kevin's not...'

'Not what? Like other men? That's nonsense, Dr Lynton, and you know it. This love business...'

'Love business...' Sophie was wallowing way out of her depths. She didn't understand what on earth was going on to cause the bitter barbs being flung at her. She was caught in a conversation she wanted no part of, and yet she couldn't stop.

'Do you seriously think there's a one and only love in the world?' Reith demanded. 'If Kevin didn't arrive on Friday, would you break your heart? Oh, your pride would be hurt, and your plans for the future, but what else?'

'That's implying I'm marrying for convenience.'

'Aren't you? Doesn't everyone?'

'No!' It was a cry of anguish, no small part of which was caused by the seed of doubt that he could be right. She couldn't think that. She loved Kevin. Kevin was all she had...

'How much do you love your Kevin? Certainly not enough to prevent you reacting to me when I carried you to bed the other night.'

'I didn't react to you.'

He shook his head. 'Liar.'

'You arrogant toad.' The colour drained from Sophie's face and she faced him square. Her breath was coming in short, harsh gasps and her eyes flashed fury. 'You don't have the faintest idea. If you think for one moment I'm attracted to you...'

'Oh, not personally,' he agreed, watching her with an interest one might bestow on a rather interesting specimen in a jar. 'On any attractive male who comes into your orbit. Because Kevin isn't exclusive, is he, Sophie? He's just the one whose bank balance, lifestyle and ego match yours—'

'No!'

'It's true,' he went on relentlessly. 'You don't love him exclusively or your body wouldn't betray you. Exclusive love doesn't exist.'

'It does!' It had to. Sophie sounded like a desperate child. Who was this man to be throwing these ideas at her—to be attacking her? Who was he?

'Prove it,' he said softly, dangerously, and before she could move he had crossed to where she stood. Her arms were swept behind her, gripped like a vice, and his dark head lowered to hers. While one hand held her wrists with effortless ease, the other raked through her curls, forcing her face back. Two seconds later she was being ruthlessly kissed.

She didn't struggle. She couldn't. One of Sophie's arms was all but useless but even if both were uninjured she couldn't fight Reith Kenrick's strength. He held her in a grip of iron and his lips possessed her utterly.

Possessed…

That was how she felt. Reith was in control. He could do with her as he willed and there was no way she could stop it. His lips fastened on hers, and his mouth demanded a response with an urgency that was almost a cry from the heart.

What was he doing? Why was he kissing her like this?

The man was kissing her with such ravaging passion that it drew from Sophie a reply she hadn't thought she was capable of feeling. This wasn't the kiss of anger—or of challenge. It was the kiss of a man who was hungering for something he had never had and didn't believe existed. Reith Kenrick might swear he needed no one—but his need was there in his kiss.

It wasn't just a need. It was an overwhelming, insatiable hunger that caught at Sophie's soul.

There was no way she wanted to stop it. To her horror she felt the urgent quiver of response shudder through her body. Reith was right. He just had to touch her and her sensible resolutions were put aside.

Reluctantly but inevitably Sophie's lips parted, answering his need, responding to his urgency. Her soul was caught by him—desperate to appease his hunger in any way she knew how.

Kevin…

She had no right to appease this man's hunger when she was firmly affianced. She had no right…

The thought flashed through her mind in a jolt of desperate confusion. She jerked back, and, to her bewilderment, she was released.

There was no sound but the jerky, shallow gasps coming from Sophie's lips. Reith was watching her as a hawk might watch a sparrow, only the inner depths of his eyes reflecting a trace of uncertainty behind the cynicism. Sophie was powerless to define her feelings. She stood, hands falling uselessly to her sides, and her wide eyes looked up at Reith in dismay.

'Why…why did you do that?' she whispered at last. 'To punish me?'

'What would I punish you for, Sophie Lynton?' Reith asked and to Sophie's amazement Reith's voice was not quite steady. He put a hand out and placed it on her shoulder. 'I'd like to take you to my bed.'

Sophie moistened dry lips. 'I suspect…I suspect that your bed would be a pretty lonely place to be—for any woman.'

'You'd like to try?'

'No!'

'How do you know if you won't try?' His eyes were throwing out an enigmatic challenge and Sophie shook her head.

'I guess…I guess I'm starting to know you, Reith Kenrick. And I'm starting to think that by your side is a fairly bleak place to be.'

'Why?'

'Because you don't need anyone—except maybe for sexual gratification.'

'And Kevin needs more than that?'

'Yes.' Did he? She wasn't sure.

He must, Sophie thought savagely, twisting the brilliant diamond on her ring finger. He was marrying her, after all, and there were women enough for sex.

Such as the woman laughing behind him on the phone…

A wave of doubt and uncertainty—and maybe even pure

bleakness—must have crossed her face because the cynicism suddenly faded from Reith's eyes.

'Hey, Sophie,' he said softly. 'I didn't mean to make you unhappy.'

'Well, you have,' Sophie whispered. She took a deep breath, struggling for words. 'Like it or not, Reith Kenrick, you have. Now, if you don't mind, I want to be taken home.'

CHAPTER FIVE

SHE needn't see Reith Kenrick ever again.

Sophie lay in her bed that night and tried desperately to block out the remembrance of Reith's mouth on hers. She failed absolutely.

Kevin was coming. This was Wednesday night. In thirty-six hours she'd have Kevin by her side and Reith Kenrick would fade to a bad memory.

The thought made her twist in her bed with bleak, hopeless longing.

Good grief, Sophie Lynton, you're a twenty-eight-year-old doctor of medicine and you're behaving like some stupid schoolgirl with a crush. Just because you feel sorry for the man...

Sorry? Was she sorry for Reith?

It wasn't true. What she felt for Reith Kenrick was empathy—empathy because of her own bleak childhood.

'But I've sorted myself out,' she told the darkness. 'So can Reith Kenrick. He doesn't need me!'

He didn't need anyone.

'Says Reith Kenrick!'

Sophie twisted over and gave her pillow a vicious thump. The man had unsettled her to the point where sleep was impossible. The sooner Kevin arrived and married her out of hand the better.

Only Kevin won't marry me out of hand, she thought sadly. He'll have to fit me into his schedule...

Between his women...

Stop it, Sophie Lynton. You're being a fool. You have no real reason to think Kevin's unfaithful. If you don't trust him now, what sort of basis is there for a marriage?

I do trust him! It was a child's bereft wail and Sophie didn't believe it for a moment.

The telephone's sudden ring resounding shrilly through the dark shook her out of her misery. She buried her face deeper in the pillows while Mrs Sanderson padded down the hall to answer it.

Sophie was still the only guest in the place. Maybe this was more people wanting late accommodation. Being a guest-house proprietor must be almost as bad as being a doctor for late-night calls, Sophie thought ruefully.

It wasn't a guest. A moment later there was a rapid knock on Sophie's door.

'Are you awake, dear?'

'Yes.' Sophie sat up and swore as an alternative reason for the phone call presented itself. Kevin! It had to be Kevin ringing with an excuse as to why he wasn't arriving on Friday.

She flicked on her bedside lamp and glared at her watch. Two a.m. in Australia was late afternoon in Belgium and it wouldn't occur to Kevin to worry about waking Sophie and her landlady. 'I'll bet he hasn't even apologised to Moira,' she muttered savagely as she flung off her bed-cover.

'Coming,' she called, but Moira Sanderson was already opening the door.

'Sophie, it's Dr Kenrick,' her landlady faltered, her voice laced with anxiety. 'He needs your help.'

'Help...' Sophie stared at Moira for a split-second and then her emergency training slid into place. 'Is he still on the phone?'

'He hung up. Sophie, it's an emergency and he was moving fast. He asked...he asked if I could take you over to the Bells' place.'

'The Bells'...'

'They live up in the hills behind the town.' Moira Sanderson was talking fast, breathless with urgency. 'Trevor

Bell's a single parent and he's odd. He had some sort of breakdown in the city and he brought his little girl to Inyabarra last year. He keeps to himself, but there's talk that he's schizophrenic and the social-welfare people have been concerned about the child. Anyway, I gather their neighbour heard shots a few minutes ago, went over and found the little girl wandering around outside with blood all over her. When Ted, the neighbour, went to the door Trevor Bell shot him in the leg. Now Trevor's barricaded himself in the house and is shooting at anything that moves. Ted's wife called the police and Dr Kenrick. The police are on their way. Dr Kenrick will be there in five minutes but he says by the sound of it he'll need back-up.'

Back-up? Sophie blinked. It sounded as if what Dr Kenrick needed was the army.

'Does he have a nurse to help in emergencies?'

'There's a trained sister who lives in Inyabarra, but she's away visiting her parents in the city.'

'I'll come.' Sophie was already pulling her jeans on. 'You don't need to—'

'You'll never find the place without me,' Moira Sanderson said firmly. 'And Dr Kenrick needs you fast. I can get you there almost as soon as Dr Kenrick arrives—that is, if I don't stop to put on my corset.' She gave the trace of an anxious smile, and Sophie guessed she'd go without more than her corset rather than be left behind. 'I know you're the doctor, dear, but I've lived a good few years in these parts. There's not a lot that can shock me, and I may be able to help.'

By the time they arrived at the Bells' small cottage, there was more than just the wounded neighbour and Reith at the scene. Word had flown round this small community, even at two in the morning. The weatherboard cottage was floodlit with lights from the local fire engine. For some reason the fire chief was there in full regalia, standing nervously behind a burly police constable, and a small group of onlookers were clustered around an area where Reith worked.

Moira, splendidly garbed in crimson dressing-gown and curlers—she'd decided that without her corset she might as well stay in what she had on—pushed her way through the lot of them, weaving a path for Sophie.

'Dr Kenrick needs Dr Lynton,' she said loudly. 'Give us room.'

Reith looked up with real relief in his face. He was too preoccupied to so much as glance at the extraordinary Moira. All he saw was Sophie—another pair of trained hands.

'Dr Lynton…' It was a momentary acknowledgement of her presence before he turned back to the job. There was no time for pleasantries.

Sophie bent swiftly over the man Reith was working on, her eyes doing a lightning-fast assessment. The ground around them was liberally splattered with blood. Below his thigh, the man's leg was a pulpy mess, and Sophie winced as she realised the extent of the damage.

'A shotgun wound?'

'Mmm.' Reith was packing the wounded flesh hard with wads of dressing, trying desperately to stop the oozing flow of blood. 'I need oxygen, Dr Lynton. In my…'

Sophie was already moving, finding Reith's mask and cylinder with ease from the heap of equipment someone had hauled from his car. She adjusted the mask on the man's face, felt his pulse and grimaced. The man was ashen and his pulse was hardly there. He was bleeding to death under their hands.

'Can we shift him head below heart?' She was talking to herself, aware that all of Reith's concentration was in stopping the blood flow. She needed to answer her own question—but how?

She glanced around fast. Someone had produced a pile of thick blankets. Swiftly she folded them into a thick wad, then shoved them beside the injured man from the waist down.

As she worked, she watched Reith, waiting for him to acknowledge what she was doing. Their eyes met for a brief instant, acknowledging their teamwork. Reith was a solid, competent person to work with, Sophie thought fleetingly, remembering some of the bumbling professionals she had worked with in emergencies. There was no need to explain things to Reith. In that brief meeting of their eyes he had acknowledged her efforts and told her he was behind her. 'Now?' she asked.

Reith left his pressure pad for a split-second, moving with Sophie in a swift, professional lift to haul the man's lower body up onto the wedge of blankets. It was not much of a pad, but it was enough to elevate his lower limbs.

Better. Now what blood pressure there was would be aided in getting blood to the brain and hindered in pumping it into the legs—toward the wound and out onto the grass.

'He's lost a massive amount.' Reith was back working on his pressure pad almost before the man was lying on the blankets. 'Can you set up a drip, fast? I'm having trouble staunching the flow.' His eyes signalled to the pile of equipment. 'You'll find everything… There's plasma…'

Sophie was already moving, searching in Reith's bag for what she needed. The man's pain-dulled eyes followed her.

'Morphine?' she queried. They might as well have been in Casualty, rather than on the leaf-strewn yard of a bush cottage. Their surroundings were blocked out and onlookers ignored. There was only the desperate task at hand. With a wound such as this, the man was lucky to still be alive now. Sophie looked at the extent of the blood around them and grimaced. It gave her a fair idea of the sort of wound under Reith's hands.

'Already administered.' Reith's face was grim and intent. 'It should take effect in a moment or two.' He touched the man lightly on the hand and then went back to applying pressure. 'You'll feel relief any minute, Ted.'

The man grunted acknowledgement.

'Sophie, there's a child hurt.' Reith's voice was tight with strain and Sophie knew that, although Reith had been forced to give Ted priority treatment, he was still worried about the patient he had left untended. 'As far as I could see on a fast examination, she has a flesh wound, not as serious as this, but she's in shock. Once the drip's set up here I can work on alone while you give her some proper attention. I only gave her a cursory once-over...'

Sophie nodded. Reith would have done a rapid triage... It was an absolute rule in emergencies that all patients were seen fast before any work was done at all. Triage was the allocation of priorities, and this man's horrendous leg wound would have to be an absolute priority.

Triage wasn't always clear. This time Reith had found his choice obvious, but in an emergency there were often hard decisions to be made. If man and child had both been bleeding to death Reith would have been forced to decide which he was most likely to save, and if both were equally possible then age and all sorts of nebulous factors such as number of dependents came into it.

Dreadful decisions. The sort of decisions Sophie, in a huge London hospital with back-up teams and other hospitals minutes away, never had to face. But a lone doctor like Reith... It was an awesome responsibility.

'How old's the child?' Sophie asked.

'Four.' Reith was still desperately fighting the blood flow. 'I need more wadding, Dr Lynton. Hell, there's not nearly enough here.' There was the edge of desperation in his voice, as if he was losing the fight. Sophie badly wanted to help him, but she had to get the drip running first. It was her job to replace the plasma. Priorities...

She inserted the intravenous needle for the drip quickly,

thanking her stars for the man's lean, work-worn hands with veins that etched themselves like lines on a contour map. Moments later the plasma bottle and tubing were attached.

'Plasma's going through now,' Sophie told Reith as she taped the drip onto the back of the man's hand and watched the thick fluid start dripping into the vein. Usually in this situation they had to use saline, but Reith had come prepared. Plasma until they could cross match his blood.

Plasma wasn't usually found in doctors' surgeries but then Reith Kenrick's surgery was no ordinary clinic. Reith Kenrick was no ordinary doctor...

Now she could concentrate on Reith's needs. Wadding... She looked around the group of open-mouthed neighbours. If they had to have spectators then the spectators might as well make themselves useful.

'I want shirts,' she said. Behind her, the crimson Moira was doing her best to comfort a sobbing woman in the crowd. Moira looked up and her eyes questioned Sophie. 'Moira, can you organise any man wearing a soft shirt or singlet—or woman wearing cotton or cotton-mix lingerie? I want them now!'

'Sure—'

A shotgun blast from the house made them all jump. The onlookers moved nervously back, and Moira moved among them, bullying the shirts from their backs. Then, with a defiant glance across to the house—as if to say, Shoot me if you dare—she stalked across and handed them to Sophie.

'Is there a problem with the woman?' Sophie asked. The woman Moira had been attending was now threatening hysterics.

'If I had a bucket of water handy I'd toss it over her,' Moira said darkly. 'Elvira Pilkington lives four doors down and is only here to get maximum drama. If nothing happens she'll invent the drama herself. What else needs doing, Sophie?'

'Could you find out where the wounded child is?'

Moira nodded, the amazing crimson dressing-gown moving off with purpose. The curlers bobbed all the way out of floodlight range.

'Did I ask if we're out of range of the gun?' Sophie asked Reith as she ripped the shirts into manageable sections. Tomorrow she'd have to account for these, she knew. From Casualty experience, Sophie knew to destroy people's possessions, no matter how grave the emergency, always led to trouble. Tomorrow she or Reith would have to face at least one person claiming that she'd torn his most expensive shirt and was she going to pay for it or did she prefer to listen to a lawyer? Reith gave a strained smile.

'Yeah. The good thing about shotguns is they haven't the range of rifles, and Ted here says Trevor's only got a shotgun.'

Ted... Their patient...

Ted was trying to talk now, fighting off the oxygen mask. Sophie lifted it slightly and bent to listen.

'He's a mad bastard,' the injured neighbour whispered through gritted teeth. 'Threatened to shoot me a few weeks ago because one of his chooks wandered over to my place. I took the thing back and the crazy coot threatened to shoot me if I came near the place again. And tonight I took his daughter back...'

His words trailed off to a pain-filled gasp and Sophie felt his pulse. What she felt reassured her. It was still faint but steadying. If only Reith could stop the blood flow...

'Got it,' Reith said harshly. He looked up to Sophie. She was adjusting the drip rate to maximum. 'Blood flow's stopped. I need some tape to hold all this in position.'

Reith needed a theatre nurse in this improvised theatre. Sophie finished what she was doing, fished in his bag for tape, cut lengths and handed them across.

'Is there any medical help within reach?' she asked as he taped. She didn't want to ask what was really in her mind while Ted was still conscious and listening, but with a wound like this the blood circulation to the leg would be cut. Ted would need vascular surgery and grafting within hours if he wasn't to lose the leg. 'An ambulance?'

'I've got the fire chief to radio Melbourne for the air ambulance,' Reith said grimly. 'They're locating the nearest one now. At most they'll take an hour to get here and an hour back to Melbourne—providing we don't have to wait for more patients.'

Sophie nodded. She stood, casting a nervous glance across at the cottage. There were no lights—nothing. Only someone standing behind closed curtains with a loaded shotgun...

Would it be better just to leave him alone with his shotgun—get all of these people out of here and wait for sanity to return?

It was a decision for the police, and one Sophie didn't envy them. On the one hand, patience could mean less bloodshed. On the other—if they left him be and he stormed out into neighbours' homes...

That was the police constable's job. The policeman was behind his car, closest of all of them to the house, and as Sophie glanced across she saw him raise a megaphone. How to talk to a madman...

'I'll check the child.' She looked down at Reith's long fingers carefully adjusting the tape. Reith couldn't leave yet. With a wound like this and a drip in place at least one of them had to stay in attendance—at least until they were sure the bleeding had stopped for good.

'I wish you would...'

Moira had found the child. As Sophie stood, uncertain of where to go, the brilliant dressing-gown and curlers bobbed out from the trees and signalled Sophie.

'Mandy's over here, Sophie. Mrs Vickers—Ted's wife—has her next door, out of sight of the cottage.'

An excellent idea. Sophie blinked at the coolness of Mrs Vickers—to leave her injured husband in Reith's care and think calmly enough to remove the child from view.

It was important. If the man doing the shooting was the child's father and he emerged from the cottage shooting... Well, it certainly wasn't the place for his four-year-old daughter.

Sophie slipped through the undergrowth at the bottom of the cottage garden, following the redoubtable Moira. It was a clear moonlit night, which was lucky, as Sophie didn't have a torch. As it was, she stumbled through the overgrown garden.

Not Moira, though. The corsetless Moira was in her element. She reached the fence between the two houses, hitched up her dressing-gown, hoisted her legs over and stood and waited for Sophie.

'Do you want a hand?' she asked Sophie kindly and Sophie shook her head.

'I can manage,' she said faintly. It was a three-foot fence and Moira had scaled it with the agility of a ten-year-old.

The child Sophie was looking for was on the neighbours' veranda, cradled in the arms of a gaunt woman in her late thirties. Both woman and child were in nightclothes, and there was blood over both nightgowns.

'Sophie, this is Mary Vickers, Ted's wife,' Moira said briefly as she and Sophie walked up the front steps to the lighted front veranda. Sophie nodded in greeting. The woman's face was set hard, in an expressionless glaze of fear. She was hugging the child to her as if desperate for contact. 'And Mandy.'

Triage... Sophie glanced at the bloom of blood on the child's shoulder. The nightgown had been torn away to reveal a flesh wound, bleeding sluggishly but almost stopped. By the look of it, the shotgun pellets had merely grazed the flesh. Mary Vickers, though… She looked as though she would topple over at any moment.

Sophie touched the woman's face gently with her fingers and knelt until she was looking straight into the woman's agony-filled eyes.

'Are you hurt?' she asked gently. 'Is any of this blood yours?'

'It's Ted's.' Mary Vickers' voice was a harsh, agonised whisper. 'I held him until…until Dr Kenrick arrived.'

So it was only fear…

'Mary, Ted's going to be OK,' Sophie said firmly. 'Dr Kenrick's stopped the bleeding, and is dressing Ted's leg now. We've called the air ambulance from Melbourne because the shotgun pellets have damaged the artery—he'll have to have an operation tonight to repair it—but Ted's pulse is steady, we've set up a drip to replace the blood he's lost and he definitely will live.'

Ted might end up losing his leg, but this wasn't the time to say that.

Mary Vickers stared at Sophie for a long, long moment. The terror-filled glaze slowly died from her eyes and they focused.

'R-really?'

'I promise.'

The woman burst into tears.

There hadn't been a sound from Mandy. Now Sophie lifted the child away from the weeping woman, leaving the way for Moira to enfold Mary in all-enveloping crimson comfort. The child came unresisting into Sophie's arms, too shocked to resist.

Sophie swiftly checked her and then nodded to Moira. 'I can manage here, Moira.' She'd have to check the wound and make sure there was nothing else wrong, but she could do that by herself. 'Would you take Mary back to her husband?' Mary Vickers needed to see her husband recovering his colour almost as much as Ted Vickers would need Mary, Sophie thought.

Mary Vickers dragged herself to her feet. 'I'd... I'd like that. I wanted to stay...but when Dr Kenrick arrived and took over looking after Ted I knew I had to take Mandy away...I was so frightened someone else would get shot and the little one was there... She's just a baby...'

And no one else would help. Sophie bit her lip. There were two types of people in an emergency—those who did what had to be done, like Moira and Mary Vickers, and those who came to gape and wonder. Take photographs while people died around them...

Sophie gathered the limp child to her. 'Can I take her inside, Mary?'

'Sure—'

Mary's word was cut off short. There was a shout of horror from the next-door garden, lights blazed out, a blast of gunshot, then a short, staccato command boomed through the megaphone.

'Don't be a bloody fool. Stop, man—'

Then suddenly Reith's voice, as though the megaphone had been wrenched from the policeman.

Instead of urgency, Reith's voice held calm—as though there was all the time in the world.

'Trevor, we're not here to harm you. No one's going to hurt you. The only reason we're here is that you've got a gun and everyone's nervous, but we're here to help you. You know me, Trev. I'm the local doctor. I'm not a policeman. There's no need to shoot.

'Mandy's out here, Trevor. Your little girl. She's hurt but she's OK. She needs you, Trevor. She's asking for you. Trevor, put down the gun and come—'

The words were cut off by a savage, explosive blast of gunfire.

Then silence.

Reith...

Mary Vickers was the first to break the horrified silence on the veranda. 'Oh, God… Ted…' The woman gave a sob of despair and took off in a desperate run through the darkened garden.

Moira looked wildly around at Sophie. One curler had come askew and was dangling crazily over her eyes, and as she shoved it back another fell down to roll uselessly away down the veranda steps.

'Will I look after Mandy?' Moira whispered in breathless horror.

The little girl had gone rigid in Sophie's clasp. Sophie felt for her pulse. Shock had taken its toll. She hadn't examined her. She didn't know for sure there was no other wound. She couldn't leave her…

'Go with Mary, Moira,' Sophie said harshly. 'And come back fast.'

'But if he's shot Doc Kenrick… It sounded like—'

'Then yell for dear life and I'll come. Go!'

Reith Kenrick had been behind the megaphone when Trevor had shot. Maybe he was still out of range, but it sounded as if the man had emerged, gun blazing. The obvious target for a shooter was the man behind the megaphone. Reith…

Sophie's heart lurched in sickening dread and the child moved convulsively in her arms, sensing her panic.

Mandy… Concentrate on Mandy…

'Hush,' she told the little girl in her arms, and it was the hardest thing she had ever done, to keep her voice even and free of horror. 'There's nothing wrong. I think your daddy's shooting things with a gun. He shot you by mistake, but I guess he's out shooting rabbits or something else now.' How to say that and make it sound completely normal? Somehow she did. 'Now, Mandy, let's get you inside and warm, and find something to put on your sore arm.'

Reith...

Your priority is this little one, Sophie Lynton, she told herself harshly. Until they come back and tell you otherwise, your priority is Mandy.

CHAPTER SIX

BAD news travels fast. Sophie told herself that over and over in the endless minutes as she carried the child inside and carefully examined and soothed her. There was no more sound of gunshots.

Surely the silence was a good sign? If there was bad news, surely Moira or someone else would burst through the trees and tell her she was needed?

Or they're all dead...

Crazy thought. Concentrate on Mandy. No news is good news...

The arm was the only wound on the child except for one dark bruise on her back. The bruise was recent—inflicted in the last twenty-four hours. Mandy didn't speak—just lay, limp again and lifeless, her tiny eyes reflecting the night's horror.

Sophie found milk in the kitchen. Leaving Mandy huddled in blankets by the stove, her huge eyes watching her as she worked, Sophie carefully warmed it and then found chocolate to sweeten it. It was simple work, but getting fluids into Mandy would alleviate the shock, and administering them to a frightened child via mouth was more comforting, and infinitely preferable if she could manage it, than the strangeness of a drip. There had been little blood loss. It was only fear that was causing the shock.

It was comforting to make the hot chocolate too, normal action blotting out in part fear of what lay outside. Domesticity as a shield to horror. If they needed her they'd be back by now, Sophie thought. If they weren't all dead.

No news is good news...

Sophie knelt by Mandy and held the mug to her lips.

81

To her surprise, the child reached out and grasped it, gulping it down with a thirst that made Sophie's eyes widen.

'M…more,' the child whispered and held out the empty mug.

'Are you hungry, little one?' Sophie asked, filling the pan with more milk.

'Daddy wouldn't let me have tea. Or lunch. He hit me and made me cry. Daddy…' Her voice faded again, fear taking over.

'Mandy, it sounds like your daddy is ill,' Sophie said gently. 'Sometimes, when people are ill, they do things that they don't want to do. If your daddy's head was hurting, maybe he wouldn't even know he was hurting you.'

'My daddy has to take pills,' Mandy said seriously. 'Every day.'

'Has he been taking his pills lately?'

The child's fearful eyes focused on Sophie. 'I don't…I don't think so.'

'Then I think that's what's wrong,' Sophie told her. 'I'm a doctor, Sophie, and I think what's wrong with your dad is a sickness, just like a horrid, sniffly cold. When your Daddy's not taking his pills then his head doesn't work properly. I think when he hit you and shot at you—maybe he really did think you were a rabbit and not his beloved little Mandy.'

'I think so too,' Mandy whispered in a tiny voice. 'He wouldn't shoot me.'

'Of course he wouldn't.'

Two more huge mugs of chocolate and the edge of fear faded from the child's eyes. The warmth from the stove and blankets was creeping through her body. Her eyelids drooped over the horror. She jerked herself into wakefulness once, twice, and then it was too much.

She slept.

When she was sure Mandy's sleep was deep and not

likely to end, Sophie finally let herself walk out onto the veranda. The place was as quiet as death. Nothing moved.

Maybe he'd shot everyone, she thought. Maybe even now he was down there in the undergrowth…

Nightmare scenario. Impossible. There hadn't been enough gunshots. There had been no gunshots since Mary and Moira had left.

So why didn't someone come?

The urge to leave the sleeping child was almost overwhelming but Sophie refused to give in to it. If Mandy's father had shot her and Mandy's father was indeed out there…

There was no sound. The wind had come up and was blowing enough to disguise the sound of cars and normal voices in next door's garden. Someone must come soon and tell her what was going on. She was going mad.

Then, above her head, she heard the distant noise of a helicopter, growing louder. Once again floodlights flashed out from next door, this time aimed into the sky and then down, as if to show a clearing. Sophie took a sobbing breath of thankfulness. At least someone else was alive in the nightmare.

It was a massive helicopter, sent by the army, by the look of the painted insignia showing in the floodlight. Reith has the army he needs, Sophie told herself firmly and crossed everything she possessed in the hope that he was able to appreciate it.

Still no one came. The helicopter hovered, obviously waiting for the locals to light flares and signal a safe place to land. It finally descended on the other side of the neighbouring house.

There was silence again for five minutes. Five minutes stretched to ten, and Sophie's nerves were stretched to breaking. Then, with a reverberating clamour, the machine roared into life and rose high into the night sky. It moved fast, disappearing into the distance until its light was just another star in the night sky.

And still Sophie stood, staring out into the mind-numbing darkness. She was going mad... Casualty in London was never like this. How much longer could she hold her breath?

And finally he came, not Mary or Moira, but Reith himself, striding swiftly up through the garden as though it weren't night and the garden weren't overgrown. For a moment Sophie wasn't sure—but her eyes had adjusted to the darkness and as he appeared in the moonlight she'd have known his lean, athletic figure anywhere.

Sophie gave a sob of pure relief and then her hands gripped the balustrade of the steps hard. Her knees were water. Reith was alive, and for some crazy, crazy reason that was all that mattered. Reith...

Reith stopped at the base of the steps. He stood, looking up at her, and in his eyes she saw the same horror she had seen in Mary's, and Mandy's—and maybe it was even reflected in her own eyes. Sophie clutched the balustrade for all she was worth and made herself speak

'What...what's happened?'

'He's dead.' Reith's voice was flat and emotionless— the voice of a surgeon who had just lost a patient after long hours of heartbreaking surgery, or a doctor who had just lost a child after months of cancer. The voice of a doctor who cared so much that it was eating into his soul.

'He...he killed himself?'

'No.' Reith shook his head, indescribably weary. 'He came out shooting, walking straight for us, shooting all the time. The police constable killed him. He had no choice.'

His words were flat, emotionless fact. Only the horror in his eyes gave him away.

Silence. The horror grew and grew, and Reith's face stayed rigid with self-control.

And suddenly Sophie could bear it no longer. She

walked slowly down the steps, twisted her hands around his neck and pulled Reith Kenrick's head down to her breast.

For one long minute Reith stayed rigid, the self-control fighting, fighting for supremacy. Then she felt his rigid body give a long, long shudder of release, and Reith pulled her into him as though he were a man drowning.

It must have been ten long minutes before they surfaced. They stayed together for what seemed eternity. Neither wished to break the moment. Closeness was all that mattered.

Reith was safe. He was alive and Sophie knew she hadn't realised how much she cared until that moment. Until now. Until he was less than a heartbeat away and his heart was beating in tandem with hers with a strength that made her own heart dissolve in gratitude and...

And love. Love...

What was she thinking? How could she love a man she had known for less than a week?

She could hardly form the thought. There was only the moment. There was only now—and the wonder of the warmth flooding through her body.

There was wonder in the way he was holding her. There was wonder in the feeling surging around her heart. It was a feeling she had never known before—a feeling she hadn't known existed.

It was a feeling that she had found her home...her heart...that this heart beating so strongly against hers was part and parcel of hers—that to separate his heart from hers would require something sharper than a scalpel.

'Sophie...' Reith's lips were in her hair, and his hands held her close, seeking comfort from the horror. There was nothing more than that need in his hold, Sophie told herself harshly. Nothing more.

Finally, unwillingly, Reith drew away, holding Sophie

at arm's length and looking down into her face with concern.

'I dragged you into a nightmare.'

'The nightmare was yours,' she said gently. 'I wish… I wish I could have done more. If you knew how helpless I felt—being here…'

'You helped save Ted's life. It was touch and go when you came. If I hadn't had your help…'

His voice dragged to an exhausted halt. Reith put a hand to his face as though wiping away thoughts that were too dreadful to face. Sophie had to physically hold herself back from reaching out to hold him once again. His need was almost a tangible thing, and her need matched his.

'Mandy,' he said at last. 'What's the damage?'

'She's asleep,' Sophie said gently. 'The pellets just grazed her shoulder and there's no other significant injury. She's been lucky.'

Reith shook his head. 'She's been abysmally unlucky. To lose her dad…' Once more that hand moved to his face in a gesture of exhaustion. 'I should have stepped in earlier.'

'You knew there was trouble?'

'Trevor's been under psychiatric care for years but refuses to take medication. His wife walked out when Mandy was a baby—who could blame her? But I do blame her for not taking Mandy. There was an incident in the city that made Social Welfare move in and threaten to take Mandy into foster care, and when things settled down Trevor moved here. The authorities contacted me and asked me to keep an eye on things. I tried… God knows, I tried. He seemed stable—only just but not unbalanced enough to justify removing Mandy. And he certainly loved her…'

His face closed in pain and Sophie nodded in slow comprehension. Every doctor's nightmare—deciding when to suggest the risk was great enough to remove a child from a parent.

'I didn't think he'd hurt Mandy,' Reith said. 'He had a shock when they threatened to take Mandy away in the city and I'm sure he hasn't touched her. Heaven knows, I've watched the child, dropping in on the slightest pretext.'

'There's bruising on her back,' Sophie told him. 'Only the one bruise, though.'

'I wonder whether that was what finally drove him over the edge,' Reith said flatly. 'If he struck Mandy then he would have horrified himself. He was terrified of Social Welfare. He wasn't going to let them have Mandy—no matter what—and if they knew he'd struck Mandy… Well, maybe his mad brain thought she might as well be dead.'

'Poor little mite.' Sophie was watching Reith's face, seeing the pain for other people's agony etched deep. It was a lie that this man wasn't involved with people. She sighed, aware suddenly of an almost overwhelming weariness. 'What happens now?'

'We lock up here and take Mandy home.'

'Home?' Sophie flashed Reith a startled look. There was no going home for Mandy.

'To your home,' Reith said. 'Or, rather, the guest house.' He shrugged. 'I forgot—you won't know what's happened, how we've tied the ends up for the night. It seems the army reserve is running field exercises thirty miles from here. When all hell broke loose the police sent for back-up. They sent their field ambulance—the helicopter. It's taken Ted and his wife off to Melbourne. The police are still busy in the cottage, but I've certified Trevor dead and my job's over. Now…now I've talked Moira into having Mandy for a while—not that it took much persuasion.'

'Wouldn't Mandy be best being sent to Melbourne? Are there any relations?'

'None, as far as I know. Social Welfare have been trying to contact her mother for years with no success.' Reith sighed and ran his hand through his hair. 'But I've an idea about her long-term care.' He shrugged. 'It may come to nothing but if she's shuttled off to foster care in Melbourne then she's lost another chance.'

'You do care about her, don't you?'

'She's a nice little kid. If they can't find her mother, and I don't see how they can succeed now, then she's faced with not being able to be adopted. Even at four she looked after her dad when he was moody and irrational. She deserves parents.' He shook his head. 'Let's lock up here and get her back to Moira's. She's gone ahead to have a bed ready—took a few of Mandy's toys and things.'

Who thought of that? Sophie thought, startled, and knew instinctively that it was this man. Reith Kenrick was starting to have depths she hadn't known. Depths she hadn't known in any man...

Moira was waiting for them on the guest-house veranda, still resplendent in crimson. Her curlers, Sophie was pleased to see, had been taken out. With the bouncing they'd received tonight Sophie had thought they'd be so twisted they'd have to be cut out.

'Bring her upstairs,' Moira told Reith as he lifted the sleeping little girl from the car. She cast a quick, concerned glance at Sophie. 'I've put her next to you, Sophie. There's an adjoining room.' She blinked. 'I'd put her in with me but I sleep like the dead—if she wakes I mightn't hear.'

'That's fine by me,' Sophie told her. 'I'll wake if she does.'

'Well, I'm not charging you for tonight's accommodation,' Moira said roundly. 'Not if you're acting nursemaid.'

'I don't mind,' Sophie told her, following Reith into the house. She shrugged and a small smile washed across her face. 'Dr Kenrick told me my bill for his services would be large. It seems he wasn't exaggerating.'

To her surprise Reith turned and flashed her a smile. The smile lit his face, glinting deep within his eyes, and the smile made Sophie gasp. It was a caress in itself. It took away some of the horror of the past few hours and lit her within.

Reith Kenrick... Something inside Sophie was growing with the speed of a bushfire. Something she didn't have any control over.

It frightened the life out of her.

She looked away from him but Reith must have seen the flickering look of fear. He slowed his steps, waiting for her to come up to him.

'What's wrong, Sophie?'

'N-nothng,' she whispered. 'It's just...it's just been a long day.'

'You've had longer days than this in Casualty. Unless the English medical system treats its juniors kinder than the Australian one does.'

'I know,' Sophie agreed. 'I'm just out of practice.'

It wasn't true. She could stay up all night and still operate near to capacity the next day—it was something most doctors learned to do very early in their careers.

What she couldn't do was cope with the emotional rollercoaster she was on now. It was something she had never had to deal with, and wasn't sure she wanted to know how.

They tucked Sophie into bed, opened the door to Sophie's room and then Moira tiptoed off to her own bed.

'I don't know about you two young things,' she told them, 'but I'm exhausted. I don't know how I'll sleep after the...after the goings-on tonight, but I'll sure give it a try.'

Sophie and Reith stood looking after her. The traces of a smile were still playing around Reith's mouth.

'Redoubtable lady,' he said softly and Sophie smiled in agreement.

It was crazily intimate to stand in this darkened bedroom with Reith beside her. There was a bedlight in the corner playing a soft glow over the sleeping child, but that was all.

'She is that.' She looked down at the sleeping Mandy. 'Reith, if you're thinking Moira can look after Mandy long-term—'

'I'm not,' he told her, seeing the doubt on her face. 'Moira Sanderson is some lady, but taking on a four-year-old at sixty is no mean task. It's Ted and Mary Vickers I'm thinking of.'

The Vickerses... Sophie thought back to the haggard lady she had seen that night and her wounded husband, and a small crease played around her eyes. 'Do you have any reason for suggesting them?'

'I have about ten.'

'But you're keeping them to yourself.'

Reith grinned. 'I guess I'm not used to sharing my professional thoughts with a colleague.' He shrugged. 'A novelty.' He touched her face with his finger and could hardly have known the effect his touch had on her. It was all Sophie could do to conceal the tremor that ran from head to toe.

'So...so tell me.'

'Simple, really,' he said. 'Mary and Ted have been trying to have children for years. They're stable, happy, not very well off—but that's no bar to being great parents—and they love kids. They've both loved having Mandy living next door. Sadly, Mary's infertile. They're not suitable for IV techniques, and they've been categorised as too old to adopt. I don't know what the waiting list for adoption's like in your country but here it's impossible.'

'And you think they'll want Mandy.'

'Lots of adoptive parents would want Mandy,' Reith said. 'She's a great little kid, maybe scarred by what happened tonight but young enough to heal with love. Ted and Mary, though—well, Mandy's been in and out of Mary's kitchen since they moved here. The number of times Mary's been in my clinic worrying about what was happening to Mandy... One of the reasons I let Mandy stay with her father was that I knew Mary was next door keeping an eye on things.'

'And you think they might want her long-term?'

'The problem won't be Mary and Ted, but Social Welfare,' Reith said. 'Ted and Mary aren't blood relatives, and there's no reason for them to get favourable treatment—unless I can prove fast that there's a strong emotional bond already. If Ted's surgery goes well Mary will be back here in a couple of days. They run a small farmlet and there are animals to look after. By the time I contact Social Welfare about Mandy, I want Mandy to be ensconced in Mary's kitchen, in an environment where she already feels secure and loved and where her dad's going to be talked about with love and sympathy. I don't think we could do any better than that for Mandy, do you?'

'N—no,' Sophie said wonderingly and looked up at Reith in amazement. 'Did you think all that up before the helicopter took Ted and Mary away? Before you made a decision not to send Mandy?'

'Pretty much.' Reith smiled. 'Even when she was scared out of her wits about Ted, Mary had the time to be anxious about Mandy's fate. I was going to suggest Mandy go in the helicopter too and then realised that Social Welfare would have to collect her as soon as she arrived in Melbourne, and things sort of fell into place.'

'You're quite some doctor, Reith Kenrick,' Sophie said softly. 'You know that?'

'Mutual-admiration society,' Reith told her, his hands reaching out to take hers in the night. 'Thank you for helping tonight, Sophie. It made a difference.'

A difference? To what? To the outcome for Ted Vickers? Or to Sophie's future?

The night was warm around them. The horrors of the night faded to nothing. Beside them Mandy slept on, losing in slumber the emptiness waiting for her in the morning.

Not complete emptiness, Sophie thought. Because of this man. This man who cared…

Her heart twisted inside her. She reached up and touched Reith lightly on the lips with hers.

'I think you're wonderful,' she whispered. She couldn't help herself. The words came from within of their own accord and Sophie could no more prevent them than fly.

There was a long, long silence. The world, it seemed, held its breath and Sophie's was held with it. She so wanted a response from this man, and finally she achieved it. With a sigh that was almost a groan he pulled her into his arms and kissed her as she wanted, as she ached to be kissed.

The sweetness was indescribable. There was passion behind the kiss, but it was first and foremost a kiss of affirmation—affirmation of a bond that was growing stronger by the moment. Could he feel it? Sophie wondered. Did Reith Kenrick's heart reach out to touch hers as hers melted toward him?

She put her arms around him, feeling the muscles of his broad back through the thick cotton of his shirt and revelling in the feel. She smelt the masculine smell of him and gloried in it. She wanted him so much. She wanted him closer to her than she had ever wanted a man in her life before…

'Sophie…' He broke off to breathe her name and then deepened his kiss. Like hers, his hands were exploring the contours of her back, running down over her slim hips, holding her hard against him. His lips devoured her and she sank closer, closer…

His fingers came around to unfasten the buttons of her blouse, lifting to cup the swelling mounds of her breasts. She'd dressed in a rush and hadn't bothered with the confines of a bra, and his fingers revelled in the freedom of her breasts, fingering each nipple in turn until she gasped with pure pleasure. Her body writhed against him, declaring its need with a sureness that she couldn't regret.

What was she? Some sort of wanton hussy, making love to this man with a passion that matched his? She didn't care. She couldn't. All she knew was that she wanted this man as she had never wanted anything in her life before and she was fighting with everything she possessed.

He pushed her away then, holding her at arm's length and looking down at her with the twisted, enigmatic smile that made Sophie melt inside. She tried to return the smile, but her look was all love—heaven knew if she was smiling as well. Her eyes were two flames of dark desire that matched his own.

'Can I take you to bed, my Sophie?' he murmured, his fingers coming up to brush lightly through her curls. 'Will you let me love you?'

Love… Was that what he was offering?

'I'm starting to think…' Sophie's voice was the thread of a whisper, hoarse with desire. 'I'm starting to think, Reith Kenrick, that I want you as much as you seem to want me.'

The smile twisted further. 'Regardless of the absent Kevin?'

Kevin…

Sophie licked suddenly dry lips, a wave of doubt sweeping over her at the lightness of his asking. What was Reith saying? That she was being unfaithful but he didn't mind? That he would love her tonight and then hand her back to Kevin on Friday as used property?

'I guess…I guess…' she whispered through lips that would hardly move. 'I guess I have to let Kevin know I've made a mistake.'

There was a long, long silence. The twisted smile slowly disappeared and Reith's eyes became expressionless.

'Sophie, I'm not offering you marriage,' he said slowly. 'I want, badly, to make love to you, but I'm offering you no long-term commitment. Not now. Not ever. I don't want you breaking off an engagement because of me.'

'Then what are you suggesting?' A wave of cold washed through Sophie so thoroughly that she felt herself tremble. 'That I make love to you and then go off and marry Kevin, regardless?'

'What you do long-term is no concern of mine.'

There had never been crueller words. A vice was closing on Sophie's heart.

'You…you think I'd do that?' she whispered. 'Make love to you and then marry Kevin as though nothing had changed?'

'Nothing has changed, Sophie. Just because we want each other now—it means nothing. Tomorrow there'll be nothing.'

'Is that what you believe?'

'It's the truth.'

Sophie closed her eyes. She took a step back, trying to move away—and feeling the pain of the scalpel. This man was so scarred by his past… She could never reach him. How on earth had she thought she could ever try?

'I think you'd better leave,' she whispered and the words were a physical agony.

'Because I won't promise marriage?'

Sophie shook her head. 'I don't want marriage, Reith Kenrick. Believe it or not, I want you. And if you think that tomorrow there'll be nothing then…then you're right. In the morning…in the morning I'd have known I'd done the wrong thing. So…so I'm engaged to another man, Reith Kenrick; you've reminded me of that just in time. So will you please leave? Now.'

'You mean that?'

'Yes.'

He nodded. 'Maybe it's best at that,' he said simply,

and only his eyes showed regret. He shook his head, as though ridding himself of a feeling he didn't understand. 'God knows, Sophie, I don't want to hurt you.'

'Just go.'

CHAPTER SEVEN

IT WAS a dreadful night. Somewhere toward dawn Sophie drifted into troubled slumber but woke feeling as if she'd had no sleep at all.

Through the open door Sophie could see Mandy stirring. She rose swiftly, gathering Mandy close and taking her back to her big bed as confusion and doubt flooded into the little face. The child looked up with eyes troubled by what seemed a bad dream.

'I want my daddy,' she said in a trembling voice. 'Or my Margy and Ted…'

It took time to settle the child, to talk through what had happened in the night, to achieve a measure of calm and finally to bring a tremulous smile to those pale cheeks. By the time she succeeded, Sophie was starting to think Reith was right: Mary and Ted Vickers were obviously more than neighbours to this child.

'May it work,' she whispered to herself as she nestled down in bed with the child curled in the crook of her arm. 'May Ted and Mary want her. May her future be secure…'

And what of Sophie's future? Her plans with Kevin were in turmoil and as far as she knew Kevin was on the plane right now, winging his way to Australia to marry his devoted bride.

'But I'm not Kevin's bride,' she whispered to herself, another image flitting through her mind—the painting in Reith's living-room-cum-studio… Bush bride… That was what she wanted to be.

I could do better than Reith's mother, she told herself. If only…

If only Reith would give her the chance. If only Reith would let down the barriers and expose himself to love.

What chance was there? One in a billion, she told herself bleakly, and then looked up as a beaming Moira came into the room bearing a loaded breakfast tray.

'So you're awake, you pair of sleepyheads. It's about time—another hour and I'd have brought you lunch.'

To her delight, Sophie heard Mandy give a soft chuckle. The resilience of children never ceased to amaze, she thought.

They sat up in bed, Moira ensconced in the armchair beside them, to demolish fried eggs and bacon, toast lavishly spread with bluegum honey, fresh squeezed orange juice, hot chocolate and brewed coffee.

'You two match,' Moira announced to the pair of them, looking at Sophie's and Mandy's bare bandaged arms.

'We've been in the wars,' Sophie agreed.

'What happened to you?' Mandy asked shyly.

'I tried to lift a koala.'

Mandy shook her head in disgust, her opinion of this pretty lady doctor obviously taking a dive. 'You dingaling!'

They all laughed, and Sophie gave her a hard hug. The child would be OK.

It was confirmed a moment later.

'Mary Vickers has been on the phone,' Moira told them.

'My Mary?' Mandy looked up with interest.

'Your Mary,' Moira agreed. 'She rang to say Ted was operated on last night and the surgeons are confident they've saved his leg. She rang, though, because she was worried about you, Miss Mandy. She said she thinks it's best for you to stay here with me until she gets back to Inyabarra, and then she'll take you home. That's fine with me if it's OK with you.'

'That's OK.' Mandy swung her small toes out of bed.

'I'm going to get dressed now, Mrs Sanderson. Then can I go and talk to your cat?'

Moira chuckled ruefully as the child walked out of the door. 'She knows this place—but heaven, Sophie, I thought she'd be a lot more upset than this.'

'She's not really facing it yet,' Sophie told her. 'She asked once whether her father was dead but was hardly interested in my reply. Small children are good at facing only what they're strong enough to cope with. It'll be up to Mary and Ted to gradually teach her to live with what's happened.' Sophie frowned. 'Not that the next few days— week, really—won't be hard. She won't be able to block everything out, and I'd guess there'll be a few dreadful times before she comes to terms with it. If she's uncertain or lonely or insecure…'

'I'll have her stick by me,' Moira promised. 'Only…' Her face clouded. 'I'll worry about her in the night after you leave.'

'What if I stay until Mary returns?' Sophie suggested.

'Won't your Kevin have something to say about that?'

Kevin…

Kevin was becoming not her security but an obstacle in her life. Was Kevin on the plane even as they spoke? What on earth was Sophie to do about Kevin?

'We agreed to stay here a week together,' Sophie said doubtfully. 'Just because Kevin's late doesn't mean we should change that, so we'll stay a week from the time he arrives.'

Only she didn't want him to arrive. She wanted Reith…

'So what will we do with our Mandy today?' she thought out loud, pushing both men firmly out of her head.

'I'm preserving apricots and she can help.'

It sounded good to Sophie. A way to occupy the mind— to keep it from Reith. 'Sure.'

The telephone interrupted them. Moira departed to answer it.

'For you,' she called, and then destroyed Sophie's calm by calling out, 'It's Dr Kenrick.'

It was hard for Sophie to keep her voice calm as she picked up the telephone and greeted the man on the other end. Reith Kenrick, on the other hand, was having no such trouble. He sounded as if there was nothing between them at all. Tomorrow there would be nothing. Not ever. Cool, calm and professional.

'Is Mandy OK?' he asked.

'She's fine. Mary Vickers rang from Melbourne...'

'She rang me too. Sophie, I phoned to remind you about lunch.'

'Lunch?' A flare of absurd hope flickered in Sophie's heart, only to die with Reith's next words.

'With Mrs Lee. Remember, she invited you for lunch? I think it's important you still go.'

'You're going to get maximum use out of me while I'm here,' Sophie snapped, anger flaring. That he could kiss her as he had and then calmly talk as if there was nothing between them...'What a waste that I won't go to bed with you as well.'

Sophie bit her tongue on the words. What a dreadful thing to say. What a dreadful thing to think!

'I'll ring her and tell her you're not coming, shall I?' Reith demanded and his voice was cold as he ignored what she had just said. Emotional outbursts, it seemed, were not Reith Kenrick's forte.

'I'll go.' She could match him for coldness. 'I said I would.'

'If you feel under an obligation there's no need—'

'It's got nothing to do with your need, Reith Kenrick,' Sophie snapped. 'I accepted an invitation from Margaret Lee and I intend to keep it. Who knows, if she'd got it in for you I might just find myself wholeheartedly agreeing with her sentiments?'

That was stupid. Sophie replaced the receiver with trembling fingers. The man was properly under her skin, forcing her to behave in a way she abhorred. Somehow she had to fight for some of Reith's detached calm.

Lunch! The last thing she wanted was a polite lunch with someone she hardly knew, but she'd promised.

'I have to try to ring Kevin before I go,' she told Moira, explaining that the apricots would have to be bottled without her.

'Won't your Kevin already be on his aeroplane?'

'I hope not.' Ignoring Moira's raised eyebrows, Sophie crossed to the hall and lifted the phone again. Ten in the morning equalled about one a.m. in Belgium, she thought. If Kevin wasn't on the aeroplane then maybe she'd wake him up. The thought gave her a quite unfair sense of satisfaction.

She didn't wake him. The doubts surrounding Sophie's heart were cementing into solid certainty as Kevin's hotel answered and she asked for him. If he wasn't already on the plane...

'Mr Carson booked out quite some time ago,' the hotel receptionist told her. 'We believe he's flying to Australia...'

Mrs Lee was delighted to see Sophie. As well as someone Dr Kenrick didn't like and a fellow Englishwoman, Sophie had been present at the shooting the night before and knew everything that had happened. Sophie couldn't have been made more welcome.

As Reith had promised, Margaret Lee had roast dinner waiting—a standing rib roast beef with all the trimmings and apple pie to follow. After Moira's vast breakfast Sophie had trouble finishing, but struggled gamely. At the other end of the table Margaret Lee watched her in satisfaction, though she ate very little herself.

Conscious of the role Reith had assigned her, Sophie swung the conversation firmly in the right direction. She might be angry with Reith Kenrick but if she was here and there really was something wrong then she could hardly do less than try.

'You served up a tiny amount to yourself, compared to what you've given me,' she pointed out. 'Margaret, I hope you're not going without to feed me.'

'Oh, I never eat very much,' the lady told her.

Sophie raised her eyebrows. 'You're trying to diet?'

Margaret gave a harsh laugh. 'I don't have to diet. I've lost so much weight… More apple pie, dear?'

Sophie smiled and shook her head. One more mouthful and she'd burst. 'Why have you lost weight?' she asked curiously.

'God knows.'

'Have you seen a doctor?'

The woman took a deep breath, as though fighting an inner fight—and losing.

'And have them muddling up my insides?' she said, and her voice held a quaver of fear. 'No way. If I'm dying then I intend going out my own way, without a lot of chemotherapy and radiotherapy to make me sick in the process.'

There was a long, long silence. Margaret Lee stared across the table at Sophie in horror, hearing what she'd voiced, maybe for the first time. A fear, Sophie guessed, she'd kept hidden from everyone. With a stranger, though, she'd finally let down her guard.

'You think you have cancer?' Sophie asked gently, and Margaret burst into tears.

'Oh, I shouldn't have said it. I haven't told anyone— not even my son. I've just bottled it up for so long—and I'll keep it quiet in the future for as long as I can. You won't tell anyone, will you, dear? I'm determined not to let doctors near me. I want to die with dignity.'

Sophie paused, searching for the right words. This was a fear she had seen often. The fear of dying without dignity was often a greater fear than the fear of the disease itself.

'Why do you think you have cancer?' she asked. 'If it hasn't been diagnosed…'

'You don't lose weight like this without there being something major wrong.' Margaret shook her head. 'The weight just seemed to drop off, even when I was eating. Now, though, it's such an effort to eat, even when I can be bothered to go shopping. I'm tired all the time—so tired. If I manage to get out to the shops then I come home and sleep. This morning I didn't get out of bed until eleven and I'm tired now.'

'That could be caused by your weight loss,' Sophie told her.

'No.' Margaret took a long drink from the glass of water before her and filled her glass again from the jug. 'I was sleepy even before I lost the weight. It's not the weight loss that caused the tiredness—it's the other way around. I can't lose much more weight without something happening—it's as if my body's being eaten away from the inside.'

'What sort of cancer do you think you have?' Sophie asked bluntly, knowing the woman would have thought it through. 'Do you have any pain?'

'Liver cancer.'

'You're very sure.'

Margaret shrugged. 'It's the only one that makes sense. I don't have any pain or discomfort and yet I'm definitely sick. It's as if it's growing down there, squeezing my bladder. I have to go to the toilet so often and I'm so thirsty…' She gave a frightened gasp and retreated to drink more water. 'This isn't…it isn't a conversation for the dinner-table.'

'I've finished my dinner,' Sophie smiled. She reached for the water jug and looked at it thoughtfully. It had been full at the start of lunch and the large jug was now close to empty. Sophie had had one small glass. She refilled her glass and emptied the jug.

'There's no growth or anything, is there, Margaret?' she asked cautiously. 'Nothing you can feel?'

'No. There's not with liver cancer. It just eats away at you, and there's nothing you can do. I've read all about it—and I'm not having chemotherapy. It makes you so sick. I want to die with my hair on.'

Sophie smiled. 'So do I,' she agreed. 'Though they make some great wigs these days. I've always fancied myself with a carrot-red beehive hairstyle.' She hesitated again, unsure how to proceed. She could take her findings back to Reith, but Margaret had asked her not to tell anyone. So…so she'd plug on alone. A couple more minutes of non-professional interest might pay dividends.

'Do you think you're getting worse quickly?' she asked. 'Are you sleeping more?'

'More and more.' Margaret rose to clear the table. 'I don't know how much longer I can live by myself,' she said sadly. 'I frighten myself even now.'

'Why?' Sophie stood up and started helping.

'Well…' The woman was still clearly reluctant to voice her fears, but to an overseas tourist she hardly knew and wasn't likely to see again it seemed safe enough. 'Well, take yesterday. I had lunch with Jenny and the baby and then I drove home. I'd just pulled into the garage when I felt all dizzy, weird. The next thing I knew it was dark and I was still sitting in the garage—four hours later.' She gave a frightened gasp. 'It was so quick. I'm not game… well, now I'm not game to get in the car again.'

Sophie put the plates she was carrying down on the sink and turned to Margaret. What now?

The easiest course would be to tell Reith or Jenny what she knew but then she'd betray Margaret's confidence—and she was ninety per cent sure Margaret was dangerously ill with something that could be controlled.

'That's why you're afraid of Reith Kenrick?' she said

softly. 'You think he'll notice and insist on chemother-apy?'

'It's not that so much,' Margaret admitted. 'He's always been a fine doctor—and I know he'd do his best by me. It's just…'

'Just what?'

'Just that all these doctors, they think they're so darned clever and can cure everything, and yet when you really need them—when you have something really awful wrong with you like liver cancer—they can't do anything. I can't see a doctor now without seeing red. I know it's unfair, but it's just—why can't they cure it, Sophie?' She let the plate she was holding drop into the sink and burst into tears.

Sophie let her have her cry out. At a guess, Margaret Lee didn't give in to tears too often. She stood and waited, and finally Margaret gave a watery sniff and turned to her with the trace of a smile. A brave lady, Sophie thought.

'I'm sorry. What a dreadful lunch—'

'It was a lovely lunch.' Sophie took Margaret's hands in hers and propelled her into a chair. 'And I'm glad you've talked honestly about you, because I'm going to talk honestly about me. I'm here under false pretences.'

'False…?'

'I'm one of your hated doctors, Margaret. You're quite right when you say Reith Kenrick's a fine doctor. He cares about this community in a way I've seen no other doctor care. He's noted your weight loss and your fear of him, and he cares about you. He asked me to find out if there was something worrying you—something maybe we could do something about.'

Margaret was looking at Sophie in horror. 'Then you'll tell him…'

'No. I won't. You invited me here as a friend and if you don't want me to talk to Dr Kenrick about you then I'll respect that. But I'm going to tell you what I think. I can't be sure without doing blood-sugar tests, but I'm willing to bet my air ticket back to England that what you're suffering from is not liver cancer but diabetes. Every symptom you've described is the symptom of acute, uncontrolled diabetes mellitus. You have frequency of urine output; you seem constantly thirsty; you drift into coma and you're losing weight. Losing weight is the only symptom you have which is consistent with liver cancer, and if it was liver failure that was causing this amount of weight loss then you'd also be jaundiced. There's not a trace of yellowing about your skin.' She smiled. 'And I've been watching really, really hard.'

'But you're a doctor.'

It was a flat accusation and Sophie sighed. Had Margaret heard anything else she'd said?

'Yes.'

The silence stretched on. The big clock in the kitchen ticked with relentless rhythm while Sophie held her breath and waited.

'Diabetes, you say?'

Sophie's breath was exhaled. 'Yes.'

'But you can't be sure?'

'No. I can't be sure. But you can't be sure of liver cancer either, and I know if I was choosing between illnesses which one I'd opt for. Mature onset diabetes is usually easy to treat, often by diet alone. Once you're on treatment, your symptoms may well totally disappear, giving you a long and healthy future.'

'Diabetes...' Margaret was turning the suggestion over and over in her mind. 'You mean I won't be able to eat chocolate?'

Sophie grinned. 'Well, your chocolate-eating will be restricted, that's for sure. But with liver cancer there's not a lot of chocolate-eating in front of you either. I'd go for diabetes if I were you.'

Margaret sniffed, reached for her handkerchief and blew her nose. 'I've been... I've been stupid.'

'You've been frightened.'

She nodded. 'I guess...I guess I need to find out for sure... That I haven't got cancer, I mean.'

'It'd be wise,' Sophie told her. 'In fact it would be sensible to do it straight away. If, as I suspect, you're falling into diabetic coma then you might injure yourself badly by losing consciousness at a worrying time. You really can't trust your body while your blood-sugar levels aren't monitored.'

'OK.' Mrs Lee took a deep breath. 'I'll need to make an appointment with Dr Kenrick, then.'

'I can take you to the surgery this afternoon if you like,' Sophie suggested. She wasn't going to push, but if Margaret was falling into coma then she really wasn't safe to leave alone. 'How about we wash these dishes and then I'll drive you down?' She didn't want the lady behind the wheel of a car until this was sorted out either.

'But he might be busy—'

'Then I'll test your sugar myself. But I think Reith Kenrick will be very pleased to see us.'

Pleased to see *you*, she should have said. After last night...

It won't make any difference to Reith at all, she told herself sadly. I don't affect Reith Kenrick the way he affects me. I bet he'll be courteous and scrupulously polite and he'll thank me very nicely for my help.

Toad!

Reith was courteous, scrupulously polite and thanked Sophie very nicely for her help. He was also so good with Margaret that Sophie felt her heart somersaulting all over again.

His afternoon clinic was just beginning as Sophie took Margaret in. Reith met Margaret with a smile of real friendliness and put aside her embarrassment as of no importance. He listened to Sophie's brief explanation, saw the fear in Margaret's eyes and apologised to the patients he had waiting. Margaret's fear was nerve-snapping.

Without wasting time on reassurance, Reith pricked Margaret's finger and checked the blood sample in the glucometer immediately. The glucometer showed sugar levels of three times the normal levels and Margaret burst into tears of relief.

'I'm so stupid,' she said over and over again.

'You're not stupid,' Reith told her. 'There's nothing more worrying than your body doing things you don't understand.'

'I guess...' Margaret Lee looked nervously out at the patients waiting in the reception area '...I guess now I know I can just make an appointment for some convenient time to find out what I should do...'

'No.' Reith shook his head and raised his eyebrows at Sophie. 'I'm sure Dr Lynton agrees with me on this, Margaret. Diabetes is straightforward enough to control, but with blood sugars as high as yours you're likely to drift into coma at any time. There's no guarantee you won't lose consciousness while you're holding a boiling kettle or in the shower or in the time between turning on the gas and setting the flame. What I want is to admit you to hospital—now if possible. If you agree I'll get the ambulance to take you across to Lamberton and have the physician there do a thorough assessment. They'll try you on medication and adjust it until they have it right.'

'But...now?'

'Tell me,' Reith said gently, 'are you really confident of being by yourself at home until we have this thing controlled?'

'N-no. I guess I've been scared—'

'Well, then...'

'But I don't want to go in an ambulance,' Margaret declared. 'I'd feel a fraud. And my son's taking a school excursion to Melbourne today and Jenny's still worried about the baby…'

'I could drive you,' Sophie told her, her eyes carefully averted from Reith. She was doing anything but look at Reith. She couldn't look at the man and keep her voice steady, and the tremor in her voice was infuriating. She felt about ten years old.

'You could do that, Dr Lynton,' Reith said gravely. He was watching her, she knew, but she wouldn't meet his eyes. 'If you were to drive Margaret to Lamberton, you could solve a problem for me.'

'A problem?' She was staring at her toes.

'I sent an urgent call for help to Lamberton last night. They had a road smash on their hands and could send only an ambulance car with one officer. When the helicopter arrived it had a doctor on board but no paramedic, so the ambulance officer went in the helicopter to assist. The ambulance is therefore still here.'

'So you want me to drive it back to Lamberton?'

'It'd save someone a job—and with one of their officers still in Melbourne Lamberton are short-staffed.'

'How would I get back?'

'There's the neat part,' Reith told her. 'I have a very old lady in the hospital in Lamberton who I badly want to see. She's dying and her daughter sent a message that she wants to talk to me. I thought I'd drive over after clinic— so I could bring you back. I'd take Margaret over then, but to be honest, Sophie, with a blood sugar as high as she has, the sooner she's in hospital the happier I'll be. She's a walking time bomb. This arrangement seems to suit us all.'

'Very neat,' Sophie said waspishly. She ventured a look at Reith, and to her fury found that the look on his face was one of amusement.

'But I won't go in an ambulance,' Margaret announced. 'Not even sitting up the front supervising Dr Lynton's performance on Australian roads?' Reith queried. 'She hasn't done too well so far. She's a danger to our wildlife if ever I met one.' The laughter in his voice made Sophie's teeth clench.

'I don't know…' Margaret hesitated.

'It is sensible,' Sophie conceded, looking at Margaret rather than those mocking eyes. There was another factor in Reith's suggesting the ambulance as a mode of transport, she knew. It would be equipped with what she needed if Margaret collapsed in a full hyper. 'I'll take you home on the way and collect your night things—and you'll let them know at Lamberton that we're coming?' How to ask Reith a question and not look at him?

'I'll let them know. And Sophie…' he put a hand out and touched her lightly on the cheek '…I do appreciate it.'

I'll bet, thought Sophie.

The journey across to Lamberton was uneventful. Margaret dozed beside her all the way, never far from sleep with her blood sugars so elevated, and Sophie was left to her own reflections.

They weren't very peaceful. Her mind was a jumble of Kevin and Reith in some crazy kaleidoscopic pattern, whirling around her mind in an agony of indecision.

How could she marry Kevin when she had discovered how she really could feel about a man? How could she marry Kevin when Reith was superimposed on everything she did? It was even impossible to summon the image of Kevin's face in her head, as Reith was there already, those dark, mocking eyes haunted with the scars of solitude…

With Margaret safely settled into hospital, treatment started and her blood sugars being monitored carefully, Sophie was free to explore the country town of Lamberton.

It was a town that lived off the sheep's back…rural, easygoing, and about twenty or thirty years behind the times, Sophie thought, and found she didn't mind a bit. What would it be like living in a place where this was the major shopping centre?

She walked slowly along the street, looking at shops selling such things as sheep dip and dog collars, and garages that sold combine harvesters and tractors. It was about as far as she could get from London, England. A whole new world…

She bought scones and jam and cream from a stall set up by the Country Women's Association and then wandered down by the river to eat them. Her sense of unreality was deepening by the moment. How could she calmly go back to practise medicine in England after this? Her heart was here, and she had a feeling that, no matter where her body went from this day forth, her heart would stay very firmly in this place.

Reith was due at the hospital at seven. Half an hour for him to do what he had to—speak to a woman who was dying. No kudos for him in that! No reason for him to make the sixty-mile round trip.

Damn the man. She was so in love with him that it was twisting her in knots. She couldn't think about him dispassionately.

Other doctors cared for their patients. Other doctors were skilled and devoted and…

That line of thinking didn't work. There was only one Reith Kenrick. He had burned himself into her heart and he was there to stay. Somehow she had to organise the rest of her life around that.

So what to do? Tell Reith he was loved? Throw herself at him?

That was the action of a fool. It didn't take many brains to know that such an action was the one thing designed to make a man run so fast that you couldn't see him for dust. Reith Kenrick had declared he wanted no one, and there was nothing Sophie could do to change that.

She was sitting on the dry-grassed river bank, idly throwing pebbles out into the still water. The ripples moved further and further out, changing the calm surface into a whirling sketch-pad of rings. One stone and the surface of the whole river changed. One man...

He didn't want her. Sophie's place was not here. It was back in London—with Kevin.

No!

She stood, looking out at the water, and her mind firmed into at least one resolution. She didn't need Kevin's odd form of security. She had moved past it. She could maybe make a life for herself on her own, feeling as she did about Reith, but that life couldn't include Kevin. It would be a mockery and a sham.

But Kevin's coming, she thought.

'It can't be helped,' she said to herself ruefully. 'He'll just have to go home again. We'll both have to go home.'

Home. Why did the word sound so bleak? It was because somehow home no longer seemed London's bustling metropolis and fog-bound skies. Home was hot and dusty and smelled of eucalypts and sheep droppings and—

'Get a grip on yourself, Sophie Lynton,' she told herself harshly. 'Get yourself together. You have to drive back to Inyabarra tonight with Reith Kenrick. You're going to have to be formally polite and distant, and then you're going to have to leave this place as fast as possible—before Reith Kenrick destroys what's left of your precious sanity.'

CHAPTER EIGHT

REITH was waiting for Sophie at seven-thirty when she made her way back to the hospital. He was leafing through journals in the reception area and stood abruptly as she entered.

'I'm sorry,' Sophie faltered, glancing at her watch. 'You said seven-thirty. Have I kept you waiting?'

He shook his head, weariness lurking in his eyes. 'No. My appointment here took less time than I'd anticipated.'

'A problem?' She guessed there was by his look of defeat.

'Yeah.' He dug his hands into his pockets. 'Blasted relatives. Do you want to go out to dinner?'

The question took her by surprise. Reith was neatly dressed in sports trousers and short-sleeved business shirt, but Sophie looked down at her casual frock with doubt. Her toes were bare in soft sandals and her hair hung free and tousled from the wind by the river.

'I'm not suggesting we go formal,' Reith said, guessing her concern. 'Friends of mine run a small restaurant north of here on the river. Thursday night's quiet.'

The doubt wasn't only because of her clothes. Sophie looked up at Reith and winced inside. She should refuse. She should...

There was little she could refuse this man. Love and good sense seemed as incompatible as chalk and cheese.

'I'd like that,' she said simply.

Reith hadn't deceived her when he had said the place was informal. The Pink Cockatoo was a tiny restaurant capable of seating only about twenty. On this balmy summer night the tables were set out under gum trees, the river

112

running deep and cool twenty feet from the restaurant's huge French windows. Around them, searching fallen gum nuts for seed, were the birds that gave the restaurant its name.

'The restaurant floods most winters,' Reith told her, seeing Sophie's look of amazement at how close the water ran. 'But Liz and Tony reckon it's worth cleaning out the mud for a view like this.'

Liz and Tony, a couple in their mid-sixties but with the bounce of a couple of teenagers, met Reith with the delight of old friends. Sophie was welcomed with warmth—and curiosity only just held in check.

'It's a quiet night,' Tony beamed, his eyes taking in Sophie's appearance with an appreciation that made Sophie blush. 'Not good for business but great for you two. Where shall we put them, Mother?'

He settled them outside, filled their glasses with ice-cold moselle and bustled off to see to their order.

'You come here often?' Sophie asked, searching for a way to break the ice. Having asked her to dinner, Reith obviously saw no need for polite chat. He sat back in his chair and looked out over the river, his face reflecting weariness.

'Yes.' With an effort Reith dragged his attention back to her. 'I shouldn't. It's a fair way from Inyabarra if things go wrong. Still…' he motioned to his mobile phone '…I can get there fast enough if I'm called and sometimes…sometimes being on call for twenty-four hours a day takes its toll.'

'Like now,' Sophie said gently, seeing the exhaustion settle over his face. 'You had little enough sleep last night. You should be home in your bed right now.'

'I wouldn't sleep,' he said bluntly. The weariness faded a little and his eyes flashed dangerous humour. 'Though if I had someone in my bed to take my mind off things…'

'Buy yourself a bedside radio,' Sophie managed. Her face flushed crimson. Drat the man…

'OK.' Reith smiled and spread his hands in mock apology. 'Enough. I should be grateful that you've agreed to have dinner with me.'

The man really was lonely. Solitude was all very well, Sophie thought with a flash of insight, but not being able to talk over medical problems must be the pits. When things went wrong professionally it was almost essential for her that she debrief herself—talk over what happened with colleagues until at least she could see the thing with clear perspective.

'So what went wrong tonight?' she asked. 'What happened to make Dr Kenrick need company for an hour or two?'

His eyebrows lifted in surprise. 'Is it so obvious—that I'm using you as debriefing?'

Their minds worked on the same channel. 'Yes. It's obvious.'

Reith picked up his wine glass, running one long, lean finger round and round the rim.

'Nothing went wrong. Medicine saved a life. It's just…well, that life didn't particularly want to be saved.'

'Meaning?'

He sighed. 'I have a very old and very gentle lady in hospital, dying of emphysema. At the weekend she suffered a cardiac arrest. May's ninety-three, she's been in hospital for months and she wants to die. Actively. Her husband died six months ago. She has cardiac failure, her legs won't hold her up any more, she has ulcers which, if she lives much longer, are going to lead to gangrene and amputation, and she's miserably lonely. So, when her heart gave out on Sunday, it was a kindness.'

'But she didn't die.'

'No. She wasn't permitted. Her niece was in the hospital when May arrested. The niece screamed blue murder until the crash cart arrived, threatened legal action all around unless the doctor on duty tried everything—so the young doctor pulled out all stops and resuscitated. They got May back without any brain damage. Now, though, May's anything but grateful. She asked me to make sure it doesn't happen next time. She wants to be allowed to go.'

'And isn't that possible?'

'It should be,' Reith agreed. 'When patients are as terminally ill as May is they can request and receive a standing order, ''Not For Resuscitation''. May already has that order written on her chart, placed there at her request. Her niece, though… Well, her niece stands to inherit May's considerable fortune and thinks the more fuss she makes at this stage the more she'll deserve the old lady's money. She's hardly visited May until the last couple of weeks, when it was clear the end was near. She's now threatening the hospital with lawsuits if they don't do everything to extend the old lady's life. In her eyes it justifies her inheritance.'

'So?'

'So.' Reith put the glass flatly on the table. 'So I had to contact a lawyer and get a statement drawn up in front of witnesses that the ''Not For Resuscitation'' order stands, and both aunt and niece are dreadfully upset…' Reith shook his head. 'The last thing May needs is conflict. I wish I'd been there on Sunday.'

'But you don't want to be a hospital doctor,' Sophie said gently.

'No. Though I've sometimes thought…'

'Thought what?'

'If another doctor could be persuaded to come to Inyabarra we could set up a four-bed clinic—just for people like May who don't want to leave the town to die. It could be useful for emergency theatre too. But…'

'But Inyabarra's not big enough to support another doctor.'

Reith gave a rueful smile. 'There wouldn't be enough money for luxuries, that's for sure. How about you, Dr Lynton? Would you be prepared to walk away from your well-paying city practice and move here? Be on call twenty-four hours a day? No highways; no bitumen; no specialists on call; no other doctors to talk to and no private schools for your kids?'

'Is that an invitation?' Sophie licked suddenly dry lips.

'You reckon you could persuade the convenient Kevin to move here, do you, Dr Lynton? It's a far cry from business trips to Belgium.'

'No,' Sophie said slowly. 'Kevin wouldn't come. But…but I might be persuaded to stay.'

'What, without Kevin?' Reith was startled.

'Maybe.'

'You're air dreaming, Dr Lynton,' Reith said brutally. 'Dreaming the classic dream of all holidaymakers. What if… What if I stayed here and made this my life? You've left your worries behind in London. You're minus the responsibility of even a boyfriend and it feels good. So…'

'So I make an offer I have no intention of honouring?' Sophie nodded, her eyes bleak. 'You may be right.'

'It was a very generous offer,' Reith said gently and Sophie's head flew up.

'Don't patronise me, Dr Kenrick,' she snapped.

'I'm not patronising—'

'Laughing, then!'

'Yes,' he said solemnly. 'I'm amused that you think you could stick this place. Plenty of stronger women than you have tried and failed.'

'Like your mother.'

'Like my mother,' he agreed and then dropped the conversation like a hot brick as his meal arrived.

Sophie had ordered at Reith's direction. 'Don't touch the kangaroo or the crocodile,' he directed. 'The tourists demand it, so it has to be on the menu, but our ancestors knew what they were about when they imported cows, sheep and pigs. The local treat here, though, is the yabbies, and you should try them.'

'Yabbies?'

'A cross between prawns and lobsters, but they come straight from fresh-water mud.'

'They sound disgusting.'

'They're not. Try and see, Dr Lynton.'

She could refuse him nothing...

The yabbies arrived in a glistening, steaming broth, tender red crustaceans in a concoction of wine and herbs that made Sophie's mouth water. The overpowering roast lunch Margaret had served seemed a long time away. She tackled the tender meat with relish, and was amazed to find herself coming back for a third helping of the warm, home-baked bread.

'This place does that to you,' Reith told her when she commented that she hadn't expected to be hungry. 'Real home-baked cooking... It's the only place I can get it.'

Sophie raised her eyebrows sardonically. 'Really, Dr Kenrick? I would have thought there would have been mobs of district ladies offering home-cooked meals just for you.'

'Yeah,' Reith said drily. 'Home-cooked meals come with strings. Mortgages and garbage on Monday nights and nappies and parent-teacher interviews...'

'Well, isn't it lucky that I can't cook, then?' Sophie told him. 'No threat, Dr Kenrick.'

It silenced him.

There was little conversation through the rest of the meal. Liz and Tony bustled around, producing mouth-watering orange and raspberry tart with clotted cream, followed by brewed coffee, chocolate and cheese. Their hosts kept a wary eye on them, as though wondering what on earth was going on.

Nothing was going on, Sophie thought bleakly. Nothing would.

They drove home in silence, through the farmland and into the bush of the National Park. Even if they had wanted to talk, it wasn't possible over the roar of Reith's engine.

'For heaven's sake,' Sophie yelled once above the noise. 'Why don't you get yourself a decent car?'

'Kevin drives a Mercedes, does he?' Reith enquired politely and Sophie almost gnashed her teeth. Kevin did.

Soon they were twisting into the mountains on the roads where Sophie had become so hopelessly lost a few days before. So much had changed since then.

Sophie ventured a look sideways at Reith's grim profile. Things might have changed for Sophie, but nothing had changed for Reith Kenrick.

'Know where you are?' Reith asked, intercepting her look.

'N-no.'

'This is just about where our friend koala nearly came to grief the other night.'

He rounded the bend, jammed his foot on the brake and swore. Sitting bang in the centre of the road was one small koala.

Sophie stared down at the little grey creature in astonishment. 'Is it…? Surely it can't be the same one?'

'An individual who likes living dangerously.' Reith steered the truck to the side of the road and parked. 'Want to try your luck at moving koalas again, Dr Lynton?'

'No.'

He grinned. 'You'll leave it to us masochistic males. Not a particularly feminist attitude!'

Sophie climbed out of the cab as Reith crossed to the koala, glad, if truth be known, to ease her body after the bone-jolting journey. She stood and watched in the moonlight as Reith expertly lifted the koala, held him in the truck lights and examined him.

'Is he hurt?'

'No. Do you fancy a walk or will you be all right to stay with the truck for a bit?'

'Why?' Sophie was startled.

'Because this animal is exactly the same one you nearly hit the other night. See the scar running down from his eye—and that patch of fur missing from his leg? He's obviously got himself a penchant for sitting on roadways. It's my guess he's carrying a few fleas and the gravel makes a nice spot to scratch his backside.'

Sophie choked on a gurgle of laughter, entranced. 'You're kidding.'

'Would I joke about something so important?' Reith smiled. 'Problem is, now he's in the habit, if he stays here he's going to get himself killed. The only thing to do is cart him a few hundred yards into thick bush where he won't be able to locate the road until he forgets how nice it is for bottom-scratching. Coming, Dr Lynton?'

'What, now?'

'What better time?'

'But…' Sophie looked nervously about her. 'Won't we get lost?'

'If you don't want to come, then stay here,' Reith said carelessly and strode off into the bush.

Sophie cast a nervous glance back at the truck. To stay here by herself in the bush…

Something behind her gave a roar like a stuck pig and she fled into the bush after Reith as if there were an electric prod at her back.

Reith was laughing when she caught up with him. The gums were huge, stretching high toward the moonlight, making it clear underfoot and easy to see a moving shadow in the darkness. That was all Reith was—a large, purposeful figure, koala held easily out in front. The koala's claws had stopped slashing—the koala obviously resigning itself to whatever fate was in store.

'Not feeling very brave, Dr Lynton?' Having caught up, Sophie was sticking close.

'It's not that. It's just—' The frightful roar broke the stillness of the night once again and it was all Sophie could do not to clutch Reith's arm. 'What on earth is that noise?'

'A koala.'

'I beg your pardon?' Sophie gazed blankly across at Reith and stumbled on a fallen branch. 'Koalas don't make a noise like that.'

'They don't in souvenir shops,' Reith agreed, waiting patiently as she regained her footing. 'I guess I wouldn't either if I was stuffed. The chap out there is declaring himself to the ladies of the district. It's romance you hear in the air, Dr Lynton.'

Sophie swallowed. 'How…how sweet.'

Reith chuckled. 'How are your feet?' He looked down at her sandals. 'Not really dressed for bush hiking, Dr Lynton. I'd sing as I walked if I were you.'

'Sing…'

'To ward off the odd Joe Blake.'

Sophie was losing it. 'J… Joe Blake?'

'Joe Blake. Australian for snake. They're a bit thick on the ground around here.'

Sophie uttered a yelp of distress and stopped moving. All of a sudden London was looking good.

'I thought you liked this place.' Reith smiled. He paused once again and turned round, his sardonic eyes glinting in unholy amusement in the moonlight. 'Am I putting you off, Dr Lynton?'

'Are there really snakes?'

'There really are snakes.' Reith relented then, seeing her real look of fear, adding, 'I wouldn't worry, though. I wouldn't have asked you to come into the bush if I was concerned. They're cold-blooded creatures and are mostly only active in the daytime. At this time of night they should be safely curled up digesting all the delicious little ground creatures they poisoned today.'

'Ugh.'

'Want to go home, Dr Lynton?'

'Yes!' The sooner the better for her sanity.

Finally, thankfully, Reith deemed they had travelled far enough from the road. He released the koala onto the trunk of a towering eucalypt. Without a backward glance, the koala headed for the heavens.

'You'd think he'd stop and say thank you.' Reith grinned.

'You probably separated him from his girlfriends.'

'Maybe I did at that,' Reith agreed. 'If so, then maybe I've done him a second favour.'

'As far as I know,' Sophie said drily, 'koalas don't have garbage nights, nappies or parent-teacher interviews.'

'Maybe they do have emotional dependence, though,' Reith told her. He turned back toward the road. 'Coming, Dr Lynton?' His hands free, he reached out and caught hers, leading her forward into the night.

'There's no need to hold my hand.' Sophie tugged to be released but his grip tightened.

'I don't want to lose you.'

'Ha!' She said it before thinking.

'Sophie…'

'What?' She snapped the word crossly, angry with herself for letting emotion show. Still he held her hand, and his grip was warm and reassuring in the loneliness of the night. If only it could go on…

'I should never have kissed you,' Reith said harshly. 'For heaven's sake, woman, it was a kiss—not a declaration of intent.'

'For you maybe…' She shouldn't say it but to have him think otherwise would be a lie.

'Sophie, this is stupid.'

'Yes, it is, isn't it?' she managed. 'I'm a happily engaged girl and you're a man who wants no one. So this feeling between us is stupid and senseless and pointless and…and will you let my hand go?'

'You won't fall?'

'I won't fall without you, Reith Kenrick.'

Brave words. If only she could be sure they were true.

It was almost eleven by the time they reached Sophie's guest house. To Sophie's surprise, the lights were all still on and Moira came hurrying out onto the veranda to meet them.

'Oh, Sophie,' she said anxiously, 'I was hoping you'd come soon. The wee one has been sobbing and sobbing— I can't get her to sleep.'

Sophie closed her eyes in distress. She had promised to stay…'I shouldn't have gone to Lamberton.'

'Of course you should have,' Moira told her roundly. 'Dr Kenrick needed you.' It was a reason that overrode everything with Moira, Sophie realised—Dr Kenrick's need…

'I'll come.' Sophie scrambled out of the truck, aware that Reith too was climbing out. 'There's no need for you—'

'Mandy's my patient.' Reith took the veranda steps two at a time beside Sophie.

Mandy was past reason. She had been sobbing for hours, the blind, unreasoning sobbing of a child frightened past logic. The wails were weak with fatigue and the tiny shoulders heaved with desperate abandon. Mandy was bereft of everything, and the night had brought the weight of a vast and frightening world down upon her.

'Mandy…' Sophie knelt to gather the child to her, but Mandy would have none of it. She held her little body rigid with distress.

'She's been like this since dark,' Moira told them. 'I

didn't know what to do. I darn near called you, Dr Kenrick.'

'You should have,' Reith said briefly. 'I was carrying the phone. We could have been back three hours ago.'

'Well, I didn't want to disturb you,' Moira told him, with a sideways glance at Sophie that had her wondering just how much the lady guessed of what Sophie was feeling. 'And she's not sick.'

'She will be if she keeps this up.' Reith lifted Mandy's rigid body up from Sophie's arms and carried her outside. Wondering, Sophie and Moira followed.

The coolness of the night breeze hit Mandy's flushed, swollen face like cool water. It caught at the child's consciousness, penetrating her misery enough to let her pause for breath. Reith took immediate advantage.

'I want no more noise, Mandy Bell.'

The child's chin wobbled. Tears slid down the woebegone face and her lip quivered in readiness of further crying.

'I mean that,' Reith growled. 'I'm walking down the stairs out into the garden right now, and it's dark. You'd better keep very quiet and still and let me concentrate or you'll have us both upside-down in Mrs Sanderson's prickle bush.'

There was enough of the unknown in what was happening for Reith to gain the child's full attention. Mandy glanced fearfully, uncertainly up at Reith's face and stayed silent.

'Now,' Reith told her, 'no more noise, my Mandy, and I'll tell you what's going to happen. Listening?'

There was the merest quiver of agreement in the rigid body.

'Right.' Agreement was assumed. 'Mrs Sanderson is going to bed. Right now,' Reith growled, at Moira's quick shake of her head. 'The lady was up half last night and is exhausted and she's been getting more and more tired try-

ing to stop you crying, Miss Mandy. You want Mrs Sanderson to look after you until Mary gets back, don't you,
Mandy? If you do, then she goes to bed now.'

He cast a stern, directing glare at Moira, who opened
her mouth to protest, thought better of it and retired from
the lists.

'Next,' Reith told the child in his arms, 'Dr Sophie and
I are going to sit on the big log swing with you until you
go to sleep. But if you start crying again it's going to be
very, very uncomfortable for all of us, so I want you to
stay quiet. Can you do that, Mandy?'

'Y…yes.' It was a terrified quiver and Sophie's heart
wrenched inside her.

'We're not going to leave you, Mandy. That's a promise. There will always be someone here with you, wherever
you are, asleep or awake. Soon it will be Mary and Ted,
but for now it will be Mrs Sanderson, Dr Sophie or me.
Right. We're going to swing and swing and swing until
your little eyes finally close, and after you go to sleep
we're going to tuck you into bed beside Dr Sophie and let
you sleep until morning. When you wake up, Dr Sophie
will be here, and Mrs Sanderson—people who love and
care for you until your Mary and Ted can come back from
Melbourne and tuck you home in their little house. Any
questions?'

It seemed there weren't.

The rigid little body stayed rigid, but the wails had
ceased. Mandy, it seemed, was giving them the benefit of
the doubt.

'Right, Dr Sophie…' Reith strode across the garden to
where a big log swing hung on the branches of an overhanging gum and organised his long body on the swing.
There was just enough room for two. 'Come and swing
with us.'

'I'll watch.'

'Dr Sophie…' He growled.

'Y... Yes?'

'Come here and sit!'

She sat.

It was half an hour before Mandy finally slept, and by the time she did Sophie was near to sleep herself. The warm night breeze enfolded them. Around the swing were flowering gums, and the blossoms—soft white cloud-bursts of scented honey—were intoxicating in their beauty. Sophie looked down at the sleeping child in Reith's arms and found herself inexplicably near to tears.

'I'll take her in now,' she said, and her voice was unsteady.

'Give her a moment. Wait until she's so soundly asleep that we won't risk waking her.'

Sophie nodded. 'Poor little mite.'

'She'll survive,' Reith told her. 'She'll have love and security with Mary and Ted, and turn out nicely normal and go on to a nice secure fiancé and brick veneer and kids—'

'There's nothing wrong with that,' Sophie retorted, hearing the note of derision in his voice.

'That's what you're doing, isn't it, Sophie? Looking for the next round of security. In Kevin.'

The next round... There had never been a first round.

A lump as big as a fist was wedged hard in Sophie's throat. This man knew nothing of her, and cared even less. He would never find out what was behind Sophie's need.

'She's fast asleep,' Sophie said abruptly and heard the tears in her voice. She stood up, making the swing rock as she rose. 'Give her to me.'

'I'll carry her in.'

'N-no.' She didn't want this man in her bedroom any more. She couldn't let herself anywhere near him.

'Sophie...' Reith had also risen. He stood in the moonlight, the sleeping child in his arms, and stood looking down at Sophie. His mobile eyebrows drew together, as if the great Reith Kenrick, for once, was off balance. 'What's happened between us is holiday madness,' he said gently and Sophie winced.

'Yes.' Say anything, she told herself. Just get away from here.

'You know you could never be happy here.'

She took a deep breath. 'So you say. And you're never wrong, Reith Kenrick. You judge people by your own criteria and you never open yourself to doubt. Look, just give me Mandy and just go home.'

Go home... A bleak command. It hung between them in its bleakness and the uncertainty stayed on Reith's face. As if, for one moment, he was unsure.

'Kevin's coming tomorrow?'

'Yes. No. I...I think so.'

Reith nodded. 'Well, there you are, then, Sophie. Your "happy ever after" is about to begin.'

'Kevin's not my "happy ever after".'

'He's your fiancé, Sophie. Your future.'

'No.'

The word stretched out in the stillness of the night, intense and forlorn. Why was she still standing here—fighting for something she had no hope of ever achieving?

It was almost a relief to turn away at the sound of a car, to look away from Reith's dark eyes and stare out along the track at the approaching vehicle. It seemed that Reith also welcomed the intrusion. They stood side by side and waited while the coming car slowed, turned into the guest house driveway and drew to a halt.

Sophie knew even before the car door opened who it was. It was a hire-car, but an expensive one, with the hire firm's logo discreetly shown on the Mercedes' rear window.

A Mercedes...

Kevin.

CHAPTER NINE

KEVIN stood uncertainly in the driveway, staring up at the house as if unsure he had come to the right place. From where he stood he couldn't know that he was being watched.

Sophie's fiancé was as immaculate as ever, the impeccable cut of his Italian suit obvious even in the dim light. It would take more than a two-day international flight to ruffle Kevin's grooming.

It didn't affect Sophie one bit. Usually Sophie felt a rush of gratitude and pleasure at the sight of Kevin—a gratitude that had grown as a lonely teenager when Kevin had first taken her under his wing. Now it was a real effort to move forward.

Reith was the first to speak.

'Dr Lynton,' Reith said drily down to Sophie, 'if this is your errant boyfriend, I dare say he's expecting a welcome. May I suggest you go say hello?'

To her fury, Sophie heard laughter in Reith's voice.

Drat the man…

'Kevin!' She called out and forced herself to take a step forward.

'Sophia…' There was relief in Kevin's tone as he turned. He took two steps in Sophie's direction and then stopped in astonishment as his eyes became accustomed to the dark. Finally he took in the scenario of couple and child. 'Sophia?'

'Sophia?' Reith quizzed softly, the laughter intensifying. 'Well, I never. I've never known a real Sophia before.'

Sophie swallowed and stepped into Kevin's abrupt embrace. The embrace was perfunctory. She was released in seconds and Kevin stared at Reith, waiting for introductions. Somehow she forced herself to make them.

'Kevin, this is Dr Reith Kenrick. Reith... Kevin Carson.'

'What the...?' There was no way Kevin could shake Reith's hand even if he'd wanted to. Reith's arms were fully occupied with the sleeping child. 'What the hell is going on, Sophia?'

'We...' Sophie was right off balance and it showed. 'Reith... Dr Kenrick is the local doctor. Mandy...this little girl's father is...is ill and we're looking after her.'

'Both of you? In the garden at midnight?' Kevin sounded incredulous, and Sophie could see his point.

'No. Mrs Sanderson...the owner of the guest house...and I have been looking after Mandy. I... Dr Kenrick and I have been busy this afternoon with another patient. We got home late and Mandy was upset...' Her voice trailed to nothing. To her fury she felt like a child caught out in wrongdoing.

'You mean you've been working?' Kevin was clearly at a loss, and reacted as he always did when things weren't going to his liking—with anger. 'Medically? Sophia, you're here on holiday.'

'On her honeymoon, I hear,' Reith said helpfully and gave Sophie a bland smile. 'You've been working in Belgium, I gather, and Dr Lynton's been working in Inyabarra. Strange honeymoon—but each to his own. Shall I put Mandy in your bedroom—Sophia?'

It was as much as Sophie could do not to grind her teeth out loud. 'Yes, thank you, Dr Kenrick. I'll come in with you—'

'There's no need.' His smile was still as bland as cream. Reith Kenrick was enjoying himself and it showed. 'I should know the way to your bedroom by now. You stay here and welcome your fiancé properly.' He smiled across to Kevin. 'Welcome to Australia, Kevin. I'm pleased for

Sophia that you finally showed.' He turned back to Sophie and the mockery faded for an instant. 'Maybe I won't see you again, Dr Lynton. Accept my best wishes for your future happiness.'

And for a trace, a fleeting particle of a second, Sophie saw a flicker of regret in his eyes.

And then he was gone.

Sophie hadn't realised how restful Moira Sanderson's guest house had been until Kevin's arrival. The rest stopped with Kevin.

By the time Sophie fell into bed she was exhausted. Kevin was incredulous, angry and belligerent.

First there had been demands to explain Reith Kenrick—and Sophie had done her best. Her explanation had left Kevin disgruntled.

Moira had come out then to find out who the strange voice belonged to—and her next statement had taken Kevin's breath away.

'I've prepared a downstairs bedroom for you,' she told him severely.

'But...' Kevin's eyes snapped annoyance. 'Sophia has a double room. There's no problem.'

'As long as you don't mind sleeping with the door open into Mandy's room,' Sophie said doubtfully, her heart sinking at the thought of Kevin in her room. She'd have to share Mandy's bed. She couldn't sleep with Kevin—but neither could she tell him that here, in front of Moira.

'I do, as a matter of fact,' Kevin snapped. 'But we can talk about that in private.' Moira's bobbing curlers were clearly not what he was used to in hotel staff. 'I'll take my luggage up now.' He would have preferred a porter, his tone said.

'No.' Moira's arms folded across her crimson-robed bosom and she stood before the stairway as though defending the honour of her house. 'The girls sleep upstairs. Men downstairs, if you don't mind, Mr Carson.'

'We booked a double room,' Kevin said silkily.

'You booked as a married couple.' The arms stayed folded and Sophie suppressed the unchristian thought that, like Reith, Moira was enjoying herself. 'Dr Lynton herself told me you're not yet married and while you're under my roof there's no hanky-panky between unwed children.'

'I'm hardly a child,' Kevin snapped between thinned lips. 'And neither is Sophia.'

'You're a child compared to me, and Sophie Lynton's an unwed girl with no mother to protect her. I know my duty. This is a decent house and I intend to keep it that way. If you want to move out then it's fine by me. There's motels in Lamberton.'

Kevin practically gaped. He glared from Sophie to Moira and back to Sophie.

Then he held out his hand to Sophie in an imperative gesture of command.

'Collect your things, Sophia. We needn't put up with this nonsense.'

Sophie swallowed. 'I can't leave, Kevin,' she said gently. 'Mandy...I promised Mandy I'd stay until...until she can go home.'

'Mandy?'

'The little girl.'

His eyes widened. 'And how long do you think that will be?'

'I don't know.'

They stood in the dim hall light, with Sophie feeling more miserable than she had ever felt in her life. She wished the floor would open up and swallow her. Heaven, she needed time to sort herself out.

Around her heart, though, was a penetrating mist of gratitude for Moira's stand. Moira had given her the breathing space she so badly needed.

'This child's not your patient,' Kevin snapped finally. 'It's not your place—'

'It is my place,' Sophie said softly. 'It is.'

She lay in her big bed alone now, and spent the night staring at patterns on the ceiling, seeing anything but.

What on earth was she to do? What?

The next day brought no answers. Kevin was rigid with fury, but his mobile phone and portable fax kept him occupied for most of the morning. Sophie's suggestion that she take him sightseeing was met with blank incomprehension.

'See what, Sophia?'

'The land around here,' Sophie said miserably. 'The mountains. Maybe…maybe I might even find you a koala. I know where to look.'

'You go,' he said uninterestedly. 'I have to finish this.'

Sophie stared at him for a long moment. 'Kevin,' she said at last, 'why did you come?'

He looked up at that. His eyes creased into the smile she'd known for so long—the smile that had reassured her as an insecure teenager that here was someone who would take the worries of the world onto his shoulders—and be her rock. They'd been each other's security for so long… A habit it was time to break.

'I came because you were here,' he said simply. 'You know I always do.'

'Eventually.'

'Sophia, I'm a busy man,' he explained patiently. 'You understand that.'

'Who was the woman in Belgium?'

'Who?'

'The woman with you when you called me.'

'There was no woman.'

It was said too fast. There was no time behind his response for thought about where he had made the phone call or who had been with him—just a harsh, flat denial that had the opposite effect to reassurance on Sophie. His snapped denial said he had been ready for the question. It was a confirmation of what she had expected.

'How long,' she said carefully, 'do you think we might stay here?'

'You've already told me—until the kid is claimed. Though why the hell you had to make promises... It's lucky I've got the fax and computer with me.'

'And then?'

'We'll go home, of course.'

'And the wedding?'

'We'll have it some-time, sweetheart.' He grinned and bent again over his laptop computer. 'After all, Sophia, we've known each other long enough. It doesn't really matter if we're married or not.'

'No.'

He didn't hear the dreary inflexion in her voice. She opened her mouth to say more but the mobile telephone rang, the fax vibrated into use with an incoming message and Kevin waved her away with his hand. Interview suspended.

So now what? Frustrated from the confrontation she'd intended, Sophie wandered outside and sat on the log swing she'd used the night before with Reith, swinging it gently back and forth as her mind came to grips with her future. A future without Kevin. And a future without Reith...

'Sophie.'

Sophie looked up. Moira was waving a tea-towel from the back door.

'Sophie, you're wanted on the telephone.'

Who on earth...? There was a tiny flicker of hope, quickly suppressed. Moira's next words doused the hope completely.

'It's Elvira Pilkington, Sophie—the woman who had

hysterics the night Mandy's dad died. I don't know what she wants with you but she's demanding to speak to the lady doctor and it's a wonder you can't hear her yelling from here.'

Moira wasn't exaggerating. Sophie picked up the receiver and the woman's shrill tone made her wince and hold the phone at arm's length.

'Dr Lynton… Dr Lynton…I want you to come straight away. Something awful is wrong with my daughter. My lovely Christabelle… She's locked herself in her room and she's crying and crying and when she walked into the house she looked like death and she vomited in the downstairs toilet but she wouldn't let me come near her and now she's gone all quiet and she won't let me in and I…I'm scared. I've been yelling at her to come out for an hour but she hasn't talked except when I said I'd get Dr Kenrick and then she yelled that if any man came near her she'd die—she'd just die—and Dr Lynton…I think she means it—'

The woman's voice cracked on a noisy sob and there was a sudden blessed silence. There was time for Sophie to think.

'Isn't Christabelle Dr Kenrick's patient?' she asked gently and held the receiver out again.

'I tried to ring him,' Elvira told her, 'but Christabelle's got a phone extension in her room and she said she'd kill herself if I so much as rang him.'

Elvira's voice had quietened a little. The distinct wobble to her words made Sophie suspect that, despite her hysterical personality, the woman really was badly frightened.

'What if I rang him?' Sophie suggested, thinking fast. Reith was much more likely to know what was troubling the girl than she was.

There was a frantic gasp on the other end of the line and a tight, terrified voice cut in. Christabelle, it seemed, was still listening.

'No! No! I don't want a man. Oh, God, I'll die... Mum, don't you dare let her ring him. No! I'll kill myself...'

The voice ended on an hysterical wail and Sophie took a deep breath. There was enough real terror in the voice to make Sophie take the girl's threat seriously. Hysterical teenage girls could be capable of anything.

'I'll come over and talk to you, Christabelle,' she said softly, and then winced as the mother's voice yelled down the line again.

'Oh, would you, Dr Lynton? A real lady doctor? You hear that, Christabelle? Dr Lynton's coming now. You'll be right...'

'I'll be there in five minutes,' Sophie said firmly and replaced the yelling receiver.

She stood in thought for thirty seconds, Moira watching from a distance. Mandy came through from the kitchen, her small face coated in chocolate-cake mix, and the two waited for Sophie to come to a decision.

'I'll go,' Sophie said finally. 'They really were frightened, weren't they, Moira?'

'They were,' Moira agreed. 'Otherwise I wouldn't have agreed to call you to the telephone.'

'How old is Christabelle?'

'Fourteen. And boy mad already.'

'Can you tell me how to get there?'

'Sure.'

'Are you going away?' Mandy asked solemnly. She took another lick of her wooden spoon and regarded it thoughtfully. 'Mrs Sanderson and me don't want you to go, but him...' She gestured with her spoon to Kevin's intent figure in the dining-room. 'He said this place is the end of the earth and he's getting you out of here as soon as he bloody can.'

'Is that what he said?' Sophie grimaced in annoyance. It sounded exactly like Kevin. She picked Mandy up, chocolate mixture and all, and hugged her hard. 'Well, he's not taking me away for a while yet, sweetheart. Not until your Mary comes back. I'm going away for an hour or two now—no more.' She nodded, firming her decision. 'Moira, could you ring Reith and tell him what's happening? If there's anything seriously medically wrong with Christabelle I'll need him. I'm not licensed to practise in this country, and I sure as heck don't have any equipment.'

'I'll tell him,' Moira agreed. 'Do you want him to come?'

'No.' Sophie shook her head. 'The girl really does sound over the edge and I'll find out what's wrong first. If it's what I suspect, then I might not need him at all.'

'What do you suspect?' Moira asked curiously.

'The most likely scenario is that she's been drinking or has taken some drug she shouldn't. Another, though, is that she's been raped,' Sophie said. 'They're the three most common reasons for girls to react like this and not let a parent near them. But it's just guesswork for now.'

Her guesswork was wrong.

It took ten long minutes before Sophie finally persuaded the terrified Christabelle to open the bedroom door. She refused to open it a crack for her mother, but finally, her mother firmly sent downstairs, she opened the door an inch and a swollen, blotched face peered out.

'I think I'm dying,' she whispered. 'Look at me.'

Sophie saw. The anxiety faded from her mind and it was all she could do not to chuckle. Instead, she put her hand through the crack and caught Christabelle's hand, establishing a link.

'Can I come in?'

Christabelle looked at her for a long moment. 'You…you really are a doctor?'

'I really am a doctor.'

'Oh…' The girl turned and fled to the sanctuary of her crumpled bedclothes. She hid her face in the pillows and burst into noisy sobs. Sophie walked in, shut the door firmly against Christabelle's mother and sat down beside the bed. Then she waited.

It took five minutes for the hysterics to subside, and they only did then because there was absolutely nothing feeding them. It was hard to keep up hysterical sobbing when no one was patting you on the shoulder, making sympathetic noises or responding in the slightest. Instead Sophie calmly waited for the paroxysms to subside.

Finally Christabelle turned her face up to Sophie, glanced wildly at her and buried her face in the pillows again.

'I wouldn't worry,' Sophie said evenly. 'I have seen chickenpox before.'

There was a deathly silence. The world appeared to hold its breath.

'Chickenpox… No! I don't believe you.' It was a faint thread of a whisper.

'Christabelle, I can see your neck and behind your ears from here. There are pustules which look for all the world like chickenpox, and there's a rash on your arms and legs that could be bigger by tomorrow.'

'Chickenpox…' The word echoed round and round the room while the girl took in the diagnosis and considered.

'I can't have chickenpox. I can't.' Christabelle's voice trembled. 'I thought I was dying of acne. If anyone sees me like this I'll die. I always have pimples and the girls tease me and these…' Her voice choked in revulsion.

'Are you feeling sick, too?' Sophie asked sympathetically.

'Yes! I feel awful!'

Sophie put her hand on the girl's forehead. She was running a fever. 'Dr Kenrick can give you something for the fever,' she told her. 'I don't know what's available in Australia or I'd tell you myself. He'll also be able to tell you what to put on your skin to stop the itch.'

Silence again. Then, 'You're sure it's chickenpox?'

'Almost a hundred per cent. It's a classic case, Christabelle.'

'And…and you think I should see Dr Kenrick?'

'I think it's only sensible. And I think we should tell your mum, too. She's very worried. She'll be very relieved it's something…' she had been about to say 'something simple' but caught herself in time; she just knew it was the wrong thing to say '…something we can treat,' she finished lamely.

Another silence.

'How long does it last?' Christabelle asked finally.

'Ten days to two weeks.'

The girl flung herself onto her back and stared out at Sophie from desperate eyes. 'I can't…I can't be like this for two weeks… And chickenpox! It's a kids' disease. How can I tell my friends I have chickenpox? I'll be a laughing stock.'

Sophie smiled, not without sympathy. 'How about telling them you have varicella? That's its true name. And I wouldn't worry about their laughing at you. Chickenpox— varicella—is incredibly contagious. Chances are that you'll be laughing at them in a week or two.'

'Really?'

'Really.'

'Varicella.' The girl looked up at Sophie in hope. 'Are there…are there complications?'

'Not often.'

'I'll read about it in Mum's medical dictionary.' The girl bounced off the bed and opened the door. 'Mum!'

She had inherited her mother's voice. The yell threatened to burst Sophie's eardrums.

Ten minutes later she was free to leave. Christabelle and her mother were happily buried in the *Family Medical Helper*, their tongues practising all the complications known to man—varicella haemorrhagica, varicella gangrenosa, ulceration, toxaemia, pneumonia, encephalitis…

'There's no way a healthy girl like you will suffer rare complications like those,' Sophie protested, only to be howled down.

'You can't be too careful,' Elvira pronounced solemnly. 'It's best to be prepared for the worst.'

Christabelle nodded in full agreement and Sophie suppressed a smile. Now the fears were behind them it was clear that Christabelle and her mother were about to dredge up every possible drop of drama from the situation.

She walked out into the sunshine and blinked. Reith Kenrick was sitting on the front stone fence, waiting for her.

'Nosing in on my patch, Dr Lynton?' he said quizzically, stretching his long legs into a standing position and intercepting her pathway to her car. 'And pinching my very favourite patients?'

'I'll bet they're your favourite patients.' Despite what the sight of the man was doing to her heartbeat, Sophie couldn't suppress a smile. 'You needn't worry. There's lots of medicine in store for you over the next two weeks from our Christabelle.'

'For instance?'

'Oh, I'd guess you'll be treating haemorrhage, toxaemia, ulceration, pneumonia…maybe even encephalitis.'

'What the deuce is wrong with the child?' Reith was clearly startled.

'Chickenpox.'

There was a moment of blank silence. Then Reith gave a shout of laughter. Sophie watched him, the pain inside twisting and twisting again into a hard knot. She found it almost impossible to laugh as well.

'You're kidding,' he finally grinned as laughter faded. 'From what Moira told me, I was expecting gang rape at the very least.'

'That's not listed as a chickenpox complication.' Sophie

smiled with a herculean effort. 'Oh, and it's not chicken-pox, by the way. Varicella or nothing.'

'I'll remember.' Reith looked toward the house. 'Am I needed?'

'Give them time to make a list of complications and symptoms,' Sophie advised.

'You won't consider staying on as their personal medical adviser for two weeks?'

'No.'

It was a flat statement and Reith heard the misery behind it. He looked down at her.

'Your fiancé not making you happy, Dr Lynton?'

'What do you think?'

'People find happiness in the strangest of places.'

'And some people never find it at all.' She made to brush past him, but Reith reached forward and took her arm. His hand gripped the soft flesh of her forearm and Sophie gave an involuntary shiver.

The hand was withdrawn.

'I had a telephone call from Mary Vickers,' Reith said slowly. He was staring down at his hand, as if the touch to her arm had affected him in a way he didn't understand.

'And?' Sophie was staring at her car, unblinking. How could someone hurt so much when not physically wounded?

'She'll be here tomorrow morning to take Mandy home.'

'Good.' Sophie's voice softened. 'Mandy needs her.'

'And you and your Kevin will be able to go.'

'As you say.'

There was a long silence. It was as if there was a vast magnetic force pulling them together but each was standing rigid. If one moved an inch...

'I hope you'll be happy,' Reith said at last.

'You've said that before.' Finally Sophie made herself move. She walked across to her car and finally allowed herself a look back. 'I hope so, too,' she said softly. 'I doubt it, but at least I'm going to try. That's more than some people do. It's more than you do, Reith Kenrick. At least I have the courage to try.'

CHAPTER TEN

'WHERE the hell have you been?'

The accusation hit Sophie almost before she was out of the car. Kevin was waiting on the veranda, his face a mask of suppressed fury.

'I've been practising medicine,' Sophie told him wearily. She didn't have the energy to even try to deflect his anger. 'A case of…a case of varicella.'

'Varicella?' Kevin looked stunned. 'What the hell is that? And why can't the local doctor… Kenrick or whatever his name is…look after it?'

'They wanted a female doctor and I was available.'

'You're on holiday.'

'Yes,' Sophie said mildly. 'And so are you, Kevin. But you don't seem to have stopped work either.'

'That's different,' he snapped. 'You know damned well we depend on my income.'

'*We* don't,' Sophie said flatly. 'You do.'

'Well, what if we start a family? Look, Sophia, I've put work off for two weeks already—'

Kevin stopped dead, a trace of unease appearing behind the bluster. The suspicions Sophie had tried to ignore rammed home as solid fact.

'You put your work off for two weeks while you had holidays in Belgium,' Sophie said gently. 'In the time that was supposed to be our honeymoon.' She sighed, depression settling over her at the knowledge of what their relationship had become. 'Kevin, this is a farce.' She tugged the expensive diamond from the third finger of her left hand. 'And I think it's time we put an end to it.'

Kevin's jaw dropped a foot. The bluster sagged out of him.

'But Sophia...' He shook his head, searching for a response. 'I need you.'

Not 'I love you', but 'I need you'.

He did. Kevin was a mover and shaker and Sophie had been his security for a long time now—a place to prop up his ego and ready him for the next foray out into the exciting world. A world that included other women.

And Kevin had been security for Sophie.

'I needed you when I was seventeen,' Sophie said gently. 'Kevin, you were the family I never had, and I'm grateful. But I'm a big girl now and I have different needs. I need...I need to be treated as a person—to be loved as an equal. No matter what I do in life, with you I'll always be the little woman, waiting at home with slippers at the ready.' She bent forward and kissed him lightly on the lips. 'I've been your friend, Kevin. I'd like... I'd like to stay that way. But I don't want to be your wife. I don't want to be your woman.'

Kevin's face had been incredulous—stunned. As Sophie watched, it now ranged through the full gamut of emotions.

Anger won. It always would.

'You trollop,' Kevin gritted between his teeth. 'You lying little tart. It's Kenrick, isn't it?'

'Kevin, don't—'

'You're sleeping with him. You let me come all the way to Australia—'

'After you went all the way to Belgium to be with...with who, Kevin?'

'Is that what this is all about?' Kevin's face cleared. 'I don't know who the heck told you about her, but there's nothing in it. Sophia, I came here, didn't I? For heaven's sake, girl, I never offered to marry Jane. It's you I want.'

She hadn't wanted his infidelity thrown at her quite so

baldly. Sophie took a step back and her hands rose to her face, as if in defence.

'Kevin, I don't want to hear about…about Jane. And I haven't slept with Reith Kenrick,' she whispered. 'But it doesn't matter whether I have done or not, because what's between us—you and me—is over. I tried too late to stop you coming to Australia, but when you did—well, I wondered whether there was anything we could make a go of. There isn't. So…so it's time you left. I'm sure you'll think of some way to make the trip tax-deductible—or maybe…' by the looks of his face, she guessed she had it right. 'Or maybe you already have.'

She handed Kevin the ring, walked back to her car and drove out of the guest-house grounds as fast as she could.

She didn't look back.

It was late afternoon before Sophie finally ventured home. She stopped at the gate, checking for Kevin's Mercedes, and it wasn't until she'd assured herself it was well and truly gone that she turned into the drive.

Mandy catapulted from the house as a relieved little whirlwind.

'Sophie, you said you'd only be an hour or two,' the child accused. 'And you've been hours and hours and Mrs Sanderson said you came back while I was having a nap but I didn't see you and she said you and Mr Carson had a…a difference of opinion…and you drove off again—and Mrs Sanderson said she bets she knows why—and Mr Carson's gone and Mrs Sanderson says he won't be missed, and I don't miss him at all but he's your friend, isn't he, Sophie?'

Sophie climbed out of the car and took Mandy's small hands in hers. She looked at where the Mercedes had been. There was no regret. She should have done this years ago. She should have had the courage.

And Reith Kenrick's given it to me, she told herself

softly. Even if…even if he can't return my love, maybe he's done me a massive favour.

So she should remember Reith with gratitude?

She could remember Reith Kenrick with nothing but aching, desolate loss for what might have been.

'You look really sad,' Mandy said solemnly, tugging her inside the house. 'Don't be sad, Sophie. Mrs Sanderson and me didn't like Mr Carson very much anyway. And we've made the most enormous chocolate cake and put on heaps and heaps of icing and Mrs Sanderson wouldn't let me have even the littlest, littlest bit until you came home— so that has to cheer you up, doesn't it?'

'It sure should,' Sophie agreed, reaching down to give Mandy a hard hug. 'It sure should.'

Mary Vickers arrived on Sunday morning to relieve Sophie of her last responsibility. There was no mistaking her suitability as a mother for the little girl. Mary drove into the guest-house driveway, and Mandy flew out of the door and into her arms like an arrow straight to her heart.

From the veranda Sophie watched them, woman and child, clinging together with the fierceness of absolute possession. Heaven help the social worker who tries to part these two now, she thought and knew that it would never happen.

Her thoughts were backed by Mary two minutes later.

'I didn't like leaving Ted,' Mary Vickers confessed, 'but he insisted. Mandy's been our little girl from the time she moved next door. Her dad's been so ill—if it hadn't been for us the welfare people would have whisked her away months ago. Though it might have been better if they had.'

'You can't blame yourselves for what happened,' Sophie said gently. 'You weren't to know.'

'No.' Mary shook her head. 'He was such a nice boy, Mandy's dad. When he was well he tried so hard. It was only when the illness took over that he couldn't cope and

Mandy needed us. And this way…well, Mandy had her dad for four years and that's more than a lot of kids have.'

Sophie nodded. This would be OK. Mandy would grow up being reminded of her father with love and the terrors of that one awful night would drift into unimportance.

'We're just so grateful to Dr Kenrick—and to you, too, of course,' Mary said. 'You both saved Ted's life. And then Dr Kenrick…to go to all that trouble…'

'Trouble?'

'He's spent hours and hours over the past few days arguing with Social Welfare—giving us time. He told them Mandy was ill but safe and not to be disturbed until tomorrow—and tomorrow I'll have her tucked up in her own little bedroom at home. It's a shame Ted won't be with me but Dr Kenrick has dispositions from all sorts of respectable people telling Social Welfare what good parents we'd make, how much time we've spent with Mandy already and how much we love her. He's organized certificates from the *in vitro* fertilization people saying we've been trying to have a baby for ages, and located the forms from when we applied for adoption years ago. The welfare services judged us suitable then—but there wasn't a baby available and now we've passed the right age. I don't know where Dr Kenrick's dug all these forms from. He seems to have people all over the state working for us. I even had a doctor contact me who Dr Kenrick persuaded to go into the IV clinic yesterday—*Saturday*—to collect files.' Her eyes filled with tears. 'Doc Kenrick…well, he's the most wonderful doctor, the most wonderful person I know, and, thanks to him, Ted and I will have our Mandy.'

They went off together soon after, Mandy sitting as close to her Mary as the seat belt would permit, and Sophie blinked back tears as she watched them go.

Happy ever after for one little girl and two loving parents—because of Reith Kenrick.

She wanted a happy ever after, too.

'And now what about you, Sophie, girl?' Moira asked as they watched the receding car. 'You're shot of that fiancé for good, I hope?'

'I guess I am,' Sophie said dully and Moira stared.

'You're never pining for him, are you, girl?'

'N-no.'

'I should think not. That man was a user if ever I saw one, and a woman is better off with no man than one who treats her as a doormat.'

'I know. I should...I should have seen it years ago.'

'But you didn't want to be alone. And now you're alone again and it's scaring you,' Moira guessed. She peered closer at Sophie's closed face. 'But that's not all that's making you miserable, is it, Sophie, dear?' Her eyes narrowed. 'It wouldn't be...' She took a deep breath as though daring herself to continue. 'It wouldn't be our Dr Kenrick, would it, Sophie?'

'No.'

The calm grey eyes didn't lose their intentness. 'Liar,' Moira said evenly and smiled. Her eyes were bright with the trace of tears from bidding Mandy goodbye and now they glistened in sympathy. 'Oh, Sophie...'

Sophie shook her head. 'Moira, I'm twenty-eight years old. You sound as if I'm ten. I'm old enough to know better than to fall head over heels for a man who needs a woman like he needs a new truck!'

She heard what she'd said. Sophie caught her breath and gasped and Moira broke into a delighted chuckle.

'That man needs a truck nearly as much as he needs a woman,' she pronounced. 'And that's desperately.'

'He won't buy one.'

'He will eventually. And he'll realise there are women he can trust. A woman...'

'I bet he can patch up that old truck with string and glue for years yet,' Sophie said darkly.

'Someone could sabotage it,' Moira suggested. 'Maybe

the same thing can be done for his need of a woman. Maybe there's sabotage already afoot—making our Dr Kenrick realise just how bleak his life is without you.'

'I...I don't know what you mean.'

'I mean, you're not planning on leaving here right this minute, are you, dear?' Moira asked blandly.

'I should.'

'But you won't.' Moira smiled with affection. 'And I'll help any way I can. Sophie, for your information, I've stopped charging you for accommodation. I charged your horrid Kevin like a wounded bull, and he's more than covered expenses for both of you. So from now on you're here as my guest. Just for a day or two,' she begged. 'Just till you get the stitches out of your arm. I don't like the idea of you driving all the way to Melbourne with stitches in your arm.'

'I should go...'

'But you'll stay?'

'Moira, there is no chance of anything happening between me and Reith Kenrick. No chance in a million years.'

'If you go now there won't be,' Moira said darkly. 'A coward would walk away. But a girl who's fighting for a future that's important to her...'

'He won't even see me.'

'He won't see you if you're in England.' Moira spread her hands. 'Two days, Sophie. The rest will do you good, without your dratted Kevin. Two days to swim and sleep and walk and think about your future. It makes sense to me. How about it?'

She didn't leave. Of course she didn't leave. To get in the car and head back to the airport would be like ripping herself apart, and mutilation wasn't something Sophie was good at. She swam and walked and let her tired mind rest, and to her amazement on Sunday night she slept like a

baby. If she couldn't have Reith, it seemed that the decision to shed herself of Kevin was a good one.

She slept late on Monday morning, swam and walked
again, but by mid-afternoon she was starting to get restless.
She wasn't good at holidays. She didn't know what the
heck to do with them.

She sat on Reith's swing with a book, trying hard to
concentrate on the murder mystery in front of her, but the
words wouldn't focus. She read the same page three times
before Moira emerged from the house and she looked up
in relief.

'Are you busy?' Moira called.

'Frantically.' Sophie threw the book aside in disgust.
'Right in the middle of an action-packed afternoon. What
can I do for you?'

'Well…' Moira took a deep breath as though searching
for courage. 'It's what you might do for Dr Kenrick.'

'What I might do?' Sophie stood up. 'Exactly…exactly
what did you have in mind, Moira Sanderson?'

'Now, I'm not plotting.' Moira wiped her hands on her
tea-towel as she walked across the lawn to the swing. 'It's
just…there's some drama going on up at the school and I
thought…I thought you might like to help.'

'Drama?'

'My friend Muriel lives next door to the school,' Moira
explained. 'She rang just then. It seems…it seems they
have an epidemic on their hands. A girl fainted and had
to be taken out of class and then another and there are
about fifteen girls affected at the moment with vomiting
and fainting and more by the minute, and Reith's on his
way, but Muriel just rang to say he might need you if you
were still here.'

Her voice rose in an absurd, birdlike expression of hope.
She stood looking so much like a nonchalant sparrow that
Sophie burst into laughter.

'Moira Sanderson, you are as transparent as glass.'

'I'm not making this up,' Moira said, wounded.

'You swear?'

'Scout's honour.' She held up three floury fingers. 'Why don't you just go down there and see?'

'Why don't I just ring the headmaster and see if they need me?'

Moira brightened. 'Oh, yes. The headmaster's Jenny's husband—David Lee. A nice, sensible man, but it sounds as if he'll really need you.'

He did. The headmaster's response was sharp and to the point.

'I don't know what the hell is going on,' he told Sophie, clearly desperate to finish fast on the phone and get back to his crisis. 'But they're certainly ill and I don't think one doctor can cope. Dr Kenrick's here and we've called for ambulances from Lamberton but—'

'I'll be right there,' Sophie told him. The phone crashed down before she finished speaking.

Sophie didn't stop to change, deciding that jeans and blouse would do in a crisis. She drove herself. Moira had scones in the oven, and clearly didn't regard vomiting teenagers worth burnt scones.

'It'll be them dratted hot dogs they sell in the school canteen that's done it,' she pronounced darkly. 'You see if I'm right. You just have to look at the colour of them to know they're disgusting. The last one someone tried to give me was bright pink. Pink food! The blasted sausage was so plastic you could tie a knot in it without it breaking. You can't tell me kids can eat those things without muddling their insides.'

Food poisoning. It could be, Sophie thought as she drove down into the little town. A batch of bad meat...

There was a teacher in the front office, clearly sent to wait for her. She took Sophie's arm with relief and led her through to the backyard.

'We've put them outside,' the teacher told her. 'In the

shade of the trees. We thought if it's infectious they're better in the open. We've asked the parents of non-affected children to take them home.'

Sensible precautions—as long as the children sent home didn't develop symptoms. Sophie had a nightmare flash of children all through the mountains becoming ill.

If it was food poisoning then the problems depended on what sort it was. A staphylococcal poisoning produced symptoms almost immediately and they'd quickly know the extent of the problem—but if the bacterium causing problems was salmonella then symptoms could occur between twelve to thirty-six hours after eating.

'Is Dr Kenrick here?'

'Yes. He got here fast.'

He would. This could be a real disaster. 'Does he think it's food poisoning?'

'I don't know.' The young teacher seemed really distressed. She seized Sophie's arm tighter before they went through the outside door. 'Dr Lynton…'

'What's wrong?' Sophie asked gently, seeing the fear.

'N…nothing. Well…well, I think I'm about seven weeks pregnant. I haven't had a pregnancy test yet but I'm pretty sure and…and we do want this baby. I've had two miscarriages already. If I catch whatever the girls have…'

Sophie stopped dead. She turned to the woman and noted her pale, fearful face. 'Do you have any symptoms?'

'N…no. I vomited this morning—but then… I've vomited every morning this week.'

Sophie smiled. 'They reckon morning sickness is a sign of a robust baby,' she said firmly. She caught the girl's hands. 'Still, I agree, it's no use taking chances. I think you should go home now and stay home until we figure out just what's going on here. OK?'

'OK.'

The girl went. Sophie watched her retreat, took a deep breath and opened the door outside.

Good grief.

There were bodies everywhere. Girls…they were all teenage girls by the look of it, some hysterical, some moaning and clutching their stomachs and one girl hunched into a foetal position screaming that she was going to die. A couple of teachers moved helplessly among them—and staring out over the whole disaster, his brow as black as thunder, was Reith Kenrick.

Sophie walked quietly up to him and touched his arm. 'What needs to be done?'

Reith turned to her, incredulity written in every line of his face. 'You!'

The word made Sophie cringe. There was no delight here that she wasn't back in England as he'd thought.

'It looks as if you need help,' she managed.

'You might say that.' Reith's mouth was set in a tight, hard line.

'Do you know what's happening?'

'I think I do.' He turned to the girls. 'Let's see if you can discover it, too, Dr Lynton?'

Sophie's green eyes flashed anger. What stupid game was this? 'Do you mind telling me what's going on?'

He smiled then, his smile sardonic and angry. 'You try answering a few questions, Dr Lynton. For instance, what do we appear to have here?'

Sophie frowned, gazing over the sprawled bodies. 'Fifteen or so girls—'

'Funny, that,' Reith snapped. 'No boys. Ages?'

Once more Sophie stared. The girls were all in their young teens—thirteen to fifteen, at a guess. 'Teenagers.'

'That's right. Teenagers. We have a comprehensive school of both sexes from four to seventeen, yet the only ones ill are thirteen-and fourteen-year-old girls. There's been no party or gathering of the girls where they might have eaten the same food. Their symptoms—apart from the odd hysteria-induced vomit—seem to be fainting, clutching of stomachs, threatening to die and wanting their mothers. Suggest anything to you, Dr Lynton?'

'Hysteria,' Sophie said slowly. She'd seen it before. One teenage girl became genuinely ill and the rest of the group went out in sympathy—not deliberately to gain attention, but because they genuinely believed they were ill.

'Do you know what's triggering this?' she asked cautiously.

'You.'

Sophie gaped. 'I beg your pardon?'

'You gave Christabelle Pilkington varicella. Not nice, common or garden chickenpox, but awful, life-threatening, scars-for-life varicella. The complications are horrible, I hear. Encephalitis, haemorrhage, pneumonia, sterility—'

'Where did she get sterility?' Sophie gasped, finally realising what Reith was talking about. 'It's not a known complication—'

'So you did tell her the complications?'

'She looked them up in the medical encyclopaedia. I didn't give them to her.' Sophie's voice was practically a wail.

'But you did tell her she had varicella instead of chickenpox?'

'It made her feel better.'

'Well, I gather,' Reith said dangerously, 'that our Christabelle has spent the entire weekend telephoning her friends, telling them what a ghastly, potentially fatal and highly contagious disease she'd just gone down with. It took a few hours of the girls' being together and comparing symptoms before some of them started feeling very strange indeed. Then someone heard someone vomiting in the women's toilets and there you are. They collapsed like ninepins.'

'Oh.' Sophie stared, daunted, out over the moaning throng. 'Oh…'

Her lips twitched. She tried really hard…

It was impossible. Before she could stop herself, Sophie burst into a peal of delighted laughter. Catastrophe turned to farce in ten split-seconds.

The teachers were staring up at her as if she had gone mad.

'Are you quite done?'

Reith's voice was like a douche of cold water. Only a faint crease at the corners of his eyes told her that he, too, saw the ridiculous side of the situation. 'It's hardly the time for levity, Dr Lynton.'

Sophie bit her lip and managed to assume an expression of suitable solemnity. 'No, Dr Kenrick. What…what should we do now?'

He flashed her a suspicious look, hearing the laughter threading through her voice. 'I should leave you with the whole mess.'

'I'll get onto the first plane back to England,' she threatened and her lips twitched compulsively.

'Laugh once more, and I'll throw cold water on you.'

'We could do that to the lot of them.'

Reith shook his head glumly. 'Wouldn't work. They all genuinely think they're ill. The symptoms are so genuine that it took me six examinations before I was sure I was right.'

'So…'

He sighed. 'So we see each of them individually. Alone. Without any of them feeding hysteria off the others. We tell them exactly what's wrong with Christabelle; bother the girl's nicer feelings—it's going to be chickenpox. We suggest that what they're experiencing might be the first symptom of chickenpox so that they come out of this with some pride intact, and then we send them home with individual parents. And we tell the individual parents what's going on.'

'It'll take hours,' Sophie said, horrified.

'Well, maybe you should have caught your plane back

to England yesterday,' Reith said darkly. 'Because if you leave now, before this mess is sorted out, I'll drag you back by the hair of your head. Caveman stuff, Dr Lynton. Now, shall we put these teachers out of their misery and get on with it?'

'I suppose so,' Sophie said doubtfully.

'There's no "suppose". Move, Dr Lynton.'

It was three long hours before the last girl departed with her parents. The final girl had clung persistently to her symptoms, growing more and more agitated at every attempt to calm her. Finally Reith had administered a sedative.

'Take her home and let her sleep it off,' he told the girl's over-anxious parents. 'Telephone me in the morning if she's not clear of symptoms.'

Finally they were left in the bare staff-room, looking at the debris of blankets and muddle left from the chaos.

'That's that,' Reith said wearily. 'Let me know when you're intending to diagnose varicella in the near future, Dr Lynton. I'll go on holidays.'

Sophie smiled and shook her head. 'I won't.' Even if she did, it wouldn't worry Reith. She'd be back in England.

He looked across at her. 'So...you and Kevin are still enjoying your holiday, then?' It was a casual question, carefully phrased.

'Kevin's gone home.'

There was a long silence.

'More business?' Reith said finally. 'You're not having much luck with your honeymoon, Dr Lynton.'

'No.' Sophie stood up. 'I have to go.' She walked toward the door but stopped as the harassed-looking headmaster walked through the door.

'All finished?'

'Yes,' Reith told him. He glanced at his watch. 'I'm overdue for clinic. We'll leave you to it.'

'Thank you both,' the headmaster said gratefully. He hesitated. 'There is one thing, though.'

'Yes?'

'Our young maths teacher… Lisa Carvis. Dr Lynton sent her home and I wondered why. Was she ill? Surely Lisa wouldn't be influenced by the general hysteria?'

'Oh…' Sophie bit her lip. She'd forgotten the frightened young woman.

'Why on earth did you send her home?' Reith demanded, and Sophie thought fast. It wasn't her place to tell these two men that the young teacher was pregnant.

'Lisa really did have an upset stomach, but her symptoms were different from the girls'—and totally genuine,' she said finally. 'She was ill this morning—in fact, her vomiting might have triggered the rest off. With the fuss happening here she was safer at home.'

'But…' The headmaster was clearly puzzled.

'I'll go and see her at home now if you'll give me her address,' Sophie said quickly, trying to deflect the queries she saw behind the headmaster's frown.

Reith nodded thoughtfully at her. 'You do that, Dr Lynton. It can be your final atonement for creating this mess.' He smiled at her then and the smile softened the severity of his words. It took Sophie's heart away all over again. 'And then come back and report to my clinic.'

'I'll telephone.'

'The clinic's on your way home from Lisa's,' Reith said firmly. 'I want to talk to you in person before you go home.'

Sophie took a deep breath. 'Yes, sir,' she said faintly and raised two fingers in mock salute. 'Any more orders?'

'That'll be all for now, Dr Lynton,' Reith grinned. 'Dismissed.'

CHAPTER ELEVEN

IT WAS a fast process to reassure Lisa.

The girl listened carefully to Sophie's explanation and, like Sophie, burst into relieved and delighted laughter.

'Oh, and I've already had the chickenpox. I could have stayed and helped. What on earth will the rest of the teachers think of me, turning tail and running?'

'They'll understand when they know you're pregnant.'

'Mmm.' Lisa patted her very flat stomach with complacency. 'Well, I won't tell them about junior for a while yet—just in case—but I have a good feeling about this pregnancy.'

'You know something?' Sophie smiled. 'So do I.'

'You don't fancy staying around for the next few months, I suppose?' Lisa asked shyly. 'I wouldn't mind a woman doctor.'

Sophie's smile faded. 'I wish I could,' she said softly. 'I just wish I could.'

Reith was still seeing patients when Sophie arrived at his clinic. He motioned her to a chair and a pile of magazines.

'I'm in a hurry,' Sophie said abruptly. 'I'd rather just tell you about Lisa and go.'

'I'd like to talk to you, though, Dr Lynton.' Reith had picked up his next patient's card and was ushering an elderly man into his surgery. 'I telephoned Moira and told her you'd be late—so there's no hurry at all.'

'But—'

'Could you come right in, Mr Hardcastle?'

He assisted Mr Hardcastle through the door and closed it, leaving Sophie fairly gnashing her teeth after him.

She could leave a nasty note and walk out…

The patients still waiting smiled at her with friendly interest. Sophie's presence hadn't gone unnoticed in the district, it seemed, and she was very welcome.

It would be childish to scrawl angry words and stalk out.

Did she really want to?

Sabotage…

Moira's word flew into her head. Moira had suggested she should sabotage Reith's lonely future by refusing to go. By clinging and hoping…

This wasn't sabotage. This was Reith Kenrick wanting to see her. Sophie gave a virtuous sniff, smiled round at the curious faces and picked up the *Woman's Mirror*.

'I didn't think you'd wait.'

The last patient had finally gone. Reith walked out, closed his surgery door behind him and lifted the magazine from Sophie's fingers.

'Do you mind?' Sophie demanded indignantly. 'Lorissa's about to confess to Jed she's not really his sister, and Dave, who Jed thinks is Lorissa's lover, is Lorissa's best friend's husband and what's the bet Jed and Lorissa fall straight into each others' arms and live happily ever after?'

Reith grinned. He held the magazine open to where she'd been reading and, with one deft pull, ripped out the page. Folding it with care, he tucked it down the unbuttoned neckline of her blouse.

'There you are, Dr Lynton. Never let it be said that I came between star-crossed lovers.'

'Oh, great,' Sophie said. Her voice sounded slightly breathless. The folded paper was sliding down against her bare skin and it was as though Reith was touching her. 'Now the rest of your patients will get to the last page and find the happy ending gone.'

'That's life,' Reith said sagely. 'It's time you had those stitches out, Dr Lynton.'

'Is that why you wanted me to wait? I can very well take them out myself.'

'I like to check my own handiwork. Sit down.'

Sophie glared.

'Sophie…' He shook his head as he would at an exasperating child. 'Do you want to sit or do you want to be sat?'

'Neither.'

'I'll bribe you with jelly beans if you like.' He smiled and Sophie's heart twisted within. 'There's really nothing to fear,' he said kindly.

'I'm not scared.'

'Then sit down.'

She sat. There seemed little else she could do.

Reith bent over the stitches, his small surgical scissors working with care. 'Very nice,' he said, admiring the neat line of scarring he revealed as the stitches fell away. 'Even if I do say so myself.'

'If you don't praise yourself, who will?' Sophie asked with careful sarcasm, and Reith grinned.

'Very true.' He snipped the last stitch. 'Great. Now, Dr Lynton, suppose you answer a few of my questions?'

'L-like what?'

'Like, why did you send Lisa home from school?'

'I was worried she'd catch what the girls had.'

'Why?'

Sophie shrugged. 'I can't tell you that, Dr Kenrick.'

Reith nodded. 'Very professional. How many weeks pregnant is she—and why on earth hasn't she seen me yet?'

Sophie raised her eyebrows. 'That's pure supposition, Dr Kenrick, and you know you're treading on professional ethics by asking.' She relented a little. 'But I wouldn't be surprised if you saw her tomorrow.'

'Excellent.' He smiled down at her. 'I have to tell you that was a fine spot of counselling back at the school, Dr Lynton. If you hadn't caused the whole drama, I'd say you'd done very well indeed.'

'How kind,' Sophie snapped. 'Can I go now…sir?'

'I have another question.'

'Well, ask it fast.'

'Where's Kevin?'

Sophie winced.

That *he* should ask… Reith, who had pulled her life apart.

'I have no idea,' she said bleakly. She stood abruptly. 'Thank you for removing the stitches. I'll go now.'

Reith reached forward and took her hand in his. He lifted her ring finger.

'Not engaged any more, Sophie?'

'What do you think?'

'I think…' he showed no sign of releasing her fingers, and his eyes held her even closer '…I think we might go out for dinner again, Dr Lynton. On unengaged terms.'

'Unengaged?'

'Without Kevin in the background,' he said simply. 'For both of us.'

Sophie took a deep breath. The world stood still. Please…

'I'd like that,' she said simply. 'Very much.'

Reith didn't take her to a restaurant. He made a fast telephone call, led Sophie out to the truck and drove north, high into the mountains. Five minutes from town, he stopped outside a cottage, left Sophie in the car while he went inside and re-emerged carrying a laden picnic basket.

'From one of my patients,' he explained, seeing Sophie's look of astonishment. 'Gilda's Gourmet Goodies. Bush picnics are Gilda's specialty.'

'Is that what we're having? A picnic?'

'We sure are. In my very favourite place.'

It was the place where *Bush Bride* had been painted.

Sophie climbed out of the truck and gazed around in awe. Such a place! She hadn't dreamed such a place existed. The painting had been magnificent in its beauty, but no painting could approach this. The tiny lake reflected the mountains around as though the world were upside-down. The sun was setting over the distant peaks, and crimson fire was everywhere.

'I thought we'd make it in time,' Reith said in quiet satisfaction. 'Sunset is the best.'

Sophie didn't answer. She was absorbing the beauty into her heart. How could she leave this place? How could she? The splendour went on and on—endless in its loveliness. Endless...

'Sophie.' Reith swung her round to face him. 'Don't cry, Sophie,' he said gently. He put a finger up and wiped a tear from her cheek.

'I'm not c-crying. I never cry. It's just...it's just that it's so beautiful.'

'It is, isn't it?' Reith agreed, and he wasn't looking at the scenery.

'D-don't.' She pushed his hand away, unable to bear it. This beauty and Reith—here, now... How could she not reveal what was in heart?

'P-please...are we here to eat?'

He stood looking down at her, his face grave. Finally he nodded.

'OK, Sophie,' he said gently. 'We're here to eat.'

The picnic was perfect—homemade quiche still warm from the oven, crispy rolls, avocado and lemon and some sort of lettuce that was frilled with purple and tasted of basil and oregano and indefinable herbs that Sophie couldn't identify and was too absorbed to try.

Despite the delectable food, Sophie ate little, and ended up feeding most of her salad to the wallabies that swarmed around them as soon as the picnic was produced.

'Since this has become a national park the kangaroos and wallabies have emerged from the bush in their hundreds,' Reith told her. 'It's as if they know guns have now been banned.'

Sophie smiled. She was lying full-length on her stomach, hand-feeding a tiny joey whose nose just emerged from his mother's pouch. The mother wallaby was holding a lettuce leaf between two dainty paws, nibbling in contentment and watching her baby being fed with maternal indulgence.

'I wish Kevin could have seen this,' Sophie said impulsively and then wished she hadn't.

Reith was packing up the last of the picnic. The sun was sliding down behind the mountains, only a sliver of tangerine and gold on the horizon now marking its path. The night was descending with the softness of velvet.

'You'll miss him?'

Sophie shook her head. 'No. No, I won't.'

'Then why were you going to marry him?'

It was a fair question. Sophie broke her last remaining lettuce leaf into shreds, eking out her baby's feed to last as long as possible.

'I guess…I guess Kevin was my security,' she said at last. 'Security seemed important.'

'So I was right?' Reith said drily. 'You moved from the security of your parents to the security of Kevin.'

'Not quite.'

There was a silence. Reith corked the wine bottle and replaced it in the basket. Sophie finished her feeding and then turned over on the picnic rug to lie on her back. She put her hands behind her head and looked up to the heavens. The evening star was just twinkling into existence.

'You're not the only one who had a bad childhood,' Sophie said at last. 'My mum…well, the only use I was to my mum was as leverage for money from my father. I was in her way. My father didn't want to know me and threw money at me to ease his conscience. Kevin came along when I was seventeen. He gave me an anchor that I'd never had, and I desperately needed it.'

'And now you've sent your anchor back to England.'

'That's right.'

'So where does that leave you, my Sophie?'

My Sophie… The words drifted on the night and Sophie closed her eyes. If only she was.

'I don't know,' she whispered. 'I don't…' The pain in her words was there for him to hear. She couldn't hide it. The gentle night enfolded her, but the pain was still there.

'Sophie…'

He moved then, leaning forward so that his arms were on either side of her, and he was looking down into her face. She opened her eyes and he was between her eyes and the stars.

'Reith,' she whispered. 'Reith…'

For one long moment he held out against her appeal. Her face was white in the twilight and her eyes were drowning pools of pain. He put a finger on her hair and twisted a curl around and around.

The magnet was there, pulling so hard…pulling…

He'd be less than human if he resisted that pull.

With a groan Reith sank to gather her close, letting the magnet do its will.

The magnet's force was supreme. Sophie was powerless to move as Reith's head lowered over hers and his lips gently claimed hers. She didn't want to move. Her hands closed over his dark hair, deepening the kiss, tasting and wanting this man so much that her whole body cried with desire.

She had felt this way since she'd first met him. Her body was his body, and his body hers.

One. Two halves of a whole. How could she feel like this and Reith not feel the same?

His tongue was moving into her mouth and she welcomed the taste of him with joy. His hands were searching for the buttons of her blouse. She arched slightly, helping him, wanting him…

Then his fingers were on her breasts, touching the nipples, taunting them into peaked and throbbing points of fire. When his head moved and his lips fell downward to gently caress and kiss it was all she could do not to cry out with joy.

Joy and sadness. This was her place. This was her man and she was Reith's woman as surely now as if he had placed a wedding band on the third finger of her left hand. Reith was making no promises, she knew, and maybe…maybe what was happening here would have to last for the rest of her life.

So be it. If this was all she could have of Reith she would take it with gratitude and with love—and she would live with this night in her heart forever.

He drew back then, one hand still gently cupping her breast.

'Sophie…' He whispered her name and gently kissed her on the lips. 'God knows I shouldn't, Sophie, but I want you…I want you as I've wanted no woman before.'

'I love you, Reith,' she told him simply.

That stilled him. His body stayed motionless. 'Sophie, I can't—'

'You don't believe you can love?' She smiled tenderly up at him, loving him with every fibre of her body. 'I know. It doesn't stop me loving you, Reith Kenrick. Tomorrow…tomorrow I'll leave and be gone from your life forever, but for tonight…tonight I'm your bush bride, Reith. Yours. I promise you no strings, but tonight my love is yours, and I want you more than I've ever wanted anything in my life. And maybe…maybe my love is strong enough for both of us.'

'Dear God…' He groaned, his body rigid above her. 'I should take you home now. This is madness.'

'I wouldn't go, Reith Kenrick,' Sophie whispered, her fingers carefully unbuttoning the front of his shirt. 'You'd have to drive me with a whip and even then I'd cling and cry. So, you see…you'll just have to make love to me, my love…whether or not you want to.'

'Sophie—'

'You're wasting time with your protests,' she whispered. 'You know you want me. You know the force pulling us together is stronger than both of us.'

He smiled then, his lean face twisting into gentle, uncertain laughter. 'You shameless woman!'

'I am, aren't I?' She laughed up at him, marvelling at herself even as she spoke. Was this really Sophie Lynton— this woman offering her body without shame? This woman fighting for what was hers with every fibre of her soul? This woman working sabotage as though her life depended on it?

Her life did depend on it. If the fight was lost, what was left?

'And if I make you pregnant?'

There would be nothing but joy, Sophie thought, to carry Reith Kenrick's child.

'I'm protected,' she told him, and her voice held a trace of regret.

He pulled her into a sitting position, his fathomless eyes holding hers in the light of the rising moon. His face searched hers.

'You're sure of this, my Sophie?'

'It's the only thing I am sure of,' Sophie whispered. 'I'm only sure that I want this. For tonight…this is right. You must feel it, too.'

'I do feel it,' he said roughly. 'You drive me to the edge of madness, Sophie Lynton. A sane man would get into his truck and drive away fast—right now.'

'A sane man would never get in your truck,' she teased him and watched his eyes crease into laughter.

'Wanton…' His hands lifted her blouse from her shoulders.

'Yes,' she whispered in agreement.

'Shameless…' Somehow her jeans were disappearing and she felt them go with pleasure.

'That too.'

'Beautiful… Bewitching…' His eyes were devouring her, making love to her without so much as touching her, and her body was on fire.

'If you say so. Reith?'

'Mmm.'

'Shut up and love me.'

'If you say so, ma'am.'

He pulled her to him with a savage groan, and suddenly it was no longer Sophie who was doing the seducing. Reith was in control, taking his love with a fierceness of possession and joy that left Sophie breathless.

Her arms pulled him tighter, tighter as skin met against skin.

Her love… Her love and her life…

For this moment and for always.

The twilight faded into darkness, the moon rose to look serenely down on two bush lovers and the night enfolded them with the magic of love.

Sophie woke some time after midnight. Something was wrong. Something.

It wasn't where she was that was the problem. Sophie was enfolded in the curve of Reith's body, wrapped in a cocoon of soft blanket and Reith's arms. She could feel the warm curve of him, and his arms holding her with a possessiveness even in sleep.

The night was warm and still, and just out of arm's reach the wallabies were grazing on the lush grass.

It was the telephone. Here of all places. Its strident ring was sounding from the truck and Reith groaned and stirred.

No...

She didn't say it. Sophie's whole body screamed it, but duty had been instilled too deeply in her by her medical training to do what she would like to do—hurl the dratted telephone to the bottom of the lake.

Reith was this district's only doctor. He had to answer it.

He swore softly, his arms lingering for a fraction of a moment on the softness of Sophie's body, and then pulled away, reaching for his trousers in the dark.

'I wouldn't worry about dressing for the telephone.' Sophie smiled into the night. 'The wallabies don't seem to be shocked—and they've seen worse tonight.'

Reith chuckled but his mind was on the telephone. Swiftly he strode across to answer it.

Sophie lay as quiet as a mouse, saying a silent prayer that wasn't answered.

'What?'

'Chest pain,' Reith said regretfully. He returned and reached down to pull Sophie to her feet. 'Duty calls, my love.'

'I'll stay in bed and wait for you.' Sophie smiled but knew before she said it what his answer would be.

'If I'm delayed you'll still be here in the morning—and all you need is a troop of local scouts dib-dibbing through here at six a.m. to be in a real pickle.' He grinned and pulled her up close to him, his hands caressing the nakedness of her thighs. 'Let's get you dressed, Dr Lynton, and I'll take you home.'

Home...

Sophie just knew whose home it would be. Not Reith's.

She sat silently beside him in the awful truck, cold and increasingly fearful. Reith's face, in the dim light, was an intent and distant mask—as though he had put away something beautiful with regret, but with finality. Now on with the rest of his life.

She knew she was right when he stopped in Moira's front yard. He pulled her into his arms and kissed her with the fierceness and passion of a man going to war. A man leaving his woman—maybe forever.

'Goodbye, Sophie,' he said roughly as he finally put her away from him. He touched her face. 'You're the most beautiful woman I've ever known. I wish to God...' He shook his head. 'I wish to God it could somehow work.'

'You won't risk trying to make it work?' Sophie's voice was trembling. Despite the heat of the night, she felt cold to the marrow.

'Sophie, it's going to be bad enough when you leave now.'

'I don't have to leave.' She sounded about six, Sophie thought. Bereft.

'Yeah...' Reith's tone changed. All of a sudden he was the bushman again—the stranger Sophie had first met. Cynicism dropped down like a shield. 'You don't have to leave tomorrow. But you will have to leave eventually. You're booked on a plane tomorrow, so you might as well get on with it.'

'Let me stay.' Dear God, was that Sophie speaking—independent career woman? Pleading for her future?

Pride and love... They were as opposite as black and white and there was no mingling grey.

He laughed then, a harsh, cynical laugh that hurt. 'No.' He turned and caught her hands. 'Hell, Sophie, I should never have let things go this far. I've been a selfish bastard—but then, that's what I have to be because when you finally go...if you stayed and got any closer to me...' He sighed. 'I think I'd go mad.'

'I'm going mad, anyway,' Sophie whispered.

'Then the sooner you leave, the sooner the pain stops.'

'Is that what you really think?'

'Yes.'

He was wrong. The sooner she left, the sooner the pain

started. It was here now, knifing through her with an agony worse than any chest pain.

He had a patient to go to. He had his life.

Without her...

Sophie clenched her fingers into her palms so hard that she broke the skin. Then, somehow, she made herself open her eyes, lean forward and kiss him very softly on the lips.

'You know where I am if you ever need me,' she whispered softly. 'England's only half a world away—'

Her voice broke on a sob. She couldn't bear it. Reith's hands came out to hold her but she was too fast for him.

Somehow she was out of the truck, the door slamming behind her, and she was stumbling up the veranda and into the sanctuary of her bedroom.

Reith was left staring after her, his face as bleak and hard as ever.

Moira greeted her at breakfast with quiet concern.

'You look dreadful, girl,' she said frankly. 'What happened?'

Sophie shrugged. She poured herself a coffee and took a sip. It tasted of mud—yet it was the beautiful percolated brew that Sophie had tasted at other times with delight.

'I'm going home today,' she said flatly.

'To Kevin?'

That startled her. 'No.' Unthinkable. At least Reith had given her that. Given her a freedom from being Kevin's little woman.

Freedom. How come it had such a sour taste?

'I'll pack and go now,' Sophie said listlessly. 'My plane doesn't leave until tonight—but I might do a bit of sight-seeing on the way.' How to confess that she couldn't bear to stay here? She couldn't bear to hear Reith's truck rattle along the road and not come in. She couldn't bear to be within a long walk of his home...of her heart...

'Oh, Sophie...' Moira's kindly face was a picture of

distress. She guessed all, this good-hearted woman. 'I so hoped... You and Dr Kenrick—'

'It was an air bubble,' Sophie said brutally. She rose, sloshing her coffee in the saucer. 'You know he doesn't want anyone. How could I possibly delude myself he could ever change for me? That he could ever want me?'

She left soon after, throwing her belongings into her hire-car with savage despair.

She was going to have to pull herself together. Somehow she was going to have to build a life out of this mess.

Thank heaven for her work. At least she had her medicine. She'd go back to working in Casualty, she decided. The rush and urgency of her work there would help to drive away the ghosts of Reith Kenrick.

Who was she kidding?

Reith Kenrick would stay with her forever.

Ten minutes later Sophie pulled her car off the main gravel road. An inconspicuous sign read 'Brand Lookout'.

You have to see Brand Lookout, Moira had told her on her first day here, and Sophie had never found time. Now...

Now she was clear of Reith and she had hours of time before she needed to be speeding toward the airport. She could either sit in an airport lounge and stare at a book, or she could be a tourist.

Neither held very much attraction, but how long would it be before Sophie came to Australia again? Maybe never.

So be a tourist here for the last time.

It was worth the detour. Brand Lookout was a ridge overlooking the entire valley. The mountains rose above and around her in blue-purple majesty. Somewhere below was Reith's lake, and these peaks would still be reflecting their beauty long after she'd gone. Long after Reith was just a bittersweet memory.

How long she sat there she wasn't sure. Sophie left the car and walked along the ridge, then sat and swung her legs back and forth from a seat on a fallen log. The sun was hot on her face. Back home it was winter. She put her face up to the sun, drinking in its heat with a need that spoke of inner cold. She was cold to the soul.

The soft wind wafted around her, fading to nothing and then gusting in short bursts of force. Sophie's curls blew around her face. It was as if the wind was caressing—trying its darndest to heal her pain.

If she could sit here forever...

Crazy dream. She stood, and then stared. The wind had sprung up in a sudden gust, and hurtling toward her from the sky was a vast red bird.

It wasn't a bird. Sophie blinked twice and then realised she wasn't seeing things. It was a brilliant flame-coloured hang-glider, hurtling down toward her ridge from one of the peaks behind her.

He was badly out of control. For some reason, here in this chasm between the mountain ranges the wind was doing strange things, sweeping up and then blowing down, down...

He was caught in such a gust now. For one horrid moment Sophie thought he would crash into the rocks at her feet. She cringed backward; the wind relented for a split-second, the hang-glider lurched up, and then down again over the edge of the ridge where Sophie sat. It dived straight down, down into the trees below.

From somewhere beneath her, Sophie heard a crash of undergrowth and then a scream that made her cringe. The scream echoed round and round the valley and died away to nothing.

Nothing.

CHAPTER TWELVE

SOPHIE stood and walked slowly to the edge of the cliff. There was a handrail holding her back from the very edge, and beyond the handrail was a drop of a hundred feet or more. After that sheer drop the ground sloped outward again, to mountainside covered in thick bush.

He must be dead…

No. The sails of the glider would break his fall a little. The wind was driving him down, but he wasn't in free fall.

So where was he? Somewhere below?

As if in answer to her thoughts, a cry came bellowing up.

'Is someone there? Help me…for God's sake, help me!'

Whoever it was must have seen her as he had hurtled down out of the sky. She would have stood out where she sat on the ridge, she knew, in her white blouse and light lemon skirt.

She should go for help. There was no way she could climb down…

The yell from below suddenly changed in its intensity; it rose as an agonised scream…

Had he fallen further? Sophie wondered.

It would take half an hour to find help and bring rescuers back. If she could see…

Sophie lay flat on her stomach and inched forward. She wasn't good at heights at the best of times, and this was no exception. The drop made her feel sick.

It wasn't impossible, though.

Inching her nose carefully over the cliff face, Sophie saw that the drop was only sheer under the actual look out. Fifty yards from her on either side there was bush and sloped ground. The rail was placed to get the best view without the trees. If Sophie made her way through the bush at the top and then down...

The scream came again, sharp, agonised and cut off short. Then another.

It made the decision easy. In seconds Sophie was bashing her way through undergrowth, and then clambering down fast.

It was hard going. The drop wasn't absolutely sheer but it was close to vertical, with only enough slope to allow growth. Stunted trees fought for root space in rocky toe-holds. Sophie struggled her way from one tree trunk to another, forcing her way down in the direction of the hang-glider.

She couldn't see him. She could only hear. The agonised screaming had given way to anguished sobs—a sobbing that told Sophie that, wherever he was, the man was in agony. She fought her way down fast, scratching her hands and legs, and tearing her flowing skirt in the process. Where in heaven's name was he?

And then, maybe two or three hundred yards down the cliff where the trees started growing high again, she stopped and looked up—and her breath was driven out of her body.

The man was hanging upside-down in a tree. Above him, twisted in the canopy of leaves, was what was left of the hang-glider.

How on earth was he caught? Sophie couldn't see. Was he somehow holding on by the knees? Maybe a broken arm was stopping him pulling himself up?

She stared up at the tree, measuring herself against the lowest hanging branch. She hadn't climbed a tree in twenty years, and she wasn't all that keen on trying now.

There was no choice. The sobbing started again. It cut right through her.

'I'm down below and coming up,' she called. 'Hang on.'

Of all the stupid things to say—he was hanging on for dear life.

It stopped the sobbing, though. The man froze, immobile, his body not moving an inch.

'Is…is someone there?' There was agony in his voice. 'Is someone—?'

'I'm coming.' Sophie cast a rueful look down at her pretty skirt, ruched it up into her knickers and started to climb. Now was hardly the time for decorum.

It took five long minutes to reach him. The man was caught thirty feet up. Sophie reached his level and stared out along the limb where he hung.

Then, as she realised why he still hung there, she sucked in her breath in dismay.

A smaller branch—almost a twig—was growing out and up from a major branch. This thick twig had pierced the man's calf. He was caught, totally helpless, the wood going right through his leg.

Her fear of heights forgotten, Sophie crawled out on the major branch with the speed of a frightened koala. The man was hanging from the injured leg. Any minute now it could tear and he'd crash to the ground.

The man could hear her coming—maybe he could see her. His view was distorted. Hanging head down as he was, it would only be a matter of time before he lost consciousness completely.

'I'm coming…'

It was a frightened whisper.

It wasn't quite as bad as Sophie had first thought—but bad enough. When Sophie finally reached him she realised that he'd been able to hook his uninjured leg over another small branch and take at least some of his weight.

'OK…I'm here.'

Sophie looped her own legs around the thicker branch and clung for dear life. Then she reached down. 'Give me your hands.'

His hands came up and clung as hard as Sophie's legs were clinging to the branch. She was this man's lifeline, and she knew that, having proffered the lifeline, she couldn't withdraw. She either pulled him up or she'd be pulled down herself.

She pulled and clung with all her might, hauling him sideways up to her. She was pulling the man's whole weight.

His leg was still solidly pierced but the small branch causing the trouble was pliable. It should bend as he moved.

It did. The man's body lifted forward and sideways and he came up with a rush that nearly sent Sophie tumbling backward.

She held on to branch and man for dear life. The world swayed and toppled and life had never seemed so good. The alternative was falling for both of them—death.

The man screamed again as the pressure on his injured leg changed. Sophie gritted her teeth, mentally blocked her ears and clung. She had never done anything so close to physically impossible in her life before.

And finally she had him. The man's body came to rest, stable enough where he lay against her, his leg still in a crazy position, but at least he was upright and she had hold of him. His head and shoulders lay across her legs, his leg still held by the offshoot of wood.

'You're safe,' she said unsteadily. 'Just lie still and don't move your leg.'

'I...I won't.' It was a grinding whisper of pain. 'Who...who are you?'

He was a boy—no more than eighteen or nineteen, desperately young and desperately frightened. It must have been the worst kind of nightmare to have hung there alone, Sophie realised. The boy had bright red hair and freckles on ash-white skin and his lean frame trembled like a leaf in her arms.

'I'm Sophie,' Sophie told him, trying for cheerfulness in her voice and nearly succeeding. 'Sophie Lynton. And who do I have the pleasure of er...cuddling?'

She almost succeeded in making him smile. The pain-filled eyes creased.

'M-Mike. Mike Letherbridge.'

'Pleased to meet you, I'm sure.' Sophie's legs were aching already from the effort of holding to the branch. She had Mike's full weight straining against her but, if she let go, the offshoot through his leg would pull him down again. 'Mike, we appear to be in a bit of a predicament.'

'You...you could say that.'

He had courage, this lad.

'Mike, do you have friends on the mountain who'll have seen where you landed?' Sophie kept her voice deliberately even, trying not to sound anxious. If he didn't...

He didn't.

'N-No. I'm hang-gliding by myself.'

By himself. He had to be kidding. Surely someone knew where he was.

It seemed someone didn't.

'I came up here by myself. I know you're not supposed to—it's against the rules of the club I belong to—but I just got a new glider. I brought my glider and a motorbike to Inyabarra, left the motorbike at the bottom of the mountain where I intended to land and brought the glider up on the trailer. It would have worked really well...'

Except for the wind. To hang-glide in gusty conditions and alone...

It was hardly the time for a lecture. The boy's voice was tight and laced with pain.

'Will someone look for you tonight?' Keep the desperation out of your voice, she told herself harshly.

'N-No. University's on holidays and I told my parents I was going away with friends. Otherwise they'd worry.'

Fancy that, Sophie thought.

So…so there was no one missing this boy. And there was no one missing Sophie. For how long?

Sophie's car was on the ridge. And this boy's car was higher still. Surely someone would see?

They'd assume whoever had left the car was off doing a spot of bushwalking. Camping even.

Could she somehow wedge the boy so she could go for help?

She couldn't. Sophie looked down at the wood piercing his leg. It was too thick to break. If she tried to pull it through the leg, chances were she'd tear an artery, as well as kill him from pain. And if she released him…well, he'd fall sideways before she was halfway back to the car. His leg would rip and he'd fall.

You couldn't even see the scarlet hang-glider from above, she thought desperately, remembering looking down and searching for a sign. It had crashed far enough through the canopy of leaves to be invisible.

So…

So hang on and wait.

The boy gave a soft moan and stirred in her arms. Morphine…she wanted morphine.

She wanted Reith.

'Reith,' she whispered over and over to herself and it was almost a prayer. 'Dear God, Reith, help me…

It was the longest day Sophie had ever known and afterwards she didn't know how she had found the strength to endure it.

'Leave me,' the boy groaned over and over again. 'Go and get help.'

He was in too much pain to realise what Sophie knew for sure—that if she left him he'd die. All he knew was the agony in his leg. He drifted in and out of consciousness during the day, calling for his mother.

A big, macho male, Sophie thought ruefully, with his car and his motorbike and his hang-glider. The macho image didn't quite ring true. He had to be an indulged and beloved son, to own all this while still a student—and still a child at heart. She couldn't leave him.

She couldn't hold on forever. Her legs were cramping badly, and the whole base of her spine seemed numb. How long? How long before she fell asleep as well and fell sideways?

She was in no danger of falling asleep yet—not with the pain in her cramping legs and the ache in her arms. At least the boy wasn't heavily built—but he was heavy enough.

The day dragged on and on. Impossible situation. Impossible to stay. Impossible to go. This was crazy—to stay here. This way they could both die.

If she left he'd die almost straight away.

Reith...

It was a prayer—a mantra—a plea of supplication over and over again.

Useless. Reith and Moira thought she was safely on a plane to England—and even at the other end there was no one to worry when she didn't arrive.

She'd end up a skeleton dangling from a tree...

Oh, for heaven's sake! Sophie gave an hysterical laugh, and winced as the boy in her arms stirred. This was the way of craziness.

The sun crossed the sky with maddening slowness, shifting the shadows under the leaves. How late? Four o'clock? Five?

Then came dusk. About now she should be boarding a plane for London.

Reith...

The darkness was absolute. Mike was half asleep, half unconscious in her arms. Sophie was almost jealous. The pain was everywhere—in her arms, her legs, her back...

'Reith... Dear heaven, bring help...' She wasn't sure

who she was talking to. Anyone. Anything. She couldn't
keep holding—

'Sophie!'

The call was so faint that at first she thought she was
dreaming. It echoed again and again—maybe a dozen
times—before she finally realised it wasn't an extension
of her pathetic pleas. It was her name that was being
called.

She wasn't crazy.

The pain receded. She pulled herself to sit upright, and
stared up the cliff face.

She wasn't dreaming. There were lights beaming
down—torches...

'Sophie...' The name echoed again out over the valley,
and she knew it was Reith.

Reith...

His call was a cry of desperation. It rang out again and
Sophie caught her breath. It held horror and hopelessness
and sheer and absolute desolation.

It was the cry of a man who had lost everything he'd
ever held dear in his world. It was the cry of a man bereft.

'Sophie...'

Sophie closed her eyes. She took a deep breath, filling
her lungs with the sweet night air. Life was suddenly, im-
measurably good.

'Reith!' she yelled with every ounce of power left in
her exhausted body. 'I'm over here, Reith.'

Mike shifted in her arms and she clung tighter. 'Hold
on, Mike. He's coming. Reith's coming. Reith!'

There was a moment's long silence and then the torch-
lights swung slowly toward the sound of her voice.

'Sophie?' Reith didn't sound as if he believed what was
happening. He was a long way away, and his voice was
dreamlike. Like Sophie, he hadn't expected respite from
hopelessness.

'Reith...oh, Reith...I'm here...'

'Sophie!' It was a shout of joy, and then there was the smashing of bodies through the undergrowth, swearing and crashing, and her name yelled over and over again.

And then Reith was swinging up the tree as if he had been born in the treetops, his lithe body moving fast and furiously.

She was in his arms. The weight was taken from her. Reith touched her as if he could scarcely believe she was human.

She knew how he felt. Reith...

Another man was there then, clambering up the tree behind Reith, and then another. She was being passed from man to man, and the pain in her legs and arms and back could finally take over.

Her whole body cramped in spasm. She cried out as she reached the ground, and Reith was swearing, and then she was drifting toward the blessedness of dark.

She couldn't let go...he'd fall—

'You're safe, my Sophie.' Somehow through the mist of pain she heard it. 'You're safe. We have you both. You can let go now, sweetheart. I have you safe.'

She closed her eyes and let the darkness do its worst.

She woke in her own bed.

Her own... It was the bed she'd stayed in for just over a week at Moira's. The bed she thought of as home more than her bed in London.

Sophie opened her eyes to the familiar pattern of light through the leaves and everything felt absolutely normal.

It was only when she moved that it didn't.

Ouch!

Her breath sucked in as the pain knifed through her. She must have made a tiny sound. The door flew open as though someone had been listening.

'Well, my love,' Moira beamed. 'Awake at last. Oh, Sophie...'

Sophie was enfolded in a massive embrace and Moira wept.

'We thought you were dead,' she sobbed. 'I've never been so frightened in my life. The airline rang when you didn't arrive for your ticket, and I started worrying. And I knew you were so upset, and I just thought…well, I just thought I might go for a drive. And I found the car by the lookout and I thought…oh, Sophie…and then…I thought I had to tell Dr Kenrick and I telephoned him and I think…I think he went a little bit crazy…'

And Moira burst into tears on Sophie's coverlet.

They'd thought she'd suicided.

Of course. Sophie thought of the sheer drop from the lookout—of her unhappiness, and the car abandoned at the top of the cliff.

'Oh, Moira, I'm so sorry,' she whispered.

'Sorry!' Moira's head came up at that. 'There's no need to be sorry. You saved that boy's life. They say it's a miracle you held him there as long as you did and they don't know how you did it. They had to cut the branch to get him down—and they flew him straight to Melbourne with the branch still in his leg and they've just phoned to say it's removed and there's no long-term damage and it's all down to you, my dear, and you say you're sorry?' She paused, bereft of speech, and shook her head. 'Oh, my dear…'

'And Reith?' It was hardly a whisper.

'He's here. He sat here all night. I tried to persuade him to go home, but he wouldn't have a bar of it. The Melbourne doctors rang to talk to him about the young hang-glider and he's in the hall taking the call now, but it was as much as I could do to get him to go to the phone. Like I said—he was a bit crazy. I don't know… And then, when we found you…'

Moira gulped and grabbed for her handkerchief. Then

she paused. From the hall below, a loud tinkle announced the end of a telephone call.

'He'll come up now,' she said. 'I tried to make him go home for a shower and change—but he wouldn't. I said if you woke and saw him the way he is—his clothes ripped and scratched and bleeding—you'd faint all over again. Honest, I thought he'd rip the bush apart to get to you.' She stood, and her smile changed.

'I'll get you some breakfast,' she promised. 'Don't faint when you see Dr Kenrick. Promise?'

'I...I promise.'

She disappeared and Sophie hardly saw her go. Reith...

Sophie heard a hard, anxious demand on the stairs and then the footsteps she knew so well.

And then Reith was there. He stood in the doorway, his eyes not reassured. His face was a still, watchful mask, as though even now he was expecting to have what was precious snatched away from him.

'Reith...' Sophie raised herself painfully on one elbow. She knew that face. Dark and unshaven, his eyes narrowed, creased, hard with anxiety.

It wasn't a forbidding face. It was a face that expected pain.

'Reith,' she whispered and held out a hand, and he crossed the room in two long strides.

She was gathered to his heart, and her body's aches melted to nothing. Sophie flung her arms around him with a sob of love, and held him close. As close as she could be.

'My Sophie,' Reith whispered in a ragged, tearing voice. 'Oh, God...I thought you were dead.'

'You should know I couldn't suicide,' she whispered. 'You should know.'

'Why should I know that?' He put her away from him then, holding her at arm's length. 'You crazy, crazy girl.

Why the hell should I know that? The car was there…'
His voice broke, nightmare flooding back.

'I couldn't die,' she whispered simply. 'Because as long
as I live I have you in my heart. Even if you don't want
me, I have you with me.' She touched his beloved face.
'So I intend to live for a very long time.'

The room around them faded to nothing. The whole
world, it seemed, held its breath.

Then Reith swore, very softly, and pulled her against
him.

'You'll have me more than in your heart, my precious
Sophie,' he growled, his voice husky with emotion. 'I
didn't know one crazy woman could tear me in two. I
didn't know it was too late to send you away. The damage
was done. To lose you was like losing life itself—worse.
From here on, my love, my life, you'll have me in your
life forever. If you'll have me.'

Sophie's eyes widened. That he could say that to her…
If you'll have me…

'I'll have you, my Reith,' she whispered. 'With all my
heart.'

CHAPTER THIRTEEN

SOPHIE woke with the dawn.

The warm breeze was blowing gently through the half-open flap of the tent. It caressed Sophie's body—the small amount of naked skin that wasn't already being caressed.

Reith had found thick feather-down bed-rolls for his bride. They billowed round the couple now in a pile of feathery softness. Satin sheets were there to cover them and there were light wool blankets to keep any chill at bay.

The sheets and blankets hadn't been needed. Their wedding night had been all Sophie had dreamed it could be, and Sophie needed no other cover than her beloved Reith.

He slept on now beside her, his harsh face easing its look of solitude in sleep.

There was no more solitude for Reith.

Sophie lay entwined in his arms, letting her mind drift over the previous day. Her wedding day.

Moira had hostessed their wedding, proudly organising the marriage of her beloved Sophie. She bullied Sophie into traditional white, aided by Gilda from Gilda's Gourmet Goodies—who also turned out to be Gilda, seamstress extraordinaire. Sophie had been married in a mist of white tulle and satin, with Mandy as flower-girl accompanying the bride in a swirling flounce of pink pride.

Half the valley had been there, and a few others. Mike Letherbridge, her rescued hang-glider, had been there on crutches and minus anything remotely macho male. Mary and Ted had been glowing over their flower-girl daughter. Margaret Lee had arrived extolling the virtues of a sugar-free diet. Even Christabelle and Elvira Pilkington had been

183

there, free of chickenpox and content, for once, to let Sophie be the centre of attention.

Though she hadn't been the centre of attention, Sophie thought blissfully.

Reith had. How could he not have been in her eyes, impossibly handsome in his black dinner suit, with one red rose in his lapel proudly declaring his love?

He hadn't needed the rose. His love had been there for all to see, holding Sophie in thrall. The beautiful ceremony washed over her in a mist of happiness and she could remember little. All she saw was her Reith.

Sophie remembered the car, though. When it was time to drive away Sophie had looked for Reith's awful truck and found it gone—a luxurious, four-wheel-drive sedan in its place.

'You can't take a twenty-year-old truck on a luxury honeymoon,' Reith had teased, refusing to reveal his plans. 'Nothing but the best for my Sophie—from this day forth.'

She would have gone anywhere with him, in a wheelbarrow if necessary, but when she had been where he had taken her Sophie's heart had cried out with delight.

Her lake and her mountains. The setting for *Bush Bride*.

'I've organised a locum for a month and in two days we'll fly to London to face your mother,' Reith had told her. 'Maybe after that we'll go to Italy…maybe luxurious hotels then, my love. But for these two days I thought we could stay here. This is where we belong, my Sophie.' And then his eyes creased in sudden doubt. 'I'm not wrong, am I, my love?' he asked anxiously, gathering her bridal beauty close. 'You did say you loved it here—but, if you want, we can go somewhere else.'

Sophie gazed down at their camp site through a mist of tears. The lake was reflecting its crimson splendour. The sun was setting on her first day of married life and she couldn't think of anything more perfect.

'But this is my place, my Reith,' she whispered and held him close. 'I'm your bush bride. Now and forever…'

They were the last words she had spoken for a long, long time.

The recollections faded. Sophie stirred, stretching her body languorously in the warmth. Reith was so close…he was part of her, and she knew that tomorrow and tomorrow and tomorrow he would always be here.

She could ask for no more.

Then she stiffened. From outside the tent came a massive roar—a roar she had heard only once before.

Reith's eyes opened and his arms tightened around her. 'Afraid, my Sophie?' He had felt her stiffen.

'It's…I know it's only a koala.'

Reith grinned, sat up and flung the tent flap wide. There on the grass before them sat a small grey koala.

A very familiar koala…

Sophie stared at the scar running down from his eye. She looked at the patch of fur missing from his leg in absolute amazement. It couldn't be. Could it?

'The very same,' Reith smiled, shaking his head in disbelief. 'You get around, fella.'

The koala glared.

'Look, I know it was you who brought us together, and I'm sorry to be unsocial, mate,' Reith grinned, 'but you can go practise your mating calls somewhere else. This lady's taken.'

Reith closed the tent flap, fastening it tight. The koala was left staring in indignation. Then Reith turned to Sophie. His dark eyes gleamed wicked intention down at his bride.

'Well, my love?'

'W-well?' Her heart was pounding at the look of him. Her naked Reith… Her husband…

'Do you need the odd growl to get you in the mating mood, my heart?'

Sophie smiled up at him. Her hands reached out to hold him—to pull him down to her. His heart...

'No growls,' she whispered, and her voice was husky with love and desire. 'My Reith, I've mated with you for the rest of my life.'

LIVE THE EMOTION

Modern Romance™
...seduction and
passion guaranteed

Tender Romance™
...love affairs that
last a lifetime

Medical Romance™
...medical drama
on the pulse

Historical Romance™
...rich, vivid and
passionate

Sensual Romance™
...sassy, sexy and
seductive

Blaze Romance™
...the temperature's
rising

30 new titles every month.

Live the emotion

MILLS & BOON®